She Walks in Love
Protectors of the Spear

MaryLu
Tyndall

She Walks in Love
Protectors of the Spear 2
by MaryLu Tyndall

Library of Congress Cataloging-in-Publication Data is on file at the Library of Congress, Washington, DC.

ISBN-13: 978-0-9991763-9-9
E-Version ISBN: 978-0-9991763-8-2

Cover Design by Ravv at raven.com
Editor: Louise M. Gouge

RANSΦM
PRESS

For I am persuaded that neither death nor life, nor angels nor principalities nor powers, nor things present nor things to come, nor height nor depth, nor any other created thing, shall be able to separate us from the love of God which is in Christ Jesus our Lord.
Romans 8:38-39

Author's Note

Dear Reader, I labeled this novel a Medieval Fantasy Romance. However, don't be confused by the fantasy title. This is not a fantasy as most people would classify that genre. This is a Medieval Romance that is not set in an historic real place. In other words, I took license with places, names, and also with some language. Hence, do not read with the intent of learning Medieval history! However, the fantasy label in no way can be attributed to the powerful acts of God described in the story. Those are quite plausible for those who follow Him.

If you wish to see character pictures and scenes from the book while you're reading, visit my Pinterest page at

https://www.pinterest.com/mltyndall/protectors-of-the-spear/she-walks-in-love/

CHAPTER ONE

Luxley Castle, Northland Goodryke

"**P**rithee, whose wedding is it?"

"'Tis yours, my lady," the curious maid who buzzed around Cristiana D'Clere answered. "Do you not remember?"

Mine? Closing her eyes, Cristiana attempted to shake the fog from her mind as the maid adjusted a circlet laden with flowers, atop her head. When she opened her eyes, it was to the blurred image of a woman in a looking glass. *Her?* Nay, not possible.

She peered closer. Honey-streaked brown hair, braided with golden threads, tumbled over her shoulders and down her back, framing what could be considered a comely face, though a bit thin and pale. She wore an exquisite wedding gown of blue Samite silk with a jeweled belt hung about her hips. Her wide bell sleeves were embroidered in gold and embedded with glistening pearls that matched the adornment hanging about her neck. Light brown eyes—misty and vacant—stared back at her.

The maid lifted a white veil over the lady's head and draped it down her shoulders.

Cristiana's vision became snowy. She lifted her hand to rub her eyes, and the woman across from her did the same. Horror squeezed the breath from her lungs. She stumbled back from the looking glass as the truth sank in.

My wedding?

The maid gripped her elbow. Another woman scurried up from behind and caught her waist ere she fell. A wave of heat swamped her. One of the maids lifted her veil and set it gently atop her circlet.

"Are you all right, my lady?" Her face appeared overly large and distorted before it suddenly disappeared. Blinking,

Cristiana glanced over the chamber—*her* chamber, the room she'd occupied alone for the past seven years.

Ever since her sister, Alexia, had abandoned her.

Light flowed in waves through the small window and over a stone floor before firing glistening arrows atop a large bed set against one wall. A table and chairs perched beside a glowing hearth, and in the corner, two large chests sat open, overflowing with all manner of fine attire.

Several women, dressed in too-fine clothing for maids, scurried about with various tasks of which Cristiana could make no sense. Some set vases of fresh flowers on the tables and mantel, others dusted and swept, some placed lit candles about, while others flung rose pedals on the bed.

Nothing, in truth, made any sense.

One of the ladies handed her a mug. "Here, my lady. A drink will settle your nerves. 'Tis normal to be nervous on your wedding day."

The tapestries decorating the high walls spun around her. "Who are you?"

The lady's brow twisted. "I'm Gelda, your bridesmaid."

Bridesmaid. "Who...who..." Cristiana took a sip of the spiced wine and attempted to draw a breath. "Where is Seraphina?"

"Your lady's maid? Never fear, my lady. She's about somewhere. Prithee, be at ease. We must finish getting you ready. Sir Walter will be here anon to escort you to the ceremony in the great hall."

Setting down the cup, Cristiana gaped at the woman. Surely this was but a dream—a terrible, horrible dream. Lord knew she'd had many a nightmare the past few years. Some even whilst she was awake. Aye, that must be it. Closing her eyes, she prayed to wake up, but her head grew light again and she wobbled.

Firm hands gripped both her arms ere she fell. Mayhap 'twas not such bad news...not if she were to marry Sir Jarin the Just. Was he not her hero? Her knight? The only man who caused her heart to leap at the mere thought of him? Besides, had she not always desired above all to be married to such a man? To be protected, cared for…cherished? Alas, why could she not recall the courtship…the engagement? She pinched the bridge of her nose, desperately trying to remember.

"Who am I to marry?" she finally asked.

Some of the ladies giggled.

"Why, Sir Cedric LeGode, my lady. A fine man, if you ask me."

Cedric? She gasped for air that seemed to abandon the chamber, whilst the scent of tallow, rose water, and wine stole her hope that 'twas but a dream.

The room became a tunnel, the end reaching far into the distance, distorting the ladies into odd shapes and sizes and twisting shadows into ghouls.

She was ill again. After so long. How had she become ill again? "I don't feel well," she murmured.

A rap on the door preceded the entrance of a man she knew all too well, and one she feared more than any other. Sir Walter LeGode, dressed in a silk tunic of forest green, a leather belt inlaid with jewels, and fine woolen hose leading down to green velvet shoes adorned with pearls, marched into the room as if he were lord of the manor. Which was his goal, after all. Was it not?

'Twas no dream, then.

"Ah, you look lovely, my dear. Cedric will be most pleased." His sickly-sweet smile loomed large in her blurred vision as he peered into her eyes searching for…what was he searching for? Her sanity? As was she, for she seemed to have misplaced it in the fog invading her thoughts.

Muted sounds of music floated in from the open door, along with laughter, the clank of plates and bowls, and the spicy scents of roasted pheasant and wild boar.

Sir Walter whirled to address one of the ladies. "Has she taken her potion?"

"Aye, my lord. But she protests."

"She drank all of it?"

"Aye, my lord."

"Hmm." Sir Walter looped his arm through hers and gestured toward the door. "Shall we?"

She stumbled forward. One of the ladies took her other arm and helped her through the door.

"I cannot marry Cedric," she heard herself say.

"Of course you can. You've been betrothed for over a month now. Do you not remember?"

She squeezed her eyes shut for a moment, searching for a shred of reason. There was something…something important she must remember…but what?

Tugging her arm from his, she staggered backward toward her bed. "I wish to see my sister, Alexia."

Sir Walter stiffened, then slowly turned to face her. "You poor dear. You don't remember, do you? No doubt grief has cushioned you from the truth."

"Grief?" Cristiana grabbed a lock of her hair, twisting it around her finger. Her legs turned to potage, and she staggered, slapping away one of the women who reached for her.

Sir Walter took a step toward her. His scent of spice and vinegar caused her nose to twitch. "Alexia was caught and tried as a witch at the king's court. She was burned at the stake two months past."

"Nay." Blinking, Cristiana tried to focus on his face, seeking the lie written therein. But his hideous visage whirled in her vision, coming in and out of view. Her sister burned as a witch? Nay! Sweet angels, what devilment was this? Even so, her heart grew so tight, she thought it would crumble to dust and blow away with the next word he spoke.

Thankfully, it wasn't to her, but to one of the women.

"Lady Miriam, I beg you, would you go to the apothecary and fetch Lady Cristiana's medicine? She is not quite herself today, and we must see to it she is well for the ceremony." Facing the others, he clapped his hands. "Now, off with you!" All of them scurried out save for one, whom he gestured to remain.

"Drink your medicine, my lady." He lifted Cristiana's hand and kissed it ere she could retrieve it. "I shall delay the guests and return anon when you are recovered."

With that, he pivoted on his velvet shoes and pranced from the room, leaving Cristiana in a fog of fear and confusion. The remaining lady came to assist her, but she waved her away.

"Leave me. I wish to rest."

But the lady didn't leave. She merely retreated into the shadows and sat in one of the chairs by the hearth. An ache rose to throb behind Cristiana's temples, and she rubbed them as she lowered to her bed. *Concentrate, concentrate!* Her sister dead? Marry Cedric? She was ill. There was something deep in her memory about being ill. But what? Tears blurred her vision even further, and she gripped her stomach, resisting the urge to cry in front of this stranger. If Alexia was dead and Cristiana was sick again, what hope was there for anything?

She was tired, so very tired. Her eyelids drooped, her breathing became as jumbled and erratic as her thoughts.

Scraping sounded in the distance, as if two stones rubbed against one another—large stones. Slowly, Cristiana turned her head toward the other lady in the room. She had risen and was staring at another woman. The intruder grabbed her and placed a cloth on her mouth. Her struggling ceased within seconds, and the woman lowered her gently back into the chair. What an odd dream. Maybe Cristiana truly was ill and needed her medicine, after all. With a heavy sigh, she closed her eyes again.

Two hands grasped her arms and yanked her to sit. "My lady! My lady! Wake up. We must leave!"

"Seraphina?" Cristiana knew that voice, recognized the snowy hair tumbling over her shoulders like an icy waterfall.

"We haven't much time. Come, my lady."

Cristiana felt herself hoisted up as Seraphina positioned her shoulder beneath Cristiana's arm and all but dragged her across the stone floor.

"Where...why...?" she managed to squeak out.

"To save you from Sir Walter and Cedric. Come. They have lied to you."

Aye, lied…deceived. Of course. They want power and…! Cristiana caught her breath and clutched Seraphina's arm. "The Spear!"

"Never fear, my lady. I have it." Seraphina continued toward the door, passing the lady slumped in the chair.

"What of…?" Cristiana gestured toward the woman.

"She will recover." Seraphina led Cristiana through an opening in the wall, then propped her against another wall as she pulled a leather strap on the stone door and enclosed them in darkness—frightening darkness. And silence, save for the *drip-drip* of water in the distance.

"Where are we going?"

"To safety, my lady." Seraphina took her arm and led Cristiana down a dark tunnel.

CHAPTER TWO

Nine months later, Braewood Castle, Gavinshire

Robin Praxis, Lord Braewood, was indeed gone. 'Twas the first time he'd left Braewood Castle in three months. Cristiana stood at the window of her chamber as a half-moon rose to dribble milky white atop the trees. Ten hours past, she'd watched as the forest swallowed up his carriage, along with the two soldiers on horseback who guarded him. She should be elated, excited even, for this was her one chance to escape. Or so Seraphina repeatedly told her. But all Cristiana felt was terror.

The wooden door creaked open and in rushed the lady herself, eyes lit with urgency. "The time is upon us, my lady." Clutching her skirts, she moved to the window and followed Cristiana's gaze. "'Tis the first time he has ever left us alone and unguarded."

"Because he trusts us...*me*." Guilt pricked Cristiana. Lord Braewood had been naught but kind to her and Seraphina, ever since he'd found them in the nearby village, shivering in the cold, their attire stained and tattered. They'd been near to starving as they prayed for people in exchange for scraps of food.

Sighing, Seraphina backed away from the window, her sapphire-blue eyes filled with both concern and fear. A braid of hair the color of glistening snow dangled down the back of her emerald green tunic. "Which is precisely why we must leave. *Now.* Ere he returns and decides *not* to trust you."

Cristiana retreated from the window and grabbed a lock of her hair, her thoughts awhirl. She glanced over her chamber, full of everything she could want. Light from several candles fluttered over a wardrobe overflowing with fine gowns, a glowing hearth constantly kept her warm, a case laden with books that had provided months of reading, and a canopied bed that was as soft and feathery as the clouds. "Alas, look how well he treats me. And you as well, Seraphina."

Cristiana clutched the edges of her Camelot surcote and spread out the rich vermilion fabric. "He dresses us in the finest attire, provides every luxury, and we feast like royalty. And what does he ask in return? Merely that I heal those who are ill. Those who come to us for prayer. How could there be evil in such a man?"

Seraphina flattened her lips. "He charges money for your skills, my lady. Large sums which sentence those who come for healing to a life of poverty."

Cristiana lowered to sit on her bed. "So you have said."

"Do you not trust me?"

"Oh, Sera, of course. You are my lifelong friend." She reached for her. "The only person who has not abandoned me."

Seraphina took her hand and sat beside her.

"If he does take payment," Cristiana continued, "what of it? He no doubt uses it for our care, as well as Thebe's." She stared at her friend. "You wish to leave that precious child?"

"Nay, my lady. I wish to take her with us. 'Tis not safe for her here." Seraphina bit her lip and stared into the coals of the hearth. "I have seen it. Danger and darkness await us if we remain."

Cristiana knew Seraphina had the gift of sight and had oft predicted future events. The lady also knew things she could not know by natural means. But, in good sooth, mayhap her disdain for Lord Braewood had stifled those gifts in this matter.

Seraphina turned to face her, squeezing her hands. "I beg you, my lady. He is gone only this one night. I have prepared everything. But we must leave now."

"But the guards."

"Naught to fear, my lady. 'Twas an easy task to convince the steward to grant them extra mead at this evening's repast. Especially with their lord gone. Hence, they are no doubt slumbering at their posts. 'Twould be of no account to take Thebe and two horses and leave by the back gate."

"Horses? Where are you to procure those? And what of the guard who stands at the gate each eve?"

Seraphina smiled. "He will be engaged elsewhere. I have paid Mistress Eleanor to lure him aside with her charms. And we both know the stable boy is quite taken with me."

Cristiana couldn't help but laugh. "I fear a devil dwells beneath your angelic exterior, Sera."

"Call it what you wish, but I have vowed to keep you safe, my lady."

"And how would I be any safer out there?" Cristiana gestured toward the window as a gust of wind whirled inside, spinning the candle flames and bringing with it the scent of horses and earth. "Where we have no provision or protection. Do you not remember the six months we spent wandering from village to village, sleeping on the cold, damp ground, begging for even the scraps fed the chickens?"

"Of course I do. 'Twas the worst time of my life. But we didn't die or starve. Nor were we even accosted. God took care of us."

"Aye, by bringing Lord Braewood across our path."

Sighing, Seraphina stood. "We were doing well enough after you discovered the power of the Spear to heal."

Cristiana rubbed her wrist and gazed at the mark that had miraculously appeared there when her sister Alexia had transferred ownership of the relic to her. The Spear of Destiny—the tip of the spear which had stabbed Christ's side. 'Twas said to have powers for war and against one's enemies. Which was why so many sought it, including the king himself. And the King's Guard—powerful knights who served only him. But she had no idea the Spear possessed powers to heal as well until she had prayed for a crippled lad in the village of Savinne. She'd only done it to silence his mother, who had discovered them hiding in a church, pronounced Cristiana an angel, and demanded she pray for her son.

When the lad's twisted leg had straightened and he began laughing and running, his mother had all but worshiped Cristiana. But 'twas God who had performed the miracle.

Through the Spear. It had to be. For Cristiana could never have done such a feat.

Seraphina strolled to the hearth and held out her hands to the warm coals. "People were offering food and shelter in return for your prayers for their sick. We could have eventually afforded a home of our own."

"Mayhap. But protection? Lord Braewood offered both," Cristiana countered, hating to argue with her dear friend.

"He uses you for gain." Seraphina faced her. "Why can you not see that?"

"Then why take in Thebe at my request? She brings no value to him. She is but a lowly child, orphaned in the fire that struck the village six months past." Cristiana rose and hugged herself.

"I wish you would trust me, my lady. He is not the man you believe him to be. His intentions are far from benevolent."

The woman's gnawing persistence reminded Cristiana that Seraphina was a friend, aye, but also a servant. "Do you take me for a fool? Have I traded one evil lord for another? At least I am not forced to take potions which keep my mind befuddled and my body abed. You have no idea how wonderful it is to regain my strength." She exhaled a deep sigh before continuing. "To have a clear mind, to be in control of my thoughts again. After so many years."

Seraphina approached, desperation spiking her tone. "Then use those thoughts to choose the wise path. Let us go home, I beseech you."

"Home to what? With my disappearance and Alexia wanted for witchcraft, Sir Walter has no doubt petitioned the king for ownership of Luxley." After their escape, Seraphina had informed Cristiana that her sister was still alive, much to her utter glee.

"The king is wise. He will not grant it ere he has proof of your death."

"Sweet angels! Indeed. Another reason not to return to a man who would happily seek my end."

"And what of your sister?" Seraphina arched a condemning brow. "Would you leave her to face such danger alone?"

Cristiana stared at the coals, hating the guilt rippling through her. "Alexia is strong, much stronger than I have ever been. If anyone can regain Luxley, 'tis her."

"Mayhap she needs your help. At least bring her the Spear."

Cristiana patted her thigh where she had strapped the relic. 'Twas the only place to keep it safe and always with her.

Seraphina huffed. "'Tis well you at least heed my advice to keep it hidden. Should Lord Braewood discover it, he would have no further need of you."

Cristiana stared at her friend, anger rising. "'Tis a folly you speak so ill of him."

Seraphina lowered her head. "Forgive me, my lady." She wandered to the window again. "And what of Sir Jarin?"

Jarin the Just, the knight who had stolen Cristiana's heart. The name that still sent a bolt of warmth through her. She could picture his dark hair curled at the tips as it hung to his shoulders, the trimmed beard lining his chin and jaw, his brown eyes so full of strength and concern, the deep timbre of his voice, and the way his roguish smile sent her heart careening in delight. But he'd abandoned her. Like everyone else. "What of him?" she spat out. "We found no trace of him or any of them in Emerald Forest."

"We didn't search long enough. I know Alexia and the friar have a hideout there."

Suddenly chilled, Cristiana moved to the hearth and dropped to a chair. "Should we have stayed until Sir Walter's soldiers found us? They were fast on our trail as you remember. Even so, 'tis obvious by now that Sir Jarin does not search for me. He has no doubt moved on to another."

"And your sister and Sir Ronar LePeine?" Seraphina asked, her tone a spear of reprimand.

"Hopefully in hiding from those who wish her burned at the stake. I place no blame on her for not coming to my aid."

"Then let us go find *her*, my lady." Seraphina knelt before her. "And Sir Jarin, Sir Ronar, and Sir Damien LaRage. Let us join their cause."

As much as Cristiana longed to see her sister and ensure she was safe, the thought of leaving the only place she'd ever felt secure and venturing into the unknown again made every inch of her seize with panic. Most of her eighteen years had been fraught with uncertainty, fear, betrayal, and death.

A knock on the door saved her from declaring her cowardice to her friend. Cristiana's maid, Muriel, entered, Thebe in her arms. At the sight of Cristiana, the two-year-old girl wiggled free to the floor and darted toward her. "Cristi, Cristi!" She leapt into her arms, and Cristiana squeezed her tight. "Why are you not abed, dear one?" She glanced at Muriel, whose nervous gaze shifted to Seraphina. "Nor in your night dress?" she added, taking in the girl's gown and woolen cloak.

Seraphina rose. "I had Muriel prepare her for our journey. We must leave. We have but a small window of time ere the guard returns to his post."

Cristiana kissed Thebe's forehead, her ire rising. "You will not only subject me to danger, but this child as well?"

"There is far more danger here, my lady. Prithee, you must believe me."

Cristiana glanced at the maid, who remained at the door. "And what do you think, Muriel? You have served Lord Braewood for years."

"I do not think, my lady. I merely do as I am told."

"Hmm. Do you wish to escape this place?"

Muriel's eyes shifted between Cristiana and Seraphina ere they lowered to the floor. "Nay, I have a home here."

"Tell her what you overheard, Muriel," Seraphina ordered the maid. "Mayhap she'll believe *you*."

The young girl, who could be no older than thirteen, shifted her feet across the floor but never raised her eyes. "I heard my lord arguing with Lady Braewood two nights past. His mother wished him to wed you as soon as possible."

"Peace froth!" Cristiana laughed, jarring Thebe, who had laid her head on her shoulder. "He has no such romantic notions."

"Indeed, my lady," Muriel added, "for he said he had no desire to wed. Rather he wished to discover the power behind your healing and acquire it for himself. He made mention of gaining a fortune by doing so."

Cristiana swallowed. The revelation slowly wormed its way into her heart, depositing a lesion of doubt. Muriel had no reason to lie about such a matter. "I bid you, Muriel, give me your troth that you speak the truth."

The maid finally raised her gaze and nodded.

Another betrayal. Would they never cease? She kissed Thebe's forehead as confusion and heartache stirred a wicked brew within her. Yet there was no time to decide the right course. She must trust Seraphina. "Then we shall leave." With the child still in her arms, she rose and nodded for the maid to grab her woolen cloak. "My things." Terror suddenly took hold of her as she glanced around the chamber at all the comforts she would leave behind.

"I have packed a bag for each of us already." Seraphina started for the door. "Just carry the girl. This way."

Cristiana followed her, glancing at the maid. "Come with us, Muriel."

"I cannot, my lady. I wouldn't know what to do in the world." Tears filled the young girl's eyes. "Godspeed."

"And to you."

Down the winding stairs, Cristiana fled. Past the great hall where several people slept on reed pallets near the massive hearth, past the dark kitchen, and out into the bailey.

The chill of the night permeated Cristiana's thin tunic even as her heart froze in fear and uncertainty. Should she leave this safe place on the word of one maid? Nay. 'Twas also Seraphina's word. But where would they go? How would they care for this precious child that was even now growing heavy in her arms?

Seraphina disappeared into the stables and emerged moments later with two palfreys, saddled, bridled and ready to ride.

"Hurry." Taking the reins, she led her horse through the courtyard toward the back where a half-moon revealed no guard stood at the post. Pushing open the gate, she led her horse through, the creaking sound reverberating like a gong through the night.

Cristiana stood frozen in place, staring at the open gate as Seraphina tied their bags to the back of her saddle, then mounted the horse with an ease that surprised her. Beyond, only darkness rose from a forest that surrounded Braewood Hall. The scent of earthy loam, hay, and horses filled her nose, whilst the howl of a distant wolf prickled the hair on her arms. Outside that gate were wars, hunger, cold, predators, evil men, and danger. Yet inside these walls were secrets, lies, and betrayal.

"Come, precious." Cristiana kissed Thebe and started to lift her onto the saddle. "I'm going to put you on the horse now."

"Ride horsey?" the sleepy child said gleefully.

"Aye, dear. Ride horsey."

"Nay, dear, no horse ride for you this night." The voice snaked an icy trail down Cristiana's back. She spun to see three figures emerge from the shadows. Lord Braewood, flanked by two of his knights.

Cristiana drew the child back to her chest and retreated a step, her heart banging so hard against her ribs, she thought it would break through.

Seraphina groaned as her horse pawed the dirt.

"Don't just stand there!" he ordered his men. "Grab her!"

The men started for Seraphina. Cristiana couldn't breathe. Thebe started to cry.

And Seraphina did the one thing Cristiana never thought she would do. She slapped the reins against the horse's neck, and after giving Cristiana one last glance of remorse, kicked her heels against its sides and sped off into the darkness.

"Should I go after her, my lord?" one of the knight's said.

"Nay. She will trouble us no further." Then turning to Cristiana, Lord Braewood pasted on a smile that curdled her stomach. "Now, my dear, where were you running off to in the middle of the night?"

At that moment, two horrid things occurred to her. One, she was the biggest fool that ever lived, and two, along with everyone else in her life, her best friend had just abandoned her.

CHAPTER THREE

Luxley Castle, Northland Goodryke

No one of rank ever took note of a servant. Especially a male servant whose face was scarred and deformed by war. 'Tis what Jarin the Just relied upon as he hobbled into the study of Sir Walter LeGode with a pail full of hot coals. Hunching over to hide his height, he hoped his tattered cloak also hid his broad shoulders as he made his way to the brazier, dragging his worn shoes over the stone floor.

"'Tis about time!" Sir Walter barked at him from behind his desk. "Devil's blood! I could die of cold ere my servants attend their tasks." He held a folded parchment up to the candlelight as though he could see through the paper. The missive had just been delivered by a lad who stood by the open door awaiting instructions.

Jarin dipped his head and started toward the iron brazier in the corner. Sir Walter was right about one thing. 'Twas chilled in this room. But the gooseflesh prickling over Jarin's skin came not merely from the cold. Evil surrounded him. Dark, malevolent evil—a heaviness that pressed on him and threatened to send him darting out the door. Forsooth, and he, a knight! One of the famous King's Guards. Rather he used to be. Still, he had fought and subdued the fiercest warriors on the battlefield. Bosh! What devilment was this that sped his heart in fear? Mayhap 'twas one of Lady Falcon's elusive spirits. He smiled as he knelt before the brazier and opened the iron grate. Poppycock!

"From the king?" Bishop Montruse yawned in his chair before Sir Walter's desk, the sapphire ring on his hand glistening in the candlelight as he brought a glass of wine to his lips. "Open it, you fool."

Jarin began shoving hot coals into the brazier as slowly as he could.

The sound of a torn paper preceded a moment of silence ere an eruption spewed from Sir Walter's mouth more vile than any curses Jarin had heard on the battlefield. The bishop only laughed. "You wake the devil with such language, LeGode. Tsk-tsk."

"You think he is not already astir with such an affront as this?" Sir Walter shook the paper vehemently in the air.

Jarin continued filling the brazier. Indeed. If there *was* a devil, he was definitely present in this place. Another chill gripped him as Sir Walter continued his rampage, unleashing his vitriol onto the poor lad who'd brought him the missive. "What are you still doing here? Out with you!"

The boy's footsteps barely hit the floor as he fled.

"I take it the king has not granted your request for Luxley?" The bishop's tone was mocking.

Sir Walter growled. "Nay, Your Grace." He tossed the parchment down and grabbed a mug from his desk. "He wishes proof that Cristiana D'Clere is dead. How am I to provide that when my men have been unable to locate her? The vile wench! She is a witch like her sister."

"At least you haven't had to deal with the first witch. 'Twould appear her fear of the stake has kept her far away. Mayhap for good, if she possesses a brain in that pretty head. Hence, you have but one witch to do away with." Bishop Montruse gave a superior grin. "*If* you and your fluff-headed soldiers can find her."

"*When,* you mean to say. Though I grant you, she appears to be as elusive as her sister." Sir Walter dropped back into his chair, mug of wine in hand. "I still don't see how she and those infernal knights could have evaded our combined forces."

Montruse fingered the gold cross around his neck. "Never fear. They will not evade us for long. We have God on our side."

Sir Walter's mouth twisted, but he made no reply.

"I must find that Spear!" The bishop's calm demeanor swiftly vanished. "One of them has it." He rose and swept aside his long, embroidered tunic as he marched toward Jarin.

Jarin continued his work, ducking his face in the shadows. Red silk shoes appeared in his vision, but the bishop paid him no mind.

"I cannot"—the bishop continued, fingering his elaborate maniple—"nay I *will not* be banished to this...this...barbaric, paltry estate! Curse those King's Guard and the witches who beguile them!"

The room reverberated with his blasphemy and filled with tension at the affront done the steward.

Jarin stirred the coals, releasing heat that quelled the icy shroud surrounding him.

Sir Walter slowly rose. "You make too free with your insults, Your Grace. Luxley is a vast holding and one which many covet."

Bishop Montruse spun about and uttered an indignant huff. "Mayhap for the likes of you, but I am accustomed to the king's palace. *And* I will make free with whatever I wish. You would do well to remember that, sir."

"Of course." Sir Walter dipped his head. "Then you should know that the Spear has not made an appearance in this castle for months."

Jarin remained stooped before the brazier, though his task was complete.

"And how do you know such a thing?"

"I have my sources."

The bishop snorted. "Your son? Is that where Cedric has disappeared to these past months? Summoning the spirits?"

Sir Walter looked surprised.

Montruse sauntered back to Sir Walter's desk. "Faith now, do you take me for a fool, Sir?"

"I would never presume, your Excellency." Yet Sir Walter's tone bore sarcasm.

Montruse flattened his palms on the top of the desk and leaned toward the steward. "I know Cedric spends much time beneath this castle. Just what are you hiding down there? Never mind." Pushing from the desk, he waved his hand through the air, his billowing white sleeves fluttering around him. "I do not wish to know. I need the Spear, or the king will have my head."

"Hurry up with the coals, you lout!" Sir Walter shouted at Jarin.

"Forgive me, my lord," Jarin closed the grate and slowly rose to a hunched position.

Retrieving the king's missive from his desk, Sir Walter held it to a candle flame. The paper instantly ignited. He watched it curiously as if it were the king himself who was burning, ere he started toward the brazier. Jarin quickly stepped aside. "I must find Lady Cristiana, and you must find the Spear. Perchance they are together." One brow rose as Sir Walter tossed the paper onto the glowing coals.

"Forsooth! The Spear with that ruffle-headed woman? Nay. She has neither the brains nor bravery of her sister."

"I do not gainsay it, Your Grace." Sir Walter wandered to the window, where even the sunlight seemed afraid to enter. "We still have a bargain, do we not?"

"Aye, the Spear for Luxley. I have not forgotten." The bishop fingered his pointed beard. "Therefore, I will help you eliminate Lady Cristiana. And together we will find and kill these Knights of the Eternal Realm, as they call themselves now." He chuckled. "Ludicrous, insolent name."

Sir Walter faced the bishop. "They continue to thwart us. Leaving meat for the villagers against our decree, even slipping in and out of Luxley undetected, like spirits of the night!"

Jarin slowly made his way to the door.

"Then use spirits to fight them, sir." The bishop's tone turned oily and sinister. At Sir Walter's look of shock, he added, "Do I surprise you?"

"I admit to being astonished, Your Grace."

"I will not accept failure, sir. I will return to the palace where I belong. With the Spear in hand."

"And you will persuade the king to grant me Luxley."

"You have my troth." Montruse held out his hand for Sir Walter to kiss his ring,

After a moment's hesitation and a flicker of disdain in the steward's eyes, he complied.

Jarin could delay no longer without suspicion. He stepped through the door just as Sir Walter said, "Then I shall employ every weapon in my arsenal."

Making his way across the great hall, Jarin barely took note of the servants spreading cloths over the trestle tables and maids scurrying about with fresh flowers and oil lamps in preparation for the noon meal. He maintained his bent posture and awkward shuffle as he entered the larder and passed through the kitchen, out into the inner bailey, where he was to meet Anabelle.

The fresh air did much to sweep away the weight of evil he oft felt inside the castle these days. But it did naught to sweep away his fear for Lady Cristiana D'Clere. They intended to eliminate her, as the bishop had declared.

And he could never allow that to happen. He was done taking orders from Ronar LePeine.

Anabelle appeared before him carrying a basket of fresh herbs. Blond curls spilled out from beneath her chaplet and circled a comely face. A year ago, he would have attempted to entice such a delicious morsel to his bed. But that was before he met Lady Cristiana.

A tiny smile curved one side of Anabelle's lips as she whispered. "I hardly recognized you."

"Then I have achieved my goal. Have you, mistress?"

Gripping the basket, she glanced around the busy bailey. "I have. At least when I have the opportunity. He has taken to his bed much of late."

"I am pleased."

"But I fear the bishop more than Sir Walter." She continued whispering as a visible shiver ran through her. "There is evil in that man."

"I quite agree. There is evil in them both. But 'tis Sir Walter's confession we need."

She nodded, and Jarin slipped his hand inside his cloak, pulled out a vial, and handed it to her.

Taking it, she hid it amongst the reeds in her basket and smiled ere she went on her way.

Finally out of the castle, Jarin drew a sigh of relief as he made his way through the village, which bustled with people going about their daily tasks.

By the time he entered Emerald Forest, he couldn't discard his disguise fast enough. Kneeling before a creek, he peeled off scars made of clay and washed Alexia's artwork from his face.

Finally able to stand tall, he drew back his shoulders and took a deep breath of pine, moss, and earth before collecting the belt and weapons he'd hidden in a bush. Anxious to report back to his friends, he strapped on the gear and proceeded on his way…when two knights leapt in his path, swords drawn.

Alexia D'Clere nocked an arrow in her bow, pulled back her bowstring, and shifted it over the forest spread beneath her.

"Tush!" Ronar growled from the branch beneath hers as he made his way from bough to bough up the tall oak tree. Gripping the hefty limb, he swung himself up to stand beside her, causing it to shake beneath her feet. "Must we always climb the tallest tree in the forest?" He brushed himself off.

"Shh." Alexia arched a brow toward him. His blue eyes met hers with a wink. The man never failed to stir her insides into a frenzy. Ronar LePeine, Lord Rivenhall, turned King's Guard, and now Knight of the Eternal Realm. And her betrothed.

Alas, she still had trouble believing that last bit. He shifted slightly ere catching his balance, then grinned her way. Dark brown hair grazed over broad shoulders encased in a thick leather doublet. All manner of weapons hung from a belt at his waist.

He scratched the stubble on his chin and lowered his voice. "I fail to see why we can't guard the forest from the ground."

Shifting her gaze to the trees, Alexia hid a smile. "Never fear, Sir Knight. With a little more practice, you shall soon be flying through these trees like an eagle."

He leaned toward her, his hot breath igniting a fire on her neck that spread down her body, causing the usual pleasurable shiver. "I am more panther than bird, my Lady Falcon. Though I am beginning to believe 'tis the only way I will get to see you."

"And is it worth your climb, Sir Knight?" She smiled.

"Only if I receive a kiss."

"Potz! Do you think I grant such favors to any knight who climbs a simple tree for me?"

"Nay." He glanced down, his eyes widening. "But I doubt many would attempt the feat for less." He faced her with that disarming smile of his. "Mayhap for your husband?"

She nudged him back, careful not to unsettle him. "You are not my lord yet."

"And why is that?" His brow wrinkled. "I fear I cannot wait much longer to make you mine."

In good sooth, neither could she. She shifted her gaze away lest she give in to his every demand. "You know we must concentrate on our mission—clearing our names, defeating Sir Walter and the evil within Luxley, and then restoring the estate to my sister."

"We can do that as man and wife." Grabbing a strand of her red hair, he fingered it as if it were made of silk and drew it to his nose.

Against her will, her blood heated. "You know I cannot enter into such happiness whilst my sister suffers."

"Which is one of the reasons I love you so." He ran a thumb gently over her cheek, and she could stand it no longer. Lowering her bow, she drew close and placed a gentle kiss on his lips. He reached around her and pulled her against him, deepening the kiss until she felt she would lose her balance and fall blissfully through the air, without a care for striking the ground.

Finally, he withdrew and gave her a victorious grin.

She frowned. "Ah, Sir Knight, you received your kiss withal."

"I always do, my love."

If she had not sensed something astir in the forest at that moment, Ronar would have found himself struggling for balance. As it was, she raised her bow again. "Hush now, knight. Something is afoot."

Opting for his knife instead of the bow and quiver of arrows slung over his back, Ronar assumed his warrior stance, studying every tree, shrub, and darting squirrel for anything out of the ordinary. Alexia had done her best to instruct him in the art of archery these past months, but the mighty King's Guard found the weapon "cumbersome and ineffectual," as he put it, much preferring his blades. His instruction, however, had provided Alexia with hours of entertainment.

The warble of birds accompanied the laughter of wind trickling through leaves. Lush greenery, brimming with wildlife, flourished everywhere she looked. Emerald Forest. Her home the past ten years. Ever since Friar Josef had rescued her from Luxley Castle when he discovered Sir Walter's plot to murder her.

"I hear naught," Ronar finally said.

Alexia closed her eyes. "Nor do I." She sought the Spirit within, and in moments the world transformed from one of bland greens and browns to stunning emeralds, jades, ambers, and bronze—all glittering and vibrating with life. Gold-dipped wings of butterflies fluttered about as the songs of myriad birds rose to the throne of God in a harmony of praise. A creek of bubbling diamonds cut across the ground past two warriors of light who guarded the foot of the tree in which Alexia and Ronar stood.

Alexia never grew weary of this privileged peek into the spirit realm. The friar said she was a seer, one of God's children gifted with sight into the next world. 'Twas not for her benefit, but to help others, as she hoped to do now. She had felt the darkness and now she saw it, lurking behind the trees, slinking in the shadows, avoiding the light. It circled around a figure in the distance, crowding in on him as if to swallow him whole.

Alexia opened her eyes. "Jarin," was all she said.

"He's in trouble." Ronar sheathed his knife and leapt down to the branch beneath them.

Swinging her bow over her back, Alexia followed, but passed him as she descended with the speed and grace of years living amongst the trees. She landed on the soft dirt and waited for him.

Shaking his head, Ronar dropped beside her. "How do you do that?" he growled.

"How did you know Jarin was in trouble?"

"You aren't the only one our Lord speaks to, my love." He kissed her cheek and sped off in the direction she would have gone.

Alexia heard the eerie clank of steel on steel echoing through the treetops long before she saw Jarin. Withdrawing an arrow from her quiver, she positioned it in the bow as she ran beside Ronar, who had drawn his sword.

Grunts and groans joined the cacophony of striking blades, urging them to increase their speed. Finally, they burst into a clearing to find Jarin battling two large, well-armed soldiers. He crossed blades with the larger of the two in a mighty clank, but their hilts caught for the briefest of seconds. Alas, 'twas all it took for the smaller soldier to thrust his sword toward Jarin's side.

CHAPTER FOUR

This cannot be the end. Jarin had no sooner thwarted one soldier's vicious attack, when out of the corner of his eye, he spotted the other soldier's blade plunging toward his side. Until now, he'd been able to use his finely-honed skills as a King's Guard to fend off the two brutes attacking him. And quite successfully, he would add, for blood saturated the arm of the smaller man, where he'd sliced the skin to the bone. If only Jarin's hilt hadn't gotten stuck with the larger soldier's blade. As it was, he knew he could not react in time.

Sudden and unusual fear squeezed his heart. What would become of Cristiana? And the Knights of the Eternal Realm? Even worse, where would *he* end up? He'd not been on speaking terms with the Almighty in quite some time. Sweat stung his eyes as he prepared himself for the pain of the sword.

Snap-swoosh, snap-swoosh. Fast and one after the other, the sounds filled the air. An arrow cut through the smaller man's arm. He dropped the sword. The other soldier groaned in agony as another arrow pierced his thigh. But 'twas not enough to stop him. With a mighty growl, he swung his blade toward Jarin.

Jarin raised his sword to fend him off just as Ronar charged the man, leveling his own sword at the man's chest. "I'd drop that if I were you."

The soldier, who appeared more beast than man due to the large amount of hair on his face and neck, sneered at Ronar, hesitating as if contemplating taking on both of them.

The other soldier, still moaning from his wound, inched his hand toward his sword on the ground, but Lady Falcon kicked it aside and pointed her arrow at him, giving him a sweet smile.

The large soldier's eyes widened at the sight of Lady Falcon—no doubt recognizing her. Surely he'd be rewarded handsomely for bringing such a prize back to Sir Walter and

Bishop Montruse. But he must have realized who he was up against, for his expression fell, along with his sword thudding to the ground.

"Begone! You may leave with your life if you leave posthaste," Ronar said, glancing at the man's wounds. "However, I advise you to hurry ere darkness falls and wolves emerge from their dens, drawn to the stink of your blood."

Jarin chuckled.

A snarl lifted the large man's lips as he glanced at his friend, who lumbered to his feet, the arrow still protruding from his arm. Together they hobbled away as fast as their wounds permitted them.

Lady Falcon, who kept her arrow pointed at them, finally lowered it and called after them. "Do tell Sir Walter, the Knights of the Eternal Realm send our regards."

Still chuckling, Jarin faced his friends. "If you must know, I had the situation quite in hand." He sheathed his blade, even as a wave of relief settled through him.

Ronar grabbed his arm and squeezed it. "I do not gainsay it. But what harm is there in a little aid from friends?"

"A little?" Jarin faced the infamous Lady Falcon. Waves of fiery hair flowed about her face and over the huntsman attire she wore that failed to hide her feminine curves. Her green eyes held a world of wisdom and spunk as she assessed him, and Jarin could see why Ronar was taken with her. "Bosh! Rescued by a woman, her two arrows fired so swiftly and precisely there was naught left for us to do. And us, King's Guards! The shame of it. My lady,"—he dipped his head in her direction—"'tis our job to rescue you, not the other way around."

Sheathing his sword, Ronar smiled at his betrothed. "Alas, a fact of which I have informed her many a time."

Lady Falcon flung her bow over her shoulder and placed a hand on her hip. "It pains me greatly that I have caused your pride to suffer, gentlemen, but if 'tis a maiden you wish to rescue, it may please you to look elsewhere."

Jarin shared a glance with Ronar, who shrugged and smiled at Alexia. "Tush, love! You cannot gainsay that I have come to your rescue more than once." Ronar grabbed the soldiers' swords off the ground and handed one to Jarin ere he approached Lady Falcon.

"Did you, Sir Knight?" She pursed her lips at her intended, an impish sparkle in her eyes. "Mayhap. Yet I trust I have more than returned the favor."

Ronar slid a finger over her cheek. "In part, I'll admit, but I hope you will repay me in full one day soon."

Jarin growled, the exchange reminding him he'd not enjoyed such amorous banter with the softer gender since meeting Lady Cristiana. "Enough of this sickening flirtation! Let's away to the cave. I have much to tell everyone." He marched off, pushing aside a shrub whilst chuckles followed in this wake.

Ronar caught up with him. "Pray, what news from Luxley?"

"'Tis not good. But I should wait until Damien and the friar can hear as well."

Ronar nodded, his expression stern in the fading light.

"How fares Anabelle?" Lady Falcon spoke from behind him.

"She is well...brave as always." Jarin glanced over his shoulder at her, but she had disappeared up into the trees. Without a sound, he would add.

"I am pleased to hear it," he heard her say from above them. He shook his head. The lady was more bird than human.

"You weren't followed?" Ronar asked.

"Nay. Nor discovered." Jarin glanced upward. "Your disguise worked, my lady." Leaves rustled, but he could no longer see her as night dropped a black cloak o'er the treetops.

No further words were said. The sound of their breaths mingled with the hoot of owls, the hum of insects, and the distant, eerie howl of a wolf.

A prickling scraped across the back of Jarin's neck. But not from the wolf. He rubbed it, trying to shake off the foreboding, when Ronar threw an arm out to halt him. Together they stood still...listening... barely breathing. Above the noise of the forest came footsteps...tentative...soft. Joined by the sound of Lady Falcon's bowstring pulled tight from a branch above.

Ronar drew his blade. Jarin did the same. Backing off the trail, they eased into the shadow of a large tree.

The footsteps grew louder. Leaves rustled. A feminine sigh followed by a slight whimper caused Jarin to loosen the tight grip on his blade. Ronar's shoulders lowered as well. Yet they remained hidden.

In moments, a shadow entered from their left and wandered down the path. A woman. A shaft of moonlight broke through the canopy and transformed her braid of hair into glistening ivory.

Leaves rustled overhead, and she glanced upward just as the name "Seraphina" loosed from Lady Falcon's lips, and she dropped onto the path before her friend.

Though the woman shrieked and leapt back, within an instant she flew into Lady Falcon's arms, crying in delight. "I found you, Lady Alexia! I found you!"

Heart leaping at the sight of Lady Cristiana's dear friend, Jarin emerged from the shadows, Ronar by his side. 'Twas indeed her! The woman who never left her lady's side.

"Where's Lady Cristiana?" Jarin approached her, though she still sobbed in Lady Falcon's arms.

Ronar touched his arm and sent him a look of censure. 'Twas obvious the woman was distraught, for they could now see her woolen kirtle was torn and stained, her hair disheveled, and her emotions awhirl.

Still, she pushed from Alexia and faced him with tears forging tracks down her dirt-stained face. "'Tis why I have come, Sir Jarin." She released a heavy breath and stumbled.

Ronar caught her. "Let's get her back to the cave posthaste. She needs care."

"Dear, dear, Seraphina." Lady Falcon embraced her again, then took one arm while Ronar grabbed the other and hoisted the bulk of her weight onto his shoulder.

"Pray tell, is my sister alive?" Lady Falcon's voice rang with the same fear Jarin felt inside.

"She is, my lady," Seraphina breathed out as they proceeded.

Feeling his fear soften a bit, Jarin took the rear, cursing his selfishness even as he grew desperate for further news.

That desperation mounted as they approached the waterfall, made their way through the prickly brambles surrounding it, leapt atop moss-laden boulders, and slipped behind the cascade of water. It further grew as they squeezed into the narrow opening behind the cleft of a rock, then felt their way along the winding tunnel leading down to the place Jarin had called home for nearly a year.

A secret knock, the turn of a latch, and the friar's kind face appeared behind the wooden door. With a gentle wave of his hand, he beckoned them inside. His smile faded to concern at the sight of Seraphina.

"Place her here by the fire." He gestured toward a high-backed bench, cushioned in red and perched beside the hearth, whilst he sped as fast as his old legs could carry him to the other side of the room, his brown robes flowing behind him.

Jarin closed and latched the door, allowing the warmth of the well-appointed chamber to sweep away the chill of the forest. Alack, his desperation remained. Yet, as light from several lamps alighted upon Seraphina, that desperation faded to mere impatience in view of her ragged condition. Aside from her torn and stained kirtle, bruises and cuts marred her arms and face—a comely face that appeared sunken, no doubt from lack of sustenance.

Dropping her bow and arrows on a table, Alexia grabbed a coverlet, flung it about the woman's shoulders, and knelt before her. Despite her obvious discomfort, Seraphina smiled at her friend, then shifted her blue eyes up to Ronar, then over the Jarin. Was it merely his own hope, or was there a flicker of eagerness in her gaze when it met his?

Friar Josef returned with a pewter mug into which he poured steaming water from a kettle hung over the fire. "Here my dear. This will soothe you. Holy saints..." He examined her cuts and bruises and turned away, no doubt to seek out salve and bandages.

"Never fear, Friar." Alexia stayed him with a touch to his arm. "I shall tend to her wounds. Let us allow her to breathe."

Seraphina sipped the tea, closed her eyes, and swallowed it, her breath still coming fast. "I need no time. Thank God I found you! I have been praying...praying...searching the forest. But in His mercy, our Lord led me straight to you."

"'Tis truly a miracle." Removing his sword from its sheath, Ronar sat in one of the chairs across from her.

Alexia slid onto the bench beside her friend, while the friar gripped the cross hanging around his neck and stood waiting off to the side.

Waiting had never been one of Jarin's skills. Shifting his gaze from the lady lest he burst out with the questions burning on his tongue, he glanced over the large chamber, still fascinated that such a place existed beneath the earth. Colorful tapestries decorated the stone walls, and fine oak chairs and tables furnished the room. One entire wall was lined with shelf after shelf of books, before which sat the friar's desk, a storm of parchment and quill pens scattered across it. A linen-clad trestle table where they enjoyed their meals stood to the right. Beyond that, a small corridor led to two other chambers, one of which was where Alexia slept for propriety's sake.

He returned his gaze to Seraphina, who took another sip of tea and appeared to be trying to settle her breathing.

"Where is Damien?" Ronar addressed the friar as he leaned forward on his knees.

As if summoned by his name, the secret knock echoed through the chamber, and Ronar rushed to admit his friend and fellow King's Guard, Sir Damien LaRage. The mighty warrior, still attired in the leather, metal, and myriad weapons of a

King's Guard, stomped into the room, a smile on his face and two dead pheasants in his hand. "Supper!" he announced. "We shall feast—" His eyes landed on Seraphina, and it seemed for a moment he believed not what they told him.

She smiled his way. "Sir Damien."

'Twas all it took to cause him to drop the birds to the silk carpet and rush forward to kneel at her feet, scanning her with a gaze that bespoke of concern and—dare Jarin guess— affection? 'Twas a rare thing for Damien to take an interest in anything save his drink and his revenge. How had Jarin missed this?

For moments they stared at one another as if they were the only two people in the chamber.

Chuckling, the friar picked up the birds and set them on a sideboard by the hearth.

"Fetch her something to eat," Damien barked.

"Nay." The woman set her tea aside. "I must speak first."

Forcing himself to stand, Damien took a spot beside Seraphina, his steely expression masking his emotions.

"What news of my sister?" Rare tears filled Alexia's eyes as she gripped the woman's hands. "Pray, 'tis not bad, is it? I could not bear it."

Jarin raised the steel fortress around his heart once again. At Seraphina's appearance, hope had lowered it slightly, but he could not allow that. He was well acquainted with bad news. In truth, he'd been battling it for years, and he would not grant his enemy another victory.

"Pray, forgive me." Seraphina squeezed her friend's hands. "Never fear. She is well, my lady. At least last I saw her. But she finds herself in a desperate situation."

"Tush! Where is she?" Ronar asked. "And where have you both been these ten months?"

Drawing in a breath, Seraphina tugged her hands from Alexia's, clasped them in her lap, and proceeded to tell them a tale of such woe, Jarin could hardly keep silent. She relayed how they had escaped the day of Cristiana's wedding to Cedric, how they'd spent six months out in the cold, hungry and frightened, then how they discovered that, the Spear gave Cristiana the power to heal.

"She healed the sick and lame without recompense, merely for scraps of food," Seraphina continued. "Until a man named Lord Braewood took us in."

Jarin knew enough about the world, knew enough about the greed and depravity of man to know this Lord Braewood had ill intentions even before Seraphina continued with the rest of the story.

Jarin could hold his peace no longer. "And she does not attempt to escape?"

Seraphina fixed him with eyes filled with despair but also determination. "She is frightened Sir Jarin. Lord Braewood offers her security, a home, her every need met. After what she has been through—abandoned by everyone she loved, poisoned and kept prisoner in her own castle—can you blame her?"

Alexia lowered her gaze, a visible shudder running through her. "I should not have ceased searching for her."

Rising, Ronar slid beside her and flung an arm over her shoulder. "We did all we could, my love. We searched high and low for three months, spoke with countless peasants, tradesmen, farmers, and clergymen."

Damien moved to stare at the fire. "Aye, and risked arrest everywhere we went."

Seraphina shook her head and gave Alexia a sympathetic look. "You would not have found us. Lady Cristiana wanted to get as far from here as she could. We hid in stables, barns, and abandoned churches, and oft in the forest. We became quite good at staying out of sight."

Damien smiled her way. "We trusted you to care for her."

She returned his smile as Alexia gripped her hand again. "I owe you everything for staying by her side."

"You owe me naught. She is not only my lady but my friend."

"Still." Alexia frowned. "I should not have given up."

"We had our battles to fight here," Ronar offered.

"And we trusted God to bring the lady back in His good time," the friar added.

Tiring of talk, Jarin stepped forward, anxious to do something. "Does this man have improper intentions toward her?"

"Nay, 'tis not like that. At least not what I have seen. He wishes only to use her power for money."

"Then she is not safe there." Jarin gripped the hilt of his sword.

A tear slipped down Seraphina's face. She swiped it away. "I doubt he would harm her. As long as she continues to heal those who come for help."

"But what happens when he finds the Spear?" Jarin huffed. "Or worse, it ceases to heal?"

"'Tis not the Spear that heals," the friar interjected.

Jarin frowned at the holy man. 'Twas not the time for his spiritual babble. "Regardless, should this power fade, what would become of Cristiana?"

Seraphina lowered her gaze. "I'll grant you I do not know the answer to that."

Ronar held his palm up to Jarin as if to calm him. "Then we have a bit of time on our side."

"Nay, the situation is most urgent," Jarin shot back. "Not only due to this vermin Braewood, but because of what I overheard at Luxley today."

All eyes snapped to him.

Shrugging from beneath Ronar's arm, Alexia stood. "Prithee, give us the sum of it."

Jarin scrubbed the stubble on his chin. "They intend to hunt her down and kill her. And they *will* find her, I assure you. They have powers of their own—dark powers. I felt them today." He stiffened his jaw. "They are stronger than ever."

"Aye." Ronar ran a hand through his hair. "I felt them as well a sennight ago when I snuck into Luxley through the tunnels. Whatever evil is there, it grows."

Damien crossed arms over his chest. "How do we fight something we cannot see?"

Friar Josef smiled. "With another unseen Being much more powerful." The man's infernal confidence and peace always grated on Jarin.

Alexia nodded. "Indeed."

Ronar stood. "Agreed."

Jarin moved to a cabinet against the wall where they stored their weapons. "Then we must go rescue her! I will not be detained further." He chose several knives, a long dagger, and an axe.

Ronar growled and moved to stand beside him. "I have not detained you, my friend. I merely advised you after we wasted three months searching for her, to remain here where we would eventually receive news of her. And hence, we have."

"All in God's good time." The friar moved to the sideboard where he gathered a piece of bread and handed it to Damien.

The large knight knelt before Seraphina and gave it to her. "I am in agreement. We cannot delay her rescue," he said to them all, though his eyes never left the lady.

Alexia shook her head. "Alas, we cannot *all* leave now. Not with the villagers depending on us for food, and the darkness soon to swallow Luxley. Our battle is here."

"You are right, my love." Ronar sighed. "Damien, I need you here."

Alexia grabbed her bow and quiver of arrows from the table. "I must go."

"Nay." Ronar's tone was commanding. "You will be caught."

"She is my sister." Alexia swung her quiver over her shoulder and faced her intended. "I will not disappoint her again."

Ronar growled. "You are wanted for witchcraft. And your face is known throughout the land. I will not lose you."

"Enough! I will go." Jarin sheathed his weapons and addressed Lady Falcon. "Ronar is right. You should remain." He gripped her hand in an effort to assure her of his determination. "Never fear, my lady. I will find her, and I will bring her back. You have my troth."

CHAPTER FIVE

Braewood Hall, Gavinshire

"**Y**ou must woo her, Robin. You must compliment her, offer her gifts, promise your devotion and protection." Lord Robin Braewood's mother, the matriarch of Braewood Castle, spread out the folds of her silk cote as she stared into the hearth, where recently-stoked flames danced like evil druids. She spun to face him, that all-too-familiar castigating frown upon her thin lips.

Robin sank to the bed with a huff. "I have tried, Mother. But you know I have no interest in the lady. She is far too refined, too prudish."

She let out a groan of disgust. "Peace froth! I will have no more of your insolent disregard! Your father would disavow you and cast you hence from Braewood."

"As well I know, Mother." But his father had taken to an early grave, a fact Robin thanked the stars for every day. At least his mother had need of him for support and mayhap bore some affection for him as her only son.

Demia Praxis, Lady Braewood approached him. The lines on her plump face and the silver in her hair did naught to distract from both the finery and fripperies of her attire, nor the authority with which she sent the staunchest servant scurrying with but one look.

The same look now scoured over Robin. "As I have informed you, my spies have returned with good news. The lady is heir to Luxley Castle in Northland Goodryke, an esteemed holding! When you marry her, 'twill be ours. Then with her power of healing, think of the wealth and status we will achieve. In good sooth, we may even be called to court." She smiled and dipped in the courtliest curtsy. "Friends of the king, can you imagine?"

But Robin saw no such glorious future. At least not for him. He swallowed down a lump of dread. "You sentence me to a life devoid of love."

Raising her hand, she slapped him hard across the face.

His head jerked to the right, and he pressed a palm over the sting radiating across his cheek into his jaw and down his neck. Alas, the sting of her callous regard hurt even more.

"Love! Bah!" she raged, waving her arm through the air. "You may have all the mistresses you wish when we are swimming in riches. Just marry the wench!"

Rising, Robin nodded, then rushed from his mother's solar and down the dank hall, swiping away the tears spilling down his cheeks. He had no choice, and he knew it. If he was ever going to gain his mother's love and approval, if he was ever going to secure their future—as was his duty—he must marry Lady Cristiana D'Clere. Whether she agreed to the match or not.

Tunic spread around her, Cristiana sat upon the woven wool rug in her chamber, Thebe by her side and two stuffed dolls in their hands. 'Twas Cristiana's favorite time of day—afternoons she spent with the little girl, playing, laughing, instructing. After Seraphina had abandoned her, Lord Braewood had punished Cristiana by not allowing her to see Thebe. It had been torture of the worst kind, and she'd quickly begged his forgiveness and his mercy in order to see the girl. His lordship had been more than kind to grant both.

Thebe giggled. "Sing, dance!"

Smiling, Cristiana began singing a song her mother used to hum throughout Luxley castle... at least what she remembered of it since she was but seven when Mother died. Taking her doll, she moved her in a jovial dance over the carpet while Thebe did the same. Together they laughed and sang until the girl grew tired. Then hugging her doll to her chest, she crawled into Cristiana's arms.

"Story," she said, as afternoon sunlight speared the colorful rug, transforming dust into diamonds in the air.

Cristiana wrapped both arms around the girl and leaned her chin on her head, pondering what tale to tell this time. 'Twas a practice they'd both embraced whene'er Thebe grew weary. A story always aided the child to fall asleep while at the same time gave Cristiana a chance to dream of lands and adventures beyond Braewood Manor, of places where life was happy and safe and nary a trouble dared tread.

She began a tale of a beautiful and powerful princess who ruled her people with goodness and love. A lady who was braver than a knight and wiser than a sage—all the things Cristiana was not but yearned so badly to be. She was halfway through the story when she felt Thebe grow heavy in her arms and heard the door to her chamber creak open.

In sauntered Lord Braewood, Muriel on his heels. With a snap of his fingers and a gesture to Thebe, Muriel reached down for the girl, giving Cristiana a reassuring smile that indicated she would take good care of the babe. A slight moan was all Thebe uttered as Muriel drew her into her arms and left the chamber.

Lord Braewood, dressed in a fine woolen surcote, trimmed in fur and clasped with an emerald brooch, smiled and extended his ringed hand. Taking it, she rose to her feet, quick in her attempt to retrieve her hand. But he refused, and instead lifted it to his lips for a kiss. The odd look in his eyes—one of a wolf toward its prey—alarmed her, and she took a step back and shifted her gaze away. Was the man still angry at her attempted escape nigh a month past? He'd informed her that his anger stemmed merely from the pain her mistrust had caused him, that she was free to leave Braewood at any time. Simply not with the babe. Thebe would not be thrust out into the cold world to starve, he had said, feigning an affection for the little girl which ne'er revealed itself in his actions.

Ergo, she was as much a prisoner in Braewood as if there were iron bars on her door. For how could she subject such an innocent babe to the cruel, frightening world when the child had her every need met here? Nor would she abandon her as everyone had done to Cristiana.

Thus, the iron bars, though unseen, were there nonetheless. And Cristiana had forced herself to be kind and compliant to the man she now knew was the monster Seraphina had believed him to be.

"Give ear a moment, my lady," he said, brushing a curl of his light hair from his face. "To the point, I fear your reputation is in danger. There is much talk amongst the townsfolk that you live at Braewood Castle without benefit of marriage."

Marriage? Cristiana attempted to hide her shock even as she wondered from whence came this sudden interest. "Surely they know I am your ward and here to heal those who are ill."

Shrugging, he raised his brows and flourished one hand through the air. "One would assume thus. But alas, people oft think the worst, as you know." He moved to the window where sunlight sparkled on the gold embroidery on the sleeves of his tunic. "Indeed, it does not bode well for me to be considered such a reprobate."

"I marvel anyone would think so, my lord."

At this, he smiled, a tight smile, which seemed forced, and she began to fear he might cast her out. *Without* Thebe.

"I care not for my reputation, my Lord," she continued, "but I am troubled yours is affected. What can I do?"

"Why, marry me, of course." He rushed to her and took her hands in his. "I love you, Cristiana. I have loved you from the first moment I saw you in town. You have my troth that I will cherish and protect you always." His tone was rote, almost as if he'd practiced what to say. And there was no love in his eyes, nor even desire. Merely a hard sheen and desperation that bespoke a disconnect betwixt his heart and his words.

"I am taken aback, my lord. I had no idea." She tugged her hands from his.

He lowered his gaze to stare at his shoes. "I cry pardon! Surely I have hinted at my affections for you."

"In good sooth, you have not, my lord." Although he had been offering her more compliments than usual, he'd made no such indication of anything but friendship, if that. She could make no sense of this sudden change in the man.

He turned his back to her. "Begad, you must pardon me there. I have been afraid of your reaction, afraid you would not return my affections."

A shiver of disgust ran through her at the thought of anything beyond a mere acquaintance with this man. Yet, how could she risk being tossed into the cold, heartless world?

Grabbing a strand of her hair, she tangled it betwixt two fingers. "My lord, I am flattered. But is this not rather rash? I fear I cannot at this time agree to marriage."

His posture slumped, and he hung his head. "You wound me deeply, my lady." Releasing a deep sigh, he faced her. A harshness had taken over his expression. "Tell me then, where are you to go? I know you run from something...or *someone.* Yet here you have all you need, every luxury, a home, protection, and of course, my love." His eyes lit as if he'd just had a thought. "And the love of Thebe. What more could a lady want?"

Was he casting her out? Without Thebe! Her heart sped to near bursting. 'Twas true she had no home to return to. Not unless Alexia could overcome and defeat Sir Walter and the bishop. But how could her sister accomplish such a feat—even with Sir Ronar's help—when she was accused of witchcraft by the king himself? Nay, her sister and her knight friends were no doubt long gone to another land or in hiding somewhere. Tears filled Cristiana's eyes at the thought she would never see her sister again. But what could she do? Even should she find Alexia, she had naught to offer to aid her cause.

Minutes passed...long minutes... during which the wind whistled against the stone walls and the setting sun withdrew its glittering rays from the window. She longed to respond to Lord Braewood's question but found her throat had closed.

"I will expect your answer anon, my lady. Otherwise, I fear, though it greatly pains me to say so, you will have to leave Braewood."

Terror threatened to choke the life from her. How could she give up a home, security, stability, and safety? Mayhap Lord Braewood didn't love her. Mayhap he merely wanted the money she made him. But he had never done her harm. Hadn't she always dreamt of marriage and children someday? Confusion spun her thoughts into a whirlwind. Surely, if he was willing to cast her off, he wasn't interested in the money after all.

As if to belie that last thought, he gave a greedy smile. "I will send Muriel to aid you in preparing for this evening's healing. There are many who await even now at the gate."

Three hours later, Cristiana sat on a cushioned chair in the great hall of Braewood Castle, Spear safely strapped to her thigh, ready to receive those who'd traveled from near and far in hopes of being healed. 'Twas truly an event she looked forward to every month, not to show off the power of the Spear nor to even bring praise upon herself but to watch the joy on people's faces when their pain left or their limbs straightened, or even on one rare occasion, they saw the world for the first time.

A fire crackled brightly in the giant hearth while minstrels played a soothing tune in the corner. By the large oak door, Lord Braewood's steward, Sir Caldwell, collected coins from those waiting in line. *That* part she hated, charging money for healing. But Lord Braewood insisted that a workman deserves his wage, or something like that, which he claimed was from the Bible. Cristiana couldn't say, for she'd not read the Holy Scriptures and knew of only a few verses Alexia had told her.

"Now, now, dear, see how they come for your power!" Lady Demia Braewood sat on a chair beside Cristiana like a queen on her throne. She clapped her hands together in glee.

"'Tis not my power, my lady. I am merely happy to help those in need."

"Faith now, of course. I make no doubt." She acted indignant.

Lord Braewood's mother had always been kind to Cristiana, had welcomed her into her home as a woman would her own daughter. But there was something about the lady that sent a spike of unease through Cristiana. She had longed for a mother figure since her own had died, but the woman hid behind a shield of ice. Now that Lord Braewood had proposed, that ice seemed to harden even more. As if one wrong word from Cristiana would make it crack.

"Master John Vottler!" A herald announced the first of the sick, diverting Cristiana's attention to the man in common threadbare attire hobbling up to her chair.

"Greetings, Master Vottler." She smiled and bade him sit on the stool before her.

He did, his eyes pools of hope and also anguish. "Good eve to you, my lady."

"What ails you this day?"

"'Tis my foot. I am a farmer, my lady, an' I broke it o'er two months past, but it didn't heal proper an' as you can see, remains crooked. I cannot till my land an' will soon be forced off by my lord. I 'ave a wife an' three wee ones to feed."

Cristiana glanced at the foot which arched at an angle away from the leg. Indeed. 'Twould be hard even to walk, let alone work his farm. Her heart ached for the man, and a love borne out of sympathy and care spilled out from her until she could barely contain it—as it always did when the Spear was about to heal. Tears filled her eyes as she rose from her chair and knelt by the man, placing her hands on his filthy foot.

The action caused a moan of disdain from Lady Braewood.

Ignoring her, Cristiana glanced up at him. "Never fear. You shall walk home this day."

Tears streamed down the man's dirty face.

"Do you believe that God can heal?" she asked.

"I do."

Then closing her eyes, Cristiana bowed her head and said, "Be straightened and healed by our Lord Christ Jesus and the power of His blood."

She felt the muscle and bone moving beneath her hand ere the man even realized what was happening. When he did, he leapt up, crying and laughing and hopping from foot to foot. "Glory to God! Thank you! Thank you, my lady!"

Gasps of shock and joy emanated from those waiting at the doorway, but not from those within. Servants of Braewood had grown accustomed to the miracles.

Lady Braewood covered her mouth in a yawn, then leaned toward Cristiana as a servant led the man away. "'Twould do you well to not waste so much time with each one. That way we can see more of them ere the night wanes."

Cristiana's jaw tightened, but she ignored the woman's greedy comment. She enjoyed the human touch, the hope and love she gave these people, even more than the healing. And she would not be put off.

Hence, the ill were led to her, one after the other, some with naught more than a persistent cough, others with gout, the flux, sweating sickness, others with bent spines, boils, withered arms, and general weakness. Cristiana took time with each one, expressing her love and care—something most were as deprived of as their health—ere she touched their maladies and watched them flee beneath the power of the Spear.

Lady Braewood grew bored and removed herself to stand on the other side of the hall, where she played the coquette with one of the young knights.

"Sir Mecum Effugium," the steward announced.

Odd name. The sound of it sent a cold wave over Cristiana, for she'd been tutored in Latin. "With me escape" was its meaning. Yet no one else seemed to notice.

The elderly man approached her, his back hunched over, his gray hair long, straggly, and embedded with twigs and God knew what else. He dragged his foot behind him.

Cristiana smiled as he approached and directed him to the stool. "God bless you, good sir," she said, seeking to look in his eyes.

But the man kept his face turned and hidden beneath a curtain of tangled hair.

"Have you come a long way?" she asked.

"Indeed, my lady." The voice was scratchy and deep, and oddly...comforting. "I come from afar."

"I welcome you from your journey then. What ails you?" Though she could determine he had many ailments, she wondered which one he needed help with first.

Slowly...slowly, he turned his face toward her, a face oddly smudged with white powder.

At last his eyes met hers—the color of strong oak, deep, impenetrable, but with an impish sparkle. "I fear 'tis my heart, my lady. It has been broken these past eleven months."

Cristiana inhaled a sharp breath.

CHAPTER SIX

*J*arin *the Just?* Swinging about, hands gripping her skirts, Cristiana paced before the hearth in her chamber. She would not believe it if her heart had not swelled to twice its size with the joy of seeing him again. Even now, it thumped against her ribs as if it could burst free and run into his arms.

Muriel stood to the side, hands clasped before her and eyes skittering about in uncertainty. "Was it truly him, my lady?" she said, her tone filled with skepticism.

"Sweet angels, I have no doubt!" Cristiana hugged herself. "That voice…those eyes…though I grant you his disguise had me quite fooled."

"What else did he say?"

"Only that if I wish to escape, I should meet him in the stables at dawn." Tearing the circlet from her head, she dropped into a chair and drew a hand to her chest in an attempt to calm herself.

Muriel approached and knelt before her, her voice etched in terror. "Tell me you are not thinking of doing so?"

Grabbing her long braid of hair, Cristiana clung to it as if it would give her strength. "'Tis my chance to escape, don't you see?"

"I marvel you would say so, my lady. Not after what you have told me about this…this knight."

Cristiana sank back into the chair, sudden tears burning her eyes. "I make no doubt he is a great trifler of women, but he has never behaved such with me."

"Mayhap he has you fooled?" Muriel's eyes searched Cristiana's, and though she knew the maid meant well, the insult pricked her ire.

"You make too free, Muriel. You do not know him."

Muriel rose and backed away, her face lowered. "I beg your forgiveness, my lady."

"Nay, 'tis I who am sorry." Cristiana stood and rubbed her temples. "Alack! I don't know what to do."

"Forgive me yet again, my lady, but did he not abandon you once before?"

The words pierced Cristiana's heart, deflating it. She released a heavy sigh and turned to stare at the simmering coals. Aye, he had. At least 'twould seem he'd never searched for her until now. What did he truly want from her? Could she trust him at all? And where was her sister? She'd had no time to ask him ere Lady Braewood approached and once again sat beside her.

Run away with an untrustworthy libertine into a world fraught with danger or remain in a place where she could have security, safety, and stability, though not love.

Her head told her to stay, but her heart—that fickle, capricious and all-controlling organ—told her to run into this man's arms and follow him anywhere.

She moved to the window where the slightest hint of gray lined the horizon beyond the forest. She must make a decision. Fast. Heart or head…heart or head. A vision of Lord Braewood approaching her bed on their wedding night was all it took for her to rush through the room, gather a few articles of clothing and stuff them in a bag, ere grabbing her cloak from a hook.

"My lady?" Muriel's agonizing wail turned her around.

"In truth, there is no choice, Muriel. I must go with him. No doubt he knows where my sister is and will take me to her. That alone is worth the risk."

Gathering what little courage she possessed, she grabbed the door latch, swung it open, and charged from the chamber—Right into a fully-armored guard, lance in hand.

Jarin the Just leaned against the wooden walls of the stables and gazed across the outer bailey toward Braewood Hall. Night hid most of the courtyard from his view and encased the large home in shadows. Though his eyelids were as heavy as anvils, he'd been unable to rest them for a moment as he waited for a glimpse of Cristiana D'Clere. He had found her! · She looked well and even more beautiful than he remembered. Back at Luxley, she'd always been ill and bedridden—due to Sir Walter's poisoning. Even then, she'd been a picture of beauty. But now, with her fawn-colored hair, dappled in glittering honey, her chestnut eyes surrounded by thick lashes, and her full rosy cheeks, she was a vision well worth the wait of these past eleven months. And it had taken every ounce of his strength to wait his turn to approach her. While he did, he found himself spellbound at the kind and loving way she dealt with each person, her smiles, her kind gestures, her gentle touch, even on those covered with pustulant sores. Why had he not realized the lady also possessed the heart of a saint?

She could heal! Jarin rubbed the back of his neck and shook his head. In truth, he had not believed Seraphina's tale in that regard. But he had seen it with his own eyes and now could not deny that Lady Cristiana possessed the Spear and its otherworldly powers.

He also had difficulty believing her reaction at seeing him—one of shock as he'd expected, but also such delight sparkling from her eyes, it made him wonder whether her affection matched his own.

And now the waiting…the night passing like a lame mare limping to her paddock, with naught but the snort of horses, snore of stable boys, and wisps of wind stirring up dust in the courtyard for company. The smell of horse flesh and dung bit his nose, along with a stench of rotted meat emanating from the butcher next door.

He angled his neck and blinked his eyes in an effort to keep them open.

His plan? To disguise Cristiana as a commoner and walk out the front gate with the other servants who left at dawn every morning to hunt, gather food from those who farmed the surrounding land, or travel into the village for supplies. Alas, in order for that to work, she had to be here soon so they could easily blend in with the crowd.

A half-moon dipped behind the wall to Jarin's left just as the faintest gray appeared beyond the towers on his right.

Where was she? Mayhap she decided not to come, preferred to stay in this prison of safety rather than trust him to protect her. How could he blame her? She hardly knew him, and aside from a brief dalliance at Luxley, she knew him only by his reputation as Jarin the womanizer. Frowning, he scanned the bailey for her once again. Could she have affection for this Lord Braewood? Nay. Seraphina labeled him a blackguard, and from what Jarin had heard in the village, the man's proclivities leaned more toward tavern wenches and milkmaids.

Regardless, Jarin had not had time to tell her that Sir Walter and the bishop's men searched for her as well, that 'twould only be a matter of time ere they discovered her whereabouts.

Enough! Jarin would wait no longer. Bosh, either something was amiss, or he must convince her of the danger in staying here. Flinging off his peasant robe, he added a leather doublet, a belt, and several weapons, along with a helmet he'd stolen from a sleeping soldier. 'Twould be far easier to dismiss a soldier wandering about at dawn than a peasant.

Now to find the lady's chamber.

With all the authority of a King's Guard, Jarin entered the stone house through the door to the main hall and began his trek up the winding stairs. The only sounds came from the kitchen where scullery maids were setting out the bread and ale to break the fast of the morning. The master's solar would be at the very top, while those of lower station would be chambered below... but not too far away for someone the lord would wish to keep watch over.

Hence, Jarin wandered down the hall on the second floor, following the few lights remaining from lanthorns perched along the way. 'Twas easy to find Lady Cristiana's chamber. It was the one with the massive guard standing out front.

Cristiana sank to her bed in defeat and lowered her gaze. "Lord Braewood *knows*. Begad! He must know."

Muriel moved to stand beside her. "I am truly sorry, my lady. Surely he only means to protect you."

"Protect?" Cristiana glanced up at her maid, her ire rising. "From whom? Nay!" She leapt to her feet and hugged herself. "He keeps me prisoner. Says one thing but means quite another. He would ne'er release such a great source of income." Hugging herself, she moved to the window. "Alas, mayhap he has discovered I am heir to Luxley."

The gray beyond the treetops transformed to gold as the sun prepared for its royal entrance. Beneath her in the bailey, servants stirred, going about their tasks. She wondered if Sir Jarin still awaited her at the stables. If so, how long would he remain ere he assumed she preferred to stay—ere he abandoned her once again.

"Did you not say, my lady, that the steward of Luxley intends to trick you into marrying his son?"

Cristiana nodded. Closing her eyes, she drew in a deep breath of fresh morning air, crisp and laden with scents of rosemary and lavender from the herb garden below.

Muriel approached. "What would happen should you bring back a husband? Would that not solve your problems and enable you to return home?"

Cristiana huffed. "He would have to bring an army with him."

"Then marry Lord Braewood, my lady. He is—"

"Nay!" She opened her eyes and faced her maid. "He is a viper. I will marry a good man, honorable, faithful, and strong." She glanced back out the window, her thoughts drifting to Sir Jarin. Then defying those thoughts, she added, "And loyal. He must be loyal, a man who would never stray or leave me for another."

A *thunk* sounded outside the door. Cristiana crept toward it and leaned her ear against the thick oak. *Whack. Groan. Thud.*

After casting a glance at Muriel, who was shaking her head in warning, Cristiana gripped the metal latch and slowly pried the door open.

There stood Sir Jarin the Just, looking like the knight she remembered, dressed in leather and metal, and sheathing a blade. The guard lay in a lump by his feet. "Never fear, my lady. He will live." Then removing his helmet, he effected a courtly bow, his dark hair scattered in every direction, his smile one to melt a dozen maidens' hearts. "At your service, my lady." Before she could respond, he straightened and held out a hand. "Shall we?"

So mesmerized at the sight of him, at his brazen courage to come to her chamber door, all Cristiana could do was stare, wondering if she was having a marvelous dream.

She started toward him, but then turned toward her maid. "Muriel, come with us."

The poor girl backed away, wringing her hands, her eyes alight with fear. "I cannot. I cannot," she repeated o'er and o'er, and Cristiana couldn't help but realize how much the girl and she were of similar temperament—terrified of everything, even good things.

"Hurry, my lady," Jarin said.

Cristiana held a hand toward the maid. "Prithee, Muriel. You can have a better life."

But the woman retreated even further. "God speed to you, my lady."

Jarin took her arm and pulled her through the door. "We have no time to waste." His normal cavalier demeanor was replaced by one of urgency.

"Nay." She halted. "I won't leave without Thebe."

"Thebe? Bosh! Another maid who won't join us?" But Cristiana had already gathered her skirts and was moving down the hall.

"We haven't time," she heard Jarin whisper urgently behind her.

"We will make time." Turning a corner, she froze, then ducked back behind the wall. Lord Braewood had posted a guard in front of the little girl's chamber as well. Smart man. She lifted a hand to her throat. The wild pump of blood racing through her veins throbbed against her fingers. Every inch of her wanted to scream out in terror. What was she doing? How could she and Thebe possibly escape with but one knight's help?

Jarin peered around the corner. "I suppose that to be Thebe's chamber?" Then moving far too close to Cristiana, he gazed down at her and raised one brow. She lowered her eyes from his disarming look of censure and stared instead at the leather doublet stretching across his wide chest. The man smelled of horseflesh, leather, and spice, and she didn't know whether to fall into those strong arms and beg him or push him back and rescue Thebe herself, as she longed to do. But bravery was not her forte. 'Twas her sister's realm of expertise.

"I won't leave without her," she said with a conviction that seemed lacking in her tone.

He gripped her shoulders, glanced back at Thebe's door, then uttered a low growl. "Stay here."

Releasing her, he sauntered down the hall as if he were lord of the manor. The knight looked up and stared at him suspiciously. "What brings you here?"

"I've been sent to relieve you. Onward to your cups and your sleep." He slapped the man on the back. "You've earned it."

The knight widened his stance. "And who precisely are you, sir?"

"As I said, your replacement." Jarin smiled.

"I've been told of no such orders." The knight stared straight ahead. "And I've never met you before."

Jarin ran a hand through his hair and sighed. "I was afraid of that." In a move too fast to see, he slammed his elbow across the man's chin. The knight stumbled to the right, and before he could gain his balance, Jarin grabbed him from behind, pressed an arm around his neck and squeezed.

The poor knight clutched Jarin's arm, gasping and choking, his face turning red. He attempted to kick his feet behind him, but with every thrust, Jarin leapt out of his reach.

Cristiana held her breath, unsure of whether to be enthralled or terrified.

Finally, the knight folded like a piece of parchment—a rather large piece of parchment—and crumpled to the floor.

Creeping out from hiding, Cristiana glanced down at the fallen knight. "I suppose he will live as well?" She tried to smile but her tight nerves forbade the action.

Jarin winked at her and opened the door.

"Thebe!" Spotting the child, she knelt with open arms, and the babe flew into them.

"A child?" Jarin spat out.

"Indeed." Ignoring his look of alarm, she entered the chamber, gathered clothes for the little girl, along with her favorite doll, and stuffed them in her bag. Then hoisting Thebe in her arms, she started out the door.

No further protests came from Sir Jarin, save for an occasional moan of displeasure as together they flew down the stairs, doing their best not to awaken anyone. Naught could be done about the servants bringing in fresh reeds for the main hall floor and stirring the coals of the massive hearth.

Some stared at them and gasped as they passed, and Cristiana knew they would soon alert Lord Braewood.

"Make haste," she all but screeched. Terror threatened to turn her about, to take Thebe back to the safety of her chamber and scatter all thoughts about ever escaping.

"As I've been saying, my lady," came Jarin's sarcastic response. He led her out into the bailey where the main gate stood open, allowing several servants to exit for their daily work. Two fully-armed knights stood on either side.

Until now, she hadn't considered what Sir Jarin's plan might be. Surely he didn't expect to stroll out of Braewood Hall without being stopped. Nay. He led them to the stables.

"Horsey ride?" Thebe said.

"Nay, dear one. Shh, now." They ducked into the barn just as a shout echoed over the courtyard. "Find them immediately!"

'Twas Lord Braewood's voice, and it was quickly followed by the captain of the guard braying further orders for the knights to search every inch of the castle grounds.

CHAPTER SEVEN

Jarin had been trained by the best knights of the realm, those assigned to protect the king himself. He was proficient in all manner of weaponry—sword, dagger, mace, flail, pole axe, battle axe, and lance. He could fight and defeat five well-armed warriors on land as well as ride a destrier bareback with no hands while dispatching enemies on both sides. He'd also been taught to make quick decisions in the heat of battle. Yet for some reason, being outnumbered and hunted inside enemy walls with a woman and child to protect caused his wits to abandon him.

The thump of soldiers' boots, along with further shouts to find the traitors and Cristiana's terrified gasp as she held the little girl close, prompted him to put aside his emotions and do what he'd been trained to do.

Defeat his enemy at all cost.

"'Twill be all right, my lady. Never fear." He grabbed the sack of clothing he'd shed earlier and hastily led her and the babe to one of twenty horse stalls, most of them still filled so early in the morning. This particular one housed an old mare.

The stable boy ran up, fear pinching his youthful features. "Sir, they search for you." His wild eyes darted to the door where a group of guards stood ready to enter.

Cristiana tightened beneath Jarin's grasp, but he'd already paid the lad handsomely for his silence.

"Should they discover I have aided you," the boy continued, "'twill be my head. I pray, leave at once, sir."

"They won't discover anything," Jarin said with as much confidence as he could muster. "I will hide the lady and child and return forthwith. No one will be the wiser." He urged a trembling Cristiana and child inside the stall, ignoring the mare's snort of complaint, and sat them against the front fencing. The lad shook his head and darted away just as several soldiers swung open the wide doors and marched into the stable.

Tugging his old torn cloak from his sack, Jarin flung it over his shoulders, and left the stall, instantly perfecting a hunch and hobble that would fool royalty. Yet even as he made his way toward the back door, his mind reeled with too many unknowns. Would the stable boy hold his tongue? Would the guards do more than peer into the mare's stall? Would Cristiana give herself away with a shriek? Or worse, the babe make a sound? If they were to get out of this alive, 'twould be God's doing and His alone. And though Jarin no longer believed God heard his prayers, he whispered a quick request withal.

Before he was noticed, he pushed open the back door of the stables and entered a paddock. There stood the old wagon he remembered from the night past that had contained barrels of ale—barrels he hoped were empty now and could hold a person. However, now a large cloth covered the wagon's contents from which a foul stink pinched Jarin's nose.

A bald man dressed in a woolen tunic with a rope belt about his waist stood tightening the harnesses on the wagon's horse. He looked up at the shouts and rustle of hay coming from the stables, and his eyes latched upon Jarin. He studied him for a moment, his one good eye registering the oddity of a peasant's cloak worn over knight's garb. And for a second, Jarin thought he would shout and give him away. Instead the man approached him, a smile revealing a row of yellowed crooked teeth.

"Pray, good sir, what is in your wagon?" Jarin asked.

The aged man lifted the cloth, revealing a dozen rotting deer carcasses, swarming with flies.

Coughing, Jarin backed away.

The man dropped the cloth, seemingly unaffected by the odor. "'Tis been a good year for huntin', sir, an' these deer were rotted ere the cook could roast em."

"Search aloft!" A shout blared over them from behind. "Find them or 'twill be your heads!"

A strange idea crept through Jarin's mind. "Where are you taking them?"

"To the village. Many people there are hungry 'nough to eat even these." He rubbed his one eye that had been stitched closed.

Jarin repressed a growl. No doubt 'twas Lord Braewood's generous way to feed the people in his village. He reached inside his doublet, pulled out a leather pouch, and dumped the coins in his hand.

The gold glittered in the man's eye.

"These are yours, good sir, if you sell me your wagon and the deer inside it."

The man drew a hand over his mouth to wipe the drool. "I could buy ten wagons wit' those coins. Gramercy to ye, good sire. May God reward ye."

Jarin returned the coins to the pouch and handed it to the man. "I pray He will. Now, if you'll allow, I have but one more request."

Cristiana could not remember a time in her life when she'd been so afraid. Not even when her sister was nigh to being burned at the stake, God forgive her. Alas, she'd been kept in a drugged stupor at the time, which no doubt aided her lack of fear. Now, however, she was in full use of her mind and in full care of the precious babe in her arms. The first one she was glad of—almost—but the second one terrified her. Biting her lip, she closed her eyes, and began counting, thinking of a time and place where she felt the safest. *One...two...three...* Sitting beneath a mound of hay in a horse stall whilst Lord Braewood's guards searched the stables, poking lances through wood, hay, and stubble, was not one of them. One peep from the child would no doubt bring a sharp blade down upon them both. Or mayhap the silly mare would give them away. She kept lowering her massive head toward them, chomping the hay that Sir Jarin had piled around them, fixing her large brown eye upon them as if she'd been assigned to guard them.

Cristiana had never realized horses had such lustrous eyelashes, for this particular mare's would be the envy of every lady at court.

Thebe was delighted, of course, and the only way Cristiana could keep her silent was by allowing her to pet the horse's face.

Four...five...six... Cristiana continued to count, searching for that safe memory that would provide shelter from her fears, but it seemed to elude her. She drew a deep breath, instantly regretting it when the sharp smell of horse dung filled her lungs. *Seven...eight...*

Men approached. She could hear them open the empty stall beside hers and kick hay about with their boots.

"'Tis no job for a soldier, treading amidst horse manure," one of them said.

Another laughed from across the way. "I'll grant you that. I doubt such a fine lady would hide in such filth."

Holding her breath, Cristiana tightened her grip on Thebe and prayed for God to keep them hidden. The man stopped before their stall. The mare raised her head to look at him. Cristiana backed against the wood, feeling his eyes scanning the area. Thebe reached for the mare, but Cristiana pulled back her hand. Thankfully, the girl did not cry out. Seconds passed like hours. The horse snorted and pawed the ground. Finally, the man grunted and stomped away.

"They aren't here! Away! Let's join the others. Milo, check out back and meet us forthwith."

A man yelled from the distance. "I just looked there. Naught but an old man and his wagon."

Footsteps retreated. Cristiana dared to breathe again, though she doubted her heart would ever return to a normal beat.

"Horsey," Thebe cooed, reaching for the mare once again.

Another set of boots approached. Had they returned? Cristiana recovered the little girl's hand, but she had already let out a giggle as the mare brushed her face against hers.

The boots stopped at their stall. Cristiana prepared herself to be arrested, dragged back to her chamber, where she'd be punished and kept a prisoner forever. And lose Thebe. She hugged the child close.

The door creaked open. The mare retreated.

And Sir Jarin, attired once again as a peasant, stepped within. He offered his hand and a smile of confidence that caused her to take it and long to trust this knight.

"Make haste, my lady." He ushered them out the back of the stable where she nearly fell over from the smell arising from a cloth-covered wagon.

"My apologies," he offered.

She was about to ask him for what when he lifted the cloth and pointed to a small section just beneath the seat of the wagon. 'Twas barely the length of a small person and the width of a child, and in front of it lay the rotting carcasses of a dozen deer. Thebe whimpered and buried her head in Cristiana's neck. "You wish us to hide in there?"

"Indeed, and quickly. 'Tis the only way."

By the time Jarin had snapped the reins and the wagon began to move, Cristiana had finally been able to silence Thebe's crying. If the sight of the dead deer hadn't been enough to upset the poor child and the smell rank enough to make the staunchest warrior gasp for air, crawling in amongst them had sent the girl into a fit of tears. Hence, Cristiana had retrieved Thebe's doll from the bag, and the child now held it fast to her chest, thumb in her mouth, and her face to the wood at the front of the wagon. A thin layer of stained cloth covered Cristiana's back—the only thing between her and the putrid carcass of a deer, a good portion of which Sir Jarin had laid on top of her. He'd also covered them with hay once again, which itched and scratched and intruded upon eyes, nose and mouth. Only this time the sharp stench stung her eyes and caused tears to fill them. Or was that merely her terror?

The wagon rumbled on, turning the corner of the stable and heading toward the gate. Jarin hummed a tune from his seat above them. He'd donned his disguise from the night past, and she wondered if he was afraid of being caught, for his punishment would be far more severe than hers. She immediately dismissed the notion. He was a member of the elite King's Guard. No doubt he'd been involved in far more dangerous intrigues. No doubt he would effect their escape with nary a problem at all.

With that assurance firmly planted in her mind, Cristiana's nerves dared to loosen a bit... when a shout echoed through the cloth, the deer, the hay and straight into her heart.

"You there!"

No sooner did Jarin turn the corner from the stables than he saw the gates closing.

"Halt there!" he shouted across the bailey. The guards looked up, and he shrugged as if to beg their forgiveness for his tardiness.

One of them called to the man in the guardroom above. "You there! Cease!" The crank and chink of the winch used to lower the gate silenced, and the guard motioned him through.

"You're late. Make haste, old man!" He continued his conversation with a knight standing beside him, barely affording Jarin another glance as Jarin snapped the reins and proceeded beneath the iron spikes of the first portcullis. The second one had stopped just above the top of his head. Halfway there, halfway to freedom...halfway to—

"Halt!" Rang out from behind him.

Jarin yanked back the reins, knowing full well they could lower the second portcullis too quickly for him to charge forward.

The captain of the guard stormed toward him, holding a hand over his nose the closer he came. "You're not the same villager who collects these deer."

"Nay," Jarin said. "'E's ill. Got the plague, they say."

This seemed to set the man aback for he retreated a step and tried to peer beneath Jarin's hood. "Show your face, man."

Jarin lifted the fabric just enough to reveal the red hue of deer's blood he'd smeared beneath his eyes and the pallor of his skin, formed from white powder he'd brought with him.

The man backed away further, stopping halfway down the wagon. He lifted the cloth, his nose wrinkling. "We search for a woman and a child. Have you seen them?"

Jarin shook his head and feigned a bout of coughing. "Nay, sir. Just deer and horses."

He broke into a cough again, and the man backed away. "Leave us, you and your rotted meat."

Jarin nodded, snapped the reins, and the wagon rumbled through the second portcullis and down the muddy pathway that descended into a valley dotted with forest and farms.

When they were well out of hearing range, he spoke up. "Are you quite well, my lady?"

After several worrisome seconds, she replied. "We are alive, Sir Jarin. But barely."

"'Twill be but a few more minutes ere we can stop and find safety."

As if to defy his statement, the sound of numerous horses' hooves striking the hard ground thundered over them. In the distance, a band of war horses, armored in steel and leather, emerged from a copse of trees like angry bees from a disturbed hive.

Jarin's heart tightened. Sweat rolled down his forehead. Still, he kept a slow pace and his head down. His thoughts shifted to a miracle he still had trouble believing—a time when he, his fellow knights and Lady Alexia D'Clere had been surrounded by overwhelming forces. She had prayed and somehow God had made them invisible. "My lady, if you have the Spear, pray, I beg you. Pray hard," he managed to say just as the men leading the band halted their horses beside the wagon.

"You there. Is this Braewood Castle?" a man attired in the field armor of a knight shouted from his horse.

Jarin peered out from beneath his hood, enough to see the heraldry of Luxley Castle on his shield and to know the voice of Sir DeGay, the captain of the guard. More horsemen halted behind them, one of them carrying the purple and blue standard of Bishop Montruse.

How had they found Lady Cristiana so quickly? Bosh! They would recognize Jarin. Kill him on the spot and drag Cristiana back to Luxley. Terror began to strangle every nerve, but he forced it away through years of practice on the battlefield. "Aye, it is," he answered as disinterested as he could.

"Is Lord Braewood in residence?"

Jarin nodded and sat waiting for them to ask his name, demand he show his face, or examine the contents of the wagon.

Instead, Sir DeGay made the motion to advance, and the troop of warriors stampeded past them. Smiling, Jarin proceeded on his way.

Not a peep was heard from Lady Cristiana or the babe, which worried him. Once safely inside the forest that circled part of Braewood, Jarin stopped the wagon before a fork in the road, leapt from the seat, quickly removed the cover, and then hoisted aside the small deer he'd lain over Cristiana.

No movement came from the cloth under which they lay. "My lady?"

She tossed the cover aside and turned ever so slowly, her brown eyes wide with fear. "Thank God 'tis you, Sir Jarin. I feared the worst."

"We are safe. Come." He jumped onto the side of the wagon and hefted two deer carcasses aside, whilst she retrieved the little girl and handed her to him. The child had fallen asleep clutching a stuffed doll to her chest.

Jarin had not held a babe since—a vision of the lifeless infant flashed before his eyes, nearly causing him to drop the child in his arms. He clung all the tighter, shaking off the image that followed—one of his mother lying on a pallet, soaked in her own blood.

The girl moaned, and he lowered to the ground. Then pressing her to his chest with one arm, he assisted Cristiana down with the other. The child's little hands gripped his cloak as she attempted to nestle into its warmth. He thrust her at Cristiana.

"She's a child, not a disease, Sir Jarin." Lady Cristiana smiled up at him with a look filled with fear and wonder at the same time. It suddenly transformed into concern as she studied him further. "Are you ill?"

"Nay." He swiped at the blood and powder, oddly wishing he could improve his appearance for this lady. But a sense of unease trickled through him—as it usually did ere disaster followed. He glanced in the direction they had traveled, then deep into the forest. Nothing. Tearing off his woolen cloak, he reached beneath the wagon seat and grabbed his weapons, strapping them on one by one.

All the while Cristiana followed him with eyes wide in concern.

Finally the pound of horse hooves shook the ground.

"Who is it?" she asked, shifting her gaze in the direction they'd come.

"Sir Walter's and the bishop's men."

"We should hide again." Terror ran from her voice as she began to climb back in the wagon.

Jarin grabbed her arm. "Nay. 'Tis too late for that. They have figured us out."

CHAPTER EIGHT

Cristiana could not find her voice. Nor could she move. All she could do was clutch a sleeping Thebe and watch Jarin the Just shed his disguise, gather all his weapons, and tie the reins of the horse to the wagon's seat. All this he did with a calmness and assurance of someone performing a daily task. Once done, he slapped the horse on the rear and uttered a shout, and the animal galloped down the left fork of the road, the wagon bouncing and trailing a putrid stench in its wake.

Why he'd released their only means of transport, she could not fathom. He faced her and smiled. Aye, *smiled*...his wild dark hair falling to his collar, the trimmed beard on his chin and jaw matching his thin mustache. Dressed in leather from his thick doublet to his knee-high boots, and strapped with all manner of weapons and belts, he was as handsome and charming as she remembered, save for the red stains beneath his eyes and traces of white powder on his face.

Why she was admiring him now, she had no idea. Mayhap because she saw their future quickly fading away as the horses' hooves grew louder behind them and the very ground beneath their feet began to tremble. She wanted to remember him thus, strong and in command, ere the men who pursued them took him away.

"What are you doing? They are nearly upon us!" She attempted to temper the fear in her voice for the child's sake, but it shot forth like a trumpet in war. Moaning, Thebe shifted slightly in her arms as Cristiana glanced behind them down the road. No sign of the evil hoard yet. "How did they discover our ruse?" Clutching the girl tightly with one hand, she grabbed her bag and started for the trees lining the road.

"No doubt they spoke to Lord Braewood and heard of our escape. 'Twas an easy deduction from there."

"But…" She turned to glance toward the place that had been her home for nearly a year. "Will they return to do him harm?"

Sir Jarin, who remained on the road as if he hadn't a care in the world, gave her the oddest look ere he answered. "I would not gainsay it. The bishop's men are brutal."

The thought saddened her. Not that Lord Braewood didn't deserve punishment for his greedy lies, but no more than a good castigation.

"Where are you off to, my lady?" Sir Jarin asked.

Swallowing her fear, she faced him. "I realize you are a King's Guard, but mayhap your arrogance does you a disservice in the belief you can defeat fifty warriors. Should we not at least hide in the brush?" Though she knew that would only delay their capture. "Or do you wish to die in front of me and this innocent child?"

"Your confidence in my abilities overwhelms me, my lady. Besides, there were only thirty." Raising two fingers to his mouth, he blew out a shrill whistle. Within seconds, a clomping sound preceded a mighty destrier plunging through the thick brush on their right. She recognized the war horse immediately as Sir Jarin's.

"Hold the child," was all he said before lifting them both atop the horse as if they weighed no more than a feather. Then leaping behind them, he grabbed the reins with one hand and wrapped his other arm around her, ere he nudged the horse and uttered a command that sent the animal into a full gallop down the right fork of the road.

For such a huge steed and at such a fast pace, Cristiana found the ride amazingly smooth. Or mayhap 'twas the mighty arm holding her and Thebe tight that kept them from bouncing hither and thither. Either way, Sir Jarin kept the pace for what seemed like an hour, past grasslands, forest and farm, past villages and manor homes perched on hills. Thankfully, Thebe remained asleep, even on those few occasions when Sir Jarin stopped to glance behind him for enemies and then inquire as to Cristiana's wellbeing.

Each time she answered that she was well, though in truth, her entire body still thrummed with fear and uncertainty. Had she really escaped Lord Braewood? Was she really with Sir Jarin the Just, the powerful knight who had haunted her dreams this past year? Perchance 'twas all a dream—a frightening, yet lovely dream.

The feel of his strong arm around her was most certainly *not* a dream, the warmth of his body so close, his scent of leather and man, and the scratch of his beard on her cheek when she turned to glance up at him. Nay. Not a dream at all. She'd never been this close to a man, and it was doing odd things to her insides. Odd things she must ignore.

By noonday, Thebe awoke, whimpering at first when she didn't know where she was. But upon seeing that she rode on a horse, she giggled and laughed and kept repeating, "Horsey ride!"

Even Jarin chuckled. He had slowed the horse to a walk, though she sensed he remained tense and alert. Surely they had outrun Sir Walter and the bishop's men by now.

The sun, which had warmed them all morning, suddenly dove into hiding behind a bank of dark clouds, sending a chill over Cristiana. "Thebe will need food and water soon. And I must change her swaddling."

"Aye," was all Sir Jarin said, but she sensed his frustration at having to care for a child.

"I thank you, Sir Jarin, for your kindness in bringing the girl along."

He snorted. "Did I have a choice?"

"I suppose not." Cristiana smiled. "But I thank you nonetheless, *and* for rescuing me."

He merely grunted, and she wondered if he regretted it. Of course he did. He was a warrior, a knight, a man who lived his life from one battle to the next, from one conquest to the next. The last thing he wanted was to be burdened with a woman and child. She had learned that much about him back at Luxley.

Drawing a deep breath, Cristiana glanced to her left where crop-laden fields flowed toward the horizon like emerald waves at sea. A group of peasants, sickles in hand, harvested wheat in the distance. Cows wandered about in another field, chomping on grass, while various trees dotted the landscape. She'd not left Braewood Castle in so long, she'd forgotten how beautiful the countryside was. Even the thick clouds rumbling toward them across the sky had a beauty all their own

Thebe whimpered. Jarin shifted in the saddle, but finally halted the horse off the side of the road before a group of trees. After dismounting, he took Thebe from Cristiana's arms and assisted her down as well.

"We can't stay long," he said, handing the child back to her.

Kneeling on the ground, she opened her bag and pulled out a small blanket and a strip of clean linen and attempted to lay Thebe down to change her soiled cloth. "Do you believe they still follow us, Sir Jarin?"

Whining and wiggling at once again being confined, Thebe squirmed from beneath Cristiana's ministrations, leapt up, and darted to a tree. "Tree, Cristi, tree."

"Aye." Sir Jarin led the destrier to a patch of grass before taking a protective stance, staring down the road. "And they won't give up easily."

Cristiana smiled at the little girl. "Aye, 'tis a tree, darling. Now come here and allow Cristi to clean you."

Thebe giggled and gave her the most precious smile— before turning and charging down the road as fast as her little legs could carry her.

"Thebe!" Gathering her skirts, Cristiana chased the girl, but Sir Jarin got to her first. Hoisting her up in his arms, he tossed her over his shoulder. "I see this little one is going to be trouble."

"I assure you, she's well-behaved. 'Tis merely that she's been sitting too long."

He gave her a look of disbelief ere picking a handful of blueberries from a shrub. Giving them to the child, he placed her back on the blanket and returned to his vigilance over the road. While Thebe plopped berries into her mouth, Cristiana took the opportunity to remove the soiled cloths on her bottom and replace them with fresh ones. 'Twas not as easy a task as 'twould seem, and Cristiana's appreciation for nursemaids rose. Finally, she set the little girl on her feet.

"More?" She held out her hand, and Cristiana led her to the shrub where, together, they consumed blueberries faster than they could pick them.

A burst of wind brought the sweet sting of rain. Jarin retrieved his horse, checked all the tack, and caressed the destrier's face.

Thunder rumbled, low and distant. *Nay*, not thunder. For it did not cease but grew louder.

Jarin looked up, his keen eyes searching the road. "Time to go." Plucking a cloak out of a bag strapped to the horse, he hefted Cristiana up, handed her Thebe, and swung behind them. He covered them with the cloak, then looped his arm around them and shouted, "Run Liberty!"

The powerful war horse took off so fast Cristiana slammed backward into Sir Jarin's chest. Thebe's chubby little fingers gripped her arm tightly, but the child uttered not a peep.

Rain pelted the cloak and began to soak through in wet splotches that dripped down Cristiana's face. She bowed her head against the onslaught in an attempt to keep Thebe dry. The steed turned this way and that, galloping down paths now transformed to mud, splashing through puddles, thumping on grassy ground and leaping over rushing creeks.

Where were they going? Did Sir Jarin have a plan, or were they to be chased all over the countryside for days? Hours passed. Her bottom grew sore. Thebe's cries turned to whimpers,

"Hush, little one. 'Twill be all right." She spoke the words but hated the lie, for she knew not the outcome of this frightening day.

Finally Sir Jarin reined in the horse and halted. Cristiana lifted the cloak to see a large wooden gate spread between two stone towers from which lanterns blazed. Thick iron crosses were embedded in the wood on both doors. Though the rain had lessened to a drizzle, it quickly saturated her face, and an unavoidable shiver carved down her body.

Sir Jarin leaned to whisper in her ear. "You'll be warm soon enough, my lady."

"Who goes there?" A voice rang down from above.

"Sir Jarin the Just!"

Liberty snorted and pawed the ground.

The eerie howls of wolves turned Cristiana's blood to ice. Where had they come from? She glanced behind them but saw naught but trees.

"Make haste!" Jarin shouted.

No further inquiries were required, apparently, for two men attired in the brown robes of monks swung open the gate.

Sir Jarin urged his horse through and commanded the men to close it immediately. It slammed shut with a solid thud, and the heavy latch was put in place just as a hundred paws pounded it from the other side. Ferocious growls and snarls filled the air.

"Sweet angels, what is that?" Cristiana asked, clutching Thebe to her chest.

"Naught to do with angels, I fear." Though his tone was unruffled, she felt Sir Jarin stiffen behind her as he turned Liberty to the right. He halted before a large wooden building from which two men emerged, also dressed in robes, and took the reins. Cristiana shivered as he dismounted and helped her and Thebe down. Wrapping an arm around them, he hurried to a nearby building, pushed open the creaking door, and entered a large room. It slammed behind them, the sound echoing through the vaulted ceiling.

Cristiana removed her cloak and was instantly rewarded by warmth wafting from a nearby hearth. Benches and chairs with red velvet covering were spread about the room, while a long trestle table stood toward the back. One wall was lined with shelves of books of every color and size. Tapestries depicting the life of Christ decorated the other walls, while hanging above the fireplace was a massive painting depicting warring angels battling a red dragon. In the corner, a monk sitting at a desk looked up from his work, but quickly glanced down again.

A boy no older than thirteen, also dressed in brown, dashed up to them, head bowed.

"Please tell the abbot that Sir Jarin is here."

Nodding, he skittered away as Jarin took the cloak from Cristiana and flung it on a hook by the door. Only then did she notice rain dripping from his doublet and breeches, forming puddles on the stone tiles. He'd used his only cloak to protect them, and now he was soaked to the bone. He shook water from his hair and raked a hand through it, making him look even handsomer, if that were possible.

She snapped her gaze back to the incredible chamber, so warm and inviting. Not something she expected to find in a monastery. But neither had she expected to find herself in such a holy place, nor especially Sir Jarin.

Before she could ask him why he brought them here, Thebe wiggled to be let down, and she set the little girl on her feet, took her hand, and proceeded to the hearth to get warm. Jarin followed, his wet boots sloshing on the floor.

The warmth of the fire felt too good to be true, and she released a deep breath and held out her hands to the flames when a "Jarin, my boy!" rang through the room.

An aged man dressed in a gray wool robe entered from a door at the other end and all but ran up to Jarin, arms extended. Despite the knight's drenched attire, he hugged Jarin so tight it left the front of his robe wet. Then taking Jarin's head in his hands, he kissed him on each cheek.

Kissed him! As if they were the best of friends. *Jarin and an abbot?* Cristiana could make no sense of it. Yet Jarin's smile couldn't be wider as he stared at the man with an affection she hadn't realized the knight possessed.

Thebe picked a reed off the floor and began playing with it.

The aged monk faced Cristiana, his eyes shifting from her to Thebe, delight brimming from them. "Faith now, lad. I see you have finally got a wife and quit your roistering!"

"Nay, nay..." Cristiana said as a tide of blood infused her face.

Jarin scratched his beard and shot her an awkward glance. "Sorry to disappoint, Father Godwin, but she is merely a lady I am rescuing from danger. The child is not hers but her ward."

"How now? If that is the tale you must tell." The abbot turned to her and smiled. "You are most welcome here, my lady. No doubt this ruffian is the cause of the danger in which you find yourself." He winked at Jarin. "My guards inform me you were in the escort of a pack of wolves?"

Jarin rubbed the back of his neck. "Indeed. Yet I had no knowledge of it till we stood at your gate."

"Hmm." Father Godwin clasped his hands together. "'Twould seem you are stirring up the dark forces, my son." He gripped Sir Jarin's arm. "And you, my lady." He faced her with a smile that gleamed from his eyes. "There is a brightness in you. I hope you shall grace an old man with your tale."

"I should love to, Reverend Father."

"But first." He knelt to look at Thebe. "I see you have need of dry attire and a warm meal."

Thebe smiled up at him. "Cheese?"

He chuckled. "Of course, little one." With a groan, he rose and clapped his hands. Two young men scurried into the room.

"Brother Silas and Brother Wayne will show you to your lodging and provide you with dry clothing. I do hope you'll join us for our evening repast. 'Tisn't much, but we gladly share what we have."

"Thank you, Father," Jarin said. "I am in your debt."

"Nay, charge it to the Almighty's account, lad. For I know He has a purpose for your returning to the order."

Cristiana blinked. The order? Jarin was a monk?

CHAPTER NINE

Dungeon, Luxley castle

S ir Walter LeGode suppressed a shudder at the cold look in Drago's lifeless eyes. 'Twould not be to his advantage to show fear before this powerful warlock. Thus far, he'd been able to hide both his terror and disdain for the...what was he? Man? Nay. Beast? Quite possibly. Monster? Aye, *monster* suited him. But the warlock's power had grown stronger, his evil intent more palpable, if 'twas possible.

"They hide in a *monastery*." He spat the last word out as if it burned his tongue.

Cedric, Sir Walter's son and apprentice of Drago, stepped from the shadows, his eyes riveted to the hot coals scattered over an iron table. "They can't stay there forever."

A chill scraped over Sir Walter. He hardly recognized his son. His light hair had darkened to a musty, dismal color. His eyes, once so full of frivolity, now were cold stones floating in stagnant waters. Instead of colorful, ostentatious attire, he wore a hooded black robe. Shadows drooped beneath his eyes over pale skin that had once been golden. Even his voice had changed. No longer gay with the excitement of life, it harbored an animosity and hatred that never failed to prick Sir Walter with guilt.

Why had he promised his son as apprentice to this... *creature*? How could any father do such a thing? Alas, he'd only wanted Cedric to grow up, quit his giddy reveling and gain the power due his station.

Drago faced Cedric. "The storm you created was not strong enough."

Cedric lowered his head. "I will do better next time, my master."

The way Drago snarled at Cedric, Sir Walter feared he'd spit on him and turn him into a snake. Instead, the warlock whirled about, his white robe fluttering about him, and walked to a shelf, from which he pulled an ancient tome.

Swallowing down his fear, Sir Walter drew a breath to steady his nerves, but a stench akin to sulfur and vinegar caused him to cough instead. He'd come down to the warlock's lair for news of their hunt for Lady Cristiana D'Clere in order to appease the bishop with some smidgen of hope. And indeed, they *had* found her—by following that peckish primcock, Sir Jarin.

An icy chill cut through him as he glanced about the familiar chamber. Steam that smelled fouler than an overused chamber pot rose from an iron cauldron hung over hot coals in the center of the room. The carcasses of bats and rodents swung from the rim of a ceiling that extended up into a dark tower. A table to the left housed mortars, alembics, braziers, sieves, and bowls, while shelves lining the wall contained bottles and jars of all sizes and colors. Candles dotted the room, offering light that never seemed to dispel the shadows hovering all around.

"Regardless, we have them!" Sir Walter dared announce. "The moment they step from the protection of that monastery."

Slamming the book shut, Drago whirled and stormed toward Sir Walter, eyes aflame. "She has the Spear, imbecile!"

Though he longed to back away from the monster, he remained steadfast, finally shifting his gaze from the hatred in his eyes to the animal feet, bird wings, amulets, and trinkets decorating the black band wrapped around the warlock's head. Long white hair as dry as hay matched a frizzled beard which Sir Walter could swear was alive with vermin.

The *Spear*, the infamous Spear. How had he let it, along with Lady Cristiana, slip from his grasp? He had need of them both. The Spear to give to the bishop so he would quit Luxley and leave Sir Walter in peace. The lady, however, would be presented with a choice—die or marry Cedric. Mayhap, now that he looked at his son, the lady would wisely choose death. Alas, to rid himself of the only heir to Luxley and her witch sister for good would be the best choice, but only if Montruse could secure Luxley for Sir Walter from the king.

So many unknowns. Yet, if all went according to plan, Sir Walter would be master of both his own estate and Luxley, more than tripling his holdings. In addition, he'd gain a greater title and the respect of his peers. He would smile at the thought save the warlock remained snarling before him.

With a foul huff, Drago backed away and returned to his simmering pot. "White livered cur! Why do I waste time helping you? Do you think I want the Spear returned?"

Sir Walter suppressed a grunt of frustration. "You know full well that with Montruse—and the Spear—gone and Luxley in my hands, you will not only continue to have Cedric as your apprentice but my protection to continue doing whatever"—Sir Walter wrinkled his nose—"evil it is you do down here. Would you rather have Luxley in the hands of those *Christ* followers?"

Cedric froze, his eyes streaked with terror.

Drago leapt back from the table as if he'd been punched. Indeed, he pressed a hand over his belly as if he had. "Never utter that name! Never speak of it!" His roar nearly shook the chamber.

Sir Walter hid a smile. He always loved to see the creature's reaction to the Holy One's title.

The room began to spin, and he closed his eyes and leaned upon the cold stone wall, suddenly fearing the warlock had cast a spell on him. But nay, Drago needed him.

"Are you ill, Father?" 'Twas his son, the barest hint of concern in a voice that had long since been stained with harsh indifference.

"Nay. Merely tired." He wouldn't tell them he'd been seeing things, hearing things that weren't there. 'Twas merely the stress, naught more.

Drago turned to Cedric. "Add a pinch of snake venom, the feather of a raven, and choose well the third ingredient. As I taught you."

Cedric stepped back into the shadows.

Shoving down his guilt, Sir Walter drew a deep breath. He still needed more information for the bishop. "What are your plans?"

Drago folded his hands before him and hid them beneath the sleeves of his robe. "Ere they step one foot out of that vile place, my wolves will devour them." His tone was devoid of emotion.

"Won't the Spear prevent such a fortuitous event?"

"As long as Lady Cristiana is ignorant of the power she holds, she cannot use it against them."

Sir Walter huffed. "Her sister well understood its power."

"She is *not* her sister." Drago spat, his eyes pinpoints of malice. "The woman is a sniveling goose."

After retrieving a vial from a shelf, Cedric poured it into the pot. Hissing and—dare Sir Walter say—shrieking emanated from the bubbling liquid. The sound prickled the hair on the back of his neck.

Drago stared into the pot and nodded. "You are learning well, Cedric."

Cedric's head shot up, his eyes focused above. Drago did the same, albeit much more slowly and precisely.

"They are here," he said, seething.

Sir Walter shook his head. "Who?"

"Those vexing Knights of the Eternal Realm."

"Bah! Here at Luxley?" Sir Walter would not believe it. His guards were instructed to capture them on sight.

Drago hissed, smoke slithering from his mouth. "They are here more than you are aware, fool! Cease questioning my work and tend your task of keeping these loathsome aberrations out of Luxley. Their very presence interferes with my work!"

Wheeling about, Sir Walter grabbed a candle, shoved open the stone door, and made his way up the winding stairway of the main tower ere he said something that would end his life prematurely.

"You, there!" He shouted to a knight standing guard at the door to the main hall. "Gather all the guards and search every inch of Luxley immediately. Arrest anyone you don't recognize. Do it, now!"

With a nod, the man rushed away.

Now, to inform the bishop of their progress in finding Lady Cristiana. But the man was not in his chamber. The lad who served him informed Sir Walter that the bishop had gone out for a ride through the countryside.

Finally, with the chink of armor and stomp of boots echoing through the castle, Sir Walter entered his study and plopped down in his chair. Anabelle knocked and entered, cup in hand.

"Your medicament from the apothecary, my lord." She set it on his desk and backed away. Smart girl. And lovely as a spring flower. Sir Walter allowed his gaze to rake over her curves and his thoughts to take license. He marveled that she continually denied him when he could do much to improve her station. But no matter. He had more important affairs to deal with at the moment.

"You may leave," he said, waving her away. Then, lifting the cup to his mouth, his lips twisted at the bitter taste ere he sat back to ponder his next move.

Alexia D'Clere knelt to move aside branches and leaves from the grating that hid the tunnel they'd recently discovered—the one that led directly to a storage room at the back of Luxley Castle. Ronar stooped to give her a hand, whilst Damien stood guard. In truth they hadn't so much as *discovered* this tunnel as Friar Josef finally disclosed its location. When Alexia chastised him for the secret, he merely shrugged and said, "I didn't wish to encourage your trips to Luxley, for you try me sorely with your disobedience."

She couldn't help but laugh. "'Twas far more dangerous for me to enter through the bailey in plain sight of all!"

"Alas, I thought the danger would dissuade you, foolish old man that I am."

"You are far from a fool." Alexia kissed his cheek and enjoyed the red flooding the wrinkled skin of his face.

Yet she had to admit the tunnel made it quite easy to enter the castle unnoticed. Apparently her parents had built it as a means of escape should they come under siege.

Ronar brushed aside the last of the branches, then hefted the iron grating and laid it to the side ere helping Alexia to her feet. "Have I told you what a lovely peasant you make." His eyes scanned her with desire.

"Once or twice, Sir Knight." She smiled. "Though I feel rather unclad without my bow and quiver." Beneath her peasant tunic, she hid two small knives and a dagger, but she still felt like a lame deer facing an army of hunters.

Ronar winked. "Never fear, my lady, you have my troth I will protect you."

Swinging her tumble of red hair over her shoulder, she arched a brow. "Mayhap 'tis I who will protect *you*."

He laid a hand on his chest. "Only from a broken heart."

"I beseech you both," Damien huffed as he approached. "Wed at once and quit this irksome dalliance. You drive me to my cups."

"Tush, you need no excuse there, my friend." Ronar slapped him on the back. "Why so dour a mood? Come now, you must agree 'tis a great satisfaction to supply the hungry villagers with meat. Especially since Sir Walter forbids them to hunt unless they betray us."

Damien grunted. "I'll grant a small moment of pleasure, but even that would be of no avail should one of the villagers come to his senses and decide the favor of a bishop surpasses that of renegades of the crown."

"Alas, you are a grim soul, Damien."

"Not so grim when he entertains Seraphina's company." Alexia put a hand on her hip and smiled at the large knight.

Damien cleared his throat. "Are we to stand here all day blathering, or do we have a steward to haunt?" He struck flint to steel and lit a torch, then leapt into the hole. Alexia followed, while Ronar took up the rear.

She'd been in this tunnel o'er a dozen times, but something was different this time…a feeling, a heaviness that hadn't been there before. She longed to close her eyes and seek the Spirit, but she must follow Damien's light as it flickered over rock, dirt, and the wooden buttresses holding up the walls. God's truth, she'd been learning how to see in the Spirit with her eyes open, and thus, she now focused her thoughts on the real world beyond this one.

Sharp-clawed hands reached for them through the dirt on all sides as if they walked through a graveyard and had awoken the dead—filthy hands, covered in rotting flesh that hung in tatters from yellowed bones. Fingers stretched to grip them, wound them, or drag them into the underworld. Alexia suppressed the urge to shriek, for she knew they could do them no harm. Instead, one quick glance behind and then before her revealed mighty warrior angels, glowing like the sun with swords in hand.

"I sense it as well," Ronar whispered as they reached the end of the tunnel, though she had made no mention of the darkness she felt nor the vision she saw.

Damien handed him the torch ere lifting a wooden plank from the floor of Luxley's root cellar. With effort, the knight hoisted himself up, followed by Ronar, who extended his hand to her.

She smiled as he helped her up onto the dirt floor. Ronar had come far under the tutelage of Friar Josef. Though he did not possess her gift of seer, he was beginning to sense things in the Spirit.

"Aye, the evil in this place grows. But we are not alone." She glanced toward one of the warrior angels whose eyes met hers ere he vanished, leaving naught but casks, crates, and barrels full of fruits, grain, and herbs surrounding them.

"Never alone." Ronar agreed.

Damien only huffed and proceeded toward the stairs.

"I should take the lead." Alexia pushed past the large knight, ignoring his protests. He was unaccustomed to a lady taking charge, but with her gift of sight, she could see things he could not. No doubt his excessive ego would recover.

The stairs led to a narrow hallway through which only servants traveled. They had merely to make their way to the end, take another circular set of stairs to another corridor where they could finally enter the maze of secret tunnels that webbed throughout Luxley.

But shouts and the thud of marching feet halted Alexia in her tracks. She glanced down the long passageway as Ronar came up beside her.

"They hunt for us," was all he said. "Make haste." Grabbing her hand, he dashed down the hall, lit only by a single lantern perched on the wall.

The footsteps grew louder.

One man shouted. "Have you searched the cellar?"

Alexia's throat closed.

Ronar halted, tossing out an arm to stop her from charging into—

"Vak! What?" Damien bumped into Ronar, nearly knocking him down.

Not willing to believe her eyes, Alexia grabbed the lantern from its hook and held it up. A stone wall stood before them from floor to ceiling.

A wall that had not been there before.

CHAPTER TEN

Jarin hadn't planned on taking Lady Cristiana to Tegimen Abbey, but circumstances had become dire. He accepted the dry attire from the boy and shut the door to the small chamber, which contained only a cot, table, chamber pot, and hook on the wall—bare-bones necessities with which he should be well accustomed after having spent three years in such a room. Three happy years, if he were forced to admit it. Ere he realized 'twas all a farce. But he'd had a warm place to sleep and plenty of food, and he'd not only learned to read and write but also the value of a hard day's work. The abbot had been a second father to Jarin, teaching him honor, chivalry, and the love of God and king. Everything but how to fight. Which was the most important thing if one were to survive this world.

Removing his weapons, he stripped off his wet attire, then hung them up to dry and quickly donned the simple linen shirt, tunic, trousers, and belt. After he dried his hair with a cloth, he sat to put on his shoes, longing to strap on his weapons again, but knowing the abbot frowned on such devices of violence.

Jarin had taught himself to fight, then joined the war and learned the hard way. People who relied on God for help in this world were naught but fools. If one were to survive, gain success and fortune, and find some measure of happiness, they had to do it for themselves. And not allow anything or anyone to waylay their plans.

Which brought his thoughts to Lady Cristiana. He couldn't help but smile. "Lovely Cristiana," he dared whisper her Christian name. She was everything he remembered, and much more. Not only a picture of grace and beauty, but possessing a heart filled with deep and precious treasures. Forsooth, the lady had even feared for the wellbeing of the man who had held her captive! He'd ne'er seen such a thing. And she was brave as well, though the lady would not agree. Yet he'd learned long ago that bravery was not bravado but rather the courage to embark on a task that brought one naught but terror.

Alas, the child. Jarin moaned and ran a hand through his damp hair. The girl was sweet and innocent, to be sure, but he had not planned on the extra burden. She would not only slow them down but keep them distracted, and quite possibly alert their enemies with her cries. 'Twas a most dangerous situation and not one Jarin would have willingly agreed to. Alas, he'd forgotten how stubborn Lady Cristiana could be.

Pushing to his feet, he opened the door and started down the long hall, making his way to the chamber he'd seen the lady and child enter. The guest rooms sat atop the stables and the distinct bite of horseflesh and hay pinched his nose. But the lady did not answer his knock. Had she fallen asleep with the babe ere they had a chance to fill their bellies? Nay. He dared to crack the door and found the small chamber empty.

Thunder rumbled through the stone building as Jarin descended the steps and emerged onto the courtyard to a blast of chilled wind. He glanced up, but a helmet of dark clouds sat atop the monastery, obscuring the moon and stars. He'd thought the rain had ended, but this was different. Not a storm at all. Yanking on the iron door handles, he cast one last glance above ere quickly entering the receiving hall of the abbot's residence. Immediately, he was rewarded with a child's laughter and the vision of Lady Cristiana, dressed in a tunic of a commoner, her honey-brown hair tumbling like a waterfall below her waist. He swallowed down a burst of longing to run his fingers through the silken strands. But this was no strumpet whom he could easily charm into his bed. Cristiana was a true lady who deserved a far more honorable man than he.

The thought disturbed him. Her smile as she turned to face him sent such a thrill through him, he'd gladly fall on his knees and swear his fealty to her then and there. A groan escaped his lips at the ludicrous notion.

Father Godwin's eyes lit and he leaned to whisper something in her ear that made her laugh.

Jarin ground his teeth. Whate'er stories his friend had to tell, 'twould do no benefit to Jarin's reputation.

"I see you two have become acquainted." He gave a tight smile as he approached them.

Cristiana laughed and glanced at the little girl playing with a doll on the couch. "The abbot has told me such tales, I can hardly believe them."

Father Godwin winked at him. "I find your lady quite charming, Jarin."

"She's not—"

"And you, Sir Jarin," Lady Cristiana said, lantern light bringing forth the gold flecks in her brown eyes. "I must say, I hardly recognized you in a common tunic devoid of the myriad blades you enjoy brandishing about."

"Those blades, my lady, have saved many lives, including my own." He dipped his head before her, taking in her feminine form, so evident beneath the simple chemise and cote she wore. Nay, he would not tell her how lovely he thought her. Instead, he faced his old friend. "Prithee, grant me at least one knife. There is evil afoot this night."

The abbot nodded. "I sense it as well. Yet we are safe in God's house. Come now, I have prepared a repast." He gestured toward the trestle table near the hearth, where young monks placed steaming trenchers and pitchers of ale.

He wanted to tell his friend that neither God nor fifty monks could stop the bishop's and Sir Walter's army, but he kept his tongue. The last thing he needed was a religious debate.

Cristiana moved to pick up Thebe. Nestling her close, she kissed the child, and for the briefest of moments, Jarin stared at them, a strange longing he could not identify welling inside him. Being in this place, he was growing weak again. And he could not allow that to happen. He had a mission to complete, and no feminine beauty, innocent child, or fable-believing monk would stop him.

Cristiana slipped a piece of warm bread into Thebe's mouth. The girl refused to sit on the bench by herself, so Cristiana held her in her lap and helped her eat the delicious repast set before them. Though but a simple meal of pottage and bread, it tasted better than the finest fare she could remember at Luxley. Mayhap due to her fierce hunger. *And* her fearful day.

Sir Jarin, the abbot, and one other monk, Brother Peter, sat across from her. The rest of the monks had already finished their nightly service and retired. Sleep. Precious sleep. She knew it would elude her until she had a chance to ask Sir Jarin the dozen questions spinning in her mind. How did her sister fare? What of Rowan and Damien? What was happening at Luxley? And how did Sir Jarin find her? She'd had little time to ask on their harrowing journey here, and now she'd be forced to wait until they were alone.

Alas, she still found it difficult to believe Sir Jarin had been a monk, or at least a novitiate. He'd left the order one year before taking his final vows. For what reason, Father Godwin would not say, though he had told Cristiana of a few of Sir Jarin's rebellious antics whilst he'd been here.

That part she had no trouble believing.

Now, as she watched the two of them eat and laugh together, she could make no sense of it. Sir Jarin, a libertine and a warrior, yet a man who had been so close to taking vows of chastity, humility, and nonviolence. That he'd left so suddenly should certainly warrant anger on the part of the abbot, at the very least displeasure, yet the monk gazed at Jarin with as much affection as any father would a son.

"More, more." Thebe pointed toward the pottage, and Cristiana gathered a spoonful and put it in her mouth. When she glanced up, Sir Jarin was looking at her with the strangest look—somewhat admiring, yet with a pinch of confusion and sorrow.

He glanced away and the loss swept over her as uncomfortable as any chill.

"Is it true, Sir Jarin, that you put fire pepper in Brother James's stew?" she said by way of gaining back his gaze.

Instead of answering her, he sighed and cast an incriminating look at the abbot.

Father Godwin shrugged. "The lady asked if I had any tales to tell. I cannot lie." He smiled at her with eyes kinder than she'd seen in a long while. Short gray hair sat full upon his chin and the sides of his head but grew thin above his forehead. A gold cross hung brightly against his dark robes.

Sir Jarin shook his head. "As you so oft told me, Father, silence is a neglected virtue."

Father Godwin laughed, joined by Brother Peter, who leaned forward to address Jarin. "In truth, we have missed your antics, Bro...forgive me...Jarin. 'Twas much livelier around here when you were present."

Cristiana drew a spoonful of pottage toward her mouth. "And what of the wild shrew you caught and released during Vespers?"

Jarin finally faced her, fingering his beard, his dark eyes full of pluck. "You are pleased to mock me, my lady."

"Nay. I am pleased to hear of the enjoyment you brought your brothers." She smiled sweetly as Thebe grabbed a strand of her hair. Tugging it from her chubby fingers, Cristiana continued. "Why leave such a comfortable life?"

Father Godwin grabbed his mug of ale and sat back in his chair. "He wanted his freedom, my lady. Saints preserve us, he was, *is* far too restless to be a monk or to stay in one place for too long, even should that life lead to a blissful eternity."

Sir Jarin frowned. "I choose to live the life I have here and now, not hope for something I cannot see or touch."

Cristiana had known this about him, but the truth brought a pain to her heart, withal.

"Alas, 'tis far too late, regardless." Jarin shrugged. "I have killed too many men. I have bed"—he glanced at Cristiana and then Thebe and halted. Alas, that he'd bedded too many women made the food in her stomach suddenly sour.

Father Godwin sipped his ale. "There is always forgiveness with God, Jarin."

Sir Jarin released a heavy sigh and stared at his food. "Mayhap, for He is far better than I, for I cannot bring myself to forgive *Him*."

Silence invaded the table. Cristiana stopped chewing and forced the bread down her throat. The words bordered on blasphemous.

Yet, the abbot merely smiled and said, "When you do, He will welcome you back."

What had happened to Sir Jarin to make him so angry at God? Alack, would the Almighty forgive such an affront? Oddly, Cristiana began to fear for Sir Jarin's soul, though, in truth, she should worry more about her own. Breaking off another piece of bread, she gave it to Thebe, but the child closed her lips, and instead, leaned her head on Cristiana's shoulder. The poor babe was beyond exhausted.

"If you will pardon me." Clutching the girl, Cristiana stood, and the three men also rose as she made her way to the warm fire and laid the child on a couch.

Brother Peter rushed over with a quilt, and Cristiana, thanked him and placed it over the girl. Within minutes, her eyes closed, and she drifted off to sleep.

Thank God. Cristiana brushed curls from the little girl's face and sat beside her. Now that the babe was asleep, she could wait no longer to inquire after her sister's welfare. She glanced toward Sir Jarin and was happy to see him heading her way. He stopped by the mantel, leaned an arm on top, and smiled at her.

Sweet angels, but the man cut a fine figure no matter what he wore. 'Twas no wonder he left a trail of broken hearts behind him.

She glanced away, determined not to become one of them. "What news of Alexia, Sir Jarin? I am desperate to hear."

"She is well, my lady. Safe, strong, and, along with Ronar, thwarting Sir Walter at every turn."

'Twas as if a heavy weight broke free from her heart and scattered into dust. "Gramercy, that is most pleasing to hear. But, pray, how did you find me? How did you know...?"

"Mistress De Mowbray," he replied with a grin.

Cristiana leapt to her feet. "Seraphina! You have seen her?"

"Aye." He approached, gently gripped her arms, then leaned toward her, smelling of damp wool and fire smoke and Jarin, a scent more pleasant than she cared to admit. "She found us and told us your situation."

Tears burned in her eyes as she dared glance up at him. He was so close she could see the concern brimming in his eyes. "I thought she'd abandoned me."

"Nay." He lifted his hand as if to stroke her cheek, but Father Godwin and Brother Peter drew near, and Jarin took a step back.

"I fear I must retire." Brother Peter nodded to them both. "I am to arise at dawn for my duties."

After saying their farewells, Father Godwin took a seat across from her, adjusting his black robe. "I understand you were chased here by wolves." His glance took in Thebe, and Cristiana realized he'd delayed the question on the child's behalf.

Jarin stooped by the fire and stared into the flames. "So 'twould seem. Though I cannot imagine an entire pack would be so famished as to chase us across the countryside."

Indeed. Most peculiar. Yet something pricked Cristiana's memory. "Did not a similar event befall my sister? I recall her telling the tale of her and Sir Ronar surrounded by wolves."

Jarin glanced her way. "Aye, I recall some fanciful tale, though in good sooth, I gave it little credit."

Nor had she. "If I remember, Alexia said they disappeared in whiffs of black smoke when she"—Cristiana lowered her gaze—"what did she do? I cannot recall."

Father Godwin grew pensive, listening to the tale, a thousand thoughts evident behind his deep eyes. "'Twould seem these wolves are not flesh and blood."

Sir Jarin huffed and rose to his feet. "Nonsense."

Father Godwin merely smiled and folded hands over his lap. "Is it? The devil would only send this kind of evil upon someone who is doing good for God's kingdom or presenting a great threat. Which are you, my lady?"

Cristiana eyed him. "Neither, Father. I am naught but an orphaned lady cast from my home and inheritance."

Sir Jarin pierced her with a gaze, and she knew he thought of the Spear. Absently, she rubbed the mark on the inside of her wrist.

Father Godwin leaned forward. "I sense good in you, my lady. Power, light, I cannot gainsay it. Though I grant you, I do not know from whence it hails." Leaning back, he stared at the high ceiling for several moments. "Evil is astir this night. It begs entrance to this holy place."

As if to confirm the abbot's statement, loud knocks on the door preceded the entrance of two monks, night cloaks over their brown robes. They bowed before the abbot.

"Father, there are more than thirty armed soldiers at our gate demanding entrance."

CHAPTER ELEVEN

"**P**otz!" Alexia blinked back her sudden fear. A stone wall as solid as any other stood before her, blocking the way—the *only* way at the moment—to the secret passages snaking through Luxley Castle. Behind her and her friends, shouts and the stomp of boots grew louder. The guards would be upon them in moments.

Groaning, Damien drew a knife from his boot and wheeled to face them.

Ronar glanced at her, his blue eyes searching hers, wise and knowing. "Walls do not appear out of nowhere." He laid palms on the stone and pushed with all his might, growling.

She nodded. But what to do? She'd never encountered so solid an obstacle. So *large* an obstacle.

"This way!" one of the guards shouted. "I hear something."

Footsteps thundered.

Damien snapped his gaze to Ronar. "At least turn and fight!"

Closing her eyes, Alexia attempted to still her heartbeat. She could never see the spirit realm when she was anxious. The friar's gentle words filled her mind. *Faith not fear. Calm not calamity.* She released a breath and sought the Spirit.

In her mind, she saw the wall begin to move as if it were alive. Like a river of mud, it oozed and bubbled before her. Eyes still closed, she drew a blade from inside her tunic and held it against the sludge.

"Any moment now, my love." Ronar's anxious words resounded from beside her.

"Are you both mad?" Damien barked.

The head of a large viper shot from the mud, fangs bared.

Alexia leapt back with a shriek and opened her eyes, breath heaving.

Ronar grabbed her arm. "What is it?"

"Naught to concern us." She smiled. Then holding her knife to the wall, she drew a deep breath, said a silent prayer, and uttered the words. "No weapon formed against us shall prosper. 'Tis the heritage of the servants of the Lord! Begone!"

The tip of the blade she pressed to the wall fell forward, along with her arm as they both swept through air.

Ronar's shocked expression transformed into a wide grin.

"Shall we?" Alexia started forward

"Come, Damien. Make haste!" Ronar slugged the knight on the arm, who remained rigid, his blade pointed toward the oncoming guards.

"Huh?" Damien whirled, knife in hand, and gaped down the hallway, his face pinched in disbelief ere he followed on their heels.

Down the passage, up another spiral of stairs, Alexia shoved aside a wooden cabinet and knelt, feeling along the stone wall. There. She pressed the latch and drew out a rope from behind it. One tug and the stone moved aside. Ronar shoved it further, and the three of them squeezed into the tunnel.

Grabbing the cabinet's legs, Ronar pulled it back in place, then yanked on the rope to secure the stone.

Just as they heard the march of boots speed past.

Darkness surrounded them. Naught could be heard save the distant drip of water and their harried breathing. A musty smell of age and decay filled Alexia's nose as Ronar struck flint to steel and lit one of many torches laid near the entrance.

"I dare not ask what became of that wall," Damien muttered.

"God's truth, you wouldn't believe it," Alexia said. "Let us be about our haunting, shall we?"

Rising, she led the way through the narrow passageway, turned left, and then rounded a corner that descended to the right and then veered left again. She knew these passages as well as she knew Emerald Forest. Cristiana and she had discovered them after their mother died, and together, they had spent hours exploring the castle and spying on the servants. They'd never told anyone, which she was thankful for now, or Sir Walter would surely have had them guarded.

Torch light glistened over moist stone, and a chill invaded Alexia's tunic, piercing her skin and seeping into her bones. Whether from the damp air or what had just occurred, she didn't know.

The wall had disappeared! Though she should not be surprised, still her mind reeled at the miracle. She knew not from whence the dark powers in this castle hailed, but they were growing stronger and more powerful every day. Which meant she and Ronar must grow stronger in their faith, must learn more of the Sacred Words of Scripture in order to do battle. For the friar had told her that they did not battle against flesh and blood, but against principalities, powers and rulers of darkness—entities that could not be defeated by sword or arrow, but only by the Word of God and the name of Jesus.

Ronar and Damien were silent behind her as the tunnel narrowed and they dropped to their knees to crawl the final distance to Sir Walter's study.

If Anabelle had done her part, which she always did, then Sir Walter should be quite befuddled by now.

Alexia halted before the hole which led into the vile steward's room. Rummaging through her pack, she found the jar, opened the cork, and smeared the white paste all over her face, neck, and the exposed skin of her arms, then handed it to Ronar and Damien, who did the same.

After tying a white cloth over her hair, she suppressed a chuckle at how ridiculous the mighty knights looked, and crawled from the tunnel to an area beneath a sideboard. There, peering from behind the cloth that covered the table, she spotted Sir Walter at his desk, his vacant eyes staring into space. Good.

"Put out the torch and allow the smoke to enter his chamber," she whispered as Ronar and Damien crawled in behind her.

Ronar gripped her arm. "Be careful."

"When am I not?"

He sighed. "Always."

Sir Walter, quill pen in hand, stared at the parchments spread over his desk. Why would they not cease floating back and forth like wheat before the wind? Blinking, he drew a deep breath and attempted to focus yet again. His stomach rebelled, and a foul smell emerged from his mouth. Tossing down his pen, he slammed his fists on the desk, yet even *that* action caused him pain.

What was amiss with him these days? What illness had overtaken him? He'd always been virile and strong. Leaning back in his chair, he rubbed his eyes. Whate'er the apothecary was giving him, 'twas of no effect. He would run to the man's chamber and curse him for a fool. If he but had the strength. Instead, fear of his own mortality clamped onto him like a vice.

"Devil's blood!" He cursed out loud. He was far too young, had far too many plans to be thinking thus. 'Twas merely a mild case of ague, and soon he'd be back to his lusty, devious self!

A scuffing sound, like wood on stone, reached his ears. The candle on his desk fluttered, though his shutters were closed. Smoke filled the room. He coughed and shook his head.

Hearing things again. Seeing things again. Sitting up, he reached for a flask of wine and attempted to pour it into a cup, but his hand shook, and it spilled, dripping from his desk onto the floor…*plop…plop…plop…*like fresh drops of blood.

He pushed his chair back in horror and looked up to see three beings moving to and fro before his desk. The room spun and cloudiness cloaked his vision. Their faces were as pale as death, and their bodies oscillated as if they were made of water. A memory taunted him. Had he not seen these three before in his bed chamber?

"Who are you?" He shriveled further into his chair, heart thundering, longing to run, but unable to find the strength.

One of the beings floated toward him and placed a parchment on his desk. "Sign this, and seal it with your ring." The voice was familiar yet muffled as if it echoed down a long corridor.

Sir Walter dropped his gaze to the paper, but the words chased each other around like children at play.

The tip of a knife appeared in his vision, pointing to a space on the bottom. "Here." The being dipped his pen in the inkwell and handed it to him.

"What is it? What does it say?"

A thousand horses' hooves pounded across his brain, and he reached up with both hands to squeeze his head. "Cease this madness, I beseech you!"

"'Twill cease when you sign this missive."

Pain spiked through his head, down his neck, and spread across his back. His breath came hard and raspy, and it took all his strength to remain upright.

He took the quill, the feather trembling in his vision, for he'd do anything to stop this pain, even cater to spirits. "Alas, I beg you, what does it say?"

"'Tis the parchment which will clear your conscience and grant you a chance for redemption," the spirit before him said, though when he glanced at it, the apparition appeared to be naught but an undulating cloud.

"Redemption! Beshrew me. What need have I of that?" He dropped the pen.

"You will have great need of it when you face hellfire," one of the spirits in the distance remarked.

"Who are you? How did you get in here?" He'd posted a guard at his door. Hadn't he? Breath coming hard, Sir Walter struggled to rise. Finally teetering on his feet, he stumbled backward and struck the wall. Hard.

"In truth, we are secret messengers from the otherworld."

"Secret messengers, forsooth!" His belly ached, and he forced down vomit rising to his throat. "You are not here. 'Tis but a nightmare."

"I'll show you how real we are!" One of the spirits started forward—the largest one—but the one in front raised a hand to stop him.

"I assure you, you vile miscreant. We are quite able to slit your throat in your sleep."

Sir Walter clutched his neck, doing his best to focus on the spirits, attempting to make out their features, but they remained twisted and malformed.

"Ergo, you will sign this parchment, or you'll meet the devil himself."

Huffing, Sir Walter's thoughts drifted to Drago. "I have already met him. Now, leave me be! I beseech you. Leave me be!"

Yet the spirits remained.

Clutching a vase from the table beside him, he hurled it at the first apparition. It ducked and the vase crashed to the floor, breaking into a dozen pieces.

The sound of the bishop's voice rang from outside the door.

Sir Walter's legs gave out, and he slid against the wall to the floor. Just what he needed. A visit from his excellent nimbycock.

More scuffling sounded, and the door swung open, slamming against the stone wall behind it.

The sound rang pain through Sir Walter's head.

"What mischief is afoot in here?" 'Twas the bishop's annoying voice. Nightmare, indeed.

Nay, no nightmare, for the real bishop circled Sir Walter's desk in a swirl of black robes and stared at him as if he would rather step on him like a bug than speak with him.

"Get up, you dizzard! Why are you sitting on the floor, curled in the corner like a whimpering tosspot?"

Pressing his hands against the wall, Sir Walter pushed himself up, held his stomach against his rising nausea, and approached his desk. One glance over the chamber revealed the spirits had gone.

"Nay. I...I..."

"Oh, do shut it, you buffoon. I hear you have good news."

Dropping into his chair, Sir Walter swallowed and studied the parchments across his desk. The one from the spirits was gone. "They have found Lady Cristiana," he moaned.

"Indeed!" The wavering form of the bishop slapped his hands together. "When will they arrive?"

Sir Walter coughed. "They do not have her in hand as of yet. But they have her surrounded."

"Surrounded! God's blood! Can you do naught right?"

"'Tis only a matter of time, Your Grace." Sir Walter muttered, though his words sounded jumbled to his ears.

"Very well. I shall expect to see the shrew back here at Luxley within a sennight." The bishop's distorted face, far too large and grotesque, appeared in Sir Walter's vision.

"Beware your drink, sir. If you can't control yourself and find the Spear, I'll seek out someone who can and give Luxley to them!"

Spinning around, the bishop stormed out, and Sir Walter dropped his head onto his desk and drifted into a tormented oblivion.

CHAPTER TWELVE

Jarin cursed himself beneath his breath. Sir Walter's knights had found them, and now the entire monastery was in danger.

Father Godwin rose to address the two monks who'd just told him an army demanded entrance at the gate. "Inform them that men of violence are not permitted to enter this sacred place. Should they wish to risk eternal damnation, they may by all means force their way inside, but only at the cost of murdering holy men of God."

Though Jarin spotted fear tighten the expressions of the two men, to their credit, they dipped their heads and sped off.

"Forgive me, Father," Jarin said. "We have brought trouble to your gate. 'Twas not my intent." Though, beshrew it, he should have considered the possibility.

Alarm skittered about Lady Cristiana's brown eyes, but she said not a word.

Father Godwin, however, waved a hand through the air. "Do you think my faith so weak that an army disturbs me? That all the armies in the world would e'er disturb God?"

Jarin stared at him, unsure whether the old man had lost his reason. "Should this particular army break through your walls, I doubt even God could save you from their cruelty." He regretted the words ere they left his lips for Lady Cristiana threw a hand to her throat and rose.

"What are we to do?" She glanced down at the babe.

"There, there, my lady, I see your faith is as feeble as Jarin's." Though reproof fired in the abbot's gaze, his tone was jovial. He closed his eyes for a moment and drew a deep breath.

Jarin knew from experience he was praying.

Whilst an army pounded on his door! And the only weapons they had were the ones Jarin had brought with him. Alas, they had but one option. They must leave lest they endanger the monks further. But how, when an army of well-trained knights surrounded them?

Lady Cristiana bit her lip and then began whispering numbers, "One, two, three…"

Was Jarin the only one here not addlebrained?

Father Godwin opened his eyes and smiled. "Nay, they will not enter Tegimen Abbey this night, I make bold to declare. And when they do on the morrow, they will not find you here."

Jarin had never known his friend to lie nor to proclaim something based purely on hope. That the man heard from God never failed to irk Jarin, for the Almighty had not graced him with such a privilege.

"Not find us here! Forsooth!" Lady Cristiana wrung her hands and approached the hearth. "I fail to understand how we are not to be found here when there is no escape."

Father Godwin followed her and laid a hand on her shoulder. "Never fear. Only believe, my lady. God always provides a way."

Jarin ground his teeth. 'Twas man, by his wit and brawn alone, who escaped danger. "Father, do grace us, I beg you, with knowledge of this *way* God will provide."

Godwin faced him, that irritating, all-knowing smile on his face. "There is more than one way into and out of the abbey, my son. Now, I am off to bed." He gestured toward a young lad standing at attention in the corner, and the boy started toward them, hobbling on one foot, whilst dragging the other.

"Brother Jeffrey will bring you more food and drink should you desire. However, I suggest you both attend to your rest, for the morrow promises to be full of adventure." He winked at Lady Cristiana, but her attention was on the crippled lad who was tossing wood onto the fire.

Jarin took a determined step forward. "Father, please. Show us how to leave anon, lest we endanger you further."

"There is naught to fear this night. Rest well, Jarin." Turning, he made his way to the door and disappeared in a mist of undying faith.

Jarin fisted his hands, shoving down his anger. If the man were a warrior, Jarin would force him to disclose what he knew. Alas, he had no idea what to do with a man of God, an abbot. *And* a friend. Trust was not something that came natural to Jarin. Not when he'd been so oft betrayed.

"You allow him to walk away?"

The angry tone turned Jarin about to Lady Cristiana, her hair glistening like amber in the firelight. "What would you have me do, threaten an abbot? Or mayhap draw my blade to his throat, bind him, and toss him into a pot of boiling water?" He regretted his insolence when a tear appeared at the corner of her eye.

"Forgive me." He took her by the arm and led her to sit.

Sniffing, she drew the back of her hand to her nose. "'Tis I who should beg your forgiveness. And the abbot's. I have brought this danger down upon us all."

"Nay." He knelt before her and took her hand in his. "None of this falls on you, my lady." He rubbed her fingers, relishing their softness. "'Tis Sir Walter, the bishop, and the malice and avarice of man that arms this threat. You...*we* have merely been caught in the middle."

"And *you* because of me."

"I am a warrior, my lady. I go where e're a battle brews."

She gave him a tender smile that spoke of disbelief. But how could he blame her? What elite knight of the King's Guard would forsake such a prestigious post and become an enemy of the king merely to see justice served in the greedy seizure of one lowly estate?

He would, apparently. Mayhap he was the addlebrained one, after all. But he'd done it for Ronar and Damien at first— the only two people he trusted in the world, his friends and fellow King's Guard. But now, as he stared into Lady Cristiana's tender eyes, longing to brush the tear from her cheek...

Nay. Releasing her hand, he rose and shook off her bewitching spell. "Since we can do naught until morning, we'd best retire."

"I cannot." She glanced toward the child. "She sleeps so soundly, I dare not move her. Besides, I doubt I shall find sleep this night." She looked up at him. "Quit us and make to your chamber, Sir Jarin. I shall remain here with Thebe."

"I will not leave you, my lady."

She glanced at him in wonder

Ere he betrayed his feelings, he added, "I gave my troth to your sister, and I dare not anger the Falcon of Emerald Forest. I've witnessed the effects of her arrow."

The lady smiled. "She is truly a formidable enemy, I'll not gainsay it. Yet she is also an inspiration to many."

Jarin longed to remark that he found Cristiana an inspiration as well but held his tongue. 'Twould do no good to give voice to the peculiar sensations spiraling through him when e'er she was near. For that would give life to something he dared not admit.

Cristiana would be loath to admit her joy when Sir Jarin announced he would stay with her and Thebe. The prospect of sitting alone without benefit of guard or locked door—even in a monastery—unsettled her nerves.

And they were already quite unsettled enough.

That she felt utterly and completely safe all alone at night with the libertine knight made her doubt her own mind. But then again, 'twas not her mind that was overjoyed.

Still, she felt uncomfortable, even indecent, lying down on the sofa beside Thebe—like a naughty girl revealing her leg to a boy for a favor. Sir Jarin had seen her oft enough in her bed at Luxley, but only when she'd been unable to receive guests any other way. Lying down to sleep in the same room as a man, 'twas simply not done. She pushed herself to sit, but Sir Jarin approached with a blanket he must have gotten from the young crippled lad, draped it over her shoulders, and forced her back down.

"You'll be no good to the girl tomorrow if you don't get your rest."

She laid her head on the pillow, feeling its softness lure her to relax.

Sir Jarin took a seat by the fire, withdrew a coin from inside his surcote and began flipping it among his fingers. Back and forth, in and out, with such speed and accuracy, Cristiana could only stare. Firelight glittered over the gold, flashing bright and dark, mesmerizing her as easily as the man so oft did himself.

"Tell me tales of your youth, Sir Jarin."

He briefly glanced her way. "I assure you, my lady, there is naught to tell."

"I do not believe you. I am sure there are many adventures that formed the man I see now."

He flipped the coin in the air and caught it, then leaned back in his chair and stared at the fire. "I grew up in a small village. My father was the town blacksmith, though in truth"—he chuckled—"he would have made a better priest for all the time he spent assisting the vicar in the local church."

"A priest?"

"Aye, a dream of his which could ne'er come true after he married young."

Apparently, she failed to hide her shock, for Sir Jarin snorted and continued, "That surprises you? With such a pious father and training as a monk, how did I become…hmm, how should I put it… a libertine and a man of violence?" His smile faded as soon as it had appeared.

She could not deny either of those charges, though she desperately longed to know what had led to them. "A very pungent question, Sir Jarin. Pray tell?"

But he did not answer. Instead, naught but the crackle of flames and whisper of wind against the stone walls filled the chamber. "Have you any siblings?" 'Twas a less intrusive question, for she merely wished to hear his voice—that deep, soothing, timbre that had the odd effect of making her feel safe in the midst of danger.

'Twas a long time ere he finally answered… and a heart full of emotions filled his simple, "Nay."

Her throat burned. Why, she could not say. Nor could she close her eyes, though they grew heavy, for she could not tear her gaze from him. Who was this knight, this adventurer and wooer of maidens? This warrior-monk with a wounded heart? Firelight accentuated the strong lines of his jaw, glistened over his dark hair, and ran along the firm muscles in his arms so evident beneath his simple linen shirt. Yet a sadness held his gaze captive to the flames, as if he were reliving some tragedy.

Moments later, the cloud of despair moved aside, and he continued flipping his coin. "What of you, my lady? Growing up the daughter of a baron in such an estate as Luxley must have been agreeable. Before Sir Walter took over."

Cristiana recalled so few happy memories, she hesitated to answer. Surely being raised in luxury would forbid her to complain to a commoner. Nor did she wish to speak of her life. For the most part, 'twas not a happy tale to tell. She closed her eyes beneath their weight, then forced them open. None other had ever asked of her childhood. Ergo, at the least, she owed him an answer.

"My father died in war when I was but five years of age. I barely remember him, though I am told I was his favorite." She smiled. "Ofttimes, after he was long gone, I used to hear his voice echoing through Luxley, his hearty chuckle, see visions of his smile when he saw me and opened his arms to receive my embrace. Alas, the memories fade with each year." Cristiana drew a breath lest she break out in tears in front of this knight. Fire smoke, ale, and a musty scent filled her nose. "My mother died two years later, leaving Alexia and me at the mercy of Sir Walter, our steward. Alack, I am told he is responsible for her death, though I can hardly believe it. Mother trusted him, leaned on him for help running the estate after Father died." She forced down her fury. How could her mother have been that naïve, that bird-witted? Yet…how could Cristiana have?

"He is a snake of the worst kind, preying on the innocent. A man devoid of conscience. I have met many like him in my travels." Jarin leaned forward, resting his forearms on his knees, still moving the coin between his fingers. But his jaw had grown tight. "I'd love nothing more than to wrap my hands around his neck and—" He glanced her way, but the look in his eyes was lost to her in the shadows.

"A year later, Alexia abandoned me," Cristiana continued, revealing the one wound on her heart that was still raw and festering. Why she was telling him these things, she couldn't say, save he was listening and seemed to care. Or mayhap she was still the fool she'd always been to think…to hope…that *anyone* cared. "I never knew what happened to her or if she was even alive. Sir Walter told me she wasn't, though he had no proof. I was only eight."

Jarin released an angry sigh. "A mere child. Left alone with a monster. And he poisoned you." He rose, slipped the coin in his pocket, and gripped the place where his sword would hang. Upon finding it empty, he crossed arms over his chest.

"Not until I became of age to take over the running of Luxley." But she didn't want to talk about it. Those two years were naught but a blur of poking and prodding by physicians and apothecaries, tossing her accounts into foul-smelling pots, spinning rooms, and horrifying visions. If not for Seraphina's constant companionship and her sister reappearing from the dead, Cristiana doubted she would have survived.

"'Tis over now, and you are well." Jarin's tone had turned soft, comforting. "We will return, regain Luxley, and punish that mewling muckrake, Sir Walter."

No longer able to stop them, her eyes closed. "First, we must escape…this…"

But her thoughts abandoned her to the blissfulness of sleep.

Jarin started to tell the lady they would find a way out of the abbey, that he'd defend her with his life. But when he glanced her way, her eyes were shut, and her chest rose and fell with deep breaths. He waited a moment, then crept closer and slipped into a chair beside where she lay. The child uttered a whimper, then turned on her side ere settling back to sleep. Leaning forward, elbows on his knees, Jarin moved his gaze back to Cristiana. Lashes as thick and dark as any forest fluttered over milky cheeks that appeared as soft as velvet. A wisp of honey-brown hair lay gently on her forehead, whilst the remainder cascaded over her shoulder and onto the sofa in a blanket of silk.

What was it about this lady that enraptured him so? In good sooth, she was extraordinarily lovely, but he'd charmed others just as comely. She was witty, intelligent, and well-bred. But 'twas more than that. A sudden longing to protect her and the babe at all costs grew to near bursting inside of him. He could hardly credit it. He'd never felt so strong a need to care for another, even above his own needs. Alas, even above his own need to survive.

And that frightened him most of all. He had plans for his life, battles to win, adventures to enjoy, women to sample. Being burdened with a lady—let alone a child—would put a halt to all of that.

Drawing a deep breath, he glanced at the lad standing by the door, wishing he could dismiss him to his rest, but knowing he would never disobey the abbot's orders. Settling back in his chair, Jarin determined to stay awake, to keep watch over this precious lady and her child. At least for now.

He must have dozed off, for sometime in the middle of the night, a woman's shriek woke him. Rubbing his eyes to clear his vision, he found Cristiana tossing about on the sofa as if she were a ship at sea. Whimpers and gasps spilled from her lips. He knelt before her and took one of her hands in his.

"Softly now, my cosset," he whispered. "Softly. All is well." He stroked her hand until she settled back to sleep, then released her and stood, lest he do what he longed to do and place a kiss on her cheek—that cheek that looked as soft as a rose petal.

Backing away, he glanced toward the high, stained-glass windows where the barest hint of gray shoved aside the night.

He'd done his duty. He'd fulfilled his promise. Ergo, he cast one last glance at her and the babe and headed out the door.

CHAPTER THIRTEEN

The first thing Cristiana saw when she pried open her eyes were the wooden beams stretching across the arched ceiling. Alarm squeezed her heart. 'Twas not the stone walls of her chamber at Braewood Castle. Nor did she hear Muriel entering to rouse her and help her dress.

Breath clambering up her throat, she sprang to sit, only then recognizing the receiving hall of the abbot's residence. The bluish glow of predawn crept through high colored windows, slinked over the wooden floor, wool rugs, and modest furniture, then eased up the stone wall to her right and landed on a tapestry hanging on the wall. 'Twas a picture of Christ surrounded by children, his hand on the head of a young boy, whilst a little girl sat in his lap. His face glowed with an affection she wouldn't have guessed He'd borne toward children, who by society's measure were naught but nuisances. Snapping her gaze from the picture, she glanced at Thebe, still snuggled under her quilt on the couch.

Cristiana breathed out a sigh as young monks entered the room, carrying platters of fruit and cheese and pitchers of what must be water or ale. Suddenly embarrassed, she flung off her blanket and stood, doing her best to press out the folds of her tunic.

Where was Sir Jarin? Had he retired to his chamber and left them here alone? Nay. She lifted her hand and rubbed it, remembering his touch, the gentle way he caressed her fingers, the whispered words of comfort.

She'd had a nightmare!

Aye, she remembered it now. Lowering to sit beside Thebe, she moved a curl from the girl's face. A terrible dream. A hand had slowly risen from beneath her blanket, curled in a fist at first. But the fingers became snakes, slithering and wiggling, their white fangs filling her vision—six of them, not five. They closed in on her neck and squeezed. The feel of their cold, slimy skin sent a chill over her even now. She hadn't been able to breathe. Or even move. Laughter had risen in the distance, the most hideous laughter—like the screech of a thousand swords rubbing together. Gasping for air, she'd attempted to pry the snakes from her throat and glanced up to see Alexia, Ronar, Seraphina, and Jarin turn and walk away.

A tremble ran through her even now. Thebe's "Cristi" aided her to shake it off and face the child with a smile. "Yes, darling." She drew her from beneath the quilt onto her lap.

"Horsey ride?"

"Mayhap." She pressed the child against her bosom and uttered a prayer for her safety. God may have abandoned Cristiana long ago, but surely if that tapestry were true, He would not abandon this innocent child.

The crippled boy from last eve hobbled up to them and smiled. "My lady, I am to escort you to your chamber to ready yourself for your journey."

Hair as black as the night surrounded a face where nary a whisker yet dare appear. Though he attempted a somber expression, playful innocence shone from his blue eyes.

"Very well." Returning his smile, she stood and hoisted Thebe in her arms and followed him out the door and into the courtyard.

Fresh, crisp air filled with the sweet scent of rain and pine battled against the odor of horse flesh and dung. No torches were needed, for the faint glow of dawn pushed back the night and stole the shimmer from stars above. Shivering against the chill, she drew Thebe close and listened for any sound of the army waiting outside the walls, but heard naught. She could only hope they'd left, but good fortune such as that rarely befriended her. Mud clung to her shoes, and she wondered how the lad was able to drag his one foot through the sludge without toppling over. But he managed well enough and halted at the stairway outside the stables.

Up in her chamber, she relieved herself, changed Thebe's soiled cloth, and donned her now-dry attire. On the way back, against all propriety, she knocked on Sir Jarin's door. Was the man so lazy as to still be abed? No answer came, nor any sound at all.

Sudden fear threatened to drain all strength from her legs. Leaning against the wooden wall, she steadied her breathing and attempted a smile for Thebe's sake. Had Sir Jarin abandoned them in the night? Her mind and heart awhirl, she descended the steps and allowed the lad to escort her back to the abbot's where a meal to break their fast had been placed atop the table.

"Have you seen Sir Jarin?" she asked the boy, but he shook his head and gestured for them to sit and eat.

Setting Thebe on the bench, she plucked a pear from a platter and handed it to her. Fresh ale, along with bread and cheese made up the rest of the meal, but Cristiana's stomach was tied in a knot at the prospect of being all alone once again.

She glanced at the lad who remained standing nearby. "Surely you are tired, Brother…"

"Jeffrey."

"Brother Jeffrey. You have been awake all night." She tried to study his foot but could see naught beneath the hem of his robe.

"I am to remain at your side until Brother Mikon relieves me, my lady."

Grabbing a lock of her hair, she twirled it around her finger, debating her next move. Something deep within her stirred at this boy's misfortune. "May I pray for your foot, Brother Jeffrey?"

At first, he remained standing, staring straight ahead, unmoving save the slight opening of his mouth. Then slowly, he turned to face her. "Gramercy, my lady, but Father Godwin and several of my brothers have already done so."

"Then what harm could it do?"

A hint of a smile graced his lips, curiosity filled his eyes, eyes that now took her in as if she were some sort of oddity.

"Surely you believe God can heal?" She raised a brow. "Didn't our Lord heal many when He was here?"

"Aye, my lady, but some of us must bear our burdens with grace."

Pain stole the life from his eyes, draining them of their youth, and an instant, overwhelming love for this young lad consumed Cristiana. 'Twas not her own love, for she was not capable of such prodigious empathy. It emanated from the Spear safely bound to her thigh.

"May I touch your foot?" Kneeling, she moved her hand toward him, though she knew 'twas much to ask of a monk.

Brother Jeffrey shook his head in horror.

"Only for a moment."

He hesitated, searching her eyes, but finally gave a little nod and took a step closer.

Placing one hand lightly on the injured foot, she bowed her head and said, "Be healed by our Lord Christ Jesus and the power of His blood."

As she had so many times before, she felt the muscle and bone moving beneath her touch. Joy filled her as she retrieved her hand and rose before him. "You are healed, Brother Jeffrey. Test and see."

He stared in wonder at her for a moment ere he slowly, fearfully, leaned his weight on his foot. When he did, his eyes snapped wide, his mouth hung open, and a look of shock and utter glee beamed from his face. Still staring at her, he tested it again, then began hopping on the healed foot, laughing. "How did you...? What marvel is this?"

Cristiana clasped her hands together in joy. "I did naught. 'Twas Christ who healed you."

"Praise be to God! Praise be to God!"

The other monks and servants in the room stared his way. A few ran up to him.

"I am healed!" He showed them his foot as he leapt and ran, whilst each gazed at him in disbelief.

Which always astounded Cristiana. From what she knew of the Holy Scriptures, Jesus had healed many people and proclaimed His servants would do the same. Yet so few believed Him.

Brother Peter entered the room, saw Jeffrey surrounded by a crowd of monks, and headed their way.

"Cristi, more food?" Thebe said, drawing Cristiana's gaze to the precious child, who had chunks of pear over her face and gown. Smiling, she knelt beside her, grabbed a cloth from the table, and cleaned her up as best she could.

"Mayhap something less messy." She broke off two pieces of bread, popped one in her mouth and gave the other to the girl, then poured water into a glass and held it to Thebe's lips.

"Forgive my tardiness, Lady Cristiana. I trust you slept well." Brother Peter's voice jerked her around.

"We did. Thank you." Ignoring the bewildered look on his face, she asked, "Have you seen Sir Jarin this morn?" Merely asking the question caused her fear to return.

Brother Peter cast a glance over his shoulder at Jeffrey, who had not ceased walking and running through the room. "What? Did you...? Brother Jeffrey says you healed him."

"God healed him," Cristiana offered. "Prithee, tell me of Sir Jarin."

He started to sit, but instead remained standing, still looking perplexed. "I have not seen Jarin. Father Godwin will be here anon. I am sure he knows the knight's whereabouts."

She might as well have swallowed a boulder, for her bread landed with a *thunk* in her stomach. Unable to hide her emotion and not wanting to upset Thebe, she rose, set down the glass, and moved to stand facing the wall to her right.

Brother Peter appeared beside her. "You believe the knight has left you?"

"Why wouldn't he?" What a fool she was. His soft words and caresses last eve were no doubt farewells, laden with guilt. "We are mere acquaintances, naught more. And surely a warrior such as he could slip out of the abbey unnoticed, whereas with a woman and child, his chances—*all our chances*—are nigh impossible."

"You have a point, I'll grant you, but I've known Jarin for years. He is not one to run from a fight. No matter the cost."

She had been of the same mind. "Mayhap this time the cost was too high." As it had been for her sister. And Seraphina. And if she admitted it, she blamed her mother and father for leaving her as well. Why had her father gone off to war? Why had her mother trusted Sir Walter with her life? Foolish choices made with nary a thought toward the children in their charge.

Brother Peter moved to stand in front of her, meeting her gaze with a pointed one that bespoke a wisdom well past his years. "Even should Sir Jarin disappoint you, Lady Cristiana, God never will. Do not think you are alone for one moment."

She held back her bitter laugh, forced away tears, and squared her shoulders. "Thank you, Brother Peter, but 'tis for *that* very reason God has disappointed me most of all. It cost him nothing to remain at my side."

Instead of shock, instead of a string of sanctimonious castigations, Brother Peter merely smiled. "I disagree. It cost Him everything."

"Then where is He? Why has my life been fraught with despair and tragedy? Why does He never answer my prayers?" She batted away a tear and lowered her gaze.

"My lady, it may *appear* that our loving Father has left you, but I give you my troth, He has not. His Word promises He never will. You have only to seek Him with all your heart."

Before she could offer a retort she would need to repent of later, a voice—a *wonderful* rich voice—turned her face to the door.

In walked Father Godwin with Sir Jarin by his side. He'd donned his normal attire, complete with leather doublet, tall boots, and myriad of weapons, and against her will, her traitorous heart leapt in her chest.

Brother Jeffrey ran up to them, gesturing to his foot, then pointing at her. Sir Jarin's eyes met hers from across the room, an undiscernible look within them.

Father Godwin rejoiced with the lad, then dismissed him, and the two men headed her way as Brother Peter gave her a knowing nod and left.

"I knew God's power rested on you," Father Godwin said as he approached, his eyes filled with kindness and wonder. "We've been praying for Brother Jeffrey since he arrived last year."

She only smiled, for she dared not tell him the truth. She'd seen the greed and bloodshed that occurred when people learned of the Spear. Jarin's knowing look told her she'd made the right choice. In good sooth, she could hardly look away from him, longing to touch him and ensure he was real. But of course he was. Her heart would not be pounding thus were he not standing so close.

Father Godwin glanced at Thebe. "I wish to know more, but time is of the essence. I have packed some food for your journey." He handed a sack to Jarin. "You must quit this place posthaste, for the soldiers will enter Tegimen any moment."

How he knew that, she could not fathom, but the words prompted her to collect Thebe in her arms, grab her own sack, and follow Father Godwin and Jarin from the room.

CHAPTER FOURTEEN

U shering Lady Cristiana and the babe before him, Jarin followed Father Godwin into a small courtyard and past the chapel and cemetery. Monks, faces lowered beneath cowls, moved about in the morning mist curling around their feet, seemingly hovering above ground as they prepared for their morning prayers.

Lady Cristiana had healed Brother Jeffrey's malformed foot!

The fact kept slipping into Jarin's thoughts, though he'd rather focus on the task at hand—an impossible task, that. Escaping a band of well-trained soldiers who had them surrounded.

Yet…she *had* healed the boy. When no other prayers had worked. Not even Father Godwin's.

Jarin had seen too much to doubt the power of this Spear of Christ. But 'twas the love and care of its present owner that had him baffled. Lord Braewood had forced her to heal. This she'd done of her own will. Regardless of the perilous circumstances in which she found herself, she thought of others, strangers even, wanting to help, heal, and restore, qualities which belied everything he believed about women of title. About most women.

Yet Cristiana differed in many ways from other privileged women he'd met. Which may have been what attracted him in the first place. She surprised him, confounded him, and even astounded him, as in the look she'd given him when he'd entered the hall with Father Godwin. A look of surprise and delight that nearly sent him running to her side.

He ran to no lady's side. In good sooth, they usually ran to him.

Tiny droplets of mist created a shimmer over her hair as she walked in front of him, making her look like some heavenly creature who dared to walk amongst mere mortals.

However, despite her angelic appearance, he could feel her fear trailing in the wake of her sweet fragrance.

Yet how could he comfort her when he had no assurance they would escape unscathed?

Wide-eyed, the babe stared at him over her shoulder, bouncing up and down with the lady's movements. Egad, but the wee one was a sweet slice of heaven. If there was such a place.

They passed the kitchen where pots and pans rattled, and the scent of oatmeal and eggs rose to lure a growl from Jarin's stomach.

Diving into a building on the side, Father Godwin grabbed a lit torch and immediately descended a stairway to the wine cellar. A chilled mustiness cloaked Jarin, and he smiled. How many hours had he and Brother Quinn spent down here drinking wine when they should have been at evening services? Too many to count.

Godwin pushed against a tall wooden rack laden with corked bottles.

"Here, help me, Jarin."

Together they shoved it aside, and Godwin retrieved a large blade from the rack and pried open one of the wooden planks lining the wall. Dank, icy air smelling of moss, dirt, and age, blasted over them.

Lady Cristiana coughed.

Father Godwin held the torch up to see Jarin's face. Sorrow lingered within his tender smile. "Make haste to Sancreet village, a stone's throw east from here. Find the spice monger's shop. Ask for Master Teagan, and tell him I sent you for Challenger. He's a sturdy palfrey."

Jarin shook his head. "I cannot take your horse."

"And I cannot smuggle a knight's warhorse out of Tegimen." The abbot smiled. "Besides, 'twill give you an excuse to return and see us again. Collect him when you are done with whate'er war you now wage." He waved a hand through the air and shook his head.

Jarin nodded. One horse for the three of them. 'Twould be difficult but better than going on foot. "You have always been…"—Jarin's throat closed as he looked at his friend. In truth he'd been a father to Jarin, the best father any man could want. "Thank you for your help."

"You are always welcome here. And you, my lady." Godwin turned to Lady Cristiana.

With hands full, she dipped her head. "Thank you, Abbot."

"Take care of this precious child." He made the sign of the cross on Thebe's forehead and kissed her.

The little girl giggled.

Father Godwin gestured toward the tunnel entrance. "'Tis narrow and low. You may have to crawl in some spots. Oh." He gripped Jarin's arm. "Should you need help on your journey, Brother Quinn, I mean, Lord Quinn resides now in Savoy village. I know he'd like to see you again."

Lord Quinn? Jarin nodded. Quinn and he had been the best of friends once. He gripped Father Godwin's arms and thanked him again ere he turned to Lady Cristiana.

"I'll carry the girl." He held out his hands, but the babe ducked her head into Lady Cristiana's neck.

"She doesn't know you yet, Sir Jarin. And she's been through much this past day. I'll manage."

"My son." The abbot's urgent tone drew Jarin's gaze. "The answers you seek are not of this world. You must seek beyond it for the truth."

Jarin had no response, nor did he want his parting words to be harsh. Hence, he merely nodded and dove into the tunnel. The abbot had been right about it being narrow and low, for most of it was only large enough to crawl through. Behind him, he could hear Lady Cristiana's moans as she struggled to keep up.

With no torch to guide the way, Jarin could only lumber along, sometimes crawling, sometimes inching forward on his haunches, a few sections nearly standing. Of a sudden, his hands struck a wall of dirt. The end of the tunnel.

Lady Cristiana bumped into him. Her breathing heightened.

He felt above. His fingers touched wood, and he shoved the plank upward and set it aside. Light blinded him for a moment ere he gripped the edge and hefted himself up, setting his pack aside. 'Twas a narrow cave, or rather, as his eyes adjusted, a cleft between two large rocks that met overhead like lovers in a kiss.

When he'd asked Father Godwin about the tunnel, he had simply replied with a twinkle in his eye, "Even monks need a way of escape from time to time."

The babe appeared in the hole. Grabbing her, he set her down next to him, then after retrieving Cristiana's sack, he helped her up as well. She clung to his upper arms as he hoisted her...mayhap a bit too quickly, for she landed in his lap. Her breath, sweet and hot, wafted over him as their eyes met just inches apart. He was a rogue of the worst kind, for he longed to take liberties and kiss her right there. And if he was right, from the look in those lustrous brown eyes of hers, she wanted the same.

He lowered his gaze to her lips and licked his own.

She inhaled a sharp breath and struggled for release.

"How dare you!" Leaping from him, she scooted back on all fours as if he had the plague, then struggled to rise.

The sound of leaves crunching halted her. A male voice echoed through the heavy air, followed by another, and then a chuckle. She bit her lip, eyes wide, and glanced over the tiny space formed by the barricade of boulders. Horror screamed from her face as she whispered, "Where's Thebe?"

Cristiana's heartbeat had finally begun to settle from Jarin's near kiss only to vault again when she realized Thebe was missing. No time to berate Jarin for his lack of attention, for she'd been just as consumed in the moment as he. Opening her mouth to call for the child, she dashed for the only gap in the rocks large enough to squeeze through, desperation and fear blinding her to all else.

Especially to Sir Jarin who leapt in her path.

A firm hand pressed over her mouth ere she could utter a word. She struggled in his grip.

"If you wish the child to live," he whispered in her ear, "be still."

Male voices resounded through the forest again. Closer, it seemed. Of course Sir Jarin was right, but how could she stand there and do naught?

Slowly, he released her and removed his hand. She pushed past him, squeezed through the opening, and emerged into a forest lush with moss-covered trunks and boulders and a bed of ferns covering the ground. Morning mist drifted among the trees allowing only sparse beams of golden sunlight to enter. No sign of a child.

A chill scraped over her.

She wanted to yell, to scream, to run about in a wild search, but Jarin emerged behind her, drew his blade and bade her to remain calm. "We will find her," he said with a confidence that surely came from being an elite King's Guard and had naught to do with the truth of their present situation.

The male voices increased. "I hope we catch the wench soon. I could use some good ale to wet my lips," one of them said.

"Aye, I'll agree with that," the other replied.

Cristiana's world twisted in a mirage of greens and browns. Forsooth, she could hear her own heartbeat, feel the mad rush of blood through her veins. *Thebe, oh, Thebe!* Grabbing her skirts, she charged forward.

Sir Jarin appeared beside her, took her hand and pressed a finger to his lips. A world of assurance drifted across his eyes, and she could see why men followed him into war.

A child's laughter bubbled through the forest like a butterfly flitting from branch to branch.

Cristiana started in that direction, trying to free herself from Jarin's grip, but it remained firm. Yanking her beside him, he proceeded toward the sound…excruciatingly…excruciatingly slow.

Thebe! At least she was alive!

Rounding the large trunk of a tree, Sir Jarin shoved aside a wall of ferns nearly as tall as she and approached the edge of a small clearing. A creek slid across the moss-laden ground like a silver snake, and Thebe sat by its edge, dipping her hand in the water and giggling as it rushed over her skin.

Thank God! Cristiana released a breath and started toward her, but Sir Jarin shoved her behind him so forcefully she dared not move. His entire body stiffened like the trunks of one of the mighty trees around them. Even his knuckles whitened where he held his sword.

The male voices grew louder.

"Did ye hear that?"

"Aye. Sounded like a child."

Cristiana grew dizzy. Her vision blurred. She stared through the brush toward the voices when two soldiers, fully armed, marched into the clearing, heading straight for Thebe.

'Twas all his fault. Jarin had put this innocent child at risk—all because of his uncontrollable passions. Now, he'd be forced to fight these two soldiers. Not that he'd have difficulty dispatching them both, but the noise of the battle could draw others to their aid. Alas, he had no choice.

Both men entered the clearing, saw the child, stood aghast for a moment, then headed toward her with sneers on their faces. Behind him, Lady Cristiana gasped and attempted to shove her way forward.

Pushing her back, Sir Jarin stepped into the clearing, blade raised, an insolent grin on his lips. "Ah-ah-ah, lay a finger on that child and meet the slice of my blade."

Shock, followed by confusion, then anger, flashed across the soldiers' faces as both men drew their blades in unison.

"Alas, has the great King's Guard been reduced to nursemaid?" The larger one cast him a contemptuous look.

The other one laughed. "Should be of little effort to disarm the lightskirt then."

Jarin grinned and cocked his head. "Come hence and find out."

Out of the corner of his eye, he spotted the babe turn at the voices, rise to her feet, and start for him. *Nay!* But Lady Cristiana suddenly appeared, swept the child up in her arms, and retreated behind him again.

"'Tis the lady the bishop seeks," the soldier said, gesturing toward her. "We'll win a fair prize for her capture."

With a sigh, Jarin gazed at the treetops as if bored. "I give you one last chance to retreat unscathed."

A moment's hesitation, a flicker of fear crossed their eyes, but the fools advanced withal.

Shrugging, Jarin met the first man's blade with a heavy *thwank* that echoed through the trees. He pushed him back, then released his sword and swung it around to strike the man's middle. He leapt out of the way just in time.

Growling like a bear, the second soldier charged, sword whirled aloft and cleaving downward. Jarin stepped to the side, spun, and clipped the man in the leg.

He shrieked as a line of red appeared on his breeches.

The first knight rushed, thrusting his blade at Jarin from left to right. But Jarin effortlessly met each thrust with a skillful parry of his own. Back and forth, high and low, each attack quelled, each swipe halted until the poor man's breath came fast and terror appeared for the first time in his eyes.

The other soldier came at Jarin from behind, but he wheeled about just in time to clash blades in a hiss of steel. Tiring of the exchange, Jarin slammed the hilt of his sword on the side of the man's head that bore no armor. He crumpled to the ground.

The confident sneer disappeared from the other soldier's face as he charged Jarin once again. But Jarin met his low thrust with a counter parry and shoved him backward. The man stumbled, arms flailing and sword waving.

Other voices resounded through the forest. More men. No time to waste. Jarin struck the soldier's blade with his own. It flew from the man's grip. Before he could recover, Jarin slugged him across the face, tossing him backward. His head struck a tree, and he toppled to the ground, unconscious.

But 'twas too late. Jarin spotted several soldiers making their way through the brush toward him.

CHAPTER FIFTEEN

Though everything within Cristiana told her to run with Thebe—to get as far away from these soldiers as possible, she found herself unable to move. Unable to leave Sir Jarin, though she doubted he could overcome two such well-trained soldiers. Still, the babe…. She glanced down at Thebe, who thankfully was playing with a strand of Cristiana's hair, unaware that her life hung in the balance. She should run, seek shelter ere these men bested Jarin. *Nay*! She should do something to help him! But what? She could not release Thebe again to wander off.

Lord, what do I do? Don't abandon me now.

Alas, barely able to breathe, she remained as the two warriors advanced on Sir Jarin. Yet he stood confidently urging them on. Audacious fool! Holding Thebe tight, she closed her eyes, unable to watch. "One…two…"

The clank and chime of steel on steel sent a shiver down her. *Thud, clunk!* Cursing filled the air. Blades rang. More cursing. She dared open her eyes, and instead of Sir Jarin on the defensive, instead of Sir Jarin being overwhelmed, he wielded his sword in such rapid precision, she thought she must be dreaming. But nay, 'twas as real as the man himself. All strength, courage, and skill. He swung his sword this way and that, dipping low and high, warding off the soldiers' attacks as if he were rowing a boat down a lazy river.

Hope dared peek its head inside her heart as Sir Jarin struck one of the soldiers unconscious to the dirt, then advanced on the other. But a sound—the barest hint of a sound—slinking through the forest forced hope back into hiding.

Men's voices. *Many* of them.

Sir Jarin heard them too, for he quickly dispatched the other soldier and scanned the forest beyond. "Three…four…"

Leather and steel appeared in splotches through the underbrush. Helmeted heads bobbed above ferns. 'Twas too late. They'd be upon them in seconds.

"Oh, Lord." All strength abandoned Cristiana as she dropped to her knees, clutching Thebe close. The girl wiggled to be free, but she managed to cling to her while touching the Spear on her thigh. "Protect us, Lord. Prithee, protect us! Five...six..."

"Over here. I heard something!" The thump of boots grew louder.

A puff of wind caressed her cheek, no more than a whisper, but with it came a cold moisture that left droplets atop Thebe's hair and dampened her cloak. Cristiana drew in a breath, saturating her lungs with the mist, and glanced up to see a forest painted in white. Fog as thick as creamy pottage blanketed the scene, hiding tree, plant, and boulder. *And* Sir Jarin. Was he even still there?

"Be still, my lady." His whisper came from close by. Aye, still there. She couldn't help but smile.

Leaves rustled. Footsteps thudded. Voices, muffled in the mist, shouted. "God wot! Where did this fog hail from?"

"A most damnable thing."

"I cannot see my hand before my face!"

"Back to the camp. Make haste!"

They were close...so close that the fog nigh two steps away stirred with their movement. Cristiana held her breath, praying Thebe would remain silent. She did. The men retreated, their footsteps and voices fading until naught but the deafening silence of the mist remained. That and the sound of Sir Jarin's breathing.

A hand reached out of the fog and touched her arm. "Are you unharmed, my lady?"

"Aye," she whispered. Thebe added her giggle and the word, "hand."

"Yes, darling 'tis Sir Jarin's hand." Cristiana rose, and the man himself materialized out of the mist, smelling of sweat and man and pine. Moisture clung to the tips of his dark hair and the beard on his chin and jaw, but 'twas his eyes as they took her in that sent an odd rush of heat through her.

"This way. Come." He swung an arm around her and led them carefully around the fallen soldiers, over the creek, and through a craggy web of branches and bushes. She dared not ask him how he knew the way without seeing, for he walked with the same confidence as always.

"This strange mist." He finally spoke when they were well out of earshot of the soldiers. "It came up so suddenly." Even as he said the words, the fog began to thin, and trees, shrubs, and even the ground they walked on emerged bit by bit.

"I prayed. I touched the Spear." She mumbled the words, only now remembering.

"You prayed?" He took her elbow and helped her over a large rock.

"I asked God to protect us."

"Humph," was his only reply, and she knew he didn't believe it any more than she did. But there was no denying what had happened. They had faced certain capture and now were safe. God had answered her prayer, but only because of the Spear. What power it possessed! No wonder the bishop desired it above all else.

Thebe wiggled in her arms, wanting to get down. "Thirsty," she said.

"Not now, little one. Soon." Cristiana reached in her pack and pulled out Thebe's doll and handed it to her. Though the child weighed less than two stone, Cristiana's back began to ache.

Though she made no complaint, Sir Jarin tugged the child from her arms before either could protest and set her atop his shoulders.

So high! She could fall. Surely the babe would be frightened. "Be care—" she began, but Thebe's laughter cut her off as he bounced her up and down, the child's fear of him dissipating like the mist around them.

Rays of sunlight speared through the remaining fog, winning the victory over darkness. Hence, by the time they emerged onto a dirt road, Cristiana turned her face to the full sun, soaking in its warmth.

Jarin started down the road, avoiding the muddy ruts. "Make haste, my lady. They won't be far behind us."

She hurried beside him, thankful to see he clung tightly to Thebe's legs as he jostled her along. "Why? How can they know we've escaped?"

"I left those soldiers alive. They will regain consciousness and tell all."

Of course. She hadn't thought of that. Ergo, her fear returned as they proceeded down the road, glancing at every tree and shadow alongside them, looking for enemies. In fact, expecting them. Yet mayhap as long as she had the Spear, God would not abandon her.

Sancreet was a quaint little village built on the side of a hill, with a large manor house in the distance. Circular towers rose on either side of the open gate, and perched upon the grand arched entrance betwixt them was a painted statue of the king. Jarin gave the monarch a cursory glance ere he walked underneath, and she wondered if he missed being a King's Guard and what he thought of His Majesty.

The stench of pigs, rotted meat, and urine caused Cristiana to draw a hand to her nose as the sounds of the village clambered for preeminence in her ears—shouts of laborers, cries of vendors, the thunderous chime of hammers, the cluck of chickens, a babe crying, and church bells.

Jarin pulled a man aside. "Good day to you, sir. Prithee, direct me to the spice monger's."

"Ah, 'tis old Teagan ye wish to see." The man whose dark hair appeared permanently matted to his head and whose face bore more lines than the ruts across the muddy road, gestured down the street. "Turn the corner at the square, and ye can't miss it." He glanced up at Thebe and then over at Cristiana. "If ye be in need of lodging, sir, for ye and your family, I run the Hollow Ox Inn just down the road. Can't miss it."

"Thank you." Jarin nodded toward the man and proceeded.

Tossing the sack over her shoulder, Cristiana did her best to navigate through the mud, pig and horse droppings, and chickens, thankful she didn't have Thebe to hold as well. Nay, the girl seemed quite happy atop Sir Jarin, which surprised her most of all. Thebe had never taken well to strangers.

'Twas an easy task to find the spice monger's shop, for it bore a sign out front carved with the images of herbs and flowers. Once inside, a plethora of scents assailed Cristiana, and she drew in a deep breath—lavender, caraway, cinnamon, garlic, mustard, and rosemary all combined into an overwhelming sensual delight. Though 'twas dim within the tiny front room, sunlight filtering in through the window revealed shelves filled with jars, bottles, and jugs of all shapes and sizes. A stained and divoted table stood to the right covered with dried herbs and mortars and pestles.

A man, as short as he was wide, waddled into the room, wiping his hands on a stained apron and approached them.

"Master Teagan?" Jarin took Thebe from his shoulders and handed her to Cristiana. The girl pointed to the herbs. "Flower."

"Aye." The man replied, his suspicious look taking in the myriad weapons strapped to Sir Jarin's belts and baldric.

"I am Sir Jarin the Just. Father Godwin sent me for your horse, Challenger."

The man's bloodshot eyes assessed him yet again, until finally a spark of relief lowered the tension within them. "Aye, I remember him speaking of ye. Come on in the back." He gestured for them to follow him past a curtain, down a hall, and through another door into a sitting parlor.

"I'll tell my wife to put on some tea."

"We cannot stay." Jarin grabbed his arm, spinning him around. "Forgive my ill-manners, but we must leave posthaste."

"Ah, you are being chased." Nodding, he blew out a sigh and settled his hands atop his rotund belly as if his statement bore no effect on his speed.

Thebe wiggled to get down, and Cristiana lowered to one of the couches and put her on the floor. "Ere we leave, Master Teagan, may I trouble you for some water for the child?"

Sir Jarin rubbed the back of his neck and snapped an annoyed look her way.

A female voice sounded from outside the room. "Hernais, a band of soldiers just rode into town. Methinks they search for someone. Should we—" Entering the room, she halted. Her eyes—or rather one eye—glanced over Sir Jarin, Thebe, and Cristiana.

"My wife, Matilda." The man introduced the woman who was as narrow as he was broad. Wispy light hair was pulled back from a long face and hollow cheeks. One eye drifted to the right whilst the other stared at them with a mixture of horror and…spite?

Thebe waddled over to a ceramic bowl sitting atop a table and started to pick it up, but Cristiana quickly snagged it from her grasp. "Nay, darling."

"In good sooth, I see the cause of your haste, sir," Master Teagan said ere turning to his wife. "Get thee hither, woman. Mind the store. If the soldiers enter to search, delay them."

"A sip of water for the babe, mistress?" Cristiana spoke up.

"We haven't time, my lady," Jarin said. "She can drink later."

But the woman had already darted off, returning in minutes with a mug of water.

"Gramercy my dear woman. May God reward you for your kindness." Taking the cup, Cristiana lifted it to Thebe's lips and smiled when the girl gulped down its contents. "And you as well, Master Teagan." Cristiana looked up at the man.

"Now, may we leave?" Jarin said, annoyed.

Cristiana gave him a pointed look as she handed the cup back to Mistress Teagan. She longed to ask the lady if she could pray for her eye, but dared not. 'Twould not only be most unseemly to mention it, but Sir Jarin was right. Time was of the essence.

"Allow me to show you to Challenger. This way." Master Teagan started out the door, but his wife drew him to the side and down the corridor toward the front.

"No doubt they would pay handsomely for them, and ye know we need the coin." Her words, meant only for her husband, made their way to Cristiana's ears, withal. And Jarin's as well, for his jaw tightened and he gestured for her to grab Thebe and rise.

"God's truth, what ails you, woman?" Master Teagan spat back in a hissed tone. "Get thee hence and do what I say. These are friends of Father Godwin."

The man reappeared, a tight smile on his lips, and led them through a door into a small fenced yard where a stable housed two horses. He dragged one of them—a pale palfrey that had seen better days—out into the yard and, with Sir Jarin's help, made quick work of saddling it and strapping on bridle and reins. Then after tying on their packs, Jarin lifted Cristiana and Thebe onto the saddle and swung up behind them.

He grabbed the reins just as the sound of Mistress Teagan's voice blared from inside the shop. "Back here, sirs! Make haste!"

Master Teagan growled. "Ah, that woman! Go now! Take the path behind the market square. 'Twill lead you to a back gate. Make haste!" He slammed his palm onto the horse's rump, and Challenger bolted forward.

Cristiana slammed against Jarin's chest and tightened her grip on Thebe just as shouts peppered them from behind.

"There they are. After them at once!"

CHAPTER SIXTEEN

Alexia rapped the secret knock on the door to the underground hideout of the Knights of the Eternal realm. Friar Josef opened it, and she pushed past him with a smile. In truth, it had been her home for the past ten years. Removing her bow and quiver, she set them on the table as Ronar and Damien entered behind her.

Seraphina rose from a chair, her eyes searching out Damien, and a noticeable breath escaped her at the sight of him.

"Judas!" Damien spat. "We were nearly caught." He made his way to the fireplace and planted his boot on the hearth.

"But we were not, Damien." Ronar poured two glasses of water from a jug on the sideboard and handed one to Alexia with a wink.

Taking it, she smiled at her intended and took a sip. "Come, Damien, surely you jest. After all that occurred, can you not see God's hand of protection upon us?"

Friar Josef gripped the cross hanging around his neck. "Indeed, my dear one. 'Tis why Seraphina and I have been in deep prayer the entire time you were gone."

Ronar plopped into a cushioned chair and raked back his hair. "Alas, we needed it, Friar. In good sooth, you would not believe what happened, even should you have seen it yourself."

"'Twas naught but trickery." Damien turned from the fire and went to pour himself some wine.

Seraphina took a step forward, her blue eyes flitting between all of them. "*I* saw it."

Setting down her glass, Alexia lowered to sit beside Ronar. She knew the maid had a gift, though the exact nature of it, she could not name. Yet ofttimes Seraphina knew events that had not yet happened and things about others no one had ever told her.

"What did you see?" Alexia asked.

Damien finished a glass of wine and poured another ere turning to face her.

"I saw a wall, a large wall blocking your way."

Ronar stared at her, blinking, then shook his head as if trying to scatter the words elsewhere.

Damien growled and halted once again before the fire.

Friar Josef's eyes twinkled. "Tell them of the snakes."

Speechless, Alexia sat back in her chair, amazed at the power of God and of His gifts freely offered to mankind if only they would believe.

"Snakes came out of the wall." Seraphina's lip began to tremble, and Damien drew a chair up for her to sit. Returning his smile, she lowered into it. "I"—she glanced at Friar Josef—"we became anxious for you."

The friar raised his brows and smiled. "Thus, the praying."

"You mock us, dear lady. How could you possibly know these things?" Damien huffed, shifting his gaze between Alexia and Ronar, though he knew as well as they that none of them could have disclosed the information.

"Are you so thickheaded, Sir Damien?" Alexia forced playfulness in her tone, for she had no desire to enrage the large knight.

A frown was her only answer as Damien shifted his attention back to Seraphina. And who could blame him? The maid had always been lovely. Even now her long hair glistened like snow in the firelight as it tumbled over her shoulder, easing over her feminine curves. But 'twas the look in her eyes as she gazed at Damien that made Alexia smile. 'Twas good to see love blossom in the midst of such tribulation.

Ronar leaned his forearms on his knees. "I can hardly credit it, Friar, but Mistress Seraphina must surely possess this gift of knowledge that you recently read to us about from the Scriptures."

"That's it!" Alexia nearly shouted. "I had not known the proper name for it."

Friar Josef smiled at Seraphina. "I will not gainsay it. You are truly gifted."

As was the friar, but he was too humble to admit it. Yet how many times during Alexia's stay in this place had he heard directly from God? Something she struggled with even now.

"Sweet saints, the wall was real, then?" Friar Josef faced her. "Pray tell us what happened to it?"

"Ah that," Alexia said with an unruffled air she had not felt at the time. "At the mention of Christ's name and the Word of God, it vanished."

Friar Josef clapped his hands together. "Praise His name!"

"Indeed." Ronar nodded, and Alexia was pleased to see him growing in the faith.

Damien, however, returned to the sideboard for more wine.

Seraphina's gaze followed him ere she spoke again, this time with more fear in her voice. "I saw something else. Darkness. Much darkness. It grows thicker at Luxley with each passing day."

"Aye." Ronar shared a glance with Alexia and took her hand in his. "We have been sensing the same every time we venture there."

"Then you will need much prayer the next time you go," the friar said. "And you must put on your armor."

Damien chuckled and took another sip of wine. "What good will armor do against walls of snakes?"

"Not that kind of armor, son. God's armor." The friar pointed at his chest, but Damien only frowned yet again. Alexia would have to step up her prayers for him.

"I suppose Sir Walter did not sign your document," Seraphina asked.

"Nay, not this time," Ronar said. "But we are close."

"Pray, what exactly does it say?"

"'Tis a statement of guilt," Alexia said, "from Sir Walter to the king, informing His Majesty that he and Bishop Montruse conspired to falsely accuse me of being a witch, though they had no reason or proof. All with the goal of Sir Walter becoming the new lord of Luxley and Bishop Montruse acquiring the Spear of Destiny." Alexia smiled at Ronar, enjoying the feel of his warm hand around hers. "It also absolves Ronar LePeine, Jarin the Just, and Damien LaRage of any traitorous activities and requests they be reinstated as King's Guards."

"Here, here!" Damien said.

"At the end," Ronar continued her story. "Sir Walter asks for clemency to return to his own estate, giving his troth to never set foot in Luxley again."

Seraphina's delicate brow furrowed. "But why would the king believe such a thing coming from the man himself? 'Twould make no sense for him to send such an admission of guilt when he believes there to be no chance of being caught. What is his motive?"

"In the document he exposes the bishop's plan to take the Spear to the Pope instead of the king. This display of loyalty he hopes will grant him his freedom."

"Is that the bishop's true desire?"

Ronar grinned. "We do not know, I'll grant you, but the bishop is an evil, ambitious man, and I would not believe otherwise."

"Still…" Seraphina frowned. "Why would the king believe such a tale?"

"He would not," Damien interjected and approached to stand beside the lady. "But the missive, complete with Sir Walter's seal, would raise enough suspicion that he would send men to investigate."

"And once they spoke with all the servants at Luxley," Alexia added, "the truth would come out. Anabelle assures me they loathe the man."

Seraphina nodded. "Then he simply must sign it," she said with the conviction of someone in power. Pausing, she glanced at Damien and then over them all. "I have other news. Sir Jarin has found Lady Cristiana."

"Found?" Releasing Ronar's hand, Alexia leapt to her feet, joy bursting within her. "Where? Is she safe? I'm going to her." She headed to retrieve her quiver and bow.

"Nay, nay, my lady. I see mere glimpses here and there. Hence, I know not where she is or how far away, only that Jarin the Just has found her, and she is safe…for now."

Halting, Alexia faced her, hiding her disappointment. "'Tis good news, Seraphina. Thank you."

Friar Josef gestured for them all to gather around him. "I beg you, we must not delay in praying for them."

"Why so urgent?" Ronar asked.

Seraphina bit her lip, fear tightening the features of her face. "I see darkness, deep, malevolent darkness. It follows close on their trail."

By all that was accursed, Cedric would earn his new name! He would no longer be Cedric LeGode, apprentice of Drago. He would be given a title worthy of his power—the dark powers he was learning to wield with such authority. But first he had to prove to Drago how much he had learned and how powerful he had become. Mayhap some day soon, even more powerful than the great warlock Drago himself! Then Cedric's father would finally grant him the respect he deserved. That or Cedric would simply put a curse on him and squash him like the rodent he was.

From beneath the hood of his black cloak, he gazed over the thirty knights and soldiers dismounting and leading their horses to drink from a creek flowing across the green pasture. They'd been chasing Lady Cristiana and that lily-livered knight Sir Jarin all day across field, forest, and farm. But to no avail. Though they'd been following their tracks, they'd seen neither hint nor hair of them.

Buffoons! Thirty warriors and they could not find one man and one pathetic woman! The woman who left him shamed and dishonored on their wedding day. Not that he'd been overjoyed to wed the shrew, but her rejection had increased not only his father's ridicule of him, but all of Luxley's, as well.

Now, as they stopped to rest the horses, Cedric's impatience bubbled to eruption. He smiled. These men knew not the danger his current temperament put them in.

His narrowed gaze slithered over them, locking onto Sir DeGay, the head of Luxley's knights, and Sir Borin, head of the bishop's soldiers, speaking to one another. No doubt planning their next atrocious failure.

Lubberworts! He'd hex them right here and now, if Drago hadn't instructed him to leave them be.

He spun, his cloak twirling around him, and pulled a black sack from his horse's saddle. Holding it to his chest, he longed to open it, grab a handful of the black dust, fling it in the air, and say the words that would transform each speck into a ravenous wolf that would do his bidding—and *only* his.

Nay, he would not waste them on these craven fops.

Strapping the bag back onto the saddle, he put his boot in the stirrup and hoisted himself up.

Demon, his black steed, pawed the ground in anticipation.

Cedric's sentiments exactly.

Then without bidding the soldiers adieu, he urged Demon into a gallop, tore across the field, and left the incompetent dolts in his wake.

He would find Lady Cristiana and Sir Jarin himself. And when he did, he'd bring them back to Drago and receive his just reward.

CHAPTER SEVENTEEN

L ife transformed into a mirage of greens, browns, and blues that swept past Cristiana as fast as the wind striking her face. *That* wind oft stole her breath, forcing her to lower her chin and cover Thebe with her cloak merely to catch a breath. All while trying to balance atop the rolling muscles of a speeding horse. In good sooth, it helped that Sir Jarin kept a thick arm wrapped around them, fastening them against his broad chest. It aided in their safety, *not* in her determination to resist the knight's charms—to *not* feel safe within his arms, to not grow to depend upon him, to not feel her insides melt at his touch.

Childish woman! Of all the men to direct her gaze upon, a philandering knight with the charm of a page and the looks of a god. When all she ever wanted was stability—to be loved and never abandoned again.

When the sun stretched high above them, they stopped in a copse of firs bordering a small pond. Thebe had begun to cry, though Cristiana was not sure 'twas the reason the knight ceased his mad pace.

"I give you but a few moments to tend the child." He grabbed her waist and lowered her and Thebe to the ground with ease ere leading Challenger to the water. Fear surrounded him. Nay, not fear. Not in this warrior. 'Twas tension...as one might feel in the silence before battle...a keen awareness of everything around them, a readiness to fight at a moment's notice.

"Have we not outrun them?" Cristiana followed him and set Thebe down on the bank.

Challenger lowered his head to slurp the water. Only then did she notice the horse's hard breathing and the foam around his mouth.

Thebe splashed her hand in the pond.

"Nay, my lady. I fear they are close behind." Sir Jarin pulled a cup from his sack and lowered to scoop up water ere handing it to her. "I haven't the time to erase our tracks." He scanned the surroundings like a hawk seeking prey, his ears tuned, his eyes taking in every detail. They finally found hers, and despite the tension emanating from him, a gentle look peered out from hiding. Sweet angels, if she didn't have her wits about her, she'd collapse against him, longing for his arms to wrap around her yet again.

"Drink, Cristi." Thebe tugged on her cloak, and Jarin frowned.

"Ensure she gets enough to drink, for we cannot stop again. Her needs kept us overlong in Sancreet, and we were nearly caught." Though his tone was not harsh, neither was it accommodating.

Anger stole Cristiana's sudden need for an embrace from this man. "Her name is Thebe, Sir Jarin." She drained the cup and stooped to fill it for the babe. Whilst the girl drank, Cristiana retrieved a clean cloth from her sack and knelt to change Thebe's soiled garment. She knew Sir Jarin never wanted the child to come along. She knew the babe slowed their progress, but she was with them now. At the very least he could speak her name, treat her kindly and not like she was a mere burden.

Turning away, Sir Jarin lowered to his haunches and drew water to his mouth.

Thankfully, Thebe's cloth wasn't too soiled. Hence, Cristiana washed it in the pond, intending to let it dry in the wind as they rode. Having completed her task, she set Thebe on her feet and took her chubby hand in hers. "She'll need to eat."

Though Sir Jarin gave not the expected groan, the news—which he should have already assumed—caused him to rub the beard on his chin and look around. Rising, he rummaged through the sack Father Godwin had given him and pulled out a small loaf of bread. "This will have to do. We must leave. Now."

She didn't argue. Thebe did, however. The poor child wished to run and play and not be once again confined to the back of a horse. But there was naught to be done for it.

Seated on Challenger yet again, Cristiana broke off a piece of bread and handed it to her. Jarin swung on behind, grabbed the reins with one hand, and wrapped the other around her, pushing her back against him. His unique scent, all man and earth and leather, filled her senses, as he prodded the horse out of the trees and down the dirt road.

Hours passed, darkness fell, and still they rode on. Thebe had long since cried herself to sleep. At least one of them rested in bliss, for though Cristiana's eyes grew heavy, and she leaned back against Sir Jarin, her slumber was chased by a thousand terrifying thoughts of her present predicament—pursued by both Luxley and the bishop's soldiers, no shelter or food to be found, outnumbered in every way, Luxley in the hands of the man who had murdered her mother, and her sister wanted for witchcraft. How would God see them out of all of this? Or would He even bother?

Finally, Sir Jarin slowed Challenger, turned off the road, and plunged into a thick forest. He dismounted and with only a "Stay here" directed at her, walked back the way they'd come, returning within minutes. Then taking the horse by the reins, he led them forward.

Clutching the sleeping babe close, Cristiana could see naught but spindly branches reaching for her like boney fingers of the night as the wind laughed through the leaves and the barest hint of a moon peeked through treetops. The chirp of night insects, croak of frogs, and the hoot of an owl accompanied them as scents of pine and hickory swirled about her.

"Why did you go back?" she asked him.

"To erase our tracks." He stopped at a small clearing and reached up to take Thebe from her, then assisted her down with his other hand. She could barely see him in the darkness as he handed the child back to her and said, "I'll make a fire."

This he did more swiftly than she could have imagined, and soon a crackling blaze centered their camp. The warmth and light drew Cristiana close as Sir Jarin disappeared into the dark forest yet again. Removing her cloak, she gently wrapped Thebe within its warm folds, adjusted the doll gripped in her arms, and laid her on a patch of soft moss by the fire.

Jarin returned with more wood and an armful of ferns, which he quickly formed into a small bed for Thebe and a pillow for Cristiana. She watched as he tirelessly performed these tasks, knowing he had to be as exhausted as she. Yet this fierce knight, this warrior, took extra measure to ensure their comfort.

"'Tis all I can do for now, my lady. If I had time, I could make a shelter should it rain." He glanced upward. "But we won't be here long enough to warrant it."

"Thank you, Sir Jarin. You have risked all to protect Thebe and me." Cristiana transferred the child onto the soft bed. Thebe made a gurgling sound but was soon fast asleep again.

When Cristiana looked up, she found Sir Jarin staring at Thebe with an odd look, which quickly dissolved when his gaze met hers. He smiled. "My pleasure, my lady. 'Tis my oath as a knight to protect those in need."

She shook off the sudden longing that 'twas more than that. "You are a worthy knight," was all she said as she settled as modestly as possible on the ground beside Thebe.

"We shall see. We are not at Luxley yet."

"How much further is it?"

"Four, mayhap five days at the most." Grabbing his sack, he pulled out some bread, salted meat, a wineskin and two cups. Breaking the bread, he handed her a chunk, along with some meat, then poured wine into her cup. "God bless Father Godwin." He arched a brow.

"Indeed." Cristiana suddenly realized how hungry she was. "Thank Thee, God, for this food," she said before biting off a piece of bread. She glanced down at Thebe, longing to give her some, but 'twas best she got her rest for now.

"I will provide a feast for her in the morn," Sir Jarin announced with as much confidence as if he had a kitchen, cook, and bevy of serving maids at his command. Yet, 'twas not that which shocked her, but that he thought of the child.

Sipping the spiced wine, she gazed at the leaping flames, praying both would help her nerves settle from the harrowing day. "We have escaped them?" She needed to hear Sir Jarin's confident tone, his assurance they were well past danger.

"For now." Unbuckling his belt, he took off his sword strapped to it and laid it within reach ere he sat beside her. Drawing up his knees, he leaned his arms on them and gave her that grin of his that could melt a fortress of ice. It had the effect of warming her insides to near searing. Alas, not simply his grin, but 'twas the look in his eyes—one of tender regard—that stole her senses.

She moved away slightly, pulled off another piece of bread, and popped it in her mouth. 'Twas most unseemly to be spending the night alone with him. Mayhap a reminder of his near-vows of celibacy would douse the flame of passion in his gaze, as well as the heat running rampant through her veins.

"I still cannot fathom it. You a monk!"

He chuckled and rubbed the back of his neck. "A lifetime ago."

"I see why a man like you would find no favor in it."

"How now? A man like me?" Playfulness in his eyes teased her as he bit off a chunk of meat.

"Aye, a wanderer, an adventurer, a fighter..." She wanted to say lover but didn't. "A life of prayer, tedious work, and devotion, not to mention being sequestered behind walls, would not suit you, Sir Jarin."

He sipped his wine. "Nay. Though none of those reasons were the cause of my leaving." He stared at the ground as if his jovial mood had suddenly fallen there among the moss and dirt.

She waited, longing to hear more, wanting more than anything to understand this man. The fire crackled and spit sparks high into the air, and she glanced up to see stars flickering between branches. She also longed to hear from God, to understand Him as well. But she found Him as elusive as this man beside her.

Sir Jarin bit off another piece of salted meat. "'Twas Who I prayed to, Who I devoted my life to that made the sacrifice of no avail."

"Forsooth! You do not mean God Himself?" Cristiana did not know whether to rebuke the near blasphemy or hasten away, lest lightning strike him where he sat.

Sir Jarin picked up a twig and tossed it in the fire. "He was not who I thought He was. I found Him untrustworthy when it mattered."

For some reason, this saddened her, though she oft thought God had abandoned her as well. For most of her life, if she were honest. The early death of her father, then her mother, and her sister abandoning her. Then being drugged by the one man she trusted most. Where was God in all of that? Yet, by all accounts, Sir Jarin was a prosperous and successful knight with everything to his credit—intelligence, brawn, bravery, skill, and good friends. Not to mention the ear of the king. What possibly could have happened to make him turn against the Almighty?

Mayhap he had as sad a tale as she.

"If you found Him so unfaithful, what made you join the monastery in the first place?"

He poured her more wine. "In truth, 'twas my father. He wanted a life of devotion in the church for me."

"Why? Did he not know his own son?"

"He loved God and received much joy from serving Him. He thought I would benefit from the same."

"And where is he now?"

"In the ground." He shrugged as if it meant naught, but his smile vanished. "'Tis for the best, I suppose, for he did not have to witness my fall from grace."

"I'm sorry."

"No more than I am for your loss. Both your parents left you at a young age."

The reminder soured the food in her stomach, and she set aside the meat, opting for more wine instead, along with a change of topic. "Surely you believe that God is with us after what happened this morning?" She sipped her wine.

"I grant you, I can make no sense of that fog, my lady." He shook his head and blew out a sigh.

"'Twas the Spear. God is with the Spear, and the Spear is with me." 'Twas the only sense she could make out of such a miraculous rescue.

"I hope you are right." He glanced her way. "If so, we shall be safe the rest of our journey."

But she could see from his tight expression he believed not his own words.

He tossed another log onto the fire, then removed his leather coat. A red splotch stained his shirt, and Cristiana set down her cup and dashed to kneel before him.

"You're injured."

He said naught, merely smiled and looked at her, their faces so close, she could see the firelight flickering in his brown eyes.

"You were hurt in the fight." She loosened the ties at his collar and peered beneath, knowing all the while a maiden should do no such thing.

A cut the length of a finger sliced across the rounded muscles of his chest.

"'Tis nothing, my lady, I assure you. 'Twill heal on its own." His breath wafted over her, all spiced wine and cinnamon, making her catch her own as her heart raced within her.

The memory of how bravely and expertly he had defeated those two soldiers made her shamelessly glance once again at the strength in his chest and the firm roundness of his arms.

Sweet angels! What was she doing? "It must needs be…It must…" Averting her gaze to the ground, she started to rise. "Cleaned. I will get a cloth."

His hand wrapped around her wrist and pulled her gently back to the ground. "No need, my lady. Prithee, do not leave.

Your close presence brings healing, for I can no longer feel the pain."

She had no doubt of that for she could no longer feel anything but the need to be in his arms.

Reaching up slowly, he caressed her cheek with the back of his hand, his eyes taking her in as if he wished to drink of her.

Her weak attempt to pull away did naught to dissuade him from continuing to caress her with both eyes and hand. She could leave if she wanted. She knew he would not keep her there by force. But she didn't want to leave. God forgive her. She didn't want to. "Alas, you tempt me overmuch, sir." Her chest rose and fell, her breaths filling the space betwixt them.

Blast him! He knew the effect he had on her, for one side of his mouth curved upward in a grin so charming and full of promise it suffocated sense and senses.

He leaned closer. She shouldn't. Nay! She shouldn't. She a maiden, and he a libertine knight. With nary a promise spoken between them.

Before she could convince herself to flee, his lips met hers.

CHAPTER EIGHTEEN

Jarin had spent many a night with a woman, but none as tantalizing, none as enchanting, as was last night with Lady Cristiana D'Clere. And oddly not for the reasons one would expect. He smiled and pushed to sit from his position on the ground beside her and the babe. In truth 'twas not beside, but a few feet away. Bosh! A man could only take so much temptation.

He rubbed his aching eyes and glanced over the trees, where the hint of dawn brought leaves and branches into focus. Birds began to warble their morning tunes, ever happy tunes. But then again they had naught but flitting from branch to branch and eating seeds and worms to fill their day—not being a mouse to a cat in a game of chase that could end up in death.

Which is why he'd hardly slept last night, keeping vigil over the precious souls entrusted to him. Rising, he stretched his back and quietly lowered to his haunches beside them. Cristiana, *dear Cristiana*, her thick black lashes fanned over lustrous cheeks as she lay on the pillow he'd formed for her, the babe tucked against her chest, her little cherub expression one of pure innocence. And Jarin's leather cloak over them both. He rubbed his arms against the chill of the morning. She wouldn't accept it when she retired, so he'd waited for her to fall asleep. Knowing they slept warm and dry had kept him warm all night.

Almost.

He should go seek out food to break their fast. He should gather wood to get the fire going again. But he could not turn away from this rare moment, a chance to stare at this angel without her knowing. To gaze upon her beauty….her exquisite loveliness—the way her fawn-colored hair lay in wisps upon her face and flowed like liquid amber over her curves, the pink hue to her lips, the color the sunshine of yesterday drew from her cheeks.

She twitched, and her lips moved, reminding him of their kiss, the sensation of her soft lips on his, the sweet taste he barely sampled ere she pushed from him, a look of horror on her face. Faith, a reaction he'd never encountered from a lady before! One kiss and he normally had a woman at his mercy. Not this lady. Though 'twas not from a lack of passion on her part. For if Jarin knew one thing, 'twas when a woman's longing matched his own.

That she'd not given herself to him pleased him more than he could make sense of. This was a proper lady, a woman of honor and morality he'd not seen the likes of in either pauper or princess. A woman of kindness and goodness and care for others.

A lady worth protecting with his life.

Thebe's eyelids fluttered ere they slowly opened. Baby blue eyes stared up at him before a smile curved the child's lips and excitement tingled in her expression.

And something hard within Jarin burst into pieces.

Angry, he rose, grabbed his sword, and charged into the forest.

Several minutes later, he returned with a pocket full of nuts and berries and five eggs he'd found in a nest. Lady Cristiana sat by the simmering coals of the fire, Thebe in her lap, brushing the girl's hair and singing a sweet song he'd not heard before. He swallowed a lump of emotion at the sight of madonna and child, the sweetness of it, the purity, the feminine allure of motherly love. Then she lifted her face to him, and the smile that lit it nearly caused him to bow before her and swear his fealty forever.

But that must never happen.

"A feast!" He strode toward them. "As promised." He would employ humor and charm with this lady, and gruffness if he had to. Whate'er it took to keep thoughts of anything more than a simple dalliance from his mind. And his heart!

After cracking the eggs into one of the cups, he broke the bread into pieces, dipped it in the yolks, and handed them to the lady, along with a selection of berries and nuts spread upon a leafy plate.

"Feast, indeed, Sir Jarin. You are a man of many talents."

"I've learned to fend for myself." He kicked dirt into the coals as he tossed a handful of nuts and berries into his mouth. The meaty sweetness lured further growls from his stomach, but a more substantial meal would have to wait.

The eerie, shrill call of a raven tainted the joyful morning birdsong. Odd. Jarin studied their surroundings, listening for any sound that shouldn't be there. Naught but the flutter of leaves in the wind, the buzz of insects, and chirp of birds met his ears. Shaking it off, he plopped to the ground and grabbed a hunk of bread. They'd have to find supplies soon, for this would not last until the morrow.

Not with the way the child was devouring what Cristiana put before her. She put berry after berry into her little mouth, and when she looked up and saw Jarin, she smiled so wide, pieces of berries dotted her white teeth as juice slipped down her lips.

He couldn't help but chuckle, and Cristiana joined him. Their eyes met, the gaiety of the moment causing a bond between them he would do anything to avoid.

He averted his gaze to the child. "You like the berries, little one?"

"Aye, Jarn. Welishious." She took a cup from Lady Cristiana and gulped down the sweet water.

He smiled at her mispronunciation, then looked at Cristiana. "Jarn?"

Shrugging, her eyes twinkled with mirth. "She has her own language, this one." Withdrawing the cup, she handed the child another piece of bread. A crumb sat upon the lady's lower lip, and Jarin reached over and brushed it off with his thumb.

At the intimate gesture, her eyes widened for a moment, and she pressed a finger to her lips, her gaze searching his. *She thinks of our kiss.*

As did he. As he had continually through the long night.

"Here." He moved the remainder of his bread and fruit before Thebe. "You can have my share, wee one."

Cristiana stared at him oddly. "You give me your cloak and now your food. I won't hear of it, Sir Jarin. You must eat as well."

"Eat, Jarn." Thebe took a berry in her chubby hands, rose, and headed for his mouth. He opened it at the last minute, and she dropped it in.

"Thank you, my lady." He dipped his head toward her, and Cristiana laughed.

Thebe returned for a nut and repeated the action, giggling this time when he promptly opened his mouth at her approach.

"You will make a good father someday, Sir Jarin." Lady Cristiana stood and brushed off her skirts.

"I never intend to bind myself to such a duty." He regretted the words ere they left his lips, along with their tone, meant only to repulse his own foolish desire.

"Whatever do you mean? Do you not wish to wed someday and have children to carry on your name?"

"I do not." He gathered his cloak from the ground, put it on, and then held hers up for her. "'Tis not a name which perforce needs to carry on."

The emotions that crossed her face could not be discerned. And he was quite good at discerning female emotions. Sorrow, shock, fury. Definitely fury.

Grabbing her cloak from him, she put it on herself, then stood before him and poked a finger at his chest. "You dare to kiss me when you have no intention of making an offer?"

Jarin swallowed down a lump of guilt and opened his mouth to answer when a low, ferocious growl filled the air, silencing the birds, and prickling the hair on his arms.

The rumbling snarl continued, grew louder, and was soon joined by others....coming from all around them.

Wolves.

Cristiana's anger drowned out whate'er sound alerted Sir Jarin, for he diverted his attention from her and set a firm gaze upon their surroundings. His entire body stiffened like the trunk of a tree, and she realized he would hear no more of her arguments even should she shout them in his ear.

Challenger whinnied and began pawing the ground from his spot where Sir Jarin had tied him to a branch.

That's when she, too, heard the growls, rising out of the mist, curling around the trees. Reaching for Thebe, she swept her into her arms and stood frozen in fear beside Sir Jarin. He pushed them both behind him and drew his sword.

Not a good sign for whate'er was coming their way. In truth, she already knew. 'Twas the ferocious wolves that had nearly attacked them ere they reached the monastery.

How did the beasts find them? What did they want? Were they even wolves? For her sister had said otherwise. Either way, whether flesh or spirit, how could Sir Jarin defeat them all?

The growling grew louder, deeper, more malevolent. Thebe whimpered and hid her face within Cristiana's cloak.

Leaves parted. Black, fur-covered faces emerged one by one, dozens of them, with sharp slit-like eyes and mouths wide, baring white fangs and salivating tongues.

Challenger snorted and whinnied, pawing the ground and shaking his head back and forth. No sooner did his reins loosen from the tree than he bolted into the thicket and disappeared.

Their horse gone!

Not a single wolf chased him. Which meant they were after other prey.

'Twas not the way she thought to die—mauled to shreds by ferocious beasts. Terror spiked through her veins. Would it hurt? Would she feel their fangs dig deep into her flesh? Or would she become numb with fear? Still the wolves crept closer, more and more materializing from the greenery, like ghouls from a forested underworld.

She gripped Thebe closer, terror whipping her thoughts into a cyclone, with only one remaining—one horrifying thought. *Thebe.* She could not let this child face such a painful and frightening death. She was but a babe. *Oh, God. Please!*

"One, two, three…" She could hear Sir Jarin's heavy breathing, feel the tension spinning tight around him.

The closest wolf snapped its jowls, growling in anticipation, and sending spittle through the air.

A stench of rotted flesh soured in her nose. She couldn't move, couldn't think, couldn't speak, or she'd surely scream with her last breath and run with all her might. "Four, five…"

Thebe began to cry.

Jarin finally spoke. "I'll take on as many as I can. When I do, run."

"I will not leave you," she returned, her voice trembling.

He snapped his gaze to her, fire in his eyes. "You will do as I say!"

Even should she wish to obey him, she could no longer feel her legs. Daring a glance over her shoulder, she spotted wolves approaching from behind. Nowhere to run. "Six, seven…"

More wolves entered the clearing, their dark eyes locked upon the three of them, almost humanlike in the hatred she saw within them.

Flesh or spirit? She searched her memory for the story Alexia had told her. How had she rid herself of them?

The Spear! Lord help her. She'd forgotten all about it. Crouching to the ground, Thebe still in her arms, she placed her hand over the spot on her leg where the artifact was strapped.

"Lord, please protect us from this evil. In Christ's name!"

The lead wolf leapt onto Jarin, his teeth sinking through his leather cloak and into his arm.

Cristiana screamed. Thebe wailed.

The sun abandoned them, along with all hope, as dark clouds roiled across the sky above. Shadows as dark as the wolves lurked about the clearing, cloaking it in deep despair.

Jarin flung the beast away while thrusting his blade through another one. It yelped in pain as more advanced, surrounding them within a barricade of fangs and claws.

Leveling his sword before him, Sir Jarin awaited their charge, bravely, stoutly.

Tears slipped down Cristiana's cheeks.

White light flashed. The brightness blinded Cristiana. Air crackled like fire. A wolf's yelp, more growls. White light again. Cristiana closed her eyes, clinging tightly to Thebe, who had ceased her wailing.

Again the stench of rotted meat, save this time, 'twas more akin to burning flesh.

Jarin gasped.

Cristiana opened her eyes. Another bolt of silver light blazed from above and struck one of the wolves. The beast disappeared into a powdery mist. Again and again, white beams flared all around them, each one striking a wolf and transforming it into dust. Thunder bellowed. The ground shook. Thebe resumed her screaming.

The rest of the wolves, not yet struck, turned and darted back into the forest.

Sir Jarin stood like a statue, his bloody blade before him, the only sign of life the rise and fall of his chest.

Holding Thebe close, Cristiana prayed she was not dreaming, that the wolves were indeed gone and would not return.

Spears of sparkling sunlight poked through the dark clouds above, pushing them back and dispelling the shadows below.

All was silent. All was still. The birds began their joyful tunes yet again.

Jarin sheathed his blade, the chime echoing across the clearing.

Thebe peeked out from beneath Cristiana's cloak. "Gone?"

"Aye, darling." Cristiana's legs wobbled, and she stumbled slightly but caught herself. "They are gone. God be praised."

Sir Jarin finally turned to face Lady Cristiana and Thebe. He hadn't wanted to look at them during the ordeal, hadn't wanted to see the terror on their faces, watch as wolves devoured their flesh. Hadn't wanted that to be his last vision ere departing this world. Now, as he took them in, unharmed and looking more beautiful than ever, he finally allowed relief to flow through him.

He allowed something else too—his arm to fling about the woman and bring her and babe close. She fell against him, leaning on his chest as if it brought her all the comfort and strength she needed. If only she knew how terrified he'd been. He'd been trained by the best knights in the realm, had fought in dozens of battles facing many enemies who resembled beasts, but nothing had prepared him for that hellish onslaught.

He held the two girls close. "'Tis over now. We are safe." At least he hoped, though he kept an ear tuned for the wolves' return.

Thebe glanced up at him and tugged on his beard. "Jarn."

Against his better judgment, he kissed her on the forehead and smiled. Before the child could further worm her way into his heart, he released them and glanced up. "The storm is past. 'Twas fortuitous it came along when it did."

Lady Cristiana breathed out a sigh. "You jest, sir! 'Twas no storm at all, and that lightning—if that is what it was— hailed from God, Himself. I touched the Spear and prayed. And He rescued us." She looked above as if she could find the Almighty and thank Him personally.

"A mere storm, my lady." Jarin glanced in the direction their horse had gone, then sought his pack on the ground.

"I suppose those wolves were mere wolves as well," she retorted.

"What else would they be?" His tone lacked conviction, for he could not deny what he'd seen. Even now, as he looked around, no carcasses littered the clearing. Yet if he accepted that the beasts had not been real animals, but instead demons conjured up from the otherworld, then he'd have to admit there *was* an otherworld, an eternal realm wherein both good and evil existed—God and the devil, heaven and hell.

Ergo, if he admitted that God had come to their rescue, then he'd have to believe God loathed him, for He'd never answered any of Jarin's prayers. Hence, he would push the incident into the realm of the unknown and unexplainable, a place getting quite crowded since he'd met Lady Alexia and her sister Cristiana.

"We must leave posthaste." He gathered his sack, stuffed the remaining scrap of bread into it, then picked up her sack as well.

"We have no horse." Lady Cristiana came to stand beside him. "However will we..." her voice trailed off in despondency.

Taking Thebe from her, he plunked the girl atop his shoulders yet again and gave Lady Cristiana a wink of reassurance of which he felt not a speck. No sense in alarming the lady further. She'd had enough fear for one day. "We shall walk until we can find another horse," he said as if the feat were as easy as plucking a flower from a spring meadow.

She frowned as he started forward, brushing aside branches as he went. Her footsteps followed. Thebe giggled above him and began playing with his hair.

They had no horse, no money, no food, and they were being chased by a troop of well-trained soldiers. Not to mention an evil he dared not admit. In truth, the odds were not in their favor, but still, nothing he had not encountered before and overcome.

Yet never with two precious lives in his care.

CHAPTER NINETEEN

"Devil's warts!" Cedric cursed and rose from the placid water of a pond he'd been staring into. The vision that had appeared after he'd poured the elixir across the surface was enough to transform the meekest warlock into the devil himself!—Sir Jarin and Lady Cristiana rescued from his wolves by lightning! Nay. Lightning would not send his beasts back to hell as these beaming shafts did. 'Twas light from above. *Pure* light. The enemy's light.

Grimacing, he grabbed his robe and wheeled about. "How did they do that? How did the enemy know of their plight so quickly?" Anger raged as he returned the bottle of elixir to his pack, his hand touching the leather pouch containing the remainder of the powder that could be turned into wolves.

His poor babies! He sank to the ground in despair. They had so wanted to taste human flesh this day. Grabbing a handful of dirt, he flung it into the air and lifted his fist to the sky. "I will have Lady Cristiana. I will have that heinous Spear of Yours! Darkness always wins!"

Merely saying the words out loud sent a surge of dark power through his cold veins. Rising, he leapt onto Demon and took off at a mad gallop.

Sir Walter LeGode swallowed hard against his rising fear as he stood before Drago. The warlock seemed to be growing in power of late, along with his disrespect for Sir Walter. A disrespect that 'twas not to be borne, for the man dwelt at Luxley only by Sir Walter's good grace. Or did he? Sir Walter was beginning to wonder whether 'twas the other way around.

Devil's blood. He would not allow it! He was the lord and master of Luxley. Ergo, all but the bishop ran in fear to do his bidding. And he would not cower before this vermin. He was but a means to an end, a rather *unpleasant* means.

The warlock finally looked up from the book he'd been reading since Sir Walter entered his dungeon lair. Another affront to Sir Walter's station. "How come you here?"

The warlock's icy stare nearly sent Sir Walter dashing for the door.

"Have you put some hex on me, Drago?" There, he'd said it. And with the force he'd intended. Now to appear unmoved by the warlock's coming outburst.

Instead, Drago chuckled and set down his book. "A hex, you say? Why, you are a bigger fool than I gave you credit for." His mirth turned to disdain. "We have a pact, do we not?" he spat out. "Why would I curse you ere our deal is finished?"

That the warlock would be free to do so afterward was not lost on Sir Walter. He diverted his gaze to the greenish ooze bubbling within the black cauldron. Whatever it was, it carried the stench of death. "I am unwell. The physicians know not what ails me. Hence, I make bold to say it must be of a more spiritual nature than physical."

"You, bold?" The warlock snickered, pointing a long, black fingernail toward Sir Walter. "Mayhap you *are* going mad. Or worse, you are being drugged, just as you did to that wench, Lady Cristiana." With a snort, he glanced back at his open book as if either event was of no consequence to him.

Though both reasons had occurred to Sir Walter as of late, neither had enough merit to fear. He was clearly of sound mind when he was hale, and Mistress Anabelle tasted every bit of his food and drink to ensure it contained no poison. The woman was the picture of health *and* beauty. Hence his question to Drago. But the warlock was being his usual menacing self.

"Should either be the case"—Sir Walter dared advance toward the fiend's table, upon which all manner of animal parts and tinctures were spread—"'twould not be good tidings for you. For if I am removed from Luxley, and those mewling fustyworts, those Knights of the Eternal Realm, take charge, you will needs find another den of iniquity from which to spew your curses upon the world."

Drago slowly raised his gaze to Sir Walter, sparks simmering in his coal-like eyes. He spoke not a word but lifted a hand to something above him. A bat dove at Sir Walter. He ducked just as the ghoulish creature swept past him so close, he felt the air move from its wings. Every nerve pinched in terror, but he could not reveal his fear. Not to this man.

"Dare threaten me again, and next time the creature will not miss." Drago seethed.

Sir Walter attempted to gather his breath. "You forget I still have the power to remove Cedric as your apprentice."

"I fear 'tis too late for that, Sir Walter." Drago huffed and moved to stare down at the iron table upon which visions of the unknown oft appeared. "Cedric is growing more and more powerful by the day. Once tasted, such power is not easily forfeited. It may please you to know he has found the girl and that heinous artifact."

"He has? Good lad! When will he return to Luxley?" Sir Walter's fear faded at the good news, for it would please the bishop greatly.

"In time."

The room spun, and Sir Walter squeezed the bridge of his nose. He hoped 'twas true, for his malady grew worse.

Of a sudden, Drago gazed up into the tower above him, a noticeable shiver shaking his white robe. "You have not stopped the light from entering Luxley."

"Me? What can I do against these knights when they do not reveal themselves?" He blew out a sigh. "What harm can they do anyway?"

"Apparently much. For you *do* look unwell." This seemed to please Drago immensely, for an uncharacteristic grin lifted his chapped lips.

"Can you not stop them? Are you not the most powerful warlock? Or should I seek another?" Sir Walter regretted the words instantly, bracing for the warlock's retort. Or worse, another bat.

But the man's attention remained above, as if he feared something far more than a challenge of his power. "They have power as well. *Great* power." He snapped his gaze to Sir Walter. "I do all I can."

"Do more, Drago."

The warlock tossed what looked like a lizard into his cauldron, causing a burst of steam to rise. "Leave me, Sir Walter, ere I do more than fling a bat your way."

Sir Walter knew better than to stay in his presence. Up the winding stairs he labored until his breathing came hard and fast. The sound of music, clank of dishes, and gay voices made him stop and utter a grunt. The evening meal already? Faith! He'd not heard the announcing horn, and no doubt the bishop would be displeased with his absence.

Trudging down the grand staircase, he forced a smile as he made his way through the crowd to his seat at the high table, thankful the evening meal was not as grand an affair as the one at noon, for mayhap he could slip away without notice. He was also thankful the bishop was otherwise engaged in the seduction of one of the serving maids. A servant arrived with a basin of water, and Sir Walter quickly washed his hands as a trencher full of stewed pheasant, cheese, and grapes was set before him and wine was poured into his cup.

His gaze sought Anabelle, and upon finding her serving bread to a table of knights, he motioned her over. She sampled each of the foods on his trencher with a smile, then took a sip of his wine ere she curtsied and returned to her duties.

The bishop leaned into him, reeking of sour wine. "By my troth, do you still believe you are important enough to be poisoned, sir?"

Sir Walter gave a tight smile. "Nay, but I take every precaution, withal, Your Grace." Should he tell him the good news about Cedric? Nay, 'twould merely give the man more to complain about should events not occur quickly enough. He sipped his wine, then broke off a piece of pheasant and popped it into his mouth.

"Humph. You would do well to learn from my example, Sir Walter, for I have no fear of those beneath me wishing me dead."

But what of those beside you? Sir Walter smiled.

Yet the pompous dizzard continued. "How do I achieve such a thing when 'tis I who wield power over them? Respect, my good sir. Respect, fear, and adoration."

Sir Walter wanted to vomit. If the man made him kiss his ring one more time, he just might.

"I shall take that into account, Your Excellency." Thankfully, another maiden drew the bishop's attention.

Sir Walter continued his meal, happy some of his appetite had returned. Below the high table, laymen of rank sat at white-clothed trencher tables, squabbling about some inane doctrine. Beyond them, knights regaled each other with tales of their bravery. Minstrels began plucking harps and tuning fiddles as they prepared to entertain. But Sir Walter had no interest in any of these things this night. He wanted Lady Cristiana and her Spear found. He wanted the bishop gone. He wanted to take his rightful place as lord of Luxley.

A minstrel began her song. A singular sweet voice that soon was accompanied by harp, fiddle, and pipe.

Nay! It cannot be!

A boulder landed in his brain, crushing all lucid thought. The banners above him twirled. Chatter became muted and hollow. Yet *that* voice. He forced his gaze to the minstrel. And found a lady clothed in a green cloak with a single braid of hair peeking from beneath her hood. *Red* hair! Nay!

She finished the song. He rubbed his eyes, and when he opened them, she was gone. He was seeing things again. Begad, it could not be that witch Alexia D'Clere. God's truth! She would not be so foolish as to appear in plain view of all. Still, he would know that voice anywhere.

Pushing from the table, he struggled to rise, but his legs gave way, and he plunged back to his seat.

"Egad, sir. Control your drink," the bishop said with disgust. "'Tis most unseemly for one of your station to make such a spectacle."

"I've imbibed but half a glass, Your Grace." Sir Walter managed to mutter as the minstrels thrummed out another tune. The great hall before him blurred, then came into focus, then blurred again. A lady floated across the room, her white tunic shimmering in the candlelight. A circlet and veil hid her face, but her hair, the color of morning snow drifted about her as she moved.

Sir Walter drew a breath and slammed his eyes shut. 'Twas whatever illness plagued him that brought forth these visions. When he opened them, the lady glanced his way, lifted her veil and smiled. Mistress Seraphina de Mowbray!

He shook his head and rose to his feet once again, this time remaining. "I cry pardon, Your Grace, but I shall retire early."

"Wise, sir. Very wise." Bishop Montruse snorted and twisted his lips in repugnance ere returning to imbibe his second trencher of food.

The small trek to Sir Walter's chamber was a blur of dizziness, nausea, and weakness. His chamberlain aided him in removing his tunic and donning his nightshirt.

"Will there be anything else, my lord?" the man asked, but Sir Walter could only shake his head ere he crawled beneath the wool coverlet.

"I don't like it." Damien announced for the fourth time since they left Emerald Forest and entered the tunnels of Luxley.

Alexia could only smile at the fear in the large knight's eyes, enhanced by the torches they held as they made their way to Sir Walter's chamber.

Seraphina halted and faced him. "I shall be fine, Sir Damien. Was I not perfectly safe in the great hall?"

Ronar, who brought up the rear, exchanged a look of annoyance with Alexia, for Damien's infatuation drove him to distraction. Alas, how soon he forgot love's blind obsession! Had his passions for her cooled so quickly? Nay. Not from the love she saw in his eyes.

Damien frowned. "Aye, but in Sir Walter's chamber? Where you could be trapped?" He glanced at Ronar. "Put by this mad scheme."

Seraphina arched a delicate brow. "How could I be in any danger with you right on the other side of the wall?"

"Indeed, Damien. Sir Walter will be in no condition to do anything save sign this document." Alexia patted the pocket of her tunic. She'd discarded her green cloak, revealing a white gown beneath, covered in a layer of shimmering gauze. With her hair braided and drawn back, she'd once been told by a servant that she was the exact image of her mother. If so, their ploy this night would bring success.

A damp chill drew a shiver from her as the scent of mold and age and stagnant air surrounded her.

"'Tis not in my nature to send women to battle," Damien grumbled. "But to fight *for* them instead."

"I am not going into battle," Seraphina announced with nary a speck of fear in her voice. "I am merely pleased to finally be of service."

"My friend." Ronar clutched Damien's arm. "We shall be but a step away should our plans go awry."

Thunder shook the tunnel walls, sending down a spray of dust and pebbles.

"Are we quite safe in here?" Seraphina's bravery fled her as she gazed up.

"Aye." Alexia pressed a hand to the stone surrounding them. "These tunnels have been here since Luxley was first built. Come, let us make haste. Our presence in the hall, along with the potion in his food, has sent Sir Walter straight to his bed. Right where we want him."

Ronar brushed past Damien and Seraphina and took Alexia's hand in his. "You make no doubt that you can be heard clearly through the wall?"

"Aye, you worry overmuch, Sir Knight. My sister and I oft listened through this very wall to my mother and father arguing in their chamber."

He chuckled. "Little imps, the both of ye."

Smiling, Alexia led the way around another corner, then up a steep ascent that grew narrower with each step. Finally, they halted before a stone wall.

"Here we are." Alexia slipped a gauze veil over her face and patted her pocket to ensure the document, quill pen, and ink were inside. Seraphina pushed past Ronar and drew a deep breath.

Thunder growled its displeasure once again.

Alexia handed the torch to Ronar. "We cannot open this door from inside the chamber without great difficulty. Ergo, should trouble befall us, I will utter the word, *Penance*."

"My destrier's name?" Ronar laughed.

"Aye. When you hear it, push on this wall, as we do now."

"I don't like it." Damien growled.

Taking the torch from her, Ronar kissed her cheek, the stubble on his chin tickling her skin. "I beg you to take care, though I know 'tis not in your nature."

"I am pleased to see you finally know me, my love."

"You as well, dear lady." Damien took Seraphina's hand and placed a kiss upon it.

Smiling, she exchanged a glance with Alexia and nodded for her to proceed.

Ronar pushed the stone door, and a blast of air smelling of tallow and something quite foul struck them as Alexia and Seraphina squeezed into Sir Walter's chamber.

CHAPTER TWENTY

Sir Walter's world became a spiraling throng of scenes, voices, and sounds—flickering candlelight; faces, some familiar, some not, some twisted into demented shapes; horses in full armor clanging and thundering across a field; a thousand swords flung at him; his shrewish wife shouting insults; Cedric's innocent smile when he was a lad; and wolves.

Black wolves.

Every time he crept closer to the bliss of slumber, his stomach revolted, and he leaned over the side of his mattress to cast his accounts into his chamber pot.

Thunder shook his four-poster bed, quivering sheets and pillows alike. Devil's blood! He would call the castle physician into his study on the morrow and dismiss him at once! Then send out his steward to seek another more capable one.

Lightning flashed silver behind his eyelids, and he rubbed them, hoping to wipe away the torturing visions. The sound of scraping stone, the rustle of fabric, and the patter of rain outside his window added to the mad cacophony.

Rustle of fabric? Blinking, he pushed himself to sit, regretting the action immediately as it forced more food from his stomach, this time onto the floor. He wiped his mouth with his sleeve and glanced over his chamber. Two shapes danced across his vision, fuzzy, billowing, like clouds driven before a winter wind.

He shook his head and swallowed, trying to focus on the closer of the two. Behind a veil, red hair streaked in gold, framed a female face, *a familiar* face, as the lady drifted through the chamber as if 'twas hers. *Hers.* Indeed, Sir Walter had moved into the solar, the chamber for the lord and lady, and made it his own.

"You!" He pointed a quivering finger at the woman.

The lady approached, a stinging smile curving her lips. "Aye, Sir Walter, 'tis I, Lady Grecia D'Clere."

"But..." Sir Walter had trouble breathing. The lady grew small, then large again, ere she split into five images that spun like a child's top. "You are not here. You died."

"How now?" Her voice sparked with sarcasm. "'Tis my chamber is it not? Where else would I be but the place where *you*"— the woman suddenly dashed for him, her face shoved large against his—"murdered me!"

Thunder bellowed. Her scent of lavender filled his nose as her hot breath slapped his face. Sir Walter tried to scream, but terror strangled him. He pressed a hand on his stomach and watched in horror as the woman retreated, floating about his bed.

"Nay. I did not murder you!" he shouted. "In truth, I was nowhere near you when you died."

"But you were the cause of it, withal, dear sir." The voice was poison.

Lightning set the chamber ablaze in ghostly white.

The other woman drew near, swirling in a haze of gleaming candlelight. Hair the color of ivory dangled like jewels from her head. *Seraphina?* Sir Walter fell back on his pillow, breath careening in his chest. The maid had disappeared the day Lady Cristiana escaped. "You both are not here!"

"But we are, good sir." Thunder shook the chamber as Seraphina whirled about the room in a dance of death.

Dread consumed Sir Walter. How did one argue with spirits? Especially since he could not gainsay their accusations.

Lady Grecia pounced on his bed to the right, while Seraphina stood like a statue of ice to his left. "We demand reparation," they both said in unison.

"Forsooth! Is that what all this is about—my nightmares, my visions?" If only the chamber would stop spinning!

"A mere prelude to your eternity in hell," came his answer from Lady Grecia.

"Hell! I cannot go to hell." He struggled to sit, then leaned back against his headboard. "I am to be lord of Luxley!"

Lady Grecia shrugged and blew out a sigh. "You make too free, I think."

"What can I do?" He shifted his gaze between them, making himself dizzier than ever. "What reparation can I possibly make now?"

Lady Grecia withdrew a document, pen, and ink from her tunic and held it out to him. "You may sign this."

"Sign…" A foul smell emerged from his lips, followed by food clambering up his throat. He pressed a hand over his stomach and searched for a breath. He remembered now. Others had sought his signature, other visions, other apparitions. His suspicions rose. "What is this document?"

"Naught but your confession, Sir," Seraphina said. "Sign it and you are well on your way to making amends."

Closing his eyes, if only to stop the walls from gyrating, he hesitated, thinking…searching for some logic, some meaning to this lunacy.

"Sign it, or you will go to hell this night!"

"Nay, nay!" He shook off the fog in his head and gestured for the lady to come forward. "Anything to stop this madness."

The lady spread the parchment before him and handed him the pen. He rubbed his eyes, squinted, held it up to the candle beside his bed. But the words skittered over the page like mice before a cat on the prowl.

Grabbing the pen, he dipped it in ink and held it over the page. His hand trembled. A drop of ink spilled onto his sheets. Lightning turned the parchment white.

A *rap-rap* pounded on his door.

"Sir Walter, is all well?" Though the words were hollow and surreal, it sounded like his guard. "Voices hail from within."

The parchment fled his sight, the pen snatched away, and the two ladies withdrew into the shadows.

The word "Penance" echoed through the room ere Sir Walter bade his guard enter.

Ronar wasn't good at waiting. And never when his lady love was in danger. Still, he leaned against the stone door of the tunnel and did his best not to betray his own agitation whilst at the same time calm his friend's. To no avail, he might add, for Damien continued to pace back and forth over the four-foot width of the tunnel.

Pushing from the wall, Ronar gripped Damien's arm, halting him. "They are safe, my friend. And if they are not, we are but one push of this stone away from their rescue."

Damien nodded, though the look in his eyes bespoke of anything but agreement.

A voice, a *word* came through the stones, dampened and hushed, as if 'twere spoken through a wall of liquid. Ronar had no doubt 'twas the word they'd dreaded to hear, *Penance.*

Which meant the ladies were in trouble.

With one nod at Damien, he gripped the pommel of his sword, and turned to push against the stones.

A thousand tiny legs skittered over his hands. The door didn't move. Yet, it *was* moving.

"Don't touch it!" Ronar all but shoved Damien behind him and grabbed the torch from its hook. Then holding it aloft, his worst nightmare appeared.

Spiders.

Hundreds of them, as big as his fist with thick, hairy legs, crawled over the stones and spread over the walls, ceiling, and floor of the tunnel.

He leapt back while Damien hacked at them with his blade. "Judas! From whence did these hail?"

"Penance!" came louder through the wall.

Ronar knew he must rush forward, knew he must push against the door and save the ladies, but despite his efforts, his feet moved in only one direction—backward. Horror buzzed in his mind, scrambling his thoughts, razored through his veins until they ached in pain. Horror like he'd never known. *They cannot be real.* He knew that. Yet…

"Ronar!" Gripping his arms so tight, pain spiraled down to his fingers, Damien shook him. "What ails you, man? They are mere bugs. We must away!"

Spiders. It had to be spiders. The one thing that frightened Ronar the most.

"The women need us! Come!" Damien jerked him forward.

The black horde was nearly upon them…a flood of biting, clawing, deadly ink that would soon swallow them alive.

"Spiders," was all he could say.

"Aye, spiders." Damien released him with a curse, then with sword drawn, charged into the nest. The creatures leapt on him, covering his body within seconds.

"Damien!" Ronar started toward him but then halted. This was not real. Like the solid wall that had transformed into snakes the last time they'd been here, this was but a trick of the enemy. An enemy that knew Ronar's biggest fear.

But he needed Alexia. He hadn't the faith to battle this on his own. He could fight a dozen warriors and put them to flight. But this? This attack came from beyond this world, beyond the reach of a sword, arrow, or dagger. He *had* to believe, but his faith was so new, so young.

Yet hadn't he seen greater things than most ever would?

Damien fell to the ground, overwhelmed by the spiders.

Nay! Ronar's anger surged, scattering his fear. "In the name of my Lord Jesus, the one and only Son of God, I command you to cease and give way!"

Instantly the spiders vanished. They did not scurry away, did not retreat, but simply disappeared as if they had never been there.

Faith and love swelled within his heart, but he had no time to consider what had happened nor worship the One who had saved them. Extending his hand to Damien, he helped the knight to his feet, ignored the look of shock on his face, and charged the stone door. He only hoped that his delay had not cost Alexia and Seraphina their lives.

CHAPTER TWENTY-ONE

Jarin, a sleeping babe curled in his arms, kicked open the broken gate and started down the path to the manor house of his friend, Quinn of Savoy. At least he hoped 'twas his friend's abode, for those in the village had told him so. Albeit with much contempt in their voices, he would add. Which gave him pause. Quinn had always been a jovial sort, full of life, lust, and vigor. There was not a monk at Tegimen Abbey who was not fond of him, though they oft found his antics irreverent. As well as Jarin's. Hence, Jarin had not been surprised to learn Quinn had left shortly after he had. Word was Quinn's father, the wealthy lord of a manor, had died, leaving his holdings to Quinn.

'Twas a fortified manor home, more akin to a small castle, and in quite a state of dilapidation, from what Jarin could see in the dim light of early evening. Broken gate, crumbling walls, a hole in one side of the roof. But he had nowhere else to go. Surely his friend would welcome them, give them a meal and place to sleep for a night or two until Jarin could procure a horse. Mayhap Quinn had a palfrey or even an old nag Jarin could borrow. The smell of horseflesh riding on the wind gave him hope.

The sound of Lady Cristiana's dragging footsteps beside him deflated it. They'd been walking for twelve hours with nary a break, and she and the babe were beyond exhausted. Alas, they'd not even had a morsel of food save some berries Jarin found on the side of the road. If he'd had time, he could have hunted and given them a meal of rabbit or pheasant, but after the incident with the wolves—be they demons or not— he'd wanted naught but to get the lady and the child to safety.

A quarter moon frowned down upon them from a sky where stars began to pop through the velvet blackness. A breeze whipped dust around his boots as he halted before a large wooden door with an iron knocker bearing, of all things, a wolf's face.

After several interminable minutes, the door creaked open to reveal an aged man sprouting more gray hair upon his chin than his head. Bags hung beneath his eyes to match his swinging jowls, and he wore attire far too large for his bony frame. He held a candle up to them and squinted. "And who be ye?"

"Sir Jarin the Just to see Lord Quinn of Savoy, if you please."

The candle came closer, the eyes squinted further as they wandered from Jarin to Lady Cristiana and then to Thebe in his arms. "My master gives no charity. Begone." Then retreating, he slammed the door with a thud.

Lady Cristiana sighed and would have sunk to the stone steps had not Jarin reached out to bear her up.

He rapped the knocker again. The same man appeared, held up his candle, and was about to slam the door yet again, when Jarin poked his boot through the opening. "I demand you announce Sir Jarin the Just to your master at once. Or, good fellow, you may lose your position forthwith."

The man snorted but withdrew and stomped away with a curse. Sir Jarin ushered Cristiana inside the receiving room and shut the door behind him. Thebe made a gurgling noise and shifted in his arms.

"I will take her, Sir Jarin." Cristiana reached for the babe. "You've been carrying her overlong."

"I have not minded, my lady. Yet, 'tis amazing how much the wee one weighs after a few hours." He could barely see Cristiana in the shadows cast by a single rushlight perched on a wall as he placed Thebe in her arms.

"I do hope this Quinn—" she began, but a man's heavy steps echoed down the hall, ere Quinn of Savoy emerged from the shadows, his servant behind him.

"Jarin!" He opened his arms and pulled Jarin into a tight embrace. The sting of strong spirits flooded Jarin's nose as his friend drew back and examined him. Eyes that had once been clear and lively wandered over him in a haze of emptiness ere shifting to Lady Cristiana. "Forsooth! Sir Jarin the Just with a wife and child. I ne'er thought to see the day!" He bowed before the lady.

"Nay. We are not..." she began in a stutter. "We are not wed."

"Not wed!" He winked at Jarin. "In good sooth, the same old rogue you've always been."

"Nay!" Cristiana protested yet again, but Jarin interrupted. "She is but a lady I am escorting home, naught more." He gestured toward her. "Lady Cristiana, may I present Lord Quinn of Savoy. Quinn, may I introduce Lady Cristiana D'Clere and her young ward, Thebe."

"A lady?" Quinn's eyes glittered as he took her hand and placed a kiss upon it. Then, giving Jarin another sly wink, he gestured down a dark hall behind him. "Prithee, come. You must be tired and hungry."

"We do not wish to trouble you, Quinn," Sir Jarin said, not willing to go a step farther until he was assured of his friend's willingness to help. "We lost our horse and food, and I dared to presume you might lend us some supplies for the rest of our journey. Father Godwin told me where to find you."

"Father Godwin!" Quinn smiled. "How fares the old monk?"

"He is well. The same," Jarin said. "As for us, I do not wish to impose upon your kindness. I know we come unannounced."

"I cry pardon. You insult me, friend. I bid you be my guests!"

Relief forced back Jarin's odd sense of discomfort as Quinn and his man led the way into the main hall where a fire blazed in a large hearth. Taking Lady Cristiana's arm, he led her to one of only two cushioned chairs perched before it and helped her to sit. The gentle smile she lifted his way did even more to improve his good humor than seeing his old friend.

That old friend now appeared in the light, staggering and snapping at a servant to draw one of the benches closer to the fire. Aside from a few lanterns and rushlights near the hearth, the rest of the hall lay in shadows, musty, moldy shadows, if Jarin's nose told the truth of it. As his eyes adjusted, the distinct shapes of four trestle tables and a long sideboard formed out of the shadows. A single banner, no doubt bearing the family crest, hung from the high oak ceiling while two tapestries sat askew on the walls.

"Bring some bread, cheese, and wine at once!" Quinn shouted at a nearby serving girl, who scampered off, stirring up rushes spread across the floor. He faced Jarin, firelight shining off his tunic of brilliant emerald slit at the sides, revealing a white cote underneath. A belt of golden circles sat around his waist, the lavish attire at odds with the condition of the house. Yet the face was the same, just as handsome, yet bearing more harsh lines than before. "Prithee, sit." He gestured toward the other chair whilst he took the bench.

"Fire." Thebe, awake now and sitting on Cristiana's lap, pointed at the flames ere shoving her thumb into her mouth.

A thousand questions stampeded through Jarin's mind. Not the least of which was how had his friend fallen so low? The house, obviously once a beautiful manor home, stood in a state of disrepair inside and out.

"How is it with you, my friend? Where have ye been so long?" Quinn grabbed a nearby mug and took a sip, which, from the way he slurred his words, was what he'd been doing ere they arrived.

Setting down his sack, Jarin removed his cloak and approached the fire, holding out his hands to the warmth. "I became a knight, as I am sure you heard."

"I did! A King's Guard. Vak, quite an accomplishment for one so lowborn."

Jarin bristled, not at the insult, for he'd come to expect such, but from the tone his friend took. One that held no joy at his good fortune and accomplishments.

Quinn tossed the remainder of his drink to the back of his throat, then shouted over his shoulder. "More mead!"

Lady Cristiana jumped at the sound, and Thebe began to whimper, fussing to get down and walk.

Quinn glanced their way, his eyes scanning the lady in a way that disconcerted Jarin.

"And you, *Lord* Quinn. I see you inherited your father's manor," Jarin said, by way of drawing his attention back to him. "A baron! Who would have expected it?"

"Not I! Sadly, my older brother died, and the duty fell to me. Alas, it has given me naught but headaches." He leaned forward, elbows on his knees, and grinned. "Ah, the times we had at Tegimen, did we not? I oft think fondly on them. 'Tis good to see you, Jarin. How many years has it been?"

Thebe finally won the battle against Lady Cristiana and took off running across the hall.

"Oh, my." Grabbing her skirts, she charged after her, making both Jarin and Quinn smile.

"Eight, I believe. Far too long." Jarin smiled at Quinn, seeking the lad he once knew beneath his now solemn exterior. "And you, lord of a manor! 'Tis the dream of many less fortunate."

Quinn rubbed his dark, pointed beard as if he were contemplating the truth of such a thing. "Aye, a true blessing." He forced a smile as Cristiana returned, hand in hand with Thebe and halted beside Jarin.

"My lady, pray, tell me from whence do you hail and how did you come to be in this rogue's company?"

Seated once more, Lady Cristiana looked up at Jarin then over at Quinn. "I am Lady of Luxley in Northland Goodryke, fallen on difficult times and forced to leave my estate for a time. Sir Jarin was tasked with my recovery and return."

"Ah, Luxley. I have heard of it. Yet why send a single knight? Why not a carriage and host of knights to escort the lady of the estate safely home?"

Thankfully, two servants arrived with platters of bread, cheese, and grapes, along with cups of water and wine, for Jarin was unsure how the lady would answer, and 'twould do them no benefit to tell of the danger following close behind them.

"Food, Cristi. Hungry." Thebe followed the servants as they spread the plates over a sideboard.

"What need have I of more than one King's Guard, my lord?" She smiled sweetly at Quinn ere she started after the girl, but Jarin gestured for her to remain seated as he went to gather the child and a trencher of food. Returning with both, he set Thebe in Cristiana's lap and the trencher on a table to the side.

"Thank you, Lord Quinn, for this repast," Cristiana said. "I fear we have not eaten today."

Quinn chuckled and took another sip of his mead. "Gadzooks, my lady, 'twould seem you have at least a need for a cook as well as a knight."

Jarin took some bread and cheese and returned to his seat as a servant refilled Quinn's cup. Grabbing it, he clutched it in both hands as if 'twas more precious than gold. But all their gazes focused on Thebe, who entertained them with *oohs* and *ahhs* as she delighted in every bite. Grapes were her favorite, and she consumed them with gusto and giggles, exclaiming, "I love gapes," until the entire cluster was gone.

"No more, my darling." Lady Cristiana held up a cup for the child to drink.

Then as happy as a well-fed cat, Thebe leaned back against the lady with a smile.

"Ah, to be young again, Jarin. When simple things brought such pleasure." Quinn's tone bore a sorrow he'd not known in the man. But then, of a sudden, his mood lifted, and his face lit as he began to reminisce of their time at Tegimen, including myriad questions of its present state. What brothers were still in residence? Did Father Godwin speak of him fondly? Were the grounds the same, the wine cellar in the place they'd left it? Jarin answered what he could, then set aside his plate, casting a glance at Lady Cristiana and the child, both of whom appeared to be sinking lower into the chair by the minute.

"My friend, would it be possible to escort the lady and child to a chamber where they might sleep? 'Tis been a long day."

"By all means. Forgive me!" Quinn pushed to his feet, swayed slightly, then clapped for one of the servants to come forth.

"Mistress Arlette, please show Lady Cristiana to the west wing chamber and provide her with whate'er she needs."

Hoisting Thebe in her arms, Cristiana cast Jarin a wary glance, to which he returned a nod of assurance. His friend may have overindulged in drink this night, but Jarin trusted him. They would be safe here. Her eyes acknowledged his unspoken pledge ere she followed the maid up a winding set of stairs.

And he felt the loss of her more than he wished to admit.

"A most lovely creature, Jarin." Quinn's eyes followed her. "I will place you in the chamber beside hers with a connecting door."

A sudden rush of indignation flooded him at the insult to the lady's honor. Why, he could not say, for he and Quinn had oft spoken thus of women when they were young. "No need. Ours is not... I am not...we..." Oh, Bosh! He was behaving like a foolish stable boy.

"You tease me, Jarin! You, a known philanderer and with every opportunity alone with such an exquisite beauty on your journey. Egad, did you take a vow of celibacy at the abbey I am unaware of?"

His friend's words cut, but only due to their truth, for even in his days at Tegimen, Jarin had tasted the forbidden fruit of a local farm girl.

"I will admit to many indiscretions in my past. However"—swallowing, he glanced up the stairs where Lady Cristiana had left—"some ladies should be honored."

As if in defiance of his statement, Quinn grabbed the young woman pouring more wine into his mug and threw her on his lap. She giggled and squirmed as he put his hands in places they ought not to be.

Jarin looked away, the food souring in his stomach.

"Never fear, my friend. I will order one of the serving girls to your chamber later."

"Nay, I fear I am far too tired this night."

Quinn shook his head as if he could not imagine such a thing, whilst the girl in his lap gazed at Jarin with seductive eyes.

"Off with you!" Pushing her from his lap, Quinn slapped her behind as she started away. "I wish to speak with my longtime friend. More wine?"

"Nay." Jarin needed to keep his wits about him. They were still being pursued, and 'twas not the time to let down his defenses. Though he had to admit, merely seeing his friend brought back memories of reveling and roistering, luring his thoughts back to a time without restraint. Why they hadn't been both tossed from the abbey was beyond him. Alack, 'twas because Father Godwin knew naught of their antics. Or at least most of them. Why did that thought suddenly pinch him with guilt?

Quinn gulped down more wine and stared at the fire, eyes that once had sparkled with mischief now dull and lifeless.

"What happened here, Quinn? Surely you bring in enough from the manor farms to live comfortably?"

He took another sip. "It provides enough, aye, but my father left me steeped in debt."

Jarin seemed to recall that Savoy Manor had been quite profitable. "It grieves me to hear such news. But take heart. I am sure you will recover in time." Though surely he'd had enough time already.

Quinn raised his glass. "'Tis the life we both dreamed of as we drank our troubles away in that wine cellar. No responsibility, no rules, no God to follow, and as lord of this manor, I have my pick of the young women in town." He blew out a snort. "Each one with hopes of marrying and improving their station."

"And none that has made you wish to settle, to wed and have children?"

"A most damnable folly, Jarin! Do you not remember our pact to remain single and free to sample any feminine delight we wish?"

Jarin *did* remember, and he had done just that these past years. Yet, in truth, not a single dalliance remained embedded in his memory, just a passing mirage of women and wine. And in the end, loneliness.

Jarin stared at his empty cup. "We were but young fools back then, were we not?"

"I marvel you would say so, my friend." Quinn looked up, his face creased with confusion. "As for me, I will not be settled. As the Holy Scriptures say, 'a man hath no better thing under the sun than to eat, drink and be merry!'"

Jarin remembered not that particular Scripture. "But are you happy, Quinn? Is this the life you hoped for?"

"Faith now! Put by this mad talk. What else could a man want—wealth, station, power, wine, and women?" The last word he slurred as he laid his head back upon the chair and closed his eyes.

Moments passed as the fire crackled in the hearth and Jarin's thoughts twisted in his head. A chill raked over him despite the flames, and he glanced at his friend, who lay with head back and mouth open, snoring. A shadow, black and fluctuating, stood behind him, then disappeared. Jarin rubbed his eyes, and yet when he opened them, more shadows slithered over Quinn, wrapping him in a ghostly restraint.

Jarin was no doubt more exhausted than he thought, for when he stood to confront them, the shadows vanished.

Two male servants approached. "I'll show ye to yer room, sir," the smaller one said as the larger one flung Quinn over his shoulder as if he'd done it a hundred times before.

Mayhap he had. Which brought more sorrow to Jarin than he expected. Why did it seem that his good friend had everything in the world, and yet in the end, nothing at all?

CHAPTER TWENTY-TWO

Cristiana brushed a curl from the little girl's face, then pulled the covers up over her shoulders. A chill permeated the chamber, which the small fire in the hearth did little to assuage. A chill permeated Cristiana as well, one she could not shake. Rising from the bed, she approached the flames and hugged herself, the night dress the maid had given her shifting about her ankles.

Quinn of Savoy…a handsome enough man, tall and muscular, with hair the color of the night, a strong jaw, and chiseled nose. But she sensed something sinister beneath the well-groomed exterior, something akin to the same feeling she got when Lord Braewood had been near, an uneasiness, a heightened awareness that put her on her guard. Foolishness! He was a good friend to Sir Jarin, and if the knight trusted him, so should she. No doubt 'twas merely exhaustion from the day's journey and the tension of being chased through the countryside. A new day's light would bring clarity and assurance.

Spinning about, she lifted the coverlet and slipped onto the bed beside Thebe, snuggling close to keep her warm. Before too long, her worries abandoned her in the sweet oblivion of slumber.

Sometime in the middle of the night, she awoke with a start. The chamber sat in darkness, all save the glowing coals in the hearth. Movement directed her gaze near the door, yet she could see nothing but shadows. The door snapped shut.

Her heart sprinted, crashing against her chest. Pushing to her elbows, she scanned the room as more things came into focus. No one was there. But someone *had* been there.

She was sure of it.

Grabbing the reins of the spirited horse, Quinn of Savoy handed the missive, sealed with his signet ring, to his servant. "Deliver this to Bishop Montruse at Luxley Castle at once. Ride through the night if you must."

The man nodded and slipped the letter inside his cloak. "Aye, my lord."

"When you return, I will pay you handsomely," Quinn added, though he knew not how. His coffers had long since been empty. But how else to inspire the man to make haste?

He released the reins, and the man nudged the horse forward and then urged him into a gallop down the path and out the main gate of Savoy Manor.

Dust flew into Quinn's face as a chill raked over him, and he stared up at the quarter moon frowning down upon him. Only adding to his shame. A shame that now rampaged through him, stealing every ounce of goodness that remained.

Shoving aside the feelings, he stiffened his jaw. He hated to betray his longtime friend, but what else could he do? Did Jarin not know that the bishop had posted a bounty on his head in the sum of twenty pounds? Quinn scrubbed a hand over his chin. That would go a long way to pay off his gambling debts and bring back some of the servants he'd been forced to release. Not to mention, once again position him in a respectable standing with nobility.

Aye, he'd be a fool to turn down such an opportunity...one that had willingly come knocking on his door.

Spinning about, he marched into the manor. Now, all he had to do was convince Sir Jarin and his lovely companion to stay long enough to be caught.

Morning sun beaming through the open window slats lit the chamber with hope and good tidings. Or mayhap 'twas Thebe's smiles, giggles, and songs that made Cristiana forget the strange visitation during the night. Though she had slept little after the event, Cristiana had come fully awake by kisses on her cheek and little hands shaking her by the shoulders.

"Wake, Cristi, wake! Where Jarn? I'm hungry."

Smiling, Cristiana rubbed her eyes as a row of tiny white teeth came into view before her, along with the excitement sparkling in Thebe's blue eyes and curls the color of soft oak jiggling about her face.

And a world full of troubles vanished before the child's innocent exuberance.

"Hungry again?" Cristiana pounced on the girl, tickling her beneath her arms and over her sides.

Giggles bubbled throughout the room, chasing away all shadows of the night.

And also bringing the lady's maid, who aided them in getting dressed after Cristiana changed Thebe's soiled cloth. The maid, per Cristiana's request last night, also brought a stack of clean cloths for their journey.

After she thanked her, the woman left, and Cristiana took Thebe by the hand. "Shall we go find Jarn and get something to eat?"

The little girl nodded her head up and down with a beaming grin as Cristiana opened the door and started out into the hall. A figure advanced toward them from her left. She barely had time to turn to see who it was when Quinn of Savoy intruded upon them so close, Cristiana took a step back.

"Lord Quinn. I didn't see you there."

"Nor I you, my lady." He bowed, grabbing her hand for a kiss ere she could withhold it. Cold lips pressed upon her skin, even as she gazed down the corridor and realized he would have had no trouble seeing her emerge from her chamber. In truth, by all appearances, 'twould seem he had waited for her to do just that.

With but a cursory glance at Thebe, he extended his elbow to Cristiana. "May I escort you to the hall, where I have ordered a feast to break your fast?"

His breath, a mockery of the morning, stung with the scent of spirits, which gave her pause. Yet how could she refuse him?

"Very well." Forcing a smile, she slipped her hand onto the crook of his elbow and followed him down the winding stairway, searching the hall when it came into view for Sir Jarin. She could not deny the relief, and dare she say *joy,* she felt when she saw him standing before the fire, one boot on the hearth, wearing his long leather hauberk, complete with sword and knives attached. Dark wavy hair fell over his cheek, brushing against his trimmed beard as he appeared to be in deep thought. Upon hearing them approach, he turned, eyes and smile lighting upon seeing her, but then frowning at Quinn so close beside her.

Her sentiments exactly, though she wondered at his reason when the man was his friend.

No time to ponder as Thebe tugged from Cristiana's hand and dashed toward Sir Jarin, flinging her arms open as she went.

Cristiana watched, concerned the powerful knight would shove aside the child's attentions, for Thebe's desires had never been tempered by decorum. But Sir Jarin knelt and received the babe with as large a smile as she'd seen on the man. Then swooping her up in his arms, he tapped her on the nose. "Sleep well, little one?"

And a warmth swept over Cristiana akin to a breeze on a summer day.

"I slept in a bed with Cristi!"

Sir Jarin's eyes snapped to hers, and the look within them sent another warm surge through her.

Frowning, Quinn sauntered toward Sir Jarin. "What need of these weapons, Jarin? Are we to hunt this morn?"

Sir Jarin set Thebe down, and the little girl picked up one of the rushes on the floor and dashed to sit by the fire.

"Nay, my friend. I fear we must be away. I am to bring the lady home posthaste."

"Peace, froth! I'll not hear of it." Quinn motioned for a servant to bring their food. "I insist you stay a few days and recover from your journey." He gestured toward Cristiana. "'Tis clear the lady is fatigued and needs her rest. As well as the child." He strolled toward Jarin, stopping before him. "Besides, we have much to catch up on, my friend. 'Tis been far too long."

He was right, of course. Cristiana was quite fatigued. However, she was also most anxious to be on her way back home to her sister. Still, 'twould be selfish of her to deny Sir Jarin a few days with his old friend. Ergo, she remained silent as Sir Jarin's gaze latched upon her, no doubt assessing her wishes.

Servants sped into the room, placing bowls of steaming oatmeal and platters of bread and plums onto a trestle table set near the fire. In the light of day, she glanced around the main hall and found it a sufficient and handsome room, well-ceilinged in oak, but desperately deficient in ornaments and tapestries one would assume the lord of the manner would wish to display. A set of family swords hung on one wall, while a painting of the sea hung on another, yet beyond that there were no painted vases or silver chalices, ivory statues, or oriental rugs.

Quinn gestured for them to sit, but Thebe had already rushed for the table and taken a spot. Laughing, they all joined her, enjoying the wonderful meal. In truth, it felt good to have her belly full again and even better to see Thebe satiated and happy. And Sir Jarin seemed most pleased as he conversed with his friend about the workings of the manor, Savoy village, and happier days at Tegimen Abbey.

Yet more oft than not, she lifted her gaze to find Lord Quinn staring at her. Alas, she could not deny the interest in his eyes, nor the way that interest made her squirm.

Finally, he turned to Sir Jarin. "I beseech you, do grace me with your presence a few more days, Jarin. I know!" His dull eyes lit. "I shall host a small gathering on your behalf this evening!"

"Nay!" Jarin said a bit too harshly, startling Cristiana. "Forgive me," he added. "We do not wish for anyone to know we are here, if you understand me."

Quinn stared at him a moment ere his eyes twinkled in mischief. "I believe I do." He finished his drink and rose from the table. "You may count on my discretion. However, you cannot prevent me from having a feast merely for us and inviting my minstrels to entertain."

Jarin smiled, glanced at her and then at Thebe ere he turned to Quinn again.

"I will not be gainsaid, my friend," Quinn said.

Jarin rose. "Very well, we shall stay another day. But only one, I'm afraid."

"That is all I ask." Quinn's smile faltered ere it reached his eyes. "Now if you'll pardon me, I shall make plans for our evening." Dipping his head in her direction, he started off, but then turned back around. "Jarin, I must needs go into the village today. Would you agree to accompany me?"

"I shall enjoy that," Jarin returned, and the man marched away.

"Do you think that is wise?" Cristiana asked as she turned to wipe nectarine juice from Thebe's face.

Straddling the bench, Jarin lowered to sit beside her, mere inches from her face. The manly smell of him rose to intoxicate her, and she avoided his gaze, fearing she'd get lost in the warmth of his eyes.

"My lady, pray, I hope it causes you no distress if we stay one more day. The rest and food will do you and the babe good ere we are forced back to our journey."

Thebe crawled into her lap and stared up at Sir Jarin.

"I agree, Sir Jarin, and I thank you for your kind thought. I only fear it gives the bishop and Sir Walter's men time to find us." *And your friend makes me most uncomfortable*, she longed to say but held her tongue.

"Nay. They would ne'er think to look here, and with no word of us in any of the villages or surrounding counties, indeed, 'tis my hope they will give up the chase." He reached for her hand but halted and gripped the bench instead. "Which is why I wish for you and the child to remain safely here today. Rest, enjoy the gardens, eat, play, and recover your strength."

"What if someone in the village recognizes you?"

Thebe reached for the belt strapped over his shoulder, curiously fingering the buckle.

Sir Jarin gently moved her hand away, but she wrapped a finger around one of his and giggled. It appeared no more than a thread circling a mighty oak as it barely encompassed his thick finger.

"I will keep myself covered," he said, staring at the oddity ere he gazed up at Cristiana again. "As I did when we inquired after Quinn. Besides, 'tis you they seek."

Moments passed as he stared at her, saying naught, yet with eyes brimming with unspoken words.

Something in those eyes, something among the words, barely perceptible—a depth, a longing for something more—caused a plethora of unnamed emotions to swirl within her. He'd declared his desire to never wed, yet he looked at her as if he were about to propose.

His gaze dropped to her lips, and her heart sped.

Thebe reached up and tugged on his short beard. "Jarn. Horsey ride?"

He laughed as the child left Cristiana's lap and crawled into his arms. Shocked at first by the action, he stiffened, but then soon embraced her. "Not today, little one. But soon."

Thebe leaned her head against his chest, and the sight of her curled up in those thickly muscled arms did naught to quell Cristiana's *unnamed* emotions.

"We will leave first thing in the morning. You have my troth, my lady."

"I shall hold you to that, Sir Jarin."

CHAPTER TWENTY-THREE

Jarin hated to leave Cristiana and Thebe, but they'd be safe enough within the walls of Savoy Manor. He also hated to delay their journey to Luxley, but he could see the fatigue dragging down the lady, and he would loathe himself should she or the babe become ill. In truth, Quinn's manor might be the perfect place to hide, for no one but Father Godwin knew of their association. And mayhap once the bishop's men lost their trail, they'd relent in their mission. At least for a time. Though 'twas a longshot to be sure.

Still, the extra day gave Jarin time to discover the reason for his friend's melancholy, though Quinn did his best to hide it. They had shared their hopes and dreams once. Mayhap the man would do so again.

Yet all Quinn spoke of as they rode on horseback through the manor lands farmed by his tenants was how great were his holdings and how far he'd risen from being the second son of a minor baron.

Sunlight dispelled the early morning mist, leaving behind sparkling drops over grassy fields and transforming the countryside into a magical place of wonder. Geese slid atop crystalline ponds as birds of every color danced among the branches of trees. And Jarin suddenly wished Cristiana was present to share the beauty. A beauty that was soon marred by the living conditions of some of Quinn's tenants. Broken-down shacks provided the only shelter for the villeins dressed in naught but rags as they went about their work.

Upon seeing their lord ride by, they gave the required bow of obeisance, but none approached to ask him for assistance in repairs. A strange sight, that, for Jarin had witnessed many a lord surrounded by adoring tenants begging for his grace with this or that. Jarin longed to ask about the shabby conditions but could hardly get a word in with all of Quinn's self-aggrandizing bluster.

Thankfully, a gust of fresh wind blew away the smell of manure and disease as they left the final cluster of farm homes and started for the small village of Savoy.

"You are most fortunate, my friend," Jarin said. "Lord of such a manor. Who would have guessed such a thing as we gulped down wine in the abbey's cellar?"

Quinn's dark hair blew in the breeze as eyes, dull from his morning spirits, found their way to Jarin. "That I would be so fortunate to have my grandfather, father, and brother die in the same day? Not I."

His callousness dismayed Jarin. "I am sorry, my friend. Was it difficult for you?"

"Nay. They bore me no affection, as you may remember. Begad! They would hate knowing I am now lord of Savoy Manor." He gave a wicked chuckle.

"Yet, here you are with land, position, and power. 'Tis what you always wanted, is it not?"

Quinn made no response, merely turned to Jarin with a wink. "Race you to the village?"

Jarin laughed and immediately spurred his horse to take off at a full gallop. Wind blasted through his hair and slapped his face, stealing his breath and making him feel as though he flew through the air. Such a sense of freedom he'd not known in some time. Quinn kept pace with him, his palfrey's muscles rolling and swelling as the beast charged forward. He laughed and smiled at Jarin, and in that smile, Jarin saw the boy he had once known.

Regardless, he could not allow him to win! Lowering his head, Jarin sped toward the small collection of buildings at the end of the road, passing Quinn by a horse-length ere he slowed the animal at the village entrance.

Quinn, however, charged straight into the village, scattering chickens, pigs, and villagers alike. One lady screamed as she gathered a child in her arms and darted out of the way.

Oblivious, Quinn lifted his hands. "I win! Welcome to my humble village, Jarin."

Humble indeed, as Jarin had noted the day before. In truth, he could see from one end to the other. Several buildings inhabited the space in between, a parish church, an inn with a pub attached, storehouse, leather worker, and apothecary. Also perched along the muddy and rutted streets were homes of wattle and daub where cow's heads poked out windows and children tramped through mud with the pigs. The smell of feces, both human and animal, along with woodsmoke and rotted meat swept over Jarin, nearly knocking him from his horse as they made their way through a procession of carts, hay wains, piemakers, and fishmongers. None spoke a word to Quinn. All quickly sped out of his way.

Ere he knew it, Quinn had stopped at the pub, dismounted, and gestured for Jarin to follow him inside. It took a few moments for his eyes to adjust to the dim lighting. It took less time for his nose to curl from the stench—much of the same as 'twas outside, but stronger and with the added sting of alcohol. A fire blazed on the far side of the room before which several benches and tables were strewn. Candles provided the only other light, including several hanging from the ceiling on a wooden chandelier.

Other things hung from the ceiling, animal carcasses, sacks full of grain, ropes, and an iron cage, housing a bird whose song could not be heard above the clamor of the men below, at least a dozen of them, some shouting, some singing, and some whispering secrets. All deep in their cups. Odd for so early an hour. Large barrels were stacked behind a wooden bar where two men poured wine for serving wenches who sashayed over straw covered floors, drawing the gaze of several salivating patrons.

Two of the women greeted Quinn with a smile as he plowed through the crowd and, upon finding an empty table, plopped down and shouted, "Wine for my friend and me!"

A woman slinked in their direction. Golden curls circled an angelic face at odds with her surroundings. Her innocent expression 'twas also at odds with her tight corset that pushed much of her chest into view, leaving little to the imagination.

She slammed two mugs on the table and then leaned forward, exposing more of herself to their view.

Jarin had not been with a woman in…how long had it been? Years? Nay. Could not be. Yet he could recall neither the date nor the face of his last tryst. Which did naught to explain why his body did *not* react to such a flagrant display of female flesh.

Bosh! What had happened to him? Had he lost his allure with women? Nay, not from the look in this one's eyes.

"She's a pretty thing, is she not?" Quinn reached out and drew the woman near ere leaning to nibble on her neck.

She giggled, but her eyes were on Jarin, luring him with their suggestive look. Then, wrapping her arms around Quinn's shoulders, she perched on his lap. "Where 'ave ye been, my lord. I 'aven't seen ye for a fortnight." Her gaze slithered to Jarin. "An' who be yer friend?"

"Mistress Dulcia, may I present Sir Jarin the Just, an old acquaintance of mine."

"Pleasure, sir." She offered her hand, which Jarin took out of politeness, attempting to keep his eyes off her half-exposed bosom. Why? He could not say, for he'd never averted his eyes from such pleasure before.

"Do ye not have a friend for Sir Jarin?" Quinn glanced around the smoke-filled room. "Where is Adelais?"

"What need 'ave ye of Adelais? I can 'andle ye both." Giggling, the woman leapt off Quinn's lap and onto Jarin's. She smelled of lilacs, sour wine, and a thousand men's hands. Despite her feminine curves, Jarin politely nudged her back to Quinn.

"If you please, mistress, I have no doubt Quinn shall be able to satisfy you fully."

Dulcia stuck out her bottom lip in a feigned pout that appeared more ridiculous than charming.

Quinn grabbed her by the waist, drained his mug, and slammed it on the table. "In good sooth, Jarin, I begin to worry for you, my friend. Dulcia, fetch me another drink." He all but shoved her from his lap, his eyes following her as she sashayed away.

Sipping his wine, Jarin studied his friend. Aye, they had dreamt of tasting all the delectable delights life had to offer, but Quinn was lord of a manor now. Surely 'twas time to put childish things away. Jarin shifted in his seat at the thought. Had he?

Dark shadows reappeared around his friend, stealing the sparkle from his eyes when his gaze returned to Jarin.

Jarin leaned forward on the table. "Get a wife and be done with all this roistering, Quinn."

"Odds life! That coming from you?" Quinn gave an incredulous laugh.

Jarin sat back, hiding his disappointment. "Our lives are different now. I am a knight. You are lord of a manor." He glanced over the trollops in the room. "A decent lady would do you good."

Quinn huffed and raked back his hair. "A lady, indeed. A woman of status and purity. Yet I cannot obtain more than a glance from such a one, though I admit they are rare in Savoy."

Jarin raised a brow at their surroundings. "And most rare in such a place as this."

"Where else to have my needs met?" Quinn shrugged and glanced toward Dulcia who was approaching with more wine.

The shadows around him moved yet again, spinning and coiling around Quinn like a dozen snakes. Jarin rubbed his eyes. Merely a trick of the flickering candlelight.

"But you, Sir Jarin, have caught the eye of Lady Cristiana."

Ignoring the leap of his heart, Jarin took a sip of wine. "Nay. The lady is far above me."

"She looks at you as if her whole world depended on your smile." Sorrow dragged down Quinn's features as he stared into his empty cup.

"Forsooth!" Jarin laughed. "You have taken too much to your cups to see clearly. She tolerates me for my protection and escort home, for I have told her I am not a man inclined to wed."

Quinn lifted his gaze. "So you have made her no promise?"

Dulcia set another mug full of wine onto the table and started to slide back onto Quinn's lap, but he sent her away with a wave of his hand.

"Nay." Then why did the thought sadden him? Even worse, why did it bring an odd smile to his friend's lips and a shiver of alarm through Jarin? He shrugged it off and glanced over the dim room. Two patrons playing cards began shouting from their table in the far corner. Oddly, a strange darkness hovered over them both.

The bird in the cage shrieked. Swinging his gaze back to Quinn, Jarin rubbed his eyes. "Come now, you have land and fortune. Mayhap you have not been called to court, but surely you can catch the eye of a woman of good standing."

Quinn gulped his wine, then fingered the mug, chin lowered. "The eye mayhap, but the empty coffers offer no incentive to wed."

Jarin stared at him, confused. "Bosh, you jest! How now?"

"I grant you, I have land and a home, but, alas, no coin to my name."

"Surely the crops from your land and rent you receive from your tenants provide a satisfactory income."

"It would, had I not gambled it away playing dice and even now owe money to lenders, along with usury. I may have to forfeit a portion of the manor and mayhap even the house itself."

Jarin pushed aside his mug and closed his eyes, his heart growing heavy at his friend's lack of restraint. But hadn't they bragged about such bold freedom when they were young? "That saddens me greatly, my friend."

"I do not suppose you could loan me a sum." Quinn looked up at him, sheepishly.

"Alas, I am as destitute as you at the moment, being no longer employed by the king."

Nodding, Quinn tossed the remainder of his wine down his throat, then slammed his mug on the table, his head swaying as if battered by the wind from all sides. He raised his hand to draw the wench's attention for more wine, but Jarin grabbed his wrist and lowered it.

"Mayhap you've had enough, my friend. Drink never solves such problems. Let's be away to the manor. Are we not having a feast tonight?"

Nodding, Quinn allowed Jarin to assist him up. Back outside, he mounted his horse with difficulty, and they walked their palfreys the short distance to the manor house.

Once they had thought lives unencumbered by responsibility and rules would bring them the pleasure and adventure they sought. Yet all that life appeared to have brought Quinn was misfortune and sorrow.

And Jarin couldn't help but wonder that, if he didn't change his ways, would he end up like Quinn someday, alone and miserable?

Feeling a bit out of sorts without Sir Jarin close by, and loathing herself for it, Cristiana spent most of the day investigating the areas both inside and outside the manor house, which included a dairy, buttery, kitchen, pantry, stables, henhouse, chapel and gardens. Thebe particularly enjoyed watching the chickens strut about, and the man in charge was kind to allow her to feed them with handfuls of dried corn. Her laughter as she watched them scramble to eat the scraps warmed Cristiana nearly as much as the sun. However, they spent most of their time in the gardens where herbs of all kinds—rosemary, lavender, lemon, meadowsweet and comfrey—blended to create a smell so pleasant, Cristiana longed to stuff it in a bottle to save for a time when she was feeling sad or afraid.

Thebe also enjoyed the flowers, most of which were in full bloom under the summer sun. Roses, daffodils, lilies, and violets created a colorful palette in the small garden as they wandered through the narrow pathways, singing songs and enjoying a rare moment of peace and joy. The sweet warble of birds filled the air, along with the buzz of bees and the distant clank of a blacksmith's hammer.

"Cristi, pink rose!" Thebe tugged from her grip and darted to the bush ere she could stop her.

"Do not touc—"

Thebe let out an ear-piercing wail, holding up her finger, where a drop of blood appeared on her skin.

Kneeling, Cristiana embraced the crying child, then nudged her back, withdrew a handkerchief from her cote, and wrapped it around her finger. "'Tis all right, Thebe. Roses have thorns. You must be careful."

Crystalline tears slid down the little girl's cheeks, and Cristiana wiped them away, suddenly realizing how much she had come to love Thebe and how hard 'twould be to ever part from her. But she couldn't think of that now.

"Why thorns?" Thebe whimpered out.

Why thorns, indeed. Why did it seem the most beautiful things in life came at such a cost? "I do not know, darling." Cristiana kissed Thebe's finger and started to rise when she spotted an old woman approaching from down the path. Dressed in stained peasant garb that fluttered in the breeze, the woman shuffled along, red blossoming on a face wrinkled from much time in the sun. She halted before them, her wide grin revealing two missing teeth.

Cristiana drew Thebe close.

"What's this now?" The woman's hooded gaze drifted from Cristiana to Thebe.

"Forgive us for disturbing you," Cristiana returned. "The child poked her finger on a thorn, 'tis all."

"Ah, you must be Lord Quinn's guests. I 'eard there was a child with ye." She brushed a wayward strand of gray hair from her face.

"Are you the gardener?"

Her eyes sparkled with a youth that belied her lined skin. "Aye, for now."

What an odd thing to say. Cristiana studied her yet felt no fear in her presence. In truth, quite the opposite.

"'Ere ye go, wee one, I'll cut a rose for ye."

"There's no need." Cristiana protested, but the woman had already plucked a knife from her belt and sliced off the loveliest pink rose from the bush where Thebe had pricked herself. She proceeded to cut off its thorns as well ere extending it to the child.

"I thank you, good lady. 'Tis most kind of you."

But Thebe retreated a step, holding up her injured finger.

"Faith now, does it still hurt?" The woman lowered her wide girth to kneel before Thebe, wrapped the finger between her palms and held it tight. Smiling, she began singing a song so completely out of tune, it made Cristiana cringe.

"God makes all things well,
Plants, flowers, trees, and critters,
And even little girls
Aye, God makes all things well…"

Thebe loved it and giggled as the woman continued to sing. Then, releasing her tiny finger, she handed her the rose yet again. This time Thebe took it with a small curtsy and a "thank you."

"You are most kind," Cristiana said. "Lord Quinn is blessed to have you."

Hand pressed on her back, the woman rose with a groan. "Ah, but does he 'ave me?" Then smiling yet again, she turned and began waddling away.

Thebe dove her nose into the petals of the rose, giggling with delight.

"Let me see your finger, darling." Unwrapping the handkerchief, Cristiana stared at the spot where the rose had pricked. No blood. Not even a mark. She glanced back down the path, but the old woman was gone.

CHAPTER TWENTY-FOUR

Thebe's little hand tightly clasped within hers, Cristiana descended the stairs into the main hall. Music and laughter drifting up to her chamber had alerted her that their evening meal was about to commence. Though she was in no humor for a celebration, she would attend so as not to embarrass Sir Jarin in front of his friend. In good sooth, she could not deny that the beautiful attire Lord Quinn had ordered brought to her chamber was an added enticement—a gown of ruby red laced in silver filigree and embedded with emeralds that matched the color of the velvet girdle about her waist. He'd also sent a silver necklace, velvet slippers, and circlet of flowers for her head. In truth, she hadn't felt this lovely in a long while.

No gowns had been sent for Thebe, nor a much-needed bath drawn for either of them, but Cristiana had done her best to make the girl presentable. Most people took no note of children, but if they did, they would see naught but the child's sweet smile and good temperament.

She expected to see a larger crowd filling the hall—those of high enough position from the manor or from the village—a steward, clerk, other members of the clergy, and a knight or two. Hence, she was surprised to find only a single vicar, a well-dressed elderly couple, another man with a face as stern as a rock wall, and two men whom she'd seen among the guards. Aside from the four minstrels plucking instruments in the corner, a bevy of servants ran to and fro with jugs of wine and trenchers full of the first course of their meal, wafting the scent of meat and spices over Cristiana.

Against her will, her eyes sought out Sir Jarin among the meager crowd—him and him alone. Apparently, either Lord Quinn had not offered him finer attire, or he had refused such, for she found him, arms folded over his sleeveless leather surcote, talking with Quinn. The same linen shirt covered his chest and arms, the same brown breeches tucked within black leather boots, the same dark hair and trimmed beard, and the same belts circling his waist from which his ever-present sword and knives hung. He seemed distracted, disinterested even, as he kept listening to his friend, glancing occasionally over the hall as if looking for something…or someone.

When she reached the bottom of the stairs, his gaze locked upon her, and a slow smile lifted his lips. Against her will, a delicious sensation trickled through her.

"Jarn!" Thebe attempted to tug from Cristiana's hand.

"Nay, Thebe, remember what I told you?" Cristiana kept her in place. "We must behave like ladies this night." Yet how could she blame the child for wanting to do something she longed to do herself, run into Sir Jarin's arms?

A man who had made it quite plain he never intended to wed.

She must remember that even now as she wove her way through trestle tables clothed in white and servants hustling about. All the while Sir Jarin's eyes remained on her as if he could look nowhere else.

Thebe finally yanked from Cristiana's grip and dashed toward the knight, who once again knelt to receive her and swept her into his mighty arms. The scene offered Cristiana little aid in erecting a fortress around her heart against the man's charms.

Lord Quinn approached and took her hand. "You wore the gown I sent." He seemed surprised at first but then a deviant pleasure filled his smile. "If I may be bold, 'tis simply ravishing on you. You are a vision of feminine beauty and grace, my lady."

"I thank you for your kindness, my lord, for I had naught else to wear but what I wore when I arrived."

"Such things should not be tolerated for so fine a lady." He forced her arm upon his and led her to her seat, giving her a chance to admire his lavish attire for which he obviously spared no expense—a tunic of fine blue wool adorned with fur at the collar and a silver belt about his waist.

"I trust my servants have provided for your every need?" he asked. "Should your clothing need mending or washing, they are at your disposal. Or mayhap a bath for you and the"—his gaze landed on Thebe still in Sir Jarin's arms, and his tone suddenly sharpened—"child."

Curious at the sudden change in the man's demeanor and blushing at the mention of a bath, Cristiana could only respond with her thanks ere the man introduced her to the other guests.

Finally, Sir Jarin set Thebe between them at the high table whilst Lord Quinn thankfully sat on Sir Jarin's other side. The vicar, elderly couple, bailiff, and two guards sat below them on another table. Servants brought basins of water around wherein everyone washed their hands, and then the feast began.

Wine was poured into goblets and trenchers full of ground lamb in a spiced wine sauce were set before them. Cristiana shared a trencher with Thebe, but the young girl, unable to stay still, leapt between her lap and Sir Jarin's, eating from both trenchers, laughing and playing as if she hadn't a care in the world.

Cristiana envied her innocence. How wonderful to be a child who fully trusted in the care and love of a parent. Something that had been stolen from Cristiana at a young age.

As the second course was served—roasted peacock in almond milk—Lord Quinn ordered the minstrels to play, and the hall was filled with the sound of lute, harp, and fiddle. Thebe clapped her hands in delight as the colorfully dressed musicians began singing and dancing, reciting poetry, and juggling.

"Go see, Cristi. Go see?" She tugged on her hand, wanting to go up close to the minstrels, but Cristiana drew her into her lap.

"We shall, darling. After we eat."

Sir Jarin maintained a conversation with his friend, stopping occasionally to smile at Cristiana and play with Thebe when she crawled into his lap. On his other side, Lord Quinn's voice grew in both intensity and incoherence as his words slurred more and more with each glass of wine he imbibed.

Much to her dismay, he would occasionally rise and move to sit beside her, inquiring how she was faring and showering her both with his wine-saturated breath and a plethora of compliments, which only caused further discomfort.

When the third course arrived, apples and pears baked in sugar, the odious man went back to his seat, giving her a reprieve. Did Sir Jarin notice the attention his friend paid her? Mayhap, for when she looked up at him, a flash of concern and, dare she say, protectiveness appeared in his eyes.

The sentiment warmed her as Thebe devoured the sweet fruit in their trencher.

Cheese and more wine completed the meal, but Cristiana had no more appetite. She had not expected such fine fare and thanked Lord Quinn ere she finally relented and allowed Thebe to drag her to stand before the minstrels.

They sang an outlaw ballad about William Wallace, two of them acting out the part of Wallace battling an English lord.

Laughing, Thebe danced before them. The troubadours enjoyed the attention and played along with her, until finally, eyes half-closed, she lifted her arms to Cristiana. Picking her up, Cristiana rocked back and forth to the tune as the other guests continued their chattering and drinking. Before too long, Thebe grew heavy in her arms, and she moved to place her on a nearby couch. The child stuck a thumb in her mouth and wiggled slightly but fell back asleep. 'Twould be impolite to retire without bidding good eve to Lord Quinn and Sir Jarin. Hence, she would return anon and take Thebe to bed. Yet by all accounts, the child slept as soundly here as anywhere, despite the noise. She stroked the girl's cheek and smiled. What Cristiana would give to sleep so deeply without a worry or care.

"Asleep already?"

Sir Jarin's deep voice turned her around, and she caught his loving gaze upon the child.

"'Tis been a long day, and she is but a babe." She scanned the hall and found Lord Quinn had cornered one of the serving maids, standing far too close, and smiling like a man intent on having his will. She pitied the woman and thought to rescue her, but the girl giggled and gave Lord Quinn a coy smile. No doubt she enjoyed his attentions along with the extra gifts and privileges that came with them.

The minstrels began playing a softer tune—a love ballad—more melodic and gentle, and Sir Jarin took her hand and bowed, a twinkle in his eye. "Will you do me the honor?"

"I couldn't. Alone? No one else dances."

"In good sooth! I did not ask *them*."

She didn't know whether 'twas the wine, the music, or the allure of this man, but she dipped her head, took his hand, and allowed him to lead her in the steps of a courtly dance she'd only seen performed and never engaged in herself. Steps forward, then back, to the side, then a spin and then back again. How a mere knight possessed the grace of a royal courtier, she could not own. 'Twas a dream every maiden longed for—the music, wine, dancing in the arms of a man such as this—a dream she had long forsaken as out of her reach.

Several times during the dance, Sir Jarin was so close, she could feel his breath upon her, sense the strength and might of him surrounding her.

Yet how gentle he was with his every touch.

"How was your day, my lady?" he asked as they drew closer.

"Thebe and I had an enjoyable time exploring the manor," she returned, stepping to the side and dipping.

"I am pleased to hear it."

"And you?"

"I fear not as pleasant as yours." She thought she saw his smile fade as he made a turn to the left.

No doubt due to spending the day with Lord Quinn. Her eyes found the man still seducing the servant. "Are we to leave on the morrow as you promised?"

He noticed the direction of her gaze. "Aye, first thing in the morning."

She smiled.

He turned her around and then drew her close, so close their bodies touched. He stood there for a moment, swaying to the music, gazing deeply into her eyes as if he hoped to find great treasure therein.

He smelled of spice and wine and Jarin, and, God help her, she never wanted the moment to end. Instead, she wanted to feel his arms around her, for him to kiss her as he'd done before, to pledge his troth to always remain by her side.

Nay! She sought to regain her senses, for she must ne'er forget the knight's reputation as one highly skilled in seduction. Nor must she forget that due to that reputation, due to his desire for freedom, he would eventually break her heart and abandon her as everyone else had done.

That she could not allow, for it would completely and utterly destroy her.

She pushed from him. "I beg your patience, Sir Jarin, but I am quite fatigued."

Cold, drafty air rushed between them, stealing away the warmth and sense of him and leaving an aching emptiness behind.

Pain crossed his eyes, and he slid a finger down her cheek. "One more dance, my lady, I beg you."

Naught but affection poured from his eyes. Sweet angels, if he but said the word there and then, she'd vow to be his lady—forever. Hence, she did the only thing left for her to do, the only thing that would dissipate the magic blossoming between them. She slapped him across the cheek.

"You use me most ungraciously, sir."

Jarin stood abashed, his skin stinging with her strike. If she'd turned into a wolf and bit off his head, he would have been less surprised, for he was sure she'd been enjoying their dance as much as he. As it was, he could only stare at her, the strange look in her eyes—one of desire and anger all mixed in a vicious confused brew—eyes that now shone with tears.

Alack, he'd been slapped before. Many times, if he were honest. Most he had deserved. This time, he'd more than restrained himself, had forbidden his fingers to wander inappropriately, offered her no vain flatteries, though he could have offered many true ones. He'd been the perfect gentleman, enjoying every minute of their amorous dance… the closeness of her, her sweet scent, and the look in her eyes—a look that bespoke the growing connection between them, one he could no longer deny.

Ah, but she was a vision of loveliness, even now in her rage. Her eyes narrowed and her lips quivered as red exploded on her fair cheeks, matching her shimmering gown. A tremble coursed through her, swaying tendrils of her hair that spilled beneath her circlet over her waist. His heart had taken flight when he'd first spotted her descending the stairs—a vision of maidenly beauty and purity. It had never alighted, even as the evening progressed, and he watched her laugh with Thebe and enjoy her feast.

But this?

"My lady, I beg your forgiveness for whate'er I have done. 'Twas not intentional. Mayhap I have been too long away from court."

She said naught, merely stood staring at him, her chest heaving, her eyes pained.

"What's this?" Quinn staggered up, his wool tunic flowing about him. "Forsooth! Has trouble invaded your *affaire de coeur*?"

The lady looked down and pursed her lips ere whirling to face Quinn. "I assure you, my lord, this is no *affaire de coeur*!"

At the lady's harsh tone, Jarin's heart finally landed.

Quinn's brows arched above eyes red and hazy with spirits. "Beshrew me. I have misspoke, my lady!" His sinister smile gave Jarin pause. "I merely—"

"Good eve to you both," Lady Cristiana interrupted with a nod and a swish of skirts as she made her way to gather Thebe.

Jarin approached and held out his arms. "Allow me to carry her, my lady."

"Nay," she said without meeting his eyes. "I shall manage."

And the way she said it made him wonder if she meant for more than that moment.

Feeling every bit as if he'd been stabbed in battle, Jarin stepped back, allowing her to leave. Both he and Quinn watched her ascend the stairway until the shadows overtook her. In truth, Quinn stared after her much longer after that, and if the man wasn't Jarin's good friend, he'd challenge him to a duel over the look he saw in his eyes.

Alas, the man was clearly drunk, which no doubt accounted for his behavior.

'Twas Lady Cristiana's behavior that still had Jarin baffled. Women!

Spinning to face him, Quinn lost his balance and stumbled, shrugging off Jarin's effort to help.

"I nearly forgot my reason for approaching you, Jarin," he slurred out, blinking as if to clear his vision. "My guards have sighted a band of armed men approaching from the east."

Alarm fired through Jarin, tightening every muscle. "Are you quite sure?"

"Aye. I'm away to check on it myself." Quinn turned to leave but stumbled again.

"My friend." Jarin gripped Quinn's arm. "You've had far too much wine for that. I do not wish to find you fallen off your horse in a ditch come morning. I shall go. If I find them and they are heading this way, I'll return forthwith, and the lady and I will leave immediately ere we bring trouble upon you."

Quinn nodded. "You are a good friend, Jarin. I shall await your return."

Smiling, Jarin doubted it. No doubt the man would be unconscious in less time than it took Jarin to saddle a horse.

More flustered and unsure of herself than she'd been in a long while, Cristiana carefully pulled back the covers with one hand whilst she clung to Thebe in the other. Gently laying the girl down, she removed her shoes and loosened the ties of her gown. If she attempted to undress her, 'twould no doubt wake the babe, and sleep was the best thing for her right now. Instead, she placed her doll in her arms and covered her with the quilt.

The maid assigned to attend Cristiana laid out her night clothes over the back of a chair. "Will there be anything else, my lady?"

Cristiana sighed and rubbed her temples where an ache brewed. Mayhap a suit of armor impenetrable to the loving glances, heated touches, and insatiable allure of Sir Jarin the Just? Or better yet, a magic carpet that would fly her and Thebe back to Luxley posthaste so she wouldn't be forced to spend another day with a man who stirred every pleasurable sensation within her.

Instead she said. "A bath. I should love a bath."

"Aye, my lady." The woman smiled, curtsied, and left the room. Indeed, never underestimate the power of a hot bath. A good soak never failed to clear her mind, set her resolve aright, and prepare her to face anything that came her way. Alas, mayhap that last thing was a wee bit of a stretch, but the rest were true enough.

Sweet angels, if it were the last thing she did, she would get her mind off Sir Jarin and back where it ought to be—avoiding the army that chased them, returning to Luxley as soon as possible, clearing her sister's name, and regaining their estate. With the Spear's help of course.

In preparation for the maids' arrival, she gathered up her skirts and began untying the binding around her thigh that kept the powerful artifact in place and hidden from all who sought it. Releasing it, she lifted it to a candle. 'Twas but the tip of a once mighty spearhead—a Roman spear, the one that had stabbed the side of Christ. Or so they said. Yet, after what she'd seen of its power, she had no doubt the tales were true. Black stained the very tip, and she dared rub her finger over it, praying 'twas not sacrilegious to do so. To think it might be the actual blood of their Savior.

She shivered and held it to her bosom, tears filling her eyes. "Holy Lord, you have allowed me the great privilege of protecting your Spear, the wonderful joy of experiencing its power…" She gazed down at it again. "And yet you abandon me in every other way." Mayhap she was not worthy of the love of One so great, the Creator, the one true God.

A knock on the door preceded two men carrying in a large wooden tub, followed by a string of maids with buckets of steaming water. The men set the tub before the fire and left immediately, not daring to glance her way, whilst the maids filled it nearly to the top and deposited soap and towels on a nearby chair.

"May I help you undress, my lady?" the maid asked.

"Nay. That will be all."

Once the last maid left, Cristiana wrapped the Spear inside its binding and set it on the mantel between a brass candlestick and a painted bowl. Candlelight shifted over the mark on her wrist, and she rubbed it. Still there after all this time. How long would she be the Spear's protector? Quickly disrobing, she stepped into the tub and sank into the warm waters, allowing them to steal the chill from her bones and the grime from her skin. Leaning back on the hard wood, she released a sigh and listened to the crackle of the fire and the wind whisking past the shuttered window. The feast must have ended, for she could no longer hear the minstrel's songs or the chatter of guests.

What she did hear were footsteps outside her door, followed by the dull creak as it opened.

"I need naught else." She waved over her shoulder at the intruding maid. "Prithee, leave me."

The footsteps continued.

Annoyed, Cristiana opened her eyes and turned to face the servant.

But it wasn't a servant. Or even a woman.

It was Lord Quinn with a sly grin on his face that would frighten the most valiant warrior.

CHAPTER TWENTY-FIVE

Jarin slowed his gelding and patted him on the neck as he made his way down the dusty road. He'd galloped at least three miles in both directions and had not seen so much as a horse-drawn dray, let alone a band of armed soldiers. Either the troop had made camp somewhere for the night, or Quinn's scout had been seeing things.

Still, the possibility of being discovered by the bishop's men reminded Jarin that they must be on their way anon, first thing in the morning as planned. He had wanted to stay and help his good friend, cheer him up, offer an idea or two to pay off his debts, get him on the right path. But from Quinn's present disposition, that would take far too long. Besides, who was Jarin to offer advice? For he lived his life in much the same carefree manner as his friend.

Turning the horse down the path that led to Savoy Manor, Jarin kept his ear tuned to hear the slightest thump of horses' hooves or the murmur of voices in the night, but all he heard was the dance of wind through the leaves, the distant warble of a night heron, and the thud of his gelding stomping down the road.

A quarter moon coated the grassy fields in milky light and transformed a nearby pond into liquid silver. Even so, shadows gathered amid clusters of trees and bushes and hovered around country homes and barns. Jarin drew a deep breath, relishing in the fresh scent that always came with the night—pine, moss, a hint of lavender, and the hope of a new day on the morrow.

He also relished a moment alone, away from the dissipation of his friend, the clamor of the manor, and the responsibility that sat heavy on his shoulders for the protection and care of Lady Cristiana and Thebe. Out in the countryside with only his sword and horse for companions, he felt free again, unfettered by the restrictions of society, the expectations of man, the commands of those above him—especially a God who demanded much more than Jarin was willing to give.

Then why was he heading back toward the manor, that dark structure he now saw sitting atop a hill, two flaming torches winking at him from the front gate? Winking at him, indeed, as if taunting him, daring him to return instead of prodding his horse into a gallop in the opposite direction. *Freedom!*

Freedom from whatever spell Lady Cristiana had cast upon him. For no other woman had ever made him consider— even for the briefest of moments—what it would be like to settle down with wife and child. Bosh! Had he lost his mind? 'Twas the one thing he had vowed never to do, never bind himself so tightly to another that he could not do as he pleased, *when* he pleased. Yet 'twas much more than that, for to truly love someone would mean his certain destruction when they were taken from him. And taken from them they would be, as had happened with his father, then his mother, and finally his sister. Everyone he had ever loved.

Thus, he had vowed never to allow himself to love a woman with the intensity he'd heard about in ballads and seen in friends—the kind of love that drove a man mad and forced him to give up everything for his lady. 'Twas far better to engage in harmless trysts now and then whene're the mood struck.

Then why, *again*, was he nearing Savoy Manor? He smiled. Because he could do naught else. Fool!

The front gate creaked open, and an old lady emerged, torchlight accentuating the lines on her face. She waddled as fast as she could up to Jarin.

"Sir Knight, Sir Knight!"

Halting his horse, he dismounted, annoyed at the interruption to his thoughts.

"How may I help you, mistress?" He nodded at the guard standing before the gate, then led the gelding through into the inner court. The woman scurried by his side and yanked on his arm to halt him.

"Your lady is in trouble, sir. You must make haste to her. There isn't much time."

🕮

Every nerve screaming in terror, Cristiana scrunched her body as close to the side of the tub as she could.

"How dare you, Lord Quinn! I insist you leave at once!" She still clung to the hope that he was so inebriated, he'd mistaken her door for another. *One...two...*

That hope spilled to the floor with the water sloshing over the edge of the tub as he continued his approach, eyes that were no longer glazed focusing intently upon her.

"I have no intention of harming you, my lady." His voice was ripe with desire.

Heart crashing against her chest, Cristiana glanced first at Thebe, praying that no matter what occurred, the child would not wake, then over to the towels set upon a chair just out of her reach. *Three...four...*

"No harm, you say?" She drew her sopping hair over her shoulder to cover her chest and glared up at him. "I believe you have every intention of doing me harm, of taking that which I do not offer."

He circled the tub, peering into the water where he ought not. And all the while grinning like he'd won a tournament prize. "You are truly a vision. And if you choose to offer, 'twill go much better for both of us."

"I would rather be strung up and flayed," she spat out, tears filling her eyes.

Reaching into the water he snatched a handful of her hair and wrenched her up.

Pain seared through her scalp. She screeched and gripped the side of the tub, doing her best to keep her body covered. *Five...six...* It wasn't working! Her terror only grew.

He released her, and she sank back beneath the water.

"If you leave now, I will not speak of this to Jarin." A sob escaped her.

With a humph, he turned to glance toward the fire. "You think I fear him? Jarin the Just!" He spat out the name, ere his tone turned mocking. "Women always chose Jarin over me. Oh, how the ladies adore him! And now he has achieved knighthood and a King's Guard at that. Jarin! With the ear of the king." He laughed. "But of course. Everything comes easy for him."

Whilst the man blustered on about Jarin, Cristiana inched along the side of the tub toward the stack of towels. If only she could reach one, it would at least provide a small barrier to his violating gaze. Numb with fear, she reached over the tub, her fingers nearly touching the cloth.

He pivoted and slapped her hand away.

She sank back. "You're jealous of him! 'Tis what this is all about?"

Fury flamed in his eyes as they narrowed and scanned her body once again. "And now he has won a true lady's affections. Do you think a man like Jarin can love you?" He cocked his head and fingered his beard. "Do you think he will wed you? Bah! Don't be a fool. He is but playing with your affections, my lady." Shrugging, he unbuckled his belt and tossed it aside, then removed his blue tunic.

Cristiana couldn't breathe. Her blood pulsed. Her fingers tingled. "I will scream. Sir Jarin will hear me. Your servants will hear!"

He smiled yet again. "I do hate to disappoint you, my lady, but my servants have been instructed to ignore any clamor emanating from your chamber. And Sir Jarin? I believe he is away from the manor in search of a phantom army."

What was left of Cristiana's hope sank to the bottom of the tub as a terror like none she'd known consumed her. "Why? What do you hope to gain?"

"I will have at least one thing that belongs to him." Lord Quinn swept off his undershirt, leaving only linen breeches. Before he fully faced her again, she spotted clusters of red rashes covering his back from his neck to his waist. She'd seen the condition before. 'Twas one caused by engaging in relations with too many partners. And now he would give the illness to her. She glanced at the Spear sitting atop the mantel, wishing she had not removed it. *Oh, Lord, if you're there, prithee help me!*

"Come, my lady." Quinn held out his hand. "Step out of the water, if you please."

"I beg you one favor, my lord."

He eyed her curiously.

"Do not harm the child." Though she had tried to hold them back, at the mention of Thebe, tears spilled down her cheeks.

He cast a quick glance toward the bed and a wry smile curled his lips. "You have my troth on one condition. Do not wake her with your screams."

Cristiana nodded and moved toward the edge of the tub, uttering the only thing left for her to say. "Sir Jarin will kill you for this."

Jarin charged into the main hall and up the spiral stairway, as tense as he'd ever been before any battle. The old woman had not told him where to find Lady Cristiana, hence he headed toward her chamber. Voices drifted through her door, calm voices. Could the woman have been wrong? Mayhap even mad? Halting, he listened, intending to knock since 'twas obvious Cristiana was awake. Then he heard Quinn's voice and a woman's sob, and without hesitation, he drew his sword and burst into the room.

Lady Cristiana sat in a bath, reaching her hand toward an unclad Quinn, intending to rise. And from what he could tell, with nary a stitch of clothing on!

They betray you! Leave at once! A voice, not his own, shouted inside of him.

But then Cristiana turned toward him, her breath coming fast, and tears streaming down her cheeks. Terror screamed from her eyes until they focused on him, and she uttered his name as if it was the answer to all her prayers.

Quinn withdrew his outstretched hand, his eyes widening as he took a step back.

"What goes on here?" Jarin finally said, his gaze shifting between them. Alas, he needed no explanation, for he could see it written on his friend's face. He charged him, leveling his sword at his bare chest. "You dare ravish my lady! What devilment is this?"

Quinn merely stared at him, the fear in his eyes transforming into anger and then... *hatred?* But that couldn't be. Once again, dark shadows swirled about his friend, faster and faster, spinning about his ears as if whispering into them.

The sound of water moving brought his gaze to Lady Cristiana. Her bare shoulders glistened in the candlelight as her creamy flesh blurred beneath the water. He quickly averted his eyes. "My lady, are you harmed?"

Quinn grabbed a candlestick from the mantel and slammed it against Jarin's sword, knocking it to the floor with a mighty clank.

Cursing himself for allowing a moment of distraction, Jarin charged Quinn, clutched his neck in a choke hold, and shoved him against the stone wall. "How dare you, you craven wastrel!"

Thebe began to cry.

Water sloshed behind him, followed by the pad of footsteps.

Quinn's eyes peered over Jarin's shoulder, but he slammed his fist on the fiend's cheek, forcing his gaze away.

Freeing one of his arms, Quinn slugged Jarin in the gut.

Bending over, Jarin backed away, all the while breathing out, "If 'tis a fight you want, Quinn, 'tis a fight you will get."

With Thebe's cries spurring her on, and with both men distracted, Cristiana took the opportunity to ease from the tub, grab her nightdress, and dart for the bed.

Slipping on her shift, she jumped onto the bed and drew Thebe into her arms. "There, there, darling. 'Tis all right."

Though she had no idea if that was true. She clutched the girl to her chest and watched as Quinn punched Jarin hard in the stomach, sending the knight reeling backward.

Of course they'd be all right. She'd seen Jarin subdue two armed soldiers. Surely he could handle a profligate like Quinn. Alack, the man was his friend! Would that make a difference?

She was shaking. Uncontrollably. And not from the cold. She drew a breath in an effort to steady her nerves when Quinn charged Jarin like a bull intent on breaking through a barn door. Together the men fell backward against the bed post, shaking the bed, and eliciting more cries from Thebe.

Cristiana rubbed the little girl's back and held her face against her chest to keep her from witnessing the brutality. "You are safe, Thebe. Jarn will protect us."

Sir Jarin pushed Quinn and slammed his fist across his jaw. Head spinning, Quinn stumbled backward.

"Why, Quinn, why?" Jarin shouted.

Quinn wiped blood from his lips and smiled. "Why not?" He swung at Jarin, but Jarin ducked, spun, and punched his friend in the side.

Moaning, Quinn growled, picked up a vase from a table and tossed it at Jarin. The knight leapt out of the way, and it crashed against the wall.

"Jarn!" Thebe shouted, drawing his gaze.

Taking advantage of the opportunity, Quinn gathered Jarin's blade and pointed it at his chest, breath heaving, and his eyes full of burning malice.

Cristiana gasped.

"Now what?" Jarin spread out his hands. "Are you to murder me, my friend?"

In a move nigh too fast to see, Jarin grabbed a towel, flung it around the blade, and jerked it from Quinn's hands. It flew into the corner.

With a mighty growl, Quinn charged Jarin, but the knight braced for the impact, grabbed Quinn by the arms, and shoved him aside.

Still he came, eyes crazed as if he'd gone mad. This time he plucked a knife from Jarin's belt and pointed it at his heart, a maniacal laugh spilling from his lips.

Cristiana drew Thebe closer, begging God for mercy.

Not a speck of fear appeared on Jarin's face as he studied his friend. "Lay down the knife, Quinn, and be gone. You are clearly outmatched."

Quinn snorted. "Yet I'm the one holding a knife to your chest."

Jarin released a heavy sigh. Lifting his arm up to block the knife, he struck Quinn in the gut and kicked his feet out from beneath him. The knife flew from his hand as his head bashed against the tub with a *thwunk.* He toppled to the floor.

Jarin caught the knife in midair.

Cristiana allowed herself to breathe.

Dismissing the fiend with a wave, Jarin turned to face them, his concerned eyes searching over Cristiana, no doubt for wounds.

Behind him, Quinn struggled to rise.

Jarin started toward the bed. Quinn rushed Jarin.

"Behind you, Jarin!" she yelled.

Wheeling about, Jarin caught the man, spun him around and held the knife to his throat. Blood trickled down Quinn's neck.

"Nay, Jarin. Nay!" Cristiana shrieked. No matter what Quinn had done, she did not wish him to die, nor for his death to haunt Sir Jarin the rest of his life.

Thebe began to wail.

Chest heaving, Jarin faced them, knife still pressed against Quinn's throat. Determined fury burned in his eyes, the likes of which she'd never seen in the knight before. But slowly the features of his face loosened, and he lowered his hand. Shoving Quinn aside, he opened the door. "Leave while you still have your life."

Much to Cristiana's relief, Quinn cast one last glance toward her, then stumbled out of the chamber.

She dared not to feel safe until Jarin's strong arms wrapped around her and Thebe—iron bands of strength and comfort. He said not a word, just squeezed tight as his warm breath came hard and fast, flooding them with his scent. Cristiana leaned her head against his chest, finding comfort in the feel of his heart thumping over her cheek. He had saved her. He had come at just the right moment and saved her. Two minutes... 'twas all that had stood between her rescue and losing her maidenhead in the most horrific way possible.

"Prithee, tell me this isn't a dream," she finally whispered, fearing that indeed she was being accosted at that very moment, and her mind had transported her elsewhere.

His chuckle rumbled through his chest. "If so, then real pain and blood invade my dreams."

"You are hurt?" Cristiana pushed from him, searching him in the candlelight and finally seeing blood staining his sleeve. "The knife. It sliced you."

"Jarn!" Thebe's sobbing having finally stopped, she freed from Cristiana's tight embrace and crawled into Jarin's lap. "You save us." She nestled against his chest as if she could burrow inside of him.

Cristiana well understood the desire.

He wrapped his wounded arm around the babe, while keeping the other around Cristiana, and drew them both close. He kissed the top of their heads, the action softening every hard place in Cristiana's heart.

"Prithee, forgive me for bringing you here. I thought...I believed he was...we were friends once."

Cristiana lifted her gaze to his. "'Tis not your fault, Sir Jarin. How could you have known?" She searched his eyes, finding a mixture of sorrow and something else she dared not hope for within them. "I gave him no encouragement, I hope you know—"

He pressed a finger on her lips. "I do."

Thebe lifted her face to Jarin's. "You brave, Jarn. Strong."

He tapped her on the nose. "Only so I can protect you."

His affection for the child nearly sent tears to Cristiana's eyes once again. *Good* tears this time.

She glanced toward the tub and a shudder ran through her. "He was so jealous of you."

"Alas, I had no idea." Reaching up, he placed a finger beneath her chin and forced her gaze back to him. "Forgive me for not being here. Quinn sent me on a fool's errand to keep me away. Beshrew me, I was a halfwit to believe him." His jaw tightened.

"But you came in time. How could you have possibly known?"

He shook his head and released a sigh. "An old woman stopped me outside the gate. Told me you were in danger."

"An old woman?"

"Aye. I'll grant you, I never saw her before. No doubt one of the servants."

Cristiana thought of the woman in the garden. "Wrinkled skin, two missing teeth?"

"Aye, that's the one. Do you know her?" He gave her a quizzical look.

"Nay. Thebe and I met her earlier in the garden. She seemed…she seemed different. I cannot explain. She healed the prick on Thebe's finger."

Jarin flinched. "Odd, that." He glanced down at the child and smiled. "I believe she's fallen back to sleep."

Cristiana smiled. "She trusts you."

Jarin swallowed as if overcome by the thought, but then gently handed Thebe back to Cristiana.

Sorrow swept over Cristiana as she lowered the girl back onto the bed and drew the covers about her. "She's been through so much."

"As have you."

The kindness in his voice turned her to face him yet again. He sat on the bed just inches from her, his eyes searching hers. She missed the feel of his arms around her, the only place she'd ever felt truly safe. Yet mayhap 'twas a false sense of safety, for Sir Jarin was a mere human with human failings.

Yet the way he'd protected them, the way he gazed at her now made her wonder if he weren't some mighty angel sent to watch over her.

He ran the back of his fingers over her cheek, tenderly, lovingly. "Did he harm you?"

She lowered her chin, embarrassed. "Nay. Merely terrified me." She looked up. "How can I ever thank you?"

A shiver ran through her. He must have noticed, for he drew her back into his arms, and she wished more than life itself that this man would love her...and love her forever.

Leaning her head on his powerful chest, she prayed the man's courage and strength would leech onto her, make her independent, in need of no one. Like him. Then no one would ever abandon her again. Alas, she was naught but a weak coward, so unlike her sister, the mighty warrior.

Against her better judgment, she glanced up at him, his trimmed beard tickling her forehead. He smelled of sweat, spice, and Jarin. And God help her, she wanted more of him.

He gently cupped her face in his hands and lowered his lips to hers.

CHAPTER TWENTY-SIX

Jarin knew he should not kiss Cristiana, knew no promise existed between them, knew she'd most likely slap him again for attempting such liberties. But ahh, he found the lady beyond irresistible, especially the way she was looking at him—as if he were the king himself, as if she admired him, trusted him, believed in him. As no one else ever had.

His lips floated above hers, waiting for her to strike him, but there was no shriek of indignation, no shove against his chest, no sting on his cheek. Instead, she touched his mouth with her own, parting her lips to receive him. Sweetness and ecstasy! He drank her in, relishing in her mesmerizing taste—more delicious than any fine wine. Wrapping his arms around her, he pressed her closer, realizing at that moment she wore naught but a nightdress. Bosh! Making it all the more difficult to restrain his growing passions, in truth a skill he had not honed these past years. But he must.

The lady, however, was not cooperating in that endeavor. Clinging to him, she moaned and continued the kiss with more passion than he'd expect from a maiden, a wonderful surprise from a lady who was so oft full of them. Finally, she withdrew and slid her cheek against his. Her breath rushed past his ear in a whiff of desire as she uttered his Christian name, "Jarin."

"Cristiana." Jarin took her face once again in his hands and gazed into her eyes, delighted at the passion he found there. A sudden urge to profess his love to her, swear his fealty forever to this lady, rose upon his lips. But he swallowed it down.

He kissed her yet again, gently this time, seductively, drunk with the heady sensation of her. She allowed him to caress her neck, run fingers through her hair, and deepen the kiss until he was mad with the need for her, never wanting the moment to end.

But end it must. And by his will. Bah! Why had she not slapped him?!

With every ounce of restraint within him, he withdrew, released her, and leapt from the bed.

She looked up at him, her chestnut hair tumbling over her shoulders to the coverlet, her eyes shimmering, her lips swollen and moist from their kiss.

And nearly every curve evident through her nightdress.

How much was a man supposed to take? Jarin snapped his gaze away. "Get dressed, my lady, and then wake Thebe. We must leave this place posthaste."

As if just realizing her state of undress, she crossed arms over her chest and nodded.

Then before he took her in his arms again, Jarin retrieved his sword from the corner, sheathed it, and left the room, closing the door behind him.

Leaning back against it, he kept a keen eye down the corridor in both directions should Quinn make another attempt. He'd be a fool to challenge Jarin again, but then he'd been a fool to do so in the first place.

Jarin examined the wound on his arm in the rushlight perched on the wall. The cut wasn't deep and would heal anon, but the cut to his heart was another matter. His friend—his good friend—had betrayed him in the worst possible way. He could make no sense of it, this jealousy Lady Cristiana spoke of. Quinn was lord of a manor, while Jarin was naught but a fallen knight without a groat to his name.

Jarin shook his head. There were no words to describe his fury when he'd seen Quinn about to ravish Lady Cristiana! He'd wanted to kill his friend, punish him for his betrayal. And he would have if the very lady the man would have despoiled had not begged him to stop.

He squeezed the bridge of his nose where exhaustion threatened to close his eyes. Through the door, he heard the lady donning her attire, and his mind went to where it ought not—to her unclad body in the water and then to the curves beneath her nightshift. His body reacted and he shoved the visions away. He must not defile the lady so with his thoughts. She was worth much more than that. Her *and* the precious child.

Holding them close on the bed, comforting and protecting them until their trembling ceased, had done odd things to his insides, evoked feelings of love and family, of being the protector and provider of such precious creatures.

He ground his teeth together. Nay! He must be more careful. His plans did not include a mundane life of responsibility. Nor did they include risking the loss of one he loved with all his heart.

Scattering thoughts of the lady, he focused on the mission at hand—leave Savoy Manor at once and make their way to Luxley Castle posthaste. They had but two or three days left on their journey. Once there, he would forfeit the responsibility of Lady Cristiana and Thebe to her sister and Ronar. And once again gain his freedom.

With Jarin's kiss still ripe on her lips and the scent of him rising from her skin, Cristiana busied herself donning the layers of her clothing. Tears trickled unbidden down her cheeks, and she kept batting them away, unsure whether their appearance was due to nearly being ravished or to Sir Jarin's abrupt behavior after their kiss. He had looked away with such disgust, she could only believe he either found her distasteful or inexperienced. Or both.

In truth, she had never kissed a man like that before. Had never allowed a man such liberties. And she in her nightdress! Sweet angels! What had she been thinking? But she hadn't been thinking at all. She'd been *feeling*—wonderful, glorious feelings of being swept away into another world where she was loved, cherished, and protected. Did such love truly exist? The kind that filled one's heart with so much joy that naught else could fit inside? The kind that loved without condition, gave without expectation, and stayed forever and ever? Mayhap that was a love that only existed in dreams and ballads.

She was a fool. A fool with no strength to resist a man who had made it plain he would never wed. 'Twas no wonder God was disappointed in her, in her constant cowardice and weakness, her shameful behavior.

She slipped on her surcote and tied up the laces, glancing at Thebe still asleep on the bed. She hated to wake her, but she must. Cristiana had no desire to stay at Savoy a second longer, nor to face Lord Quinn after what he'd done.

As it was, it took little effort to stir the child from her sleep and get her dressed. No doubt she was still unnerved from the battle she'd witnessed.

"Where going?" Thebe asked, rubbing her sleepy eyes.

Cristiana slipped on the girl's shoes. "Away from here. To a safe place."

"With Jarn?" The little girl's pleading blue eyes stared up at Cristiana.

"Aye. With Jarn."

This seemed to satisfy the little girl as she leapt from the bed and stood waiting whilst Cristiana made her way to the mantel for the Spear.

It wasn't there.

Panicked, she searched the entire mantel, groping around the brass candlestick and painted bowl. She'd put it there. She was sure of it, wrapped in its binding.

Heart thundering, she glanced down over the hearth, the floor. Nothing. Had it fallen somewhere during the fight? She grabbed a candle and dropped to her knees, peering under the chairs and in the corners.

"What looking for, Cristi?" Thebe approached.

"Nothing, darling. Just something I misplaced."

A rap sounded on the door, followed by Sir Jarin's voice. "Are you ready, my lady? We must leave posthaste."

Leaping to her feet, Cristiana rushed to open the door. "I can't find the Spear," she said ere Jarin could utter a word.

He marched into the room. "Where did you last see it?"

"I removed it so I could bathe..." Her glance took in the tub of water and a shudder overcame her. "I wrapped it in a cloth and set it atop the mantel."

Grabbing another candle, Sir Jarin joined the search, and together they scoured every inch of the chamber, tossing quilts off the bed, searching the wardrobe, the chair cushions, even beneath the rug.

Finally standing, Sir Jarin rubbed his chin. "Could Quinn have taken it?"

Cristiana shook her head, panic gripping her. "Nay. Why would he? He has no idea what it is or even that it was here."

Sir Jarin cast a quick glance at Thebe, who stared up at him with admiration. "We cannot stay here."

"I cannot leave without it. 'Tis what protects us. 'Tis what my sister needs to defeat Sir Walter and the bishop. I know that now. I should never have left Luxley with it in my possession." She closed her eyes in defeat. "And now I have lost it." She glanced at her wrist where the mark of the Spear remained. If God had deemed another protector more worthy, surely the mark would have disappeared.

Jarin released a heavy sigh. "Mayhap one of the maids took it."

"Nay. I placed it on the mantel after they left." Cristiana glanced over the room, tears blurring her vision.

Jarin reached for her hand and took it in his, giving it a squeeze that did more to comfort her than he realized. "I will ask Quinn."

"Nay. He will fight you again."

Jarin gave a half smile. "Not if he has any of his wits remaining."

Thebe reached for him. "Stay, Jarn."

He knelt before her. "I will return anon, little one. Never fear." He tapped her on the nose, then stood and headed for the open door.

The old woman appeared in the entryway, gray hair springing from her cap, dirt smudging her skirt, and a smile on her cracked lips, revealing two missing teeth.

Jarin halted. "You."

"Aye, 'tis me, handsome knight." Her smile widened as her gaze shifted to Cristiana and then to Thebe. "Are ye missing something?" She held out her hand to reveal the Spear's binding folded neatly in her palm.

Cristiana darted for her. "Where...how?" Taking it from the woman, she gently unwrapped the cloth and breathed a sigh of relief when the Spear tip glowed in the candlelight. She gazed at the woman, who still had a smile on her face. "I don't understand."

Moving inside the chamber, the old woman glanced around, laid a hand upon Thebe's head and smiled, ere facing Cristiana again. "Had to protect it, you see. It would have been found. But He wants you to have it. For now."

Sir Jarin studied the old woman but said not a word.

"Who?" Cristiana folded the cloth around the Spear once again and held it tightly in her hand.

The old woman approached and wrapped her hands around Cristiana's. Though the skin around her eyes resembled aged parchment, within those shining orbs lived a volume of wisdom, knowledge, peace, and love, the likes of which Cristiana had never seen.

"The power lives within you, child. Where God is. Not in a scrap of metal." Then releasing her, the woman winked at Jarin and headed toward the door. Before she reached it, she began to fade...slowly...slowly...until suddenly she was no more.

They all stood there for several seconds, staring after her. Cristiana blinked, wondering if exhaustion had finally consumed her senses. Jarin rushed to the door and glanced both ways down the corridor.

"Angel," Thebe said, smiling.

Jarin faced her.

"Angel," she repeated.

"How?" Jarin shifted his confused gaze to Cristiana. "I know not what just happened, but we must leave. Now."

Stuffing the Spear in the pocket of her tunic, Cristiana nodded, grabbed their sacks, took Thebe's hand in hers, and followed Jarin out the door. The rushlights along the stairway had long since gone out, leaving them to grope their way down each tread until they reached the bottom. In the flickering light of a dwindling fire, she spotted servants lying scattered over the main hall floor, curled up in blankets, whilst shadows shifted over the walls like ghoulish specters.

"I'm scared," Thebe said, and ere Cristiana could lift her into her arms, Jarin turned and hoisted her into his, chipping away yet again at the barricade Cristiana attempted to erect around her heart.

They crept around the snoring servants and made their way to the main hall door.

The eerie chink of a sword echoed through the chamber. From whence, they could not determine.

Jarin halted. Then proceeded.

Shadows consumed them again. A spark ignited and a lantern shone bright. Lord Quinn's maniacal face shone in the glow, along with ten well-armed guards blocking their only exit.

CHAPTER TWENTY-SEVEN

"**W**hat devilment is this, Quinn?" Jarin quickly handed Thebe to Lady Cristiana. "Not had your fill of humiliation?" Even as he spoke the words and gripped the hilt of his blade, Jarin knew he could not defeat ten soldiers.

"Tsk, tsk, tsk." Quinn shook his head. "Where are your manners, Jarin? You dare leave without saying goodbye? Again?"

"You know why we leave." Jarin frowned, hoping beyond hope that his old friend still existed in there somewhere. But the shadows slithering about the man spoke otherwise. "Put by this mad jealousy. We were friends once."

Thebe began to whimper, and Sir Jarin heard Cristiana attempt to console her.

"Friends do not abandon friends as you did to me at the abbey," Quinn spat, then wobbled slightly as a waft of brandy-soaked breath slapped Jarin's cheek.

He sighed. Alas, so that was it, the cause of this madness. Guilt pricked his heart, for he had indeed left the abbey without a word and ne'er returned. "For that, I cry your pardon. Upon my own, I should have…there was much…many things happened which kept me away."

His words seemed to soften Quinn's expression for but a moment ere the shadows grew darker and their swarming more intense.

Jarin rubbed his eyes. Why was he seeing these things? He did not wish to see spirits from the underworld, if that's what they were. "However," he continued. "You have no right to keep us here. Nor to accost Lady Cristiana. Hence, I bid you and your men adieu and demand you step aside or pay the price."

Quinn grinned. "You are well-skilled, I grant you. But not against ten soldiers."

"What is it you want, Quinn? To kill me for the mere crime of leaving you without word?"

"You not only left, but you became the highest knight of the realm, achieved success, fortune, and"—he glanced at Cristiana—"the affections of a true lady."

"And you, lord of a manor!" Jarin spread his arms wide toward their surroundings.

"Bah! Meaningless." Quinn huffed.

Jarin watched Quinn's expression darken as the man looked around at all he had and considered it rubbish. Peckish dolt! "If you would but cease your drinking, quit your gambling and roistering, and be kind to your tenants, you would gain the happiness and success you desire."

At this, Quinn's expression grew sour and pained. His shoulders sagged as if his bones had turned to pottage. "I fear that will ne'er happen. For I am dying."

Jarin stood abashed, unsure what his friend meant. Unsure whether 'twas another trick to gain sympathy.

Lady Cristiana appeared by his side, Thebe still in her arms. But the look on her face as she gazed at Quinn sent Jarin even further into confusion and doubt. 'Twas a look of compassion, not fear, not hatred for the man who had nearly ravished her.

"You speak the truth, Lord Quinn. I saw the sores on your back."

To his credit Quinn would not meet the gaze of the woman he accosted. "I have but months to live," he mumbled.

"'Tis the whores' scourge." Blushing at her own words, Cristiana glanced at Jarin.

Aye, Jarin knew of it. Spread by intimacy and quite painful and deadly. He wanted to express his sorrow at the news, wanted to forgive Quinn for all past wrongs, but his anger kept such sentiments at bay.

It did not keep Lady Cristiana at bay. Handing Thebe back to Jarin, she approached the insolent ravisher and laid a hand on his back.

Quinn jerked in surprise and lifted confused eyes to her.

"Would you like God to heal you?" she asked in a voice that trembled slightly but bore no ill-will.

Quinn merely stared at her, shock claiming his features. Naught but the sound of the wind whisking past open windows and the simmer of coals in the fire filled the air. "What trickery is this?" he finally said.

"God wishes to heal you."

Thebe nestled within Jarin's arms as he stared in wonder at the lady before him. He could make no sense of her actions, her kindness toward this man.

"And you would allow Him?"

Cristiana smiled. "He does what He wills, my lord. Do you agree to it?"

Swallowing, Quinn nodded, still gaping at her with confusion and suspicion.

Clearing her throat, she closed her eyes, hand still upon the fiend, and said, "In the name of Christ and by the power of His blood, be healed of all disease, Lord Quinn. I cast away the spirits of illness and death and all other evil that hovers about you."

Then retrieving her hand, she stepped back. "Now receive the grace of God."

Quinn stood still for a moment, his eyes shifting between her and Jarin ere they widened in shock and joy and his breath came fast and hard. "I no longer feel the sores that plague my back! I cannot feel them!" He reached around to rub his back. "They are gone. Begad! They are gone!"

"Thanks be to God!" Cristiana smiled.

Jarin stared dumbfounded at his friend. He'd never seen him so exuberant, so joyful. Even the shadows that surrounded him had vanished.

Quinn took Cristiana's hands in his. Trembling, she attempted to pull them away, but he shook his head. "Do not fear me, my lady. Though I know 'tis but a trifle, I am truly sorry for what I did. Even so, even after I..." His eyes filled with tears. "You healed me! How can I thank you for that?"

She finally withdrew her hands. "'Twas God who healed you. And I forgive you, Lord Quinn. Now you must give your life to God and follow Him always."

Forgive him? Jarin shook his head in disbelief. What sort of woman so easily forgave, so quickly granted such a gift to a man who would have ruined her without a second thought? Weakness! 'Twas the only explanation.

Then why did it seem more like strength?

Dismissing his soldiers, Quinn finally faced Jarin, his face twisted in anguish in the torchlight. "I have done much evil, my friend."

Jarin ground his teeth together. "Apparently the lady has forgiven you. As for me, 'twill take longer, I fear. *If* ever."

"Nay, not for that, though I am forever in your debt for such…such a horrendous act." He glanced nervously toward the door, then back at Jarin, his face filled with horror.

Alarm prickled over Jarin. "Out with it!"

"I needed the money. To pay my debts."

Jarin grabbed him by the collar. "What have you done?"

"Jarin, stop!" Cristiana said.

"I sent a rider to Luxley last night with word you are here."

Jarin shoved him against the door with a loud thud, but then released him. "Bosh! Give us horses and we will leave straightaway."

At a snap of Quinn's fingers, a soldier approached. "Prepare my two best horses immediately." As the man darted off, Quinn stepped to the side and gestured toward the door. "I hope you can forgive me someday, Jarin."

Saying not a word, lest a string of curses fly from his mouth, Jarin grabbed Cristiana's arm and hurried out the door, praying 'twas not too late to make their escape.

*Emerald Fores*t

Alexia skittered her fingers up Ronar's back as he sat before the hearth in their home beneath the forest.

The brave knight leapt up, brushing his back in haste, then halted and frowned her way. "It pleases you to mock me, my lady."

"It does," she said. "But I shall stop...someday," she added, smiling as she looped her arm through his. "When it pleases me no further."

He drew her near. "I see I shall have to teach you to respect your husband."

"When we are wed, indeed. For now, allow me my fun, Sir Knight." The smile he gave her bespoke of years to come filled with love and laughter. She could hardly wait. But for now...

"You should have seen his face!" Damien chuckled from his seat at the table, where he consumed a trencher full of stewed venison. "Judas, you would think there was a horde of armed knights attacking us. Not tiny spiders."

"They were not tiny," Ronar said. "And quite hairy, if I recall."

The friar approached, the Good Book in his hands. "We all have our weaknesses, Ronar. Even mighty knights."

Alexia stood on her tiptoes and kissed Ronar's cheek. "Though I taunt you, Sir Knight, I am quite proud of you, withal. For you realized 'twas but an attack of the enemy and did away with them by the power of Christ."

Ronar rubbed his chin. "I fear I am much better in physical battle than spiritual."

The friar lowered into a cushioned chair and opened the Bible. "Like any battle skill, it must be honed, my son. I make no doubt you are a fast student in this regard."

Ronar nodded. "I pray you are right."

Damien finished his meal and moved to stand behind Seraphina, who sat on the couch before the fire. Crossing arms over his mighty chest, he stared into the flames.

"Pray tell, Damien." Alexia cocked her head. "Have you yet seen enough of God's power to believe He exists and is with us?"

He grunted. "What I have seen I cannot explain, my lady. I await further evidence."

Seraphina stared up at him. "As stubborn as you are powerful, Sir Damien."

"I do not gainsay it, mistress." He gave her a rare smile.

The friar waved a hand in his direction. "Never fear. Even doubting Thomas came around eventually." He gazed up at them all. "But to another point, these spiders…I believe the evil in the castle grows."

"I agree." Alexia pulled from Ronar and placed hands on her hips. "It grows thick and heavy, and more powerful each time we visit. But why?"

"'Tis a warlock." Seraphina glanced over them, eyes burning with fear.

"At Luxley?" Alexia asked. "How do you know?"

"I do not." She flattened her lips and hugged herself. "And yet I do."

"Makes sense." The friar ran fingers over the pages of the Bible. "Only an emissary of Satan could do such vile works."

Alexia shuddered. To think such an evil man lived within the walls of her home. And she did not know! Yet she had been sensing him for a long while now. "His power grows, then."

"Aye." Ronar walked to pour himself a drink. "And no doubt Sir Walter consorts with him."

Damien raised a brow. "'Twould explain why we cannot get the man to sign his confession."

"Ah, Sir Damien." The friar chuckled. "You believe in warlocks, but not in God Himself?"

"I believe in good and evil, good friar."

"You call me good, sir. There is none good without Christ."

Damien snorted.

Alexia turned to stare at the fire, her resolve rising. "Wherefore all this pother over a warlock? God's power is far greater, as we have already proven."

"Aye, my dear," the friar said, "but 'tis our human vessels which are weak, our faith which falters." He flipped a few pages in the Bible. "Put on the whole armour of God that ye may be able to stand against the wiles of the devil. For we wrestle not against flesh and blood, but against principalities, against powers, against the rulers of the darkness of this world, against spiritual wickedness in high places." He looked up. "This kind of battle takes much prayer and fasting."

"Then that is what we shall do." Alexia faced them. "What else do you see, Seraphina?"

Ronar returned with two mugs and handed one to Alexia. She took a sip of the fresh water, watching her maid close her eyes for a moment as if searching for an answer.

"No more about this warlock, but about your sister." She opened her eyes, directing them to Alexia.

"Prithee, what?" Moving toward Seraphina, Alexia knelt before her, searching her eyes.

"There has been betrayal. Great betrayal."

Alexia's heart tightened. "What do you mean?"

Damien slid onto the seat beside Seraphina and took her hand.

"The bishop knows where they are," she said, voice quivering. "He sends his soldiers there even now, along with Sir Walter's."

Alexia gripped the lady's other hand. "Where? Where are they?"

"I do not know, my lady. I'm sorry." A tear slid down her cheek, and she glanced at Damien.

"Is this the evil you spoke of before? The one that follows them?" Alexia asked.

Seraphina looked away, her breath coming fast. "Nay. The evil still lurks nearby."

Ronar put a hand on Alexia's shoulder. "Jarin will protect her."

Doing her best to force down her rising fear, Alexia stood and faced him. "Even Jarin the Just cannot fight such evil forces."

"Come, child." The friar rose and set down the Holy Book. "Let us not speak without faith. God can rout any army. But He waits on His faithful to pray." He gestured for them all to come closer. "Let us bow before Him and make our petitions."

Nodding, Alexia took Ronar's hand on one side and Seraphina's on the other, and they formed a circle with the friar, whilst Damien stood off to the side. Alexia would have to increase her prayers for the doubting knight. But for now, she had more important battles to wage.

CHAPTER TWENTY-EIGHT

Jarin rode the horses fast and hard throughout the night, unsure whether 'twas his anger at Quinn, shock at Lady Cristiana's kindness, or fear of the bishop's army that made him long to escape and leave everything behind.

Even leave the lady herself, for every moment he spent with her, he lost all sense and reason. She enchanted him, mesmerized him, luring him closer and closer like a flopping fish hooked on a line, unable to free himself, only in the end, to find himself hopelessly tangled in her charms. He could not allow that to happen.

She'd rode beside him all night, with the babe in her arms, nary a complaint spilling from her lips. Now, as the hint of dawn teased the horizon, he glanced her way and guilt weighed on him for the exhaustion lining her lovely features. Thankfully, Thebe was asleep in her arms—arms that no doubt ached from holding the child.

Turning in his saddle, he glanced behind them. No sign of soldiers. No sign of much of anything all night save owls and a fox that had glared at them from the brush. He must find a place to stop and rest, at least for a short while. Mayhap he could forage for some fruit or nuts for them to eat. Regardless, the sooner they were on their way, the better, for the bishop's soldiers now had a scent and a trail to follow.

The lady glanced his way, and her gentle smile reached up to her sleepy eyes, dazzling him. And, against his will, he found everything within him wanting to protect and cherish this precious woman all his days. "I will find a place to rest anon, my lady."

"Thank you," she whispered ere opening her eyes wider and glancing over the countryside. Morning mist hovered over the green rolling hills, sparkling in the rising sun. The scent of horse flesh, earth, and lilacs showered over Jarin, awakening his senses to a new day, even as exhaustion tugged upon his eyes. He would have to find sleep later. For now, he must seek safety above all else.

Safety. He had thought Quinn's home would be such. His jaw tightened. He couldn't have been more wrong. Bosh! What a fool he'd been to trust him, to believe he was the same generous lad he'd once known. Life had been cruel to Quinn. Nay! Quinn's choices had caused the sad predicament in which he found himself. His gambling, drinking, and whoring had robbed him of his wealth, respect, and oddly...his happiness. Vak! His philandering had nearly cost him his life.

Save for Lady Cristiana D'Clere.

But hadn't that been their troth to each other in that dark wine cellar at Tegimen Abbey—that they would spend their lives seeking out the pleasure of coin, drink, and women, and ne'er allow themselves to be burdened with the responsibilities of life or the rules of an overbearing God? Alas, Quinn had done just that. But where had it gotten him?

Something to ponder later, for Thebe woke up, stretched in Cristiana's arms and smiled brightly when she spotted Jarin.

And every hard thing within him melted.

Cursing himself, he averted his gaze and spotted a copse of trees up ahead where they could hide. 'Twas difficult enough to resist the allure of Lady Cristiana, but must he also battle the innocent admiration of the most adorable little girl he'd ever met?

Cristiana handed the best part of the single nectarine Jarin had found on the ground to Thebe, whilst she did her best to nibble on the bruised part. 'Twas all they had, for no further fruit grew on the tree. Indeed, it appeared withered and diseased.

Jarin had tucked them safely within a thicket of trees and brush while he went off in search of water. She hated that she felt lost and alone without him nearby. She hated her utter and complete dependence on him. More than either of those, she hated the way her insides quivered at the mere sight of him.

Weak fool. Why couldn't she be more like her sister?

Finishing the foul fruit, she withdrew the Spear from her pocket, lifted her skirts, and proceeded to bind it tightly around her thigh once again. Thebe was engaged following an ant trail, or no doubt the girl would assail Cristiana with a dozen questions about what she was doing. Cristiana tightened the binding and pressed a finger over the precious relic. It had saved them more than once. Them, *not* her. For where had its power been when Quinn was about to ravish her? If Sir Jarin had not burst in at that moment, would the Spear have protected her? Or mayhap, she was not worthy of its protection. Mayhap her job was to use it to help others and then return it to her sister, who would make better use of its power.

Settling her skirts back down around her ankles, she opened her small pack and pulled out a comb. "Come, Thebe, allow me to rid your hair of those tangles."

The little girl lifted bright blue eyes to Cristiana, holding up her finger where an ant circled, seeking an escape. Her giggle seemed to swipe away all the terror of their predicament, if only for a second.

"He tickles, Cristi!"

Cristiana smiled. "Do put him down to join his friends. We wouldn't want him to get lost."

Frowning, the little girl did as she was told, then scooted closer to Cristiana and turned her back to her. "Like we are? I still hungry."

Sorrow stole the joy of the moment. "Nay. We are not lost. We will soon be home." She began combing Thebe's hair.

"My home?"

"Your new home, darling." Cristiana leaned down to kiss her cheek then resumed her combing.

"Ouch!" Thebe jerked forward, her hand flying to her head.

"I'm sorry." Cristiana sighed. "Come. I'll be gentler." How the little girl's hair could become such a mass of tangles in one day was beyond her.

The rustling of leaves sounded, followed by footsteps, spiking alarm through Cristiana that instantly softened when Sir Jarin's tall figure appeared, bearing a pouch of water, a handful of some sort of treasure, and a smile on his face that would suffocate her if she allowed it.

She wouldn't. She continued combing Thebe's hair, but the little girl shot to her feet and darted toward the knight, who once again knelt to take her in his arms. He squeezed her tight, the look on his face—one of pure joy—warmed everything within Cristiana. But then his expression changed, and something akin to sorrow followed by frustration trampled his features ere he nudged the girl back and stood. His eyes grazed over Cristiana, a myriad of unidentifiable emotions swirling within them. Approaching, he handed her the pouch of water and assisted her to her feet.

"'Tis all I could find." He opened his hand to reveal a dozen or so walnuts, already removed from their shells.

"Take what you want, Sir Jarin, and give the rest to Thebe." Cristiana knelt to give the girl water.

"You need your strength as well, my lady, if you are to care for her." He lowered to sit upon a fallen tree and plopped a nut into his mouth ere handing one to Thebe.

"I ate a nectarine," Cristiana replied, taking a swig of water.

Thebe sat cross-legged on the dirt beside Jarin and happily consumed the nuts he handed her, the remainder of them, from what Cristiana could see. So, the knight *did* have a tender spot for the child. Against her will, she smiled. Jarin must have noticed for he rose and went to tend their horses. "We should leave posthaste and find a safe place to sleep and food to eat."

Thebe promptly stood and followed him. "Still hungry, Jarn." She clung to his breeches and gazed up at him as if he were a king and could produce a feast with a snap of his fingers.

"Come, Thebe, leave Sir Jarin alone." Cristiana beckoned to the girl, but she was having none of it. And despite his odd behavior when he'd held her moments ago, he reached down and gathered the girl in his arms. Giggling, she nestled against him as he brushed curls from her face. "Soon, little one. We will eat again soon." Then setting her down before Cristiana, he tapped her on the nose. "Allow Lady Cristiana to finish combing your hair. A princess must look her best ere she travels."

Beaming from ear to ear and nodding her assent, Thebe sat back down before Cristiana with the obedience of a saint.

Cristiana frowned, lowered to her knees, and began combing the girl's hair again. If Sir Jarin intended to leave them after he brought them to Luxley, *or worse*, ignore them once his mission was completed, 'twould not do for Thebe to become so attached. Why, the girl gazed at him as if he were her father! And Cristiana did not wish to see the dear child's heart broken.

Nor did she wish to see her own suffer such a fate.

Thus, she did her best to ignore Sir Jarin as he poured water for the horses to drink and readied them to continue the journey.

Once back on the trail, she continued in her attempts to not stare at the knight, to not admire the way he sat tall in his saddle, his hand ready on the pommel of his sword, alert eyes scanning their surroundings, ear cocked for any sound of danger. 'Twas all for her and Thebe's protection, for he was not the one the bishop and Sir Walter sought. No doubt he had not expected such trouble when he agreed to the mission. Then why did he not abandon her like everyone else in her life had done?

They urged the horses into a gallop, which they maintained for most of the morning ere alternating betwixt a trot and walk. Sir Jarin made no attempt at conversation, merely glanced occasionally at Cristiana and Thebe, offering a glimmer of a smile and an unreadable emotion on his face.

Cristiana fought the exhaustion threatening to topple her from the horse as the world flew past in a blur of greens, blues, and browns, blasting her with wind tainted with the scents of fresh grass, wildflowers, and horseflesh. When she dared to close her eyes for a mere moment, the sun dappled light over her eyelids as it rose to its crest and enveloped her in a blanket of warmth before it began to sink again. Now, as it sat a hand's breath over the western horizon, Cristiana drew a deep breath and shook her head in an effort to keep awake.

"There's a village up ahead. We will stop there for the night, my lady." Jarin's tone was one of deep concern, and it caused her to open her eyes fully and glance his way.

He studied her. "I grant you, I have never met a woman as strong as you, nor one who did not perforce shower me with idle chatter or complaints, the latter of which you have every right."

A compliment? Indeed, it took Cristiana aback for a moment. "I dare not ask what type of ladies you normally associate with." Her tone was mocking, defying the warmth his words spread throughout her.

"None like you, I assure you." He directed his gaze forward again.

Smoke rose from a small cluster of buildings up ahead as they slowed their horses to a walk.

"Do you believe the bishop's men have lost our trail?"

"I can only hope, my lady."

"Yet you have seen no hint of them this day."

"Nay." He faced her again. "You have the Spear?"

"Aye. Bound to my leg once again."

He glanced at Thebe, asleep in Cristiana's arms. "What do you make of the old woman?"

The aged lady who had appeared and disappeared at will, healed Thebe's finger, and brought back the Spear to Cristiana? How the relic had come into her possession, Cristiana could not fathom. "Thebe said she was an angel."

Jarin snorted. "Thebe is two years old. Mere fantasies of a child."

His lack of faith irked her sorely. "It may surprise you to know, Sir Jarin, that innocent children oft see things in the Spirit ere the world infects them with its logic and deflates their hope."

He rubbed the back of his neck. "But an angel? Bosh, I'd sooner believe she was one of Quinn's spies."

"Would Quinn give me back the Spear if he knew the power it possessed?" Nor would a mere servant speak as the woman had. *The power lives within you, child. Where God is. Not in a piece of metal*, she had said with such assurance and love, Cristiana had no alternative but to believe she was not from this world. Still, the message niggled her, poking and prodding her weak faith, making her uncomfortable even now as she pondered it.

They rode on, nearing the village. Though the light from the sun was still bright, not a single person was in sight, no farmers working in the fields, no wagons carrying goods into and out of the village, no town criers could be heard, no laborers or travelers moving about.

Something was amiss.

Jarin grabbed the reins of Cristiana's horse and halted both animals.

"Pray, what is it?" she asked.

Jarin's bearded jaw stiffened as he scanned their surroundings. "'Tis the smell of death."

CHAPTER TWENTY-NINE

Cedric flung his black robe behind him and dismounted his steed, Demon. The horse panted, foam cresting around his mouth from the mad pace Cedric had maintained all day. He patted the animal's neck and led him to the stream trickling past the narrow road.

"Drink, my vile one. Rest awhile, but not for long."

Nay, not for long. For Cedric could smell Lady Cristiana's innocence polluting the air like an insidious disease. The odor nauseated him, but it meant they were not far. His elixir and a still pond had shown him they were in a manor house. He'd sent his ravens to discover which one.

Kneeling, he cupped water to his mouth, then wiped his chin with his sleeve. Devil's worts! By the time the birds had returned and led him to Savoy Manor, Jarin and the lady were gone. Just left, that nimbycock Lord Quinn had said. 'Twas the last thing he'd said, for Cedric had cast a spell upon him which stole his voice. He smiled at the memory of the man holding his throat and attempting to speak, but no sound emerged.

Why had Cedric done it? Merely for the enjoyment, for he found this current quest rather dull and tedious.

Demon finished drinking, shook his head, and walked to a spot to eat some grass. Meanwhile, Cedric examined the creek for any areas of still water in which he could spread his elixir. He found naught but a bubbling happy creek, which only increased his anger.

There had been one moment of amusement in the otherwise tiresome chase. The last time he'd stared into the water in search of Lady Cristiana, he'd seen the bishop and his father's men at Savoy Manor questioning that dolt Lord Quinn. When the man had been unable to answer them, an old woman appeared and sent them down the road in the opposite direction from where Sir Jarin and Lady Cristiana had gone. Pribbling puttocks! To think these were trained soldiers!

Cedric uttered a foul curse and laughed. No matter. He would be the one to capture the loathsome knight and his fair lady. He would be the one to bring them back to Drago and Father. He would be the one to win his master's favor and another rodent tongue to add to his badge.

Sir Jarin the Dust—as Cedric liked to call him—had ridden the lady and child all night and all day. Surely his chivalry would not allow him to continue but would force him to seek out shelter and food for his weaker travelers. "Chivalry, pish!" A waste of time if you asked him.

Rising, he walked to Demon and drew his wolf pouch from his pack. He untied it and peered inside, reaching in for a few specks of dark dust. He could not afford to waste it, but two would do nicely.

Flinging them into the air, he uttered the ancient words Drago had taught him. The specks of dust drifted down, slowly growing and gyrating, twisting and turning, taking shape and form and substance. By the time they hit the dirt, two black wolves stared at Cedric, baring sharp fangs and growling with an anger he knew not from whence it originated. No doubt the dark pit from which they came.

"Go, my pets! Go find Jarin the Dust and his lady. But do them no harm. Leave that to me."

Sir Jarin was right about one thing. The stench of death and decay clung to the deserted village like mold on a damp stone. 'Twas not entirely deserted, for as they rode through the front gate and down the center of town, eyes appeared in windows behind parted curtains, and the cries of more than one babe rang through the air like a dismal ballad. Aside from that, the only other sign of life was the smoke curling from chimneys and the snort of a large pig wallowing in the mud.

"What happened here?" Cristiana lowered her shoulders beneath the thick weight of despair in the air.

"Naught good, I assure you." Jarin shifted in his saddle and halted his horse before a two-story brick building announcing itself with a sign that said *Inn*. Still, no stable hand sped out to tend their horses, no laughter or music hailed from within. No savory scents of roasted meat wafted on the breeze, but rather the smell of rot and disease.

"We should leave." He jerked the reins to lead his horse away.

"Nay. I cannot go on another moment," Cristiana said. And 'twas true. If she didn't get some food and rest soon, she'd grow weak and ill. As would Thebe. She glanced down at the sleeping babe, her long lashes spread over her chubby cheeks and a look of complete trust on her face. Cristiana would ne'er betray that trust. She would ne'er abandon this child as she herself had been abandoned.

Jarin frowned, his jaw stiffening as he glanced from her back to the inn. "I fear 'tis the plague, my lady. If so, we should quit this place at once."

Mayhap he was right. Cristiana could not deny she had the same thought. Yet even as she pondered it, the Spear seemed to warm on her thigh. Was she imagining it? Or was it—and the God behind it—reminding her of its power? "We have the Spear," she announced with more authority than she felt.

Jarin's eyes narrowed. "Does the holy relic also protect from foolishness?"

She smiled. "Has it not kept fools like us safe thus far?"

Humor appeared in his eyes as he shook his head. "Indeed. But I've no doubt even God has His limits." He dismounted. "Regardless, I will discover what ails these people and search out some food. Stay here."

No sooner had Jarin ascended the first step of the inn than a man slipped out the front door, holding up a hand to halt the knight, whilst he glanced back and forth up the muddy street.

"Good day sire. Be fellow or friend, I bid you caution." His voice emerged scratchy and breathless, and only then did Cristiana note the sores pustulating on his neck and face and how his clothes hung on him as if they were too large for his emaciated frame. Thin, light-colored hair hung to his ears and framed cheeks that sunk into his face as if afraid to meet the light. He could be no older than forty, but he looked as near to death as any aged man.

"I urge you, good sire, mount your horse and leave this place at once."

"What ails you, sir?" Cristiana asked from her horse, unable to dismount with Thebe in her arms.

"'Tis the plague, mistress." The man shuddered. "Already killed five. Prithee, leave ere it infects you as well."

Jarin slowly backed away from the man and swung about, apparently with every intention of obeying his advice.

"Here, take Thebe," Cristiana ordered.

"Why? We're leaving." Jarin was about to brush past her to mount his horse when she all but dropped the babe in his arms, giving him no choice but to cling to the girl.

Swinging her leg over the saddle, she slid down the other side, nearly falling, but managed to maintain her dignity.

"My lady." Jarin leapt in her path. "We are but a day's travel from Luxley. You risk too much. What of Thebe?"

The man coughed and leaned on the side of the door for support. "Prithee, leave at once. There is naught but death here."

Hesitating, Cristiana brushed a lock of Thebe's hair from her face and lifted her gaze to Jarin's. Unusual fear shouted from his brown eyes. "People are dying, Sir Jarin. 'Tis within my power to possibly cure them. How can I leave?"

He huffed, looked away for a moment, then back at her, shaking his head. "You would risk us all?"

Reaching up, she dared to run fingers over his jaw in an intimate gesture that surprised even her. "The Spear protects us. We must have faith."

One side of his lips quirked. "I don't suppose I can stop you, save for tying you and the child up and making you my prisoners." He released a heavy sigh, still blocking her path. "Which I may still do, withal."

She attempted to push past him, but 'twas like trying to shove aside a brick wall. "By all means, Sir Jarin, if it pleases you to do so. Only allow me to save lives whilst you decide."

To her delight, and surprise, he stepped aside, though he uttered a growl that followed her as she approached the man.

The innkeeper shrank back and held up a hand to stop her. She took that hand in hers, amazed at how thin and cold it was. Sores scratched and dampened her palms, causing bile to rise in her throat. Forcing it down, she focused on his eyes, bloodshot and yellow. "Do you wish to be healed, sir?"

Confusion furrowed his sweaty brow. "Aye, mistress, but what can ye…" He halted to catch his breath.

The Spear warmed her thigh. Cristiana closed her eyes, fighting both exhaustion and fear, fear that this time the Spear wouldn't work, fear that this time her foolishness would cause all their deaths. "Holy Father, in the name of your Christ and the power of His Blood on the Spear, I command all sickness to depart from this man and his full health to return."

Keeping her eyes shut, she felt the warmth of the Spear travel up her leg, into her belly, through her chest, and down her arm, spreading into the man's hand.

He uttered a faint squeal of surprise as Cristiana kept her grip firm, allowing the healing power to fully penetrate his body. Sores withered and disappeared beneath her touch as warmth returned to his flesh.

"Holy Moses!" the man exclaimed, his voice strong and full of life.

Cristiana opened her eyes to see shock and joy beaming from features no longer tainted by death, skin no longer marred by disease.

"How?" Eyes, clear and bright searched hers. "How?" He fell to his knees, took her hands in his and kissed them over and over.

"The Lord has healed you, sir, not me. Get up."

Rising, he dashed into the street, raising his hands to heaven. "I am healed! I am healed!"

Cristiana smiled, her gaze meeting Jarin's and finding therein both astonishment and admiration. And something else, something permanent and deep. She could bask in that look forever, but Thebe stirred and opened her eyes, drawing Jarin's gaze to her.

The man's shouting did more than wake Thebe. It drew citizens from their homes, at least those who could walk. Out from their hovels they staggered like the blind seeing their first speck of light. A few of them crawled, some clung to each other for support. Women bore feverish children in their arms.

Sorrow threatened to crush Cristiana to the mud at the sight of so many, of so much misery. The crowd circled the man, who continued rejoicing and pointing in Cristiana's direction. Finally, pushing past them, he darted toward her.

"Can ye save them, mistress? Can ye save them all?" His gaze darted over Cristiana's shoulder to the inn. "And my family."

Jarin strode forward. "First the lady and child need food and water. We have traveled a long way."

"Cristi!" Thebe reached for her, and she took her in her arms.

"Of course!" the man exclaimed. "You are welcome. Come in, come in." He started through the door, beckoning them to follow.

Save for a few lanterns, shadows consumed the main room of the inn where empty tables and chairs were strewn about, littered with mugs and fly-infested plates. Barrels and sacks filled the corners whilst dark chandeliers hung lifeless from the rafters. The smell of dust, mold, and stale spirits pinched her nose from a long bar covered with crusty food and half-full mugs as if the plague had caught them all off guard. A dog roused from his sleep on the cold hearth and whimpered.

"Prithee, have a seat." The innkeeper hurried toward the back.

She set Thebe down on a chair. "Stay here with Jarn, little one. I'll return anon."

"My tummy growls." Thebe rubbed her eyes.

"Aye, dear. You will eat soon." Cristiana faced Jarin. "Will you tend to her for me?"

Jarin crossed arms over his chest. "I beseech you, my lady, wait until you partake of nourishment and regain your strength."

"How can I eat when so many suffer?" Even as she said the words, her head grew light, and a sound akin to a bear growling emanated from her stomach. "What if some should die whilst I am thinking only of myself."

"How can you heal if you fall ill or faint?" He grabbed her arm.

"When that happens, I will eat."

Shaking his head, he released her.

Ere she changed her mind, she pushed open the front door and stepped from the porch to a scene that made her long to run back inside, to hide from such human misery and torment, to pretend that this world could never be this cruel.

Covering the street before her like scabs on putrefied flesh were at least one hundred people, some barely standing, others sitting, a few lying in the mud. All in various stages of a plague that could end in death…*would* end in death…

If Cristiana didn't do something.

She glanced down at the mark of the Spear on her wrist. 'Twas all up to her and the Spear. And that frightened her most of all.

CHAPTER THIRTY

After ensuring Thebe had consumed her fill of the bread, cheese, and plums the innkeeper had given them, Jarin broke off a piece of bread, grabbed Thebe, and headed outside. There, he found what he'd seen so clearly from glances out the open window—Lady Cristiana passing through the massive crowd of diseased and dying people. Not just passing, stopping at each person, speaking to them in kind tones ere laying her hands on them and praying. Joyful shouts and cries of praise followed her from those whose bodies were restored to health. The more people she healed, the more the crowd pressed in, arms and hands reaching for her, desperate for her touch.

"Cristi!" The child reached out from Jarin's arms as he stood on the porch, but he clung to her tightly, not wanting her anywhere near whate'er disease plagued these poor people.

The woman never failed to astound him. Sleep deprived and starving, she put the needs of complete strangers ahead of her own. Not only that, she risked getting the same disease, for who knew how long the power of the Spear would last?

He watched, longing to stop her and give her the bread, but knowing she would not be put off. Bosh! She was as pigheaded as she was kindhearted. Still, she'd barely made it through twenty of the sick when she halted and reached up to touch her forehead, swaying on her feet.

Enough! Setting Thebe down in a chair on the porch—with an order for her to remain—he made his way toward Cristiana, nudging people aside, trying to avoid touching their open sores. He found the lady lying on the dirt, face pale and breath heaving. Pushing away the people, who continued to grope her with withered hands, he swept her in his arms and carried her back to the porch where he set her down in a chair.

The crowd followed.

"Back! Give her room!" he shouted from the top of the stairs, gripping the pommel of his blade, willing to use it if need be.

Thebe crawled into Cristiana's lap.

The mob halted, a mass of grimy rags, bones, and bloody sores. A stench that assaulted his nose swamped him until he could hardly breath.

"Allow her to eat, and I will permit one at a time to see her."

This seemed to appease them for the time being. Turning, Jarin kneeled before Cristiana and handed her the bread. She took it, offering him a slight smile. "I must have fainted."

"Cristi sick?" Thebe snuggled against her.

"Aye, but she will get well," Jarin answered. "Because she's going to eat and rest, aren't you, my lady?" He raised a brow.

To which she sighed, her gaze roving over the throng of death gathered before the inn. Obligingly she bit into the bread and chewed.

"That's it, my lady." Jarin, still stooped before her, studied this enigma before him—a mixture of heavenly angel, timid lamb, and stubborn mule. He wanted to lock her up for her own protection, this sweet woman who defied all sense, who both warmed and tore at his heart, who infuriated as well as enchanted him. Shadows hung beneath chestnut-colored eyes that still sparkled with life and love, despite her exhaustion. Even the dirt smudging her face could not hide the creamy smoothness. Wisps of tawny hair danced around her face in the breeze, making him long to reach up and brush one aside.

Wrapping an arm around Thebe, she drew her close while she continued eating the bread. The innkeeper emerged with a tankard of wine and handed it to Jarin. "All we 'ave, sire. We fear the water's been tainted."

"Thank you." Jarin lifted it to her lips, and she gulped it down.

The innkeeper remained, shifting from foot to foot. "When the lady regains 'er strength, sire, me wife an' babe are upstairs, as ill as any."

Cristiana glanced up at him and smiled. "I must beg your patience and plead fatigue, sir. But I will see to them soon."

He nodded.

Finishing her bread, Cristiana handed Thebe to Jarin. "Sit with Jarn, dear one. I must help these people." Then with a nod toward him, she drew a deep breath and indicated she was ready.

One by one, the ill mounted the steps of the inn, some walking on their own, some carried by others, all in various stages of the horrid disease. Jarin watched with bewilderment as Lady Cristiana addressed each one as if they were long lost friends ere she healed them with a touch and a word. The day waned into evening, the sun relinquishing its reign to the moon.

And still they came.

The innkeeper lit torches and lanterns, casting flickering golden light over the porch and out into the street. Jarin had long since released Thebe to run in front of the inn with several of the children her age who had been healed, dancing, and singing, and chasing each other as children do. He doubted she'd had much exposure to other children, and her innocent laughter did much to put Jarin at ease, at least for the moment, at least until he remembered they were being chased by several well-trained soldiers.

And they were wasting precious time in this place.

How long before news of these miraculous healings reached other villages and drew the interest of their pursuers? Not long, he imagined. Hence, they mustn't stay more than this night.

A night that was nearly half over by the time the lady had healed all who'd come to her. Healed! Forsooth, the Spear must truly bear the blood of Christ. He'd seen too much to deny it. Or to deny that Christ, the Son of God, cared for people, dare he say, even loved them, even peasants such as these. Bidding the crowd—which continued to celebrate through the streets with shouts, music, and laughter—good eve, Sir Jarin insisted Cristiana retire for the night.

But when the innkeeper's worried face appeared before the lady, she pressed a hand on his. "Show me to your wife and babe."

One arm carrying Thebe, one arm wrapped around Cristiana's waist, Jarin assisted the weak lady up the stairs, down a hall, and into a chamber at the far end. A single candle sitting upon a table beside the bed provided the only light in a room so clouded with misery, it nearly choked him. The still form of a woman lay on the bed, a babe swaddled in her arms.

Jarin halted in the doorway. Blood raced through his veins, gathering up memories and pain from a time long ago and forcing them into his thoughts, blurring his vision.

The innkeeper gazed upon them with both fear and love ere he faced Cristiana. "She 'asn't eaten for days, mistress. 'Ad a fever this morn, both of them."

Kneeling beside the bed, Cristiana laid one hand on the babe and one on the lady's arm. Immediately, she drew back and lowered her head, her breathing heightened.

"Alas, what is it?"

Cristiana glanced up at the man, tears streaming down her cheeks. "I'm sorry, good sir, but they are both dead."

Cristiana hadn't slept in nearly two days, and still sleep outran her every attempt to catch it. 'Twas no wonder, really. With all she'd witnessed that day. Both the delight of watching people set free from the bondage of death, and then the despair of watching the innkeeper crumble into a pile of agony from which she doubted he'd ever recover. Shock, disbelief, and then desperation had claimed his features ere he demanded she pray for them. Could she not raise them from the dead with whate'er power she possessed? He had begged.

So, she had prayed, but to no avail. Mother and child had already passed into eternity and would not be called back.

Yet 'twas Sir Jarin's reaction that had Cristiana most baffled. No sooner had she pronounced the mother and babe dead than he'd dashed from the chamber and flew down the stairs. At first she'd thought he was protecting Thebe from the sight of a dead child, but he remained distant, distracted, and tormented long after she'd descended to the main room of the inn.

Now he sat before the crackling fire, flipping a coin through his fingers and staring at the flames as if he wished to toss himself into them.

Refusing to leave his family's side, the innkeeper remained above, though his sobs poured down the stairs in a river of misery, a portent of doom and gloom that erased the joy and victory of earlier in the day. Each wail sent a shiver of guilt over Cristiana that she'd not gotten to the woman soon enough, that she'd not been able to help them at all.

Thankfully, Thebe had fallen asleep before the fire, wrapped in blankets Cristiana had found in one of the chambers above, a chamber the child refused to sleep in without Sir Jarin. Hence the reason she was curled up on the hard floor, thumb in her mouth, beside the knight. Still, she slept peacefully, for which Cristiana was grateful.

Grabbing a blanket for herself, she rose and handed one to Sir Jarin, but he waved her off.

"Nay. Thank you, my lady. Prithee, lie down with the babe and rest. We must needs leave first thing in the morning." He said all this without looking her way, his jaw tight, and his tone devoid of emotion.

"I will rest when you rest, Sir Jarin." Cristiana lowered to sit on the warm stones of the hearth and glanced up at him. "When you tell me what has you in such ill humor."

The fire crackled and spit behind her, its flames reflecting in his brown eyes as he stared at it. Moments passed. He swallowed, sighed, and then flattened his lips.

Cristiana dared intrude on his thoughts. "Was it the sight of the dead child?"

He glanced her way, continuing to flip the coin between his fingers. Finally, he caught it and slid it inside his pocket ere leaning forward, arms crossed on his knees and staring at the dirty floor. "Merely bad memories, my lady. Naught to concern you."

"But it *does* concern me, Sir Jarin. If you'll allow, we are friends, and what saddens you, also saddens me."

He rubbed his eyes, glanced at her, and sighed once again. "I had a sister once."

Cristiana waited, already knowing what was coming.

"She died in my arms. Not yet a day old."

Sorrow clamped hard on Cristiana's heart, squeezing the lifeblood from it. She said naught, merely allowed him to continue.

He looked her way, his eyes moist and full of agony. "My mother died ere I arrived home. In childbirth, the midwife said. She handed me my sister. So tiny…" He looked back at the fire. "So innocent, gasping for a breath, any breath that would keep her among the living. I held her tight, longing to breathe my life into her, would have given her my last breath, if I could." He dropped his head into his hands. "But her whimpers soon ceased, her tiny breaths halted, and she grew cold and stiff."

"I'm so sorry, Jarin." Cristiana longed to reach out to him, to comfort him in some way, but she sensed an anger rising in him that kept her at bay. "And your father? Where was he?"

"Dead." His tone had indeed turned bitter. He lifted his head. "Roving outlaws attacked our village while I was at Tegimen Abbey. My father was run through with the sword."

Cristiana's eyes flooded with tears.

"'Tis why I was called from the abbey to return home. To bury him and comfort my mother."

"How old were you?"

"Sixteen. The dirt on my father's grave was still fresh when Mother started her pains. Early, they said. Far too early. 'Twas the agony of losing my father which caused it."

Cristiana looked down, swiping tears from her face. "So you were abandoned, as was I."

The fire crackled as wind whooshed past shutters now closed for the night.

"I returned to the abbey, for I knew not where else to go. But things were different." He picked up a twig and tossed it into the fire. "The God I once believed in had proven Himself untrustworthy." He fisted his hands. "My father was a man of faith! He revered the church and faithfully tithed his earnings in its support! If God would not protect those who dedicated their lives to Him, then what good did it do to follow Him at all?"

"So you left the abbey."

"Aye, without saying a word. Since then, I've seen many good people die and many evil people succeed. This proves that either God distances Himself from the affairs of men, or He is not worthy of following."

Now Cristiana understood. She understood this man's anger toward God, his quick dismissal of anything good that might come from Him. His yearning to live a full, unrestricted life, taunting death at every turn, and ultimately his terror at the idea of tying himself to a woman and child, of loving anyone enough to put his heart at risk again.

Overcome with despair for this wonderful man, Cristiana allowed the silence to stretch between them. For what could she say to make any of this aright? After several moments, she inched closer to him and reached out for his hand.

He gave it to her, enfolding hers within his warmth.

Thebe's light snoring joined with the hiss and snap of the fire, and creak of aged floor timbers, providing the only sounds in the room. Thankfully the innkeeper's wailing had ceased.

"Who is to understand God's ways?" she finally said. "We are but to trust." She cringed at her own words, for had she abided by them herself? Hadn't she thought God had abandoned her as well? If not for the Spear, would He give her a second thought?

"*You* trust Him, my lady. I will trust in myself." He lifted her hand and placed a kiss upon it. "Now, will you rest?" He gave her a look of censure.

Nodding, Cristiana took her blanket and curled up beside Thebe, her heart and thoughts spinning in confusion and despair at Jarin's sad tale.

Sunlight and screeches of horror woke Cristiana with a start. She pushed from the floor, noting Thebe remained deep in sleep by her side. Rubbing her eyes, she glanced around and spotted Sir Jarin, also asleep, still sitting in the chair in which she'd left him.

Cries of sorrow penetrated the gray mist seeping in through the shutter slats of the windows. Tossing aside the blanket, and ensuring it remained around Thebe, Cristiana rose and moved to look outside.

Horror jolted through her.

A group of villagers assembled before the inn, several of whom she recognized from the day before as having been healed.

Only now, the same sores once again covered their bodies. *How?* Grabbing her skirts, she flung open the door and stepped onto the porch, blinking her eyes and hoping 'twas but a nightmare.

"She's a witch!" one of them shouted.

"Our illness has returned! What devilment is this?"

"Burn her! Burn her! Burn her!"

CHAPTER THIRTY-ONE

Cristiana's shriek brought Jarin instantly to his feet, blade drawn faster than he could blink. By the time his eyes focused, he saw Thebe still sleeping by the hearth, but Cristiana was nowhere in sight. She screamed again, and he darted for the open door to find her standing on the front porch, an angry mob of villagers hobbling toward her, knives and ropes in their hands.

"Halt at once if you wish to live!" Jarin moved to stand before her, brandishing his sword before him.

They stopped, eyeing him with disdain.

'Twas then that he noticed the sores had returned on their skin, along with the stench and shadow of death that hovered over them like a relentless storm from hell.

"Thank you," Cristiana breathed out.

"What goes on here?" He rubbed his eyes.

"She's a witch!" one of the ailing people shouted. "She must be burned!"

A witch? Jarin wondered if he was still asleep and a nightmare had invaded his thoughts.

Footsteps behind him swung him about, knife plucked from his belt toward the intruder, whilst he kept his sword forward.

The innkeeper raised his hands, his eyes red and swollen, but no malicious intent resided within them.

"Burn her! Burn her! Burn her!" the crowd chanted, spinning Jarin back around. From beyond the angry throng, other villagers emerged from homes, these in perfect health and approaching the commotion with confused looks on their faces.

The innkeeper brushed past Jarin and perched on the bottom step of the porch. "Silence, I beg ye!" He held up his palms.

Jarin was glad the innkeeper seemed to have some authority in the village, for the throng settled and finally quieted. "Would a witch 'eal you as this lady did?" He pointed at Cristiana.

Mumbles bounced through the mob.

"Curse me for an imposter, but the devil don't make people well. She 'ealed ye once. She can do it again."

Moans were his only response.

Cristiana gazed over the crowd, biting her lip, doubt and fear sparking from her eyes. "What if it simply returns again?" she whispered.

Jarin slowly lowered his blade and squinted into the rising sun. In good sooth, he no longer cared. His mission was clear. He must return Lady Cristiana and the Spear safely to Luxley. Naught else mattered. They were wasting time. He spotted the stone manor house perched atop a hill at the far end of the village.

"Where is the lord of this village?" Jarin asked, sheathing his sword. "Should he not send physicians to help? What of the bailiff, the rector? Is there no one else to aid these people?"

The innkeeper snorted. "Bailiff died, our rector ran off, and Lord Wykeham left long ago when the plague began. In search of help, he said. Though 'twas 'im who likely started it, I make bold to say."

"How is that?"

The innkeeper rubbed his grief-swollen eyes. "'E were a cruel overlord, demanding more taxes than we could pay, confiscating our food. And even our young women, when the pleasure struck 'im."

Cristiana glanced his way and trembled.

"When we rose up against him," a man said from the crowd, one of the healthy ones who had recently approached. "He sent an evil man here. A sorcerer, some say."

Several people crossed themselves and shuddered.

"'E cursed our water. I told ye 'e did!" The innkeeper shook his finger at the mob. "Who among ye drank of the creek last night?"

Those who still bore the plague slowly glanced at each other, affirming the truth with nods and horrified looks.

Those who remained healthy shook their heads. "We drank what's left of our wine," one of them offered.

The innkeeper groaned and his voice broke as he stared at his sick friends. "I told ye to stop drinking it. I told my wife to stop drinking it." He sobbed and lowered his chin.

A woman in rags shuffled forward. "We had naught else to drink."

"I still don't understand." Cristiana looked at Jarin. "The Spear should have healed them."

"Does it heal curses?" he answered. "Mayhap its power does not extend to such evil." He gauged the concern dripping from her sweet expression. How was he going to get this kind woman away from this village of people who needed her?

Cristiana faced the mob. "Do not drink the water from that creek anymore. Or from the wells."

"What are we supposed to drink? We'll die of thirst if this plague don't kill us first."

The moans and shouts of the crowd dimmed into the background as Cristiana felt herself grow numb. Numb with fear, with loss…with uncertainty. She had no idea what to do, how to help these poor souls. In good sooth, the Spear could heal them again, but they needed water. They'd have to leave their homes in search of it, and from what she'd seen on her travels here, 'twould be more than two days journey ere they found enough to support an entire town.

Thebe's tiny hands yanked on her skirt, and she reached down to hoist the precious child in her arms, no longer fearing she'd be burned at the stake. Not with Sir Jarin by her side. The sleepy child nestled against Cristiana's neck and yawned, oblivious to the danger surrounding her.

Oh, what Cristiana wouldn't give to have such peace!

The sun rose above the treetops in the distance, trickling golden streams over green hills and onto fields ripe with barley and oats that needed harvesting. The light brought the village more into focus, not like the hazy blur she'd seen pass by her yesterday. Though small in size, the town appeared to have all one would need—a parish church, complete with steeple and rectory, an apothecary across the way, scrivener, candle-maker, blacksmith and other shops that circled the market square. Behind the inn, she could hear the gush of a creek that flowed from the hills above down to the lake she and Jarin had passed yesterday.

How could these people leave all this behind to start over without the protection of a lord? How could Cristiana leave a cursed stream and lake that would infect any poor traveler happening this way?

She kissed Thebe's forehead and closed her eyes, silently praying for an answer. Moments passed as the crowd moaned, a rooster crowed, and Thebe's breath tickled Cristiana's neck. But then warmth radiated from the Spear, followed by the spark of an idea that ignited within her, *deep* within her, and ever so slowly made its way up to her thoughts—a ridiculous, madcap idea that made no sense at all. None. And surely one which should she voice, would cause the townsfolk to once again wish to burn her alive.

Jarin watched as Cristiana closed her eyes. He knew she was praying to her God for an answer, knew He'd most likely give her one—one that would keep them in this cursed village overlong, one that would get them caught and brought back to Luxley in chains.

One that he could not allow.

When she opened her eyes and glanced his way, the sparkle of delight in them proved him right. She faced the innkeeper.

"This curse you speak of, the order came from the lord of the manor you say?"

"Aye." He rubbed his chin.

"And he no longer lives at the manor home?"

"Nay." His swollen eyes widened. "But we dare not invade it, mistress. For surely he'll return one day."

"I have no intention of invading it, kind sir." She smiled, then glanced over the mob. The ones infected with the plague stared at her, hatred and betrayal in their eyes, whilst fear tightened the expressions of the others.

Jarin kept his hand on the hilt of his blade and his eyes keen, should they of a sudden decide to accost the lady.

"Let us away to the manor home," she stated, chin lifted, though her shaky tone betrayed her. "Sir Jarin, if you could keep them..." She studied the throng yet again.

"I will protect you with my life, my lady, have no doubt." He gently grabbed her arm. "I beseech you, the longer we delay, the greater chance we will be caught."

"I cannot..." She drew a breath. "I *will* not leave them to this curse." Then hoisting Thebe higher in her arms, she proceeded down the steps of the inn and out onto the street.

At first the villagers refused to let her pass, some reaching out for her, desperate once again to be healed.

"Follow me, and you *all* will be healed." Though her voice emerged weak and lacking in conviction, the crowd parted, muttering and moaning, to allow her through.

Keeping his hands ready to grab his weapons, Jarin shook his head and fell in step beside her. "Do you know what you are doing, my lady?"

She cast him a quick glance, not long enough for him to see whether confidence or fear lingered in her eyes. "In truth, no," she whispered back. "But I hope the Spear does."

Jarin raked back his hair and huffed. Bosh! How did it come to this, that their lives depended on hearing from an ancient piece of metal?

Hence, with her gown wrinkled and stained, her hair disheveled, eyes still puffy from sleep, and a babe in her arms, the baffling lady marched down the muddy streets, a mob of both ill and healthy shuffling behind her. To what end, Jarin had no idea.

Worse, he began to fear that if she didn't perform the miracle she promised, the villagers would string both of them up and leave them for dead.

She halted at the open gate of the manor house, its thick stone walls and steepled roof at odds with the waddle and daub homes of most of the villagers. Smokeless chimneys rose from two-story chambers decorated on either side with towers upon which statues of strange otherworldly creatures perched.

Lady Cristiana passed through the gate and crossed what once was a well-manicured garden but was now naught but a mass of weeds and thickets. A large pond, dark and stagnant, marred the landscape to the left of the house like a blistering sore. Making her way in that direction, she circled the manor home where a set of stone steps hugged the structure and led up to a door on the second story. Threads of ivy wove over brick and stone on both sides of the stairway, nearly choking it in green. Here the lady halted and gazed upward as if this particular door, this particular stairway, held all the answers.

The villagers halted behind them, still murmuring threats and doubts.

Jarin leaned to whisper in her ear. "My lady, I beg you, let us quit this place ere danger finds us."

"Jarn." Thebe reached her chubby hand to play with his beard. He took it and kissed her palm, eliciting a giggle. "For the child's sake," he added with urgency.

"I *do* this for her sake."

"Do what, my lady?" Jarin asked, shifting his stance, alert to the enemies behind them.

She blew out a sigh. "I do not know. 'Tis what the Spear wants. Here." She handed him Thebe ere he could protest further. Clutching her tunic, she mounted the stairs.

Nearly at the top, she turned to face them all.

"Egad, she thinks to become our new lord!" one of the villagers shouted as their murmuring increased.

"The lady is mad. Let us away from here!"

"We've no time for this. Heal us, woman, as you did before!"

Some cursed her, others mocked her, whilst others pleaded with her to make them well.

Holding Thebe tight, Jarin attempted to discern the look on Cristiana's face. Fear was there, to be sure. But also a peace he could not describe.

"This is where the sorcerer stood when he cursed the water," she said in a voice loud enough for all to hear. "And this is where the curse will be lifted." Then kneeling on the step, she spread both her hands on the tread beneath her and closed her eyes. With her chest rising and falling beneath heavy breaths, she whispered something he could not make out, something about living water and curses.

Seconds passed. More curses and threats shot at her from the villagers.

But then…

A gust of wind blasted over them, from whence Jarin could not determine, for the morning had been still. It stirred up dust and leaves and fluttered the vines surrounding Cristiana, tossing her hair around her. Still, she remained, kneeling on the step, unmoving—a statue of an angel far too kind for this vile world.

Then…the sound of water bubbling and gurgling filled the air.

The crowd grew silent.

The wind dissipated.

And water emerged from the steps beneath where Cristiana knelt. It started off slowly, a mere trickle, but then grew and grew until it gushed forth, swallowing the stairs in a cascading stream.

It splashed over Jarin's boots. He leapt from its path. Thebe laughed. "River! River!" she squealed.

A hush fell over the mob. They gasped and moved from the torrent as it rushed past them, down a small hill of grass, and splashed into the pond beside the manor home. Fingers of light spread over the black waters, pushing back the darkness, as the fresh stream swept over the pool.

Some of the throng followed the stream. Others remained, gazing back and forth between the stairs and the pond.

Jarin didn't know what to think. *Or* to feel. His thoughts and emotions whirled into a cyclone of unbelief.

Thebe wiggled to get down, and he set her on the ground, trying to hold her arm ere she darted off. Too late. She rushed for the brook and began jumping in the water along with a few other children.

On the stairs, Lady Cristiana rose, a smile on her lips and a light in her eyes that bespoke a wisdom and power he never knew existed. Then it was gone. But her smile remained. Their gazes locked, held by some invisible force...an intimacy he'd never experienced, an affection, a respect.

Unable to restrain himself, he charged into the water and up the stairs. There, he swept her into his arms and carried her to dry ground.

"I don't underst...I don't..." He was sounding like a fool, but shouts of joy and delight from the pond below forbade them any conversation. Splashes and cries followed, drawing their gazes down to several villagers wading into the waters, some cupping the liquid to their mouths, whilst others splashed it all over them. Sunlight glittered over the clean water spreading like a blanket of crystal toward the far end of the pond.

"I'm healed! I'm healed!" A young woman, water dripping from her hair and clothing made her way up the hill to kneel before Cristiana. "The water is cured! Thank you, mistress! Thank you!"

"'Twas not me," Cristiana said. "But the power of God. Rise."

The woman did so but still stared at Cristiana in wonder ere she backed down the hill to the pond again.

"The water, it runs beneath the wall!" an older man shouted, and a group of villagers rushed for the gate and disappeared around the corner.

In good sooth, the man was correct. The pond overflowed, gushed through a hole in the wall, and formed a rivulet down another hill that spilled into the creek running behind the village. Jarin could hardly believe his eyes. In the same way the pond had been cleansed, the creek transformed into a bright, shimmering ribbon of water.

Jarin, Cristiana, and a damp Thebe stood once again before the inn, watching all those who had been ill that morning made well by the fresh water. Only ten of them came back to thank Cristiana. A few bowed before her, but the lady was quick to give all credit to God and send them away.

The innkeeper finally approached, the sorrow of his loss washed from his eyes. At least for the moment. "I don't know what you did, mistress, but I thank ye."

Cristiana smiled. "God removed the curse on your water. Once it was gone, the illness it brought also departed. 'Twas not a plague, you see, but an evil that could only be dealt with by good."

He folded hands over his ragged shirt, his eyes misting. "I ne'er seen the likes of such a thing. May God reward ye, mistress."

Cristiana placed a hand on his arm. "May He reward you, kind sir, with peace and comfort."

Nodding, the man gave a sad smile, and Jarin knew he most likely wondered why God's mercy had not healed his wife and child. Jarin could well understand the sentiment, along with the anger and bitterness it caused. Yet, oddly, no hint of either appeared in the man's eyes. "Indeed, mistress. God be praised."

Confused, Jarin shifted his gaze away. A dark cloud toward the east caught his attention, so at odds with the other white puffs that floated idly across the blue sky. His body tensed, and he faced the innkeeper.

"I fear we must leave posthaste."

Cristiana followed his gaze to the dark cloud. "What is it?"

The black mist grew, churning and billowing as if it were alive. "Nothing good."

CHAPTER THIRTY-TWO

A lexia squeezed through the narrow opening that led from one of the tunnels into the bottlery. The sharp smell of wine and aged oak scraped over her, along with a chill. It had been raining for three days now, and the gloom had set her nerves on edge. Grunting, Ronar emerged behind her, followed by Seraphina and Damien, all dressed in black priestly robes. Save her. She wore one of her mother's favorite tunics and surcotes, items she'd confiscated from the solar's wardrobe. They had not been to Luxley Castle in three days, not since Ronar's spider attack. Regardless, Anabelle had gotten word to them that she'd been administering the potion to Sir Walter, and he was getting worse by the day. Thus, 'twas time for another attempt to obtain his signature.

Even in the midst of danger, Ronar gave her that sensuous smile that made her blood heat.

"Keep your mind on the task at hand, Sir Knight," she whispered, raising a brow.

"I can do both, my lady," he returned. "A man of many talents."

"You are a man who boasts overmuch," Damien said, brushing dirt from his robe. "Why must we wear these? I look the fool."

Seraphina, her golden hair hidden beneath a black hood, eased beside him. "I doubt that could ever happen, Sir Damien."

His glance took her in with an affection that warmed Alexia, ere he faced her with anger. "'Tis too dangerous to bring her. She is not a warrior."

"Ahh, but she is, my brazen knight," Alexia returned. "Not all warriors are bang and brawn. She has a gift, a powerful one—one of knowledge."

"I wanted to come," Seraphina spoke up. "I want to help." She rubbed her arms and looked around. "'Tis strong here."

"Evil?" Ronar asked.

"Aye. Thick, malevolent." She shook her head. "Powerful."

Alexia laid a hand on her arm and squeezed. "Never fear. Our God is far more powerful." Alexia believed that. More than anything. She'd witnessed God's power on many an occasion. Then why did fear suddenly squirm down her back?

"Come, let's be about it, then." Ronar took the lead, skirting past casks, barrels, and bottles, then out the door and down a long corridor. Up two sets of stairs and down another hall they crept, thankfully meeting no servants or guards along the way, for 'twas well past midnight.

Soon they approached the east wing of the castle that housed Sir Walter's chamber. 'Twas also where Anabelle had told them the steward wandered aimlessly during the long nights. Apparently, due to increasing nightmares, the poor man had given up sleeping in favor of drifting through passageways, alcoves, and Luxley's many empty chambers, muttering to himself. The stronger potion had also made him suspicious and frenzied as it blurred the line betwixt reality and delusion.

Which was precisely what they needed.

Many of the lanterns and rushlights had long since sputtered out, leaving but a few to guide their way. Even the moon and stars had abandoned them in favor of dark clouds, offering no light through the narrow windows. But Alexia knew this castle well and thus had no trouble feeling her way down the cold stones toward Sir Walter's chamber.

She turned to Seraphina. "Anything?"

"Aye, this way." The young maid pressed past her and Ronar and led them to the right, up the stairs, then down a narrow passage that ended in a small circular alcove. "He comes this way." She halted.

"Good." Ronar nodded and each of them retreated into the shadows at intervals down the hallway, with Alexia at the end.

Light from a single lantern cast dancing shadows over the floor and walls as the sound of shuffling footsteps sounded, and Sir Walter came into view. The white of his nightdress fluttered behind him, but he hung his head low, wringing his hands and mumbling to himself.

He approached Sir Damien first, and the knight stepped out before him. Screeching, he leapt out of the way, backing against the other side of the hallway, trembling and wide-eyed.

"Sign it," Damien said, ere he retreated into the shadows again.

"Who are you?" Sir Walter demanded, peering into the darkness, his voice cracked with fear. He stood for a moment, staring at the place where Damien had disappeared. But then he started walking again, resuming his hand wringing whilst keeping a wary eye on his surroundings.

Seraphina eased out before him. He jumped back, hand on his heart, and screamed. The echo bounced hollow over the walls, and Alexia hoped none of the guards heard.

"Who are you? What do you want? Has God sent priests to torment me before my time?" He pressed palms over his temples. "Make it stop!"

"Sign it," Seraphina said, then eased back into the shadows.

It was several moments before Sir Walter moved again, scrambling over the stone floor much faster than before.

Ronar stepped out from a dark corner, blocking his path. The man ran into him and bounced back, tumbling to his knees on the hard stones.

He began to whimper. "Make it stop. Make it stop! Leave me be!"

Alexia slipped out from behind Ronar. "You can make it stop, Sir Walter."

He looked up. "You. You again."

"Aye, the woman you murdered." Her tone was poison.

"I'm sorry. I'm sorry." He dropped his head into his hands and sobbed. "I'm sorry I killed you."

Alexia longed to pluck out her knife and end this man's life right here and now. He deserved worse for his many crimes, but especially for killing her mother and nearly destroying her sister. But the friar's words kept floating to the top of all her vengeful desires. "God will avenge you, my dear. Leave it to him."

Withdrawing the parchment, pen, and small jar of ink, she extended it toward him. "If you truly wish to make amends, sign this."

Sir Walter rubbed his eyes and stared at the paper. "I don't underst—"

"Just sign it!" Ronar ordered. "And your pain will be gone."

Not entirely, Alexia thought, for the man was tortured by more than potions.

"Very well! Whate'er this is, grant me your troth you will quit this haunting, Lady Grecia. Leave me be, I beg you."

Alexia hesitated. She found such pleasure in playing her mother to this man, in torturing him endlessly. Alas, mayhap 'twas not the best Christian attitude. She was still working on loving her enemies. "You have my troth. You will never see me again." She pointed where he should sign.

Sir Walter took the pen, dipped it in the ink, and hovered it over the parchment.

After changing Thebe's soiled cloth and receiving sacks of food from the innkeeper, along with a skin of the fresh water from the creek, Cristiana found herself atop a horse once again with Thebe sitting in front of her. Only this time, the child squirmed and wiggled like a worm on hot coals, wanting to get down to run and play and release her youthful energy.

Though Cristiana had not the same energy after very little sleep the night before, she could well understand the need to run and sing and dance in praise to God after what had just occurred. Alas, now that they'd long left the village behind and Sir Jarin kept them at a rapid pace, Cristiana began to wonder if she had dreamed the entire event, so amazing and unbelievable as it was.

The dark cloud they'd seen on the horizon grew to cover nearly the entire sky, save for tiny breaks through which light from the afternoon sun pierced the landscape. Before her, shadows drifted across the countryside she'd come to love so much, over hills and ponds, farms and forest, like dark waves upon a green sea. A burst of chilled wind wafted over her, stirring dust and leaves into eddies, and whipping Thebe's curls. Cristiana drew her close, a sense of foreboding mangling the hope she'd gained over the past few days.

"Get down?" Thebe asked. "Hungry. Look, a birdie!" Her voice changed from one of complaint to delight in an instant as she pointed to a bird, the color of a ruby, staring down at them from a passing branch. It tweeted and chirped, serenading the child with a tune that made Thebe clap.

"We will stop soon, darling," Cristiana said, glancing at Jarin.

But the knight remained as stoic and silent as he had been since they'd left the village. Could he be angry they'd delayed overlong? Nay, for he'd oft smiled at her during the day—a quick flash of kindness—ere he quickly snapped his gaze away as if looking at her for too long was dangerous. If she admitted it, 'twas a danger to *her* heart to do so as well. For there were times…there had been moments…when the knight's shield was lowered, and she saw a world of promise in his eyes.

"Jarn." Thebe stretched out her hands toward him. "Sit with Jarn?"

"Nay, little one," he said, barely offering her a glance. "We will stop anon."

Thebe shrank back against Cristiana's chest and put her thumb in her mouth.

"I'm sorry," he added, looking at them both. "I must keep alert."

So, he felt it as well, the portent of doom hanging in the air. "How long before we arrive at Luxley?"

Slowing his horse to a walk, he stretched in his saddle, hand on the pommel of his sword. "On the morrow." He glanced over the landscape, eyes sharp and focused, and rubbed his beard. "We'll find a safe place to stay the night, and then we should arrive at Luxley ere the noon meal."

Home. Cristiana had been gone for so long, she hardly knew what to feel. Excitement—certainly at seeing her sister. Fear, indeed. Uncertainty, to be sure. Alas, and a bit of sorrow as well, for her time with Sir Jarin would come to an end.

Thunder roared across the sky. Thebe shrieked and clung to Cristiana.

"Merely thunder, Thebe. 'Tis all right." The spicy scent of rain filled the air as lightning flashed.

Jarin looked at the girl and frowned. "Pray, my lady, what happened back at the village? How did you know to go to the manor steps? How did you know what to pray? That 'twas a curse?"

"I did not know." She bit her lip and glanced at a passing farm where smoke rose from a small home and pigs wallowed in mud inside a pen. "At least not in my head. 'Twas a different sort of knowing…coming from the Spear."

Jarin snorted. "Peace, froth! An old piece of metal cannot think or speak, my lady. No matter whose blood stains it."

"I make no sense of it, either," she snapped. "But as you said, how else would I have known what to do?" In truth, she hadn't been sure of anything right up to the moment she'd knelt on the stairs and uttered the words that came unbidden to her lips.

He rubbed the back of his neck.

"You cannot deny there is a God who is all powerful, Sir Jarin."

"God loves," Thebe took her thumb out of her mouth to say.

Cristiana squeezed her. "Aye, He does darling."

"Nay. I have seen too much," Jarin said. "But I have also seen that He deems to save some whilst allowing others to suffer for no cause. Good people, such as the innkeeper."

And Sir Jarin's family, Cristiana realized. Nevertheless, he had a point, one for which she had no answer.

Still, he smiled her way, that smile that made her long for more of him. That smile that thrilled her beyond all else.

"Your care, your love for strangers, never fails to astonish me, my lady. Even those who would have gladly burned you as a witch."

Thebe grabbed a lock of Cristiana's hair and began twirling it around her finger.

"How can I blame them? They were hale one minute, only to have their health stolen from them the next."

"Hence, my astonishment, my lady."

Embarrassed by his flattery, she longed to turn the topic of conversation away from her. "Why do they call you the just, Sir Jarin?" Something she had been dying to ask him, but dared not intrude.

He smiled. "The king dubbed me as such after I refused to take a bribe."

"From who?"

"Merely some knaves seeking special favors at court."

"Indeed? A poor knight who turns down coin?" She teased him with her tone, though, in truth, she found the deed admirable. Most people of power took bribes. 'Twas the way of things.

He shrugged. "Most would have done the same."

"I doubt that. You possess more honor than you give yourself credit for." She could not tell if her compliment affected him, for he said not a word, though a smile flickered across his lips.

Thunder roared again, dull at first, but increasing in both volume and tension until it seemed to shake the very ground they rode upon.

Clinging tight to Cristiana, Thebe looked over at the knight. "Hungry, Jarn."

Without stopping, the knight reached into a sack tied to his saddle and pulled out a nectarine and a block of cheese the innkeeper had given them and handed them to Cristiana. A light mist began to fall, and he glanced up at the ever-darkening sky.

"From whence hails this strange storm?"

Black, undulating clouds hung so low, it seemed they could reach up and touch them. A strange chill shuddered Cristiana.

"Let us make haste ere the rain falls." Sir Jarin prodded his mount into a trot and Cristiana did the same, clinging to Thebe.

They continued their journey, attempting to outrun the malevolent storm, stopping once to relieve themselves, stretch their legs, and change Thebe's cloth. The girl was having so much fun running about, collecting leaves and looking under rocks, that Cristiana hated to place her back on the horse again.

But Jarin would not be put off.

Finally, the storm clouds swallowed up what was left of the now-setting sun. And still no rain fell. Instead a band of ravens joined them, circling above their heads like vultures over the dead. Their eerie caws only added to Cristiana's unease.

Turning off the main path, Sir Jarin led them across a field toward what looked like the remains of an old stable. Half the roof was caved in, and all that remained of the front were jagged pieces of broken wood hanging like rotted teeth in an old man's mouth.

Dismounting, he led their horses inside, then reached up for Thebe. The sleeping girl woke of a sudden and all but leapt into his arms.

"Jarn! Hungry."

"You're always hungry, little one." He chuckled and set her down, then reached up for Cristiana.

His touch on her waist warmed her down to her toes, her reaction surprising her with its intensity. He placed her gently down before him, so close she could feel the heat from his body, smell his familiar scent that did odd things to her stomach. Swallowing, she glanced up at him, searching for his eyes in the shadows, longing to know what she'd find within them. He brushed a curl from her forehead, and for a moment, she sensed he might lean down and kiss her.

But just as quickly, he cleared his throat and moved aside, taking the reins of her horse and tying both the animals up to a nearby post.

A chill stole his warmth away as thunder growled from the angry sky. Thebe dashed to Cristiana and clung to her leg. Hoisting the girl into her arms, she carried her beneath the remainder of the roof whilst Jarin brought their sacks of food and found the candles the innkeeper had given them.

Once lit, the flickering light revealed naught but piles of hay, empty troughs, and broken-down stalls. Yet, as they unloaded their food and sat to eat, it might as well have been a feast in the great hall of a castle for all the joy and love that filled Cristiana's heart with Jarin and Thebe by her side.

A feast that, unlike so many she'd attended, she wished would never end. But the caw and screech of several ravens stole the happiness of the moment as at least six black birds swooped down and lined along a fence post just outside the stable. There they sat like demonic sentinels, eyeing them, leering as if they'd won a great victory.

Thebe leapt into Cristiana's lap and hid her face.

Sir Jarin jumped to his feet, sword drawn and ready.

"Away with you! Away!" He charged the birds, swinging the blade before him. The ravens took flight, croaking and squawking in protest.

But then another sound—one far more terrifying—rose to take their place.

The growl of ravenous wolves.

Grabbing a candle, Sir Jarin took a protective position before Cristiana and Thebe, sword leveled in one hand and the candle lifted in the other.

Two of the largest wolves Cristiana had ever seen emerged from the darkness and crept toward Sir Jarin, red, slit-like eyes glowing and white fangs dripping with saliva.

Thebe wailed and gripped Cristiana's tunic so tight, it tore.

"Get on the horse," Jarin ordered. "You and Thebe. I'll hold them back until you are gone."

Cristiana didn't move. Not out of fear, though she felt more terrified than she'd ever been. In truth, she could hardly breath, could hardly hear for the mad rush of blood past her ears. But just as she had known about the curse in the village, she now knew two things with certainty.

One, these wolves were not of this world, and therefore, Jarin could not defeat them.

And two, they wanted only her and would leave Sir Jarin and Thebe alone if they got what they came for.

Rising on shaky legs, Cristiana pried Thebe from her arms and set her down in the hay. "Stay here. Sir Jarin will keep you safe."

Ere the girl could cling to her again, Cristiana moved to stand beside Sir Jarin.

"They want me, Sir Jarin, not you. Not Thebe."

"Nay! Do as I say. Get Thebe and leave at once!"

But she could not. She would not put the two people she loved most in the world in danger. Not when 'twas within her power to keep them safe.

Brushing past Sir Jarin, ignoring her trembling legs, Jarin's protests, and Thebe's cries, Cristiana marched straight toward the wolves.

CHAPTER THIRTY-THREE

"**D**evil's blood!" Sir Walter took the final step down into Drago's lair and pushed open the door. "Devil's blood!" he cursed again, his gaze scanning the dark chamber as the door slammed behind him, the echo ringing hollow and empty.

A dark mist appeared behind the warlock's cauldron, twisting and spinning faster and faster ere taking form and shape. Drago suddenly appeared, a scowl on his face. "What has you in such a pother, Sir Walter? One of the maids reject your advance again?"

Sir Walter fisted his hands. "Nay. Far worse. I signed it." He still could not believe his own words. The bats hanging above swayed, and his head grew light. Stumbling toward a chair, he sank into it and rubbed his eyes. Maybe 'twas just a dream, one of his many recent nightmares.

Uttering a sigh of annoyance, Drago poured something into the cauldron. "You signed what?"

"I don't know," Sir Walter mumbled, staring at the dirt-encrusted floor. "Mayhap I didn't."

"Then why do you disturb me?!"

The cauldron hissed and the stench of bile and feces bit Sir Walter's nose. The warlock's white robe fluttered into his vision. Shooting to his feet, he backed away, staggering and trying to catch his balance. How did the man always approach without a sound?

"I signed something. Something important. They are here."

Drago's face twisted. "Do you think I do not know that? I have felt them since they arrived."

"Then why do you not stop them?"

"I was attempting to do so when you interrupted me, you lizard-brained whoreson! Now, what did you sign?"

"I don't know. Lady Grecia haunts me."

"'Tis not her, you fool. She is with our enemy." Flipping his robes behind him, Drago returned to his cauldron.

"They tricked me." Sir Walter wrung his hands. "They—"

"Silence!" Drago's command could wake the dead. In truth, it seemed to do just that as a row of bats took flight up the open tower.

The warlock tapped his chin, bouncing his long white beard. "Ah. I know just the thing." Spinning around, he plucked what appeared to be a dead fish off a shelf, along with a dusty book. The fish he tossed into the bubbling cauldron, the book he opened.

Sir Walter sank to the floor, blinking to clear his eyes...*and* his thoughts.

The warlock flipped through pages, halting on one that made him grin, ere he began spewing a string of Latin Sir Walter could make no sense of.

Then slamming the book shut, he waved a hand over the cauldron, around and around and around, churning the liquid into a cyclone. Finally, that liquid rose, forming a dark funnel that sped up into the tower above.

Drago laughed, a maniacal laugh that pricked the hairs on Sir Walter's arms. "They don't stand a chance."

Alexia could hardly believe she'd finally gotten Sir Walter to sign his confession! After months of feeding him the poisoned elixir, months of haunting him, she'd come to believe his stubbornness would win out. But God had come through. Yet again. When would she ever have the faith to believe for the impossible?

With the document stuffed safely in her surcote, she led the way back through the tunnels, a very pleased Ronar, Damien, and Seraphina following behind her. With this paper, sealed with Sir Walter's stolen signet ring, the king would have no choice but to send court magistrates to investigate the situation at Luxley. Mayhap 'twould not get the charges against Alexia and her friends lifted right away, but 'twas the first step.

She couldn't help but smile as she ducked and squeezed through a particularly narrow section, the cold stone jabbing her arms.

Rumbling sounded. Nay, 'twas more like thunder, distant and hollow. The tunnel walls trembled. Alexia halted and held up the torch. An odd gust of wind blasted over them, flickering the flame and showering her with the smell of mold and earth. And something else. *Water.*

Ronar squeezed beside her. "Tush, what is it now?"

The thundering increased. As did the shaking. Dust and pebbles rained down upon them.

"Earthquake?" Damien said from behind them.

"Nay," Seraphina added, her voice filled with terror. "'Tis something evil. Hurry!"

Grabbing the torch from Alexia, Ronar nudged her behind him and hastened forward as fast as the tunnel and the shaking would allow. Alexia bounced against the stone walls like a loose apple in a hobbling cart. The roaring grew louder, the shaking increased. They struggled onward, angling down toward the storage room beneath the castle where another tunnel would lead them outside Luxley's gates.

Seraphina screamed.

Alexia turned.

A wall of water rushed for them.

No time to react.

It struck them with the force of a battering ram.

Alexia slammed against the tunnel wall. Hard. Water filled her nose and mouth and gushed past her ears. Seraphina—or was it Damien—crashed into her, while she smacked into Ronar. Together, they all shot through the tunnel, carried by the mad torrent. Arms and legs failing, she managed to clutch Ronar's robe, a bastion of hope in the midst of a nightmarish flood. Her lungs ached for air, but she dared not gasp, lest water pour into them.

Lord, help!

Was this how she would die? Drowned like a rat in her own castle?

She launched through the air, and her bottom hit hard stone. Seraphina fell on top of her. Grabbing her friend, Alexia moved out of the way of the cascade pouring from the tunnel into the tiny storeroom. Damien landed beside them. Ronar was already on his feet. He sloshed through the water toward the iron chest, behind which hid the tunnel that led outside.

Alexia stood and helped Seraphina up, but the water was already at their knees.

After a quick glance at them to ensure they were all right, Damien went to help Ronar.

But the water had already covered the chest. Both knights yanked with all their might. It wouldn't budge.

"Search for anything we can use to pry it!" Alexia shouted, nodding at a trembling Seraphina beside her. "'Twill be all right. You'll see."

The maid smiled but Alexia could see in her eyes, she didn't believe her.

They waded through the rising water, searching for anything—a shovel, pickaxe—anything they could use. But there were only crates, barrels, and now-saturated sacks.

The water was at Alexia's waist now, cold, swirling water that sent a chill through her. And still it poured out of the tunnel entrance as if it hailed from a bottomless sea. Huge slabs of stone made up the tiny storeroom—floor, walls, and ceiling. Alas, even should there be a leak, a small opening somewhere, it wouldn't drain the water quick enough to save them all from drowning.

Terror choked her.

"What are we to do?" Seraphina yelled.

Alexia joined Ronar and Damien at the only door to the chamber. The knights yanked and pulled on the latch, but it wouldn't budge. The three of them kicked at it with all their might, but their efforts were futile beneath the water.

Ronar shook his head and took to feeling along the stone walls for any loose stones, any crack they could use to create an opening. Not that it would do them any good, for there was naught but dirt beyond the wall. Indeed, they were below ground, about to be buried in a tomb of water.

That water was at her chest now. A rat floated by, along with several apples, which must have loosened from a crate.

This can't be happening. How is this happening? Alexia closed her eyes and shoved past her fear and shock, seeking the peace within…seeking the Spirit.

"We are all going to drown!" Damien shouted, then growled into what was left of the air above him.

"This cannot be!" Alexia shouted over the thunderous rush. "This is not real. We must pray! Come!" She searched for Seraphina's hand beneath the water and gripped it as Ronar found hers. Damien, fear and anger marring his expression, stood at a distance for several seconds that seemed like forever ere he finally joined them.

No time for a long prayer. Alexia lifted her face to heaven. "Mighty Father, in the name of your Son Jesus, I command this water to dry up at once!"

Nothing happened. Instead, the water tickled her neck as it rose higher. "Peace, be still!" Alexia shouted. Moments passed. Was it her or did the roar of the water lessen? She opened her eyes and glanced toward the tunnel. The cascade became a surge, the surge became a flow, and the flow became a trickle.

The water around them began to recede.

Ronar started to laugh, small at first, but then it transformed into a hearty chuckle. Reaching behind her neck, he brought her head close and kissed her cheek.

She smiled. "You make a rather handsome, wet priest, Sir Knight."

"And you a lovely mermaid."

"Both of you are cream-faced loons," Damien groaned. "We nearly drowned, and you act as though we are at court."

Breathing hard, Seraphina eased beside the big knight. "We are saved, Sir Damien. Put by your ill humor."

"God has saved us once again!" Ronar shouted.

"Praise His holy name!" Alexia added. Only then did she remember the document in her surcote.

The now-saturated document.

"Nay!" Jarin darted for Cristiana as she approached the two ravenous wolves. *Foolish woman!* Sword drawn and ready to fight to his death for this lady, he was nearly upon them—when the two beasts sprang, fangs sharp and ready to clamp onto her flesh.

Thebe screamed.

Jarin thrust his blade at one of the wolves, but it struck air, and he toppled forward.

Nay, not air. A mist. Black and undulating, it spun faster and faster, consuming the wolves and Cristiana in a dark cloud.

Blinking to clear his vision, Jarin knew not what to do. Should he plunge his sword into it? What if he struck Cristiana?

Growls emanated from the murky cyclone, along with the eerie caw of ravens.

"Cristiana!" he shouted, staring at it as it whirled and lifted from the ground. Higher and higher it went, growing in both darkness and intensity, before it completely disappeared.

Cristiana and the wolves were nowhere in sight.

CHAPTER THIRTY-FOUR

Darkness surrounded Cristiana. Thick, blackness with a life of its own...breathing...gyrating....pulsing. She whirled around. Black. Nothing but black. Yet it moved, flowed like ink, thick and heavy. She took a step, reaching out for it. An icy breeze wove around her hand, so cold, she jerked it back.

"Where am I?" she shouted, sobbing.

Laughter, deep, malevolent laughter pierced her ears and sent shards of terror down to her toes.

Dropping to her knees, she hugged herself. *Oh, God, am I in hell?*

No answer came. Instead, a cloak of despair weighed upon her, threatening to crush her beneath its weight.

"Oh, God, oh God, oh God!" She kept repeating the words over and over.

A pinprick of light shattered the darkness.

"He can't help you now." The voice dripped with guile.

The light grabbed ahold of Cristiana and pulled her from the darkness out of her nightmare.

And straight into another one.

A man's face peered down at her, a grin that bore no kindness on his thin, pale lips.

"Welcome, my intended."

Who? What? Where were Jarin and Thebe?

Confusion gave way to fear, and Cristiana pushed from the dirt where she lay and jumped to her feet. Her vision whirled. She wobbled and reached behind her for something to cling to. Her hand found hard rock.

The man straightened and stared at her with eyes so dark, she found no white within them.

"Do you not recognize me, my lady?" He moved closer to the fire. Flames flickered over his black robe and the hollow features of his face, then danced over the rock walls of a small cave surrounding them.

The voice was familiar, yet it bore a confidence and authority that had been absent before. Nay. Couldn't be. She inched toward him.

Growling emanated from the shadows at the back of the cave.

"Silence, pets!" The man waved a hand through the air.

"Cedric?" she asked, still not believing it.

He smiled. "You forget so soon the man you were to wed? The man you shamed by running away on our wedding day."

A breeze laden with pine and oak and night jasmine wafted around her, and she glanced to her left where a turn in the cave surely led outside.

"Ah, you think your gallant knight will come to your rescue?" Cedric gave a sarcastic snort.

"How did I...?" The last thing she remembered was walking toward two wolves, hoping to save... "Sir Jarin and Thebe. Where are they?"

He smiled again and shrugged. "My guess? Miles from here. In good sooth, the man is surely glad to be rid of the burden of protecting you." He leaned toward her and raised a hairless brow. "We both know Sir Jarin is not a man who would allow anyone to impede his libertine tendencies. Unless, of course, there were benefits offered?" He winked at her.

It took Cristiana a moment to determine what he meant. "How dare you suggest such a thing!?"

He sighed. "Then 'tis no wonder he has abandoned you."

Abandoned. Abandoned. Abandoned. The word pummeled Cristiana like a fist. A very familiar fist that had left its bruise more than once.

"As to your other question, 'twas my pets that brought you here." Cedric glanced fondly toward the shadows, where one of the wolves slunk out, plopped down, and whined. Reaching beside the fire, he selected two bones covered in raw flesh and tossed them into the corner. A storm of snarling, yapping, and growling ensued as the beasts leapt upon their meal.

"What do you want?" Cristiana hated the weakness in her voice, hated the tears threatening to spill from her eyes.

"Why, *you*, my dear."

"I will not wed you, Cedric. Ever." She knew her words might get her tossed to the wolves next, but she'd rather die than be wife to this man…this beast before her.

He laughed and placed a hand over his heart. "You wound me deeply, my lady. Nay, as lovely as you are"—he cocked his head, assessing her—"I have no desire to marry you. Or anyone."

Cristiana's legs turned to pottage, and she lowered to sit on a rock by the fire. Despite the flames rising toward the ceiling, the warmth did naught to chase away the chill that permeated every inch of her. A chill that only increased when she lifted her gaze to study Cedric and found naught but ice in his eyes.

"What happened to you?" She remembered a young man full of life and joy, a lazy clodpole to be sure, but harmless nonetheless. He had never loved Cristiana. His father had forced him to press his suit upon her. Thus, his slide into darkness could not find its cause in her rejection.

He flung his robes around him and lowered to sit, never taking his gaze from her. Dark smudges stained the skin beneath his eyes as if the man had not slept in a sennight. Pale, hollow skin covered his face and neck. Hair that had once been light now hung to his shoulders in a tangled mass the color of dirt.

His lips lifted slightly. "I gained power. I became strong."

Strong? Yet there was an emptiness in his eyes as if all hope and joy had been leeched from him. "You think evil is strength. You are wrong."

Those eyes narrowed ere he snapped in the air and said something in a language she did not recognize. A raven appeared on his finger.

Though everything within her flinched in fear, she attempted a calm demeanor.

"I could order it to peck out your eyes, should I wish."

The bird glared at Cristiana as if longing to do just that.

Terror threatened to squeeze her heart dry. For she knew now she was not dealing with a mere madman, nor with mere flesh and blood, but with principalities and rulers of evil.

"'Tis the dark powers that aided me in finding you," he continued, petting the raven. "When a host of trained soldiers failed."

Cristiana swallowed, trying to find her voice. "What is it you want with me?"

"I am ordered to bring you back to Luxley, of course." He lifted his arm and the raven flew off, disappearing into a puff of black mist.

She gripped her hands together to keep them from trembling. How was she to fight against such evil? "So you do your father's bidding?"

"That foolish tosspot!" He roared, hatred firing from his eyes. "Nay. I no longer answer to him."

If not Sir Walter, then who had sent this fiend from hell to find her? Unless… "'Tis *your* ambition then to become Lord of Luxley?"

"Pfff" He chuckled. "I assure you, my lady, my ambitions far outweigh such a lowly station."

"Then what use am I to you?"

"To me? Naught. But a bargain was made with my master for your return."

"Your master?"

"Enough! Your prattling tongue annoys me." The wolves growled as Cedric rose from his seat like a specter from its grave.

Against her will to appear strong, Cristiana shrank back. "Prithee, just kill me and get it over with."

His smile was as sharp as a blade. "As pleasant as that sounds, there is something you have that I need. Ergo, give it to me, and I may allow you to live. If you do not, I will rip it from your lifeless flesh."

What could this vile man possibly want from her? "I have naught of value."

"In good sooth, I beg to differ, my lady. You have a relic stained by the blood of my enemy. My master fears its power. I wish to use that power against him and take my rightful position as grand warlock of the realm."

A warlock? Her blood froze in her veins. A powerful one, from the sounds of it. Poor Alexia. What she must be up against.

The Spear heated on Cristiana's thigh. For what purpose? Averting her gaze from the evil man, she stared at the fire. "I have no idea what you are talking about."

He chuckled. "Very well, lifeless flesh it is." Flinging his robes behind him, he advanced toward her.

It took nearly an hour for Jarin to fully accept that Cristiana was gone. During that time, he searched every inch of the stable, then grabbed Thebe, mounted his horse, and further searched a mile in every direction over dark fields and roads. All the while, he desperately called her name whilst trying to calm down an hysterical babe.

Finally, he returned to the stable, more despondent than ever, and plopped down in the hay, a weeping Thebe in his arms.

"Where Cristi? I want Cristi!" the poor child wailed over and over.

"I know, little one. I do as well." He did his best to console her, to hold her tight and reassure her Cristiana would be all right, but Thebe refused to be comforted. The poor child had witnessed the same thing Jarin had, two massive wolves leaping on Cristiana ere all three of them disappeared in a cyclone of black smoke.

Jarin had seen many strange things in his life—most of which had happened after he met Lady Cristiana. But he'd never seen the likes of a lady here one moment and gone the next. Something evil was afoot, something beyond this world. *And* beyond the cut of his blade. Which made him feel all the more helpless.

Thebe finally stopped crying and stuck her thumb in her mouth, though sobs still wracked her small body, each one increasing his guilt. His one job, his *only* job, had been to protect Lady Cristiana at all costs. And he had failed.

Miserably.

How does one fight against what cannot be seen? If the wolves had been real, he would have plunged his blade through both of them. If they had been men, he would have killed them ere he ever allowed them to lay a hand on Cristiana. If an army had captured and run off with her, he'd leave Thebe safe with a nearby family and dash to her rescue.

But this? He had no idea what to do, where to go, how to find her.

"Shh, shh." He rubbed Thebe's back and kissed the top of her head. "We will find Cristi, little one. We will find her. You have my troth."

What sort of man lies to a child? The accusation blared through his head over and over as he packed up the remainder of their food and water, tied Cristiana's horse to his own, swung into his saddle, and headed out with Thebe in his arms. He could think of naught else to do but return to the main road, pick a direction, and ask along the way if anyone had seen the lady.

Ridiculous idea since no person would be out in the thick of the night, and he could hardly see them if they were. Finally, after a few hours of aimless wandering, he led the horses off the main road into a patch of willows. Better to get some rest until daylight. Especially for Thebe, for the girl continued to sob and inquire how long before they found Cristi.

After making a small fire and a bed of leaves for the girl, Jarin lay beside her, hoping she would go to sleep. He had no idea how to care for a child. Did they merely fall asleep on their own, or was there something he should do? He had not paid attention to what Cristiana had done.

Thebe glanced behind her, then moved her little body right beside his, curling her back against his chest. She let out a ragged sigh and said. "Jarn, sing song."

Song? The salacious ballads Jarin knew would not be appropriate for a child. "I don't know any songs. Go to sleep."

She began to whimper again, soft and low, sending quivers through her tiny body. "I want Cristi!"

"Faith now," he whispered, annoyance rising. "Hush. I'll sing a song. Hush." He swung an arm around her and drew her close. Then, clearing his throat, he made up a song and a tune to go with it about a frog, a pig, and a sleepy little girl. To his ears it sounded ridiculous and incredibly off-tune, and he was thankful none of his friends were nearby to make sport of him. But it made Thebe laugh and snuggle closer ere she grew limp in his arms and her breathing deepened.

Jarin laid his head on his arm, breathing in her scent of flowers and innocence and feeling her small body nestled against his, so tiny against his large frame, so dependent on him for everything. And a strange feeling rose within him, an overwhelming feeling of protection, of care, of being a father to such a child, of watching her grow, teaching her, providing for her. Of guarding her with his life.

Bosh! 'Tis precisely what he didn't want!

Exhaustion finally won over his anger with himself and his fears for Cristiana, and he slowly drifted to sleep.

Jarin walked through a field of flowers. A breeze swirled about him, cooling his skin and bringing with it the sweetest fragrance he'd ever smelled, so sweet he could near taste it. Bright sunshine lit the tall, swaying flowers in sparkling colors so vibrant and pure 'twas like a painting from another world. Yet where was the sun? He could not find it in the brilliantly blue sky. Instead, light seemed to explode from all around, bright, golden light that kissed everything it touched with warmth and life.

He continued walking, his boots cushioned by the soft soil, his hands spread out to graze the passing flowers. They tickled his palms. He smiled. In the distance, beyond the meadow, green mountains rose from which poured crystalline waterfalls, the silver liquid bouncing and bubbling in delight as it splashed into a lake below.

A song danced upon the breeze like the sound of many harps, each playing a different tune, but all in harmony. Yet no minstrels were in sight. Nay. The song was not from human hands. Jarin stopped and glanced over the magnificent scene. The music came from all around him. From the flowers, grass, trees, waterfalls, and mountains. A joyous tune of peace and love and a happiness that had always eluded him in life.

Three figures appeared in the distance, heading toward him—a man, woman, and child. At first he could not see their faces, but as they came closer, he stumbled backward and nearly fell.

"Greetings, my son." The man halted before him and smiled.

"Father? Father! I'm dreaming." Jarin rubbed his eyes. When he opened them, he shifted his gaze to the woman. "Mother?" Then to the child. A girl around eight years of age.

"Your sister, Celia," his mother said.

Jarin could only stare at them in wonder. Yet how could he deny what he was seeing? His father looked the same, yet younger, stronger, devoid of the ravages of time and hard work. The last time he'd seen his mother, she'd been covered in blood, her face a twist of pain and heartache. Here, she was radiant, beautiful, healthy.

"This can't be," he said. Nay, 'twas a dream. A beautiful, wonderful dream, but one that would soon end.

His father grabbed his shoulders and drew him close in a tight embrace, a solid, warm embrace. Jarin could even smell the man's familiar scent of tallow and aged books, hear his chuckle in his ears.

"Jarin, my boy. I'm overjoyed to see you!" He backed away, allowing Jarin's mother to rush into his arms and bury her head against his chest.

He hugged them both. Tears burned in his eyes, but he dared not show the weakness, not for something that wasn't real, that would vanish without warning just as it had come.

The little girl tugged on his leather coat. Releasing his parents, Jarin stooped and gazed at her angelic face. Dark brown hair—the same color as his—fell in a bounty of curls over her shoulders. Golden eyes fringed in thick lashes stared back at him, love and laughter bursting from within them.

She said naught. Merely fell against him and wrapped her arms around his neck.

He nudged her back, kissed her forehead, and rose to face his parents. "She died in my arms."

His mother laid a hand on his arm. "Nay, my son. An angel took her from your arms and brought her here to mine."

Jarin swallowed a burst of pain. "I don't unders—"

"This is the real world. Not the one you live in now, son." Jarin's father grabbed his wife's hand as she took Celia's. "We await you."

"Wait for what?" Jarin reached out for them, but they turned and started to walk away.

"Nay! Don't leave!" Jarin started to rush after them, but some invisible force held him at back.

Beyond them, on top of a hill, a white city appeared, so bright, he blinked and shielded his eyes at the sight. Its walls were made of glimmering jewels and its gates of lustrous pearls, whilst towers made of gold rose toward the sky.

When he glanced down toward his family, they were gone.

CHAPTER THIRTY-FIVE

Cristiana shot to her feet, intending to make a dash toward the entrance of the cave. She turned, but Cedric had already grabbed her arm. *Tight.* So tight, pain spiked across her shoulders and down her back.

Hence, she spoke the first words that came to her. "In the name of Jesus the Christ, I command you to leave me be!"

Cedric uttered a cry of pain and jerked his hand off her. Rubbing it, he backed away, eyes narrowed and mouth tight. Smoke rose from charred flesh on his palm.

Cristiana slowly faced him, eyes wide, and breath coming fast. Part of her was shocked. Part of her praised God for His deliverance. Part of her longed to drop to her knees in worship. No doubt God wished to keep the Spear out of the hands of evil men.

Cedric's expression of pain and confusion soon transformed into one of hate and anger. He whirled and stormed to a pouch lying on the ground. From inside, he withdrew a small corked vial, some feathers, and what appeared to be rat tails. He tossed the tails and feathers into the fire. It spit and hissed, spewing a snake of smoke that slithered toward the ceiling of the cave.

She glanced toward the entrance. Cedric could not touch her. Ergo, she could leave, couldn't she? Yet...something kept her in place—a voice, a knowing. A peace.

He poured out the vial onto the flames, then lifted his head and uttered. "Sicut superius et inferiu. Potestatem tuam super omnes vincit in bonum."

Cristiana knew enough Latin to understand he was calling on powers below to defeat all good.

The fire leapt toward the ceiling as flames that looked more like claws reached for her.

Cristiana leapt back. Mayhap she *should* leave.

Cedric was beside her in less than a second, as if he'd been transported by some otherworldly power.

He gripped her arm once again.

And once again, he leapt back, screaming, his flesh singed. Cristiana smiled. "Praise be to God."

Cedric uttered a demonic growl as fury warped his features. Lifting his good hand, he snapped. "Come forth, pets. Your meal is prepared."

The wolves jumped from the corner and charged for Cristiana.

Holding her breath, she stood her ground. If the Spear kept her safe from Cedric, surely it would protect her from these beasts. Wouldn't it?

Fangs bared, they leapt through the air toward her.

Cristiana closed her eyes, waiting to feel their claws dig into her flesh, smell their foul breath as they bit her neck.

A whooshing sound met her ears. Then a whine, as from an injured animal. She opened her eyes to see naught but two clouds of black mist rising to the ceiling.

"What have you done!?" Cedric raged, staring upward. "My pets! My dear pets!" He sobbed and cried and screamed, shaking his fist at the sky and stomping like a spoiled child. Thundering toward her, he halted and lifted his hand to strike, his dark eyes churning like a storm at sea.

He froze. Withdrawing, he retreated to the fire and lowered to sit. "Beshrew all that is good and holy! The enemy's power is greater. Of this, I now have no doubt."

A beam of light appeared at the entrance of the cave, floating on the morning mist. Dawn had arrived. Cristiana should leave. Instead, she watched Cedric curiously, a strange sympathy for the man flooding her heart.

"He is not your enemy, Cedric."

He spat on the ground.

"Your enemy is the one who seduces you with power, with lies, and with pleasures that last but a moment. God is the One who offers real power, love, truth, and eternal life."

He said naught, merely drew the hood of his cloak over his head as if he could hide from her.

She took a step toward him. "Remember who you used to be, Cedric. A young man full of life and joy. Turn to God, repent of your evil ways, and He will welcome you with open arms."

Moments passed. The flames of the fire died to mere flickers.

"Why do you speak so kindly to me?" he asked without looking up. "I can do you no harm. You are free. Yet you remain. Why? When if I could, I'd slit your throat?"

"I stay because God loves you, Cedric, your evil deeds, notwithstanding. And because 'tis never too late to turn to Him and forsake this dark path you are on."

He finally lifted his gaze to hers. His eyes no longer churned with hatred. Instead a deep sorrow tugged upon his features. "Leave me." He waved toward the cave entrance. "I beg you. Leave me."

Cristiana swallowed, said a silent prayer for him, and then turned and made her way out of the cave.

The warble of birds in his ears and glimmer of light on his eyelids dragged Jarin from his sweet slumber. Sweet, indeed, for he'd had the best dream of his life. Sorrow threatened to batter away his joy when he realized 'twas only a dream. Or was it?

He opened his eyes to the simmering coals of a fire, rays of sunlight spearing through trees, and a squirrel on hind legs staring at him.

Deep puffs of breath rose from the precious child in his arms, and ever so gently he pushed to a sitting position beside her. The squirrel darted off. Thebe muttered and shifted slightly but remained asleep. Curls the color of a baby fawn lay gently on her chubby cheeks whilst long lashes fluttered over her creamy skin.

What was he to do with her? How was he to find Cristiana whilst caring for a babe? *Cristiana.* Jarin rubbed his eyes and stood. The horses snorted at him as terror wrapped around his heart and squeezed. What evil was she now facing? Was she even still alive? The latter thought crushed him more than he admitted. More than he *wanted* to admit. He needed help. They were so close to Luxley, mayhap he should ride there and get Alexia and Ronar. Alexia possessed powers for good, did she not? He'd witnessed them firsthand. Or mayhap 'twas only the one who held the Spear. Which gave him hope for Cristiana.

Confusion tangled his thoughts. Stepping away from Thebe, he raked a hand through his hair and stooped before the fire. Grabbing a stick, he stoked the coals, then tossed a log onto the rising flames. He'd always been a man of action. Whene'er a problem arose or an enemy attacked, he gave no thought to a plan, but simply reacted, destroyed the enemy, solved the problem. Task completed. But this. How was he to fight an enemy he could not see?

His dream filled his thoughts. It had seemed so real. Lifting his arm to his nose, he drew a breath. He could still smell his father's scent, still see the love in his sister's eyes. What if 'twas no dream at all? What if God had given him a vision of heaven, for surely 'twas what he'd seen. No other place could compare with the stunning beauty of that meadow and the city he saw beyond. A city on a hill. Could they really be there, alive and well, happy and loved?

Yes.

Jarin shot to his feet and glanced around. Where had the voice come from? Easing toward Thebe, he picked up his blade from the ground where he'd placed it and held it before him. A breeze stirred the leaves of the surrounding trees. Birds flitted from branch to branch. A squirrel scrambled up a trunk as the two horses stared at him as if he'd gone mad. Quite possibly he had.

Still, he knew what he'd heard.

And it changed everything.

Odd fancy, that. Jarin the Just hearing from God. Receiving a dream from the Almighty that proved there was indeed a world beyond this one, a world that outshone this one by ten thousand to one. The *real* world—an eternity with the Creator Who had made this place. A place that now seemed petty and trite by comparison.

He lowered his blade. Mayhap 'twas Jarin who had played the fool his entire life. For it seemed as though he'd been merely staring at a mural on a stone wall, believing that to be all there was when, in truth, there was an entire world beyond that wall. He'd been mad at God for taking away those he loved, when all this time, they'd been in a better place, a far better place—a place wherein he would see them again someday. If he didn't play the fool.

He hadn't time to ponder it all before Thebe woke.

"Jarn." She sat and reached for him with both hands.

"Good morn to you, little one." Leaning over, he hoisted her into his arms. Moisture crept onto his shirt. Jerking Thebe from him, he held her aloft, noting the patch of wet on her small gown.

Bosh! He set her down, but her lips drew into a pout, and she began to cry.

"'Tis all right, Thebe." Kneeling, he wiped her tears, but she fell against him, her chubby arms reaching around his neck.

"Very well." The sting of urine, and something else more foul reached his nose as he lifted her and headed toward the horses, trying not to think about what was saturating his shirt. Removing a clean cloth from the sack, a fresh gown, and the pouch of water, Jarin returned to the fire and laid Thebe down on the warm ground beside it.

"Jarn is going to change your cloth now. Aye?" He stared down at the little girl who smiled up at him, though a tear spilled from her eye.

He drew a deep breath. He could fight off five knights with blade, axe, or fist, scale a castle wall in ten seconds with naught but a rope and his brawn. He could win a joust, fight a battle, woo a maiden, and kill a deer all before the evening meal.

But he had no idea how to change a baby's cloth!

Lifting her skirts, he proceeded. The sight and smell that met him stole his breath and brought water to his eyes. He winced. If they could bottle this, 'twould be no need to fight wars. Simply lay the stuff out on the battlefield and watch the enemy retreat. Holding his breath, he did his best, using leaves and water, to clean Thebe's bottom ere tying on the clean cloth. All while she kicked her feet and moved about like the many squirrels darting up trees around them.

"Stay still, little one." His voice must have emerged too harsh for she started to cry yet again.

Frowning, Jarin finished his work, changed her gown, and swept her in his arms. "I'm sorry. Jarn not mad."

Egad, now he was talking baby talk.

But 'twas worth it, for in an instant, she was giggling again.

"Find Cristi? Go find Cristi." She tugged on his shirt.

He nodded. "Aye." Rising, he discarded the soiled cloth in the bushes, pitying the animals who lived there, kicked dirt onto the fire, then readied the horses.

Thebe was not her normal, curious self, roaming about, investigating all things, and begging for food. Instead, she eyed him, thumb in her mouth, as if she didn't trust that he intended to find Cristi. If the girl only knew that he'd rather die than not find Lady Cristiana D'Clere. Against his will, the lady had set up shop in his heart and sold off all his desires to be independent and free, all his desires to be a libertine, to ever glance at another woman.

"Come, little one. Let us go find Cristi." He reached for Thebe, and she flew into his arms, squeezing his neck so hard, his breath caught in his throat. "No leave me, Jarn. No leave?"

"Nay, Thebe." He rubbed her back. "I'm not leaving you." He set her on the horse and gazed up at her, forcing back his own tears that anyone could have ever abandoned this precious child. Then swinging up behind her, he led the horses back onto the main road.

The sun peered above the horizon, setting the morning mist aglitter and spreading a sheet of diamonds over farm, field, and forest. Somewhere in the distance a rooster crowed. Jarin turned right toward Luxley and eased the horses into a steady pace. What else could he do but seek out Alexia, Ronar, and Damien and elicit their help. Along the way, he would ask anyone he encountered if they'd seen Cristiana. The feckless plan weighed heavy on what little hope he had left in his heart, but there was naught to be done for it. Not until he had a clue where Cristiana was.

Reaching in his sack, he brought out a piece of bread for Thebe ere she began to complain. She consumed it within minutes as she pointed at every bird, frog, squirrel, and cow in their view. Ah, to possess such joy and excitement at sights so common, and also such trust that all would be well. Yet wasn't that what God demanded? That those who followed Him believe He would work out everything for good?

Jarin should pray. Wasn't that what people did who believed in God, and those no longer angry with Him? If the Almighty had given him such a glorious dream, surely He would answer Jarin's prayers. Particularly if they were for a woman as godly as Cristiana. A woman who held the Spear of Christ.

So many years had passed since Jarin had prayed, he wasn't sure how to proceed. At the monastery, his prayers had been recited from books, repeated so oft, he never gave them much thought. But now he sensed God expected more than rote verses.

Sighing, he bowed his head. *Lord, if you're there and you can hear me, I beseech You, help me find Cristiana. Prithee, keep her safe until I do.*

He lifted his gaze. Nothing. No voice from heaven, no sign from above pointing the way. Naught but the rising sun and the smoke from a farmhouse chimney. Feeling the fool, he shifted in the saddle and urged his horse into a faster gait.

An hour passed, or was it two? Heat from the sun moistened Jarin's skin beneath his leather surcote, and he took it off, relishing in the breeze sifting through his shirt. They came upon a field carpeted with purple, pink, and yellow wildflowers.

"Run! Run!" Thebe pointed toward the meadow. "Stop, Jarn."

He pulled the horses to a halt and dismounted. Mayhap 'twas time for a break, anyway.

No sooner did Thebe's feet touch the ground, than she ran off frolicking through the field, giggling and twirling as if she were a pauper dancing through piles of gold. Jarin couldn't help but smile. He also couldn't help but remember the dazzling meadow of his dream and the joy and peace on his parents' faces so similar to the expression of this innocent child before him.

Untying the skin from the saddle, he took a drink, then set it aside for when Thebe returned. When he looked back up, he could hardly see her through the tall grass and flowers.

"Thebe!" he shouted. "Return at once!"

Her brown curls bobbed above the flowers in the distance. *Too* far away. "Thebe!" Jarin took off after her, cursing himself for allowing the child to leave his sight. Yet surely there was naught to fear in such a beautiful field. He charged forward, noting a copse of pines in the distance.

A figure emerged from them.

A woman.

Thebe let out a yelp and headed straight toward her.

CHAPTER THIRTY-SIX

"Thebe!" Jarin raced for the girl ere she ran up to a complete stranger. After what he'd seen with the wolves, he trusted no one.

But the closer he came, the more the woman's beautiful features formed in his view. *Cristiana?*

He caught up to Thebe—several yards before she reached the woman—and hoisted the child into his arms. Halting, his breath heaving, he stared at the apparition of Cristiana walking toward him, all the while doing his best to restrain the little girl kicking and crying to be set free.

"Cristi!" she held out both hands to the lady, who smiled at them as she continued her approach.

No apparition. 'Twas the lady, herself! Jarin set Thebe down, and the girl dashed and leapt into the woman's arms.

A joy he did not know possible bubbled through him as he walked toward them both, still attempting to catch his breath, along with his heart, which seemed about to burst through his chest.

Cristiana turned Thebe around, showering kisses all over the girl's face. "I missed you, darling! I missed you so much."

"Cristi, where go? Why leave?"

"I didn't leave you. I was taken. But I'm here now." She glanced at Jarin. She looked tired, but unscathed and as lovely as he remembered. It took all his strength not to take her in his arms and kiss her all over like she was doing to Thebe.

"How did you find me?" she asked him, clinging to Thebe as if she never wanted to let her go.

"We didn't." Jarin smiled and nodded toward Thebe. "She wanted to run in the field, so I…" Jarin remembered his prayer, then shook his head and put his hands on his hips. "In truth, I have no idea."

"'Twas the Lord and the Spear," Cristiana said, squeezing Thebe tight.

"What happened to you?" he asked, still not sure he wasn't seeing things.

"Cedric LeGode." Cristiana's smile faded, and she reluctantly set Thebe down. The girl resumed her frolicking through the flowers, only this time squealing, "Cristi! Cristi!"

"Sir Walter's son? The one you were to wed?"

"Aye, the same."

"But the wolves..."

"His pets. He has turned to the darkness." Cristiana hugged herself, staring off into the distance, her joyous mood dissipating.

Jarin rubbed his chin. "I don't understand."

"Dark powers. There's a warlock at Luxley who trains him." She swallowed and wobbled slightly.

Jarin needed no invitation to rush to her side. Wrapping his arms around her, he drew her close and kissed the top of her head. "Are you harmed?"

"Nay. He did not touch me."

"Where is he now?" Jarin searched the forest behind her.

"I left him in a cave not far from here."

His jaw tightened. "He released you?"

She looked up at him and smiled. "He had no choice." Her nose wrinkled. "What is that smell?" She backed away from him and laughed.

He glanced at Thebe and shrugged.

"Sweet angels! You had to deal with her soiled cloth?" Her eyes laughed as she covered her mouth with her hand.

Jarin hid his embarrassment behind a smile. "As you can no doubt guess, I'm not skilled in that particular art."

Chuckling, she glanced at Thebe picking flowers and drawing them to her nose. "Would that I could have witnessed your attempt."

"I am glad you did not, for I prefer to maintain my dignity as a King's Guard." He gestured for her to return to him, surprised when she did without hesitation. He smoothed a lock of hair from her forehead, his eyes finding hers, searching within them, for what, he didn't know. For life, love, truth…meaning. He found all of that. And much more.

"I thought I'd lost you." He drew her against his chest again, inhaling a deep breath of her sweet scent and allowing it to chase away all his fears of the past days.

She grinned up at him, one eyebrow arched. "Finally free of the burden of our care. In good sooth, you must have been overjoyed."

"Nay." He ran a finger down her cheek, so soft, despite the smudges of dirt. "Quite the opposite, if I were to admit it."

"And are you?" Her eyes moistened again.

He could resist her no longer. Lowering his lips to hers, he kissed her, kissed her with all the passion, love, and loss, that had been building within him. Kissed her like a man who would gladly pledge his troth to this lady and never regret it for a moment.

She met his passion with equal fervor, gripping his shirt, pressing against him, allowing his kiss to deepen, explore, love, and cherish this precious lady.

Sweet ecstasy! Jarin had never known a kiss could evoke such emotions! An overwhelming desire burned within him to become one with this lady, not only in the physical sense, but spiritually, emotionally, and in every way possible.

He withdrew his kiss ere he frightened her. Pressing his forehead against hers, he allowed their heavy breaths to mingle between them in silence.

"Jarin," she breathed out. "What are your intentions, sir? For I fear should you kiss me like that again, I will lose my heart forever."

Cristiana's heart balanced on the edge of a cliff, ready to topple over the side at one word from Sir Jarin—one *wrong* word. Pulse still racing and body yet throbbing from their kiss, she looked up at him. Wind tossed his dark hair about him, wild and free, like the man himself. His shirt flapped open, revealing his thickly muscled chest and arms. Yet fear appeared in his eyes. A mere flicker as he gazed away as if afraid to answer.

She started to push from him, her heart on its way tumbling down the cliff.

But he took her arm and drew her back. The fear in his gaze had been replaced by something…something deep and permanent she dared not hope for. "My Lady Cristiana, I can make no promises as of yet, but I *will* tell you—" He cupped her chin in his hand and then caressed her cheek with his thumb. "I love you. In truth, I have loved you since the day I met you at Luxley. 'Twas why I could not leave you be, why I volunteered to find you, why I have freely put my life in danger for you and the child."

Inexpressible emotions flooded her, and she leaned into his hand. "I love you, Jarin. Promise or not, my heart is yours." She could no longer deny it.

"Can you bear with me a little longer, my lady?" He leaned toward her, his breath drifting over her face. "I fear I must grow accustomed to the idea of having a wife."

Wife. How wonderful that sounded. But if a man must grow accustomed…She stepped back. "I will not imprison you, Jarin. Love does no harm to another. Seeing you unhappy, I could ne'er live with myself."

He reached for her but lowered his hand. "How could I ever be so with you in my arms?"

"You are a warrior, a man who loves his freedom, who fears the pain of loss that love can bring." She wanted him to deny all, to bend his knee before her, take her hand and pledge his life and love to her forever.

Instead, he remained standing, confusion furrowing his brow and desperation burning in his eyes.

Tears blurred her vision. She quickly wiped them away when Thebe rushed toward her, a bouquet of flowers in her hand. "For you, Cristi! For you!"

Kneeling, Cristiana took them and hugged the girl tight. "They are beautiful, Thebe! Thank you. I love them!"

The little girl beamed and kissed Cristiana on the cheek.

Sir Jarin's jaw stiffened as he stared at the patch of trees behind them, and she knew the moment between them was lost.

"What is it?" she asked, rising to her feet.

"Cedric. You said he's nearby in a cave?"

"Aye, just beyond these trees and over a hill."

"Stay here," Jarin ordered, gripping the hilt of his sword. "Hide in the trees. I'll return anon."

"Where are you going?"

"Forsooth, you cannot expect me to leave him free. He almost killed you. He *would* have killed you. He must answer for his crimes."

Cristiana grabbed his arm, feeling the flex of his muscles beneath her hand. "Nay, Sir Jarin. Leave him be." She glanced in that direction. "I am unharmed. Let him answer to God."

"Enough of your kind heart, my lady!" He tugged from her. "If I do not end his life, he will come after you again."

"Nay." Tears glistened in her eyes. "He cannot touch me. Not as long as I have the Spear."

He raked back his hair and snorted. "Why leave him unpunished? Surely, he'll return to Luxley and fight against us."

"Or he may not. He may repent and turn from the darkness."

His expression softened. Releasing a deep sigh, he shook his head. "Another reason I love you, my lady. Your love for others—even your enemies—astounds me."

She smiled, longing to be in his arms yet again, feel their strength around her, warm, loving, protecting. Longed for another kiss, one that made her feel so many wonderful things all at once.

The way he was looking at her now, he seemed to be of the same mind.

"Hungry, Cristi." Thebe yanked on her skirt and stared up at her, and she and Jarin laughed.

"We should be on our way." He jerked his head toward the road where their horses awaited. "And aye." He reached for Thebe, and she leapt into his arms. "I will give you some bread to eat."

Walking behind him, watching his strong, confident gait, the blade at his side and knife in his belt, reminded her he was a warrior at heart. And yet...the way he was smiling and talking with Thebe, so gentle and loving, caused a bittersweet feeling to flood her. Sweet because she was in love with him, and she doubted she'd ever feel this way about another. And bitter because she also doubted a man like Jarin could ever tie himself to a wife and family.

She would not think of it now. She must keep her focus on returning to Luxley with the Spear and aiding her sister in whate'er way she could in order to defeat Sir Walter and this warlock who had invaded their home.

If only Jarin would stop looking at her like he kept doing as they continued their journey on horseback, she'd be more successful at her task.

They passed through a small village, the inhabitants of which barely paid them any mind, then across a series of farms and forests ere the sun began its descent in the west. A chilled wind, ripe with the scent of earthy loam and spicy rain wove about them, and Cristiana folded her cloak tighter around a sleeping Thebe. A bank of dark clouds drifted over the sun, casting everything in gloom.

Jarin pulled back on his reins and raised a hand for her to do the same. Dust spun eddies over the ground in the distance. Thunder bellowed. Nay, not thunder. Rather, the pounding hooves of many horses.

"This way!" Jarin shouted, jerked his horse to the left, and sped across an open field toward a line of trees in the distance.

Cristiana followed, her horse tearing up the soil as they went. Thebe woke and clung to her. But there was nowhere to hide. No building or trees close enough to duck behind. One glance over her shoulder proved her right.

At least a dozen soldiers gained on them from behind.

Jarin saw them too, drew his sword, jerked the reins to slow his horse, and gestured for Cristiana to keep going. But she didn't want to keep going. She wanted to stay with him.

He turned to face the soldiers as if he could defeat them single-handedly. He was highly skilled, a great warrior, but not even *he* could overpower such a force. And she would not see him die. Not on her account.

Pulling on the reins, she whirled her mount around. The animal thrust its front legs in the air, nearly toppling them, but finally settled. Thebe let out a frightened wail.

Jarin glanced back at them, a frown on his face.

But the soldiers were already on them, surrounding them, their horses agitated and foaming, their drawn swords shimmering in the light.

And their grins wide and victorious.

CHAPTER THIRTY-SEVEN

A thousand horses stampeded through Cristiana's brain, *th-thump, th-thump, th-thump, th-thump,* stirring up clouds of dust, obscuring her thoughts. Familiar scents assailed her—beeswax, lavender, freshly laundered linen, and....*sick,* putrid and foul. She moved her hand. A familiar softness brushed her palms. The spit and crackle of a fire met her ears, along with the whisk of wind past an open window.

With great difficulty, she pried her eyes open.

And terror like she'd never known ripped across her flesh.

She lay on a bed, decorated with four carved wooden posts and a gauze covering. A candle flickered from a stand to her left, whilst a lantern sat atop the mantel above a blazing fire. Two stuffed chairs perched before it atop a silk-embroidered rug. Tapestries and paintings lined the walls of stone that led to a narrow window through which a shaft of moonlight entered.

Her chamber.

Her chamber at Luxley Castle.

Reaching a hand to her head, she attempted to rise, but the ceiling spun, and nausea bubbled up her throat.

She was ill. *Again.*

Or was it *still?* She rubbed her temples as she tried to catch her breath. Nay, couldn't be. She'd escaped nigh a year ago, had been on the run with Sir Jarin and...Thebe!

"Thebe!" she shouted, but her voice emerged faint and distant.

Forcing her eyes open yet again, she pushed herself to sit, no matter the nausea. Sweat moistened the skin of her neck and arms. Someone had dressed her in her nightshirt. Grabbing the chamber pot sitting on the stand, her stomach convulsed, and she spewed forth its contents, sparse as they were.

Tears spilled from her eyes as she wiped her mouth. This can't be happening! 'Tis but a nightmare. Aye, that was it. She'd soon awaken in Sir Jarin's arms with Thebe by her side.

Returning the pot to its place, she drew a deep breath and prayed to wake up.

The door squeaked open. She stared at it as if she were watching a play—with interest, but as one who was not a part of the scene.

Sir Walter LeGode swept into the room with the pomp of a king, wearing a brilliant purple velvet tunic slit at the sides to show his creamy undertunic. A silver belt hung about his waist embedded with rubies that matched the brooch at his collar.

"Ah, you're awake, my dear." He approached and leaned to stare at her as if she were some odd curiosity.

His face swirled in her vision, candlelight reflecting in his lifeless eyes.

"What am I doing here?" she asked.

He raised his hands and glanced around. "Forsooth, this is your chamber, my lady."

A wave of dizziness threatened to force her back down on the mattress, but she would not give this man the pleasure. She closed her eyes. "Where are Sir Jarin and Thebe?"

"Who?"

Cristiana drew a breath. "Sir Jarin the Just and the little girl who was with us when your soldiers captured us."

"My soldiers?" He chuckled, and she heard him walk away. "If you weren't so ill, I'd think you cupshotten, my lady. Or mayhap 'tis but a dream you had, for you have not left your chamber in quite some time."

Nay! Cristiana hugged herself. She would not believe it. She *had* escaped. She had been kept by Lord Braewood, rescued by Sir Jarin. They'd hidden in a monastery, then at Lord Quinn's manor home, then the village. Then Cedric. Could it all have been a dream?

She laid a hand on her thigh where she kept the Spear. Gone. Frantically she groped with both hands over her entire leg.

"Ah, you are no doubt looking for that old relic?"

She gazed up at him. He stood at the foot of her bed, a supercilious grin on his face.

"The maids found it when they bathed you. No need for a refined lady as yourself to have such a filthy object strapped to your thigh." He snorted. "Most unseemly."

"What have you done with it?"

He shrugged and moved to the window where a faint glow began to push back the night. "As it turns out, the bishop is quite interested in it. Hence, I plan to give it to him."

"'Tis the Spear of Destiny, you fool. And neither"—her chamber retreated to a tiny point and then expanded again as her head seemed to float toward the ceiling—"you nor that vile bishop will ever be able to keep it or use its power." Blinking to clear her vision, she lifted the sleeve of her nightdress and focused on her wrist. The mark of the Spear was still there. She was still the protector!

"Indeed?" He smiled. "Alas, if the old thing is truly powerful, then why has it not healed you from your illness, my lady? 'Tis been in your possession for months now, I make bold to say."

'Twas true enough. But she'd not been ill these past...she attempted to catch her breath. Alas, what if he spoke the truth—that she'd been in her chamber all along? And all the love she'd shared with Jarin and Thebe had been but illusions of her desperate mind.

Yet, if he *was* lying and she had escaped, the Spear had not healed her before she'd left. *And* it had not protected her from being captured...or had she been captured? She couldn't think.

"Cedric," she muttered.

Sir Walter moved toward her, eyes narrowed, and voice spiked. "What about my son?"

Memories of the cave, the wolves, and ravens, and Cedric's attempt to take the Spear from her fluttered through her mind. Or had it merely been a dream? "He...he tried to get the Spear." A blade sliced through her head, and bending over, she gripped her temples. "I don't know."

Sir Walter studied her. Tension tightened around him as if he longed to spring on her. Then he smiled. "A dream, my lady. You have been quite ill of late. But be of good cheer. Today is your wedding day!"

She stared at him aghast.

"We delayed it, my lady, due to your illness, but you are on the mend now."

"But Cedric is not here."

"No matter." He leaned toward her, then retreated, pinching his nose as if he smelled something foul. "You are marrying me."

Cristiana blinked, hoping to sweep away the man's last words. "You?" Nausea bubbled again. "But your wife…"

"Oh, you hadn't heard? Of course. An unfortunate accident has taken her life. So young." He tsked and laid a hand over his heart. "They say the best remedy for a broken heart is to remarry as quickly as possible."

Cristiana gripped her throat, trying to keep from being sick again. "I won't marry you."

"You have no choice, my dear." He whirled about, his velvet tunic flapping, and headed toward the door. "Your maids will arrive soon to bathe and dress you for the ceremony."

"You are poisoning me!" she shouted after him.

"Devil's blood! Such a thing to say to your espoused. You use me most ungraciously, my lady. In good sooth, I am trying to make you well."

"Where are Thebe and Sir Jarin?"

"I truly have no idea who you are talking about, my lady, but never fear, you will feel back to yourself anon." Then, after flashing her a grin that was as fabricated as the tale he told, he left and slammed the door.

Cristiana sank into a puddle on the bed. Either she was going completely mad and she'd only dreamed the past year. Or she'd been captured and poisoned again, and Sir Jarin and

Thebe were somewhere nearby. She had to believe the latter. She simply had to.

Or there'd be no reason to go on.

Even so, the Spear was gone. What chance did she have against Sir Walter and Cedric's vile warlock? Without its power, not only could she not heal herself, but neither could she stop them from poisoning her further, dressing her, and forcing her to marry Sir Walter.

Dropping her head in her hands, she sobbed. *God, have you finally abandoned me like everyone else?*

Alexia held up the crinkled parchment to the hearth where a fire provided enough light to see that—though some letters were smeared—most of the words on the document were legible. In good sooth, it wouldn't take a scholar to read and understand the intent and meaning in those words. The only problem? Sir Walter's signature was also smeared. Not entirely. One could easily make out the *Si* and the *eGode*, just not the Walter in the middle.

She breathed out a sigh of frustration as Ronar appeared by her side. "What say you, my love?"

They had allowed the parchment to dry for several days, hoping and praying that God would transform the smeared sections back into letters. Otherwise, they would have to return to Luxley and make one more attempt to get the pompous man's signature.

"It might suffice as proof for the king as is," Alexia said. "Especially should a reputable person deliver it straight to his hand."

"And you know such a man?" Damien said from his seat on the couch beside Seraphina, his tone sarcastic.

Alexia turned to face them. "I do. A trustworthy one whose services my mother and father oft used when they were alive."

"And is *he* still alive?" Ronar asked, raising a mocking brow.

"Aye. He's the village scrivener, if you must know. A Master Garitt. And he has a rabid disdain for Sir Walter." She gave him a tight smile.

"And an appreciation for you, who delivers fresh meat to his family, if I recall," Ronar added, gazing at her again as if there were none other in the room. She doubted she could resist him if there weren't. Instead, she settled for a squeeze of his hand.

Friar Josef entered through a door at the back of their underground cave and approached, bringing with him the peaceful aura that always surrounded him after he spent time in prayer. "Greetings young knights. The Lord wishes you to know there is naught impossible with Him!"

Ronar greeted him, then said to them all. "Indeed! I say we contact this scrivener and send the post as soon as possible to the king."

"Nay." Seraphina rose, fear sparking in her blue eyes. "The scrivener will die. Wolves will attack and devour him. I have seen it."

Damien growled and leaned forward, elbows on his knees.

"Are you sure?" Alexia took a step toward the lady. "Mayhap 'twas merely a nightmare or vision from the enemy?"

"I wish that it were, my lady." She glanced over them all. "I waited until you said the man's name and that he was a scrivener, for that is what I keep seeing."

Ronar grabbed the back of a chair and slammed it down on the stone floor. "'Tis the warlock. He knows. He sees."

"Mayhap, my son." Friar Josef raised a calming hand. "But God's power is greater."

Damien looked up. "Then we send someone else."

"Nay." Alexia glanced at the friar, understanding stretching between them. "'Tis not the person, but the parchment he sees. Anyone we send would be in danger."

"Aye." Friar Joseph let out a sigh. "Anyone who is not a follower of Christ will be at great risk."

Damien jumped to his feet. "Then I will bring it."

"Egad, man." Ronar chuckled. "Have you quit your roistering and drinking and made a commitment to God I am unaware of?"

The knight sneered. "What need have I of an invisible God when I have this." He gripped the pommel of his sword. "A pack of wolves? Bah! I've single-handedly fought and killed a band of trained soldiers. I can handle a few sniveling beasts."

From looking at the knight, clad in leather and armor and strapped with a dozen weapons, Alexia had no doubt 'twas true.

Ronar, however, shook his head. "Do you forget you are a wanted man, Damien? You'd be arrested ere you reached the king. Alas, any of us would." Growling, he took up a pace before the hearth. "Tush! To come this far and be trussed like a hen."

"*I* will take it," Seraphina said, easing a braid of golden hair over her shoulder.

"Nay." Damien didn't hesitate to answer with both authority and finality.

"But I am not wanted by the authorities."

Damien faced her, his face tight with frustration. "Did you not just hear that this warlock will send wolves to devour your flesh?"

She frowned at him.

"He's right." Alexia approached the lady and took her hands. "Though I know you for a godly woman, 'tis far too perilous. Even so, a mere maid would ne'er be given audience with the king."

"Alack." Seraphina withdrew her hand and sighed. "I want to do something. I feel so helpless."

"We all feel helpless at the moment." Walking to the friar's desk, Alexia gently laid the parchment down and placed a large book atop it. "Should you have an idea, a word from God, friar, now would be the time to express it."

He shook his head. "Naught but what I normally suggest. To pray." He glanced over them all. "'Twill all work out. I know it."

"Would that I enjoyed your confidence." Ronar huffed as he continued pacing.

Still, the friar's faith put Alexia to shame. She, too, should believe that God would provide the answer. A much more difficult task when things continued to grow worse.

"Alexia!" The voice was faint, distant.

She glanced over her friends, but none of them addressed her.

Ronar swept his gaze to hers, sharp and tense.

"Alexia!"

They all glanced at the door. No one knew of this secret place. Few called her by her Christian name.

Making her way to the far table, Alexia grabbed her bow and quiver of arrows. Ronar took his sword and together, the two of them, along with Damien, started for the door. All while Alexia sought her mind for an answer as to the source of the voice.

"Wait." She held up a hand. "It has to be Anabelle. She's the only one who knows of our hideout." She'd almost forgotten that she'd told the maid—nigh two years ago now—that should she ever find herself in danger, to walk east for two miles and search for the pond beside an ivy-covered cliff over which a waterfall tumbled. There was none like it in all of Emerald Forest.

"Allow me to go to her." Alexia opened the door and started out.

"Nay." Ronar nudged her behind him. "Damien and I will go. If 'tis her, we'll bring her to you."

Alexia didn't like being told what to do. She also didn't like waiting and doing nothing, but her heart never failed to warm whene'er Ronar desired to protect her. Within minutes, Anabelle appeared in the tunnel.

"Anabelle!" Alexia ushered her inside, glancing behind her at Ronar and Damien, who followed.

"Never fear." Ronar closed the door behind him and Damien. "She is alone."

"I made sure of it, my lady." Anabelle glanced over the chamber in awe, as everyone did when they first saw such a well-appointed home beneath the ground.

"Forgive me for coming here. I know you told me never to do so, but I have important news." Anabelle gripped her throat as if the action would help her to speak.

Seraphina poured a mug of water and handed it to the woman.

She gulped it down, and set it on the table, her worried eyes flitting over them all.

"What is it?" Alexia asked.

"'Tis Cristiana and Sir Jarin. They are caught."

Jaw bunching, Ronar lowered his head and groaned.

"Judas!" Damien gripped the hilt of his sword.

"My sister? Where is she?" Alexia didn't know whether to be thrilled or terrified. She hadn't seen Cristiana in so long, *far* too long, that the thought of her being so close elated her. Yet now, she feared the worse.

"In her chamber. 'Tis all I know. Save, I believe Sir Walter poisons her again."

Alexia closed her eyes, fighting back tears, fighting back desperation *and* fury.

"And Jarin?" Ronar asked.

"In the dungeon. To be executed on the morrow."

Ronar cursed again, then apologized as he glanced at the friar.

Executed? Alexia could not bear it.

"Not if I can help it!" Damien raged and pounded his fist on the stone wall.

"Is it the bishop's doing?" Alexia asked. "Surely Sir Walter is too muddle-brained to do much of anything."

The maid shook her head. "He no longer takes the potion, my lady. He knows someone poisons him, thus he gathers his own food and drink from the kitchen."

Alexia touched her arm. "Does he suspect you?"

"Nay. I don't believe so."

Damien muttered, rubbing his leather-clad hand. "Then we can no longer get his signature."

Ronar nodded, silent. But Alexia had seen that look before. He had retreated within himself, gathering courage, making plans, hoarding anger.

He was preparing for war.

Alexia squeezed Anabelle's hand. "You have done right to come here. And at great risk. Thank you."

Anabelle glanced at the door. "I must return ere he discovers me gone."

Approaching, the friar laid a hand on her head. "Go with God, dear lady."

She cast them all one last glance, then slipped out the door.

Friar Josef gestured for them all to come near. "We must pray."

"Nay!" Damien barked. "We must go rescue them."

"Indeed." The friar's tone brooked no argument. "But first, we pray."

"Where is Cedric?" Sir Walter hesitated to make demands of Drago, but 'twould seem his son was missing.

"How should I know?" A swarm of flies hovered over Drago as he read a book spread open before him.

"Can't you spread some coals on your iron table and locate him?"

Drago lifted his gaze, his black eyes so sharp, Sir Walter swore he felt something stab his chest. "I have tried. He does not appear."

"Why would he not appear? Is he dead?" Sir Walter swallowed and wrung his hands. If so, he'd lose his leverage with this monster.

"Dead *or* he has turned to the light. Either way, I no longer sense his power." Drago flipped a page and ran a long black fingernail over the words.

"Turned, bah! The woman said he tried to take the Spear. Mayhap she bound him somewhere or sprinkled holy water on him."

A screech from above drew Sir Walter's gaze as a bat took flight up the hollow tower.

"Hell's fire! You'd better hope that is not so, for you promised him as apprentice to me." Drago's pale lips curled like the smoke rising from his cauldron, his smile frightening Sir Walter more than the threat.

"And he has been a good apprentice...powerful and very useful to you." He hated the tremor in his voice.

"Hmm." The cyclone of flies above Drago's head suddenly dove into the bubbling cauldron, their bodies hissing as they hit the liquid.

A stench akin to rotted flesh and human feces burned Sir Walter's nose, and he wondered why he tortured himself with these frequent visits below. What need had he of this devil anymore? He had the Spear *and* the girl. The Spear he'd give to the bishop and send him on his way. The girl he would marry and become lord of Luxley.

As if reading his thoughts. Drago seethed. "Do you try me for a fool, *snake*? We have a bargain. And should you not fulfill your part, I'll carve your loathsome carcass into pieces, and your fate will follow that of these flies!"

Sir Walter gulped. Terror twisted his tongue, leaving him speechless. A single fly flew out of Drago's ear and joined the others by way of demonstration.

"Sulfur and flames!" Drago shuddered and gazed up. "They are here again."

"The Knights of the Eternal Realm?"

"Do not say their name!" His bellow sent more bats screeching upward.

"Then flood them, topple a wall on them, or send a swarm of locusts to devour them." Sir Walter flung a hand through the air.

"The Spear is here, you fool! Its presence forbids me to see clearly. Get rid of it at once, or these knights may get the better of you."

"I intend to. After the bishop weds Lady Cristiana and me this eve, I will give him the Spear, and he will no doubt make haste to return to the king. To the devil with that swag-bellied pompous snod!"

"Aye, the bishop will eventually meet our master." Drago resumed his reading. "Acquit me and be about it then. I find your company tiresome."

Sir Walter fumed. The sentiment was mutual. Someday—and someday soon—he would teach this warlock to respect him. Mayhap when Cedric returned with more power than this depraved sorcerer, whose dark magic couldn't even defeat a rusted old relic.

CHAPTER THIRTY-EIGHT

A rat scrambled over Jarin's boot. He kicked it to the stone wall on his left, one of four walls that enclosed him in a prison of his own stupidity. He should have seen those soldiers coming, should have been paying closer attention. But he'd allowed his thoughts and his focus to stay upon Lady Cristiana—on their recent confessions of love, their kiss, and the conflict within him to either make her his wife or run as far from her as he could.

Forsooth! Now, he had not only lost her and Thebe, but his freedom, and quite possibly his life. If what the guard told him was true—that he was to be hanged at dawn.

Death, the ultimate loss of freedom. Or was it? Not if his dream had been real.

Rising, he walked the four steps it took to reach the far wall ere he turned and retraced his path. His boots rang hollow over the dirty stones, kicking up the odor of mold, decay, and death to taunt him. He felt for the other wall, lost in the shadows, and moist, scratchy rock met his fingers. Water trickled down a column of stones and formed a small puddle in the corner.

He turned and gazed upward where a small window far above provided a modicum of light that did naught to dispel the gloom of the place. Nor the gloom from his heart.

He'd not slept all night, alternating between pacing and crumbling to a heap. No visitors had come nor any food, and from the dimness of the light now coming through the window, he assumed the day was nearly spent.

One more endless night, and he'd be dead.

Jarin fisted hands at his waist and growled. What was happening to Cristiana and Thebe? Were they safe? Cared for? Or were they to face the same fate as he? Nay, Sir Walter needed Cristiana alive. That gave him hope. But what about Thebe?

"Oh, God, prithee, watch over the child." His pathetic prayer sounded hollow and empty, bouncing off the walls of the dismal chamber.

Would he ever see them again? Despair threatened to leech all hope from his soul.

"How could you allow this to happen, God? How?" It didn't seem fair when Jarin had started praying again. When he'd begun to believe God might not be the cruel tyrant he'd always believed.

Pacing to the other wall, he kicked it. Pain shot up his foot into his ankle. Good. It kept him alert, focused, and assured him he was still alive.

Unbidden, his thoughts drifted to all the incredible things he'd seen since he'd found Cristiana. Scenes from a play no one would believe unless they'd been there themselves. The sudden fog that had saved them from the soldiers, lightning that had transformed wolves into dust, the dark spirits he'd seen around Quinn, the angel who had alerted him of the threat to Cristiana, the healings he had witnessed, the curse on the village's water lifted. He could go on. And what of the lady herself, her love and care for others, even her enemies? In good sooth, how could Jarin deny that God was love when His love shone so brightly through Cristiana?

Nay, he could no longer deny there was a loving God, a God who cared about His children, who loved and healed and protected. He could also not deny that *that* same God stole his father, mother, and baby sister from his arms. When all they did was serve Him.

Their faces flashed before him, so young and full of joy and living in a place beyond description—a glimpse into an eternity that made this place and their time here of no import at all. 'Twas the last scene in a parade of events that God had used to get Jarin's attention.

Jarin bowed his head. "You have it, God. You have it." *Alas, now what?* For instead of all things working out for good as Cristiana so oft proclaimed, things had ended up much worse than they ever could have expected.

Jarin sank to his knees on the hard stone. "I'm sorry, Almighty God. I'm sorry, Jesus. I wandered away from you, angry and bitter. I thought I could run my own life, be master of my soul—eat, drink, and be merry until my dying day. But You have shown me that this life is nothing compared to eternity. Death is not the end for those who follow You, but merely the beginning of something far beyond compare. When You took my family, I thought 'twas cruel, but I see now 'twas a blessing, a reward, for them."

A dark shadow grew in one of the corners. Not from the waning light, but something much darker—a blackness that moved and breathed. *And* fumed. A presence. An evil that sent a shudder through Jarin. And he was not one to shudder. Two dark hands reached for him. Every nerve tightened. His breath seized. Fingers, black and pointed, curled around his neck, icy and sharp.

And he knew without a doubt that if he allowed it, the darkness would devour him.

"Nay! You cannot have me! I belong to Almighty God!" Jarin stood and fisted his hand at the mist ere closing his eyes and continuing his prayer. "And should I enter that eternity soon, I hope, Father, that You will find me worthy to join my family. My only request is that You spare Cristiana and Thebe and keep them safe and loved in this life until You bring them home as well."

The evil dissipated as if a strong wind had blown it away. Indeed, Jarin felt such a breeze, ripe with the sweet scent of myrrh. Strange. He opened his eyes. The final spire of light drifted over him from the window above.

A man appeared in his cell, glowing like a thousand candles, his hair whiter than pristine snow, his eyes burning flames, and his tunic sparkling like diamonds.

He smiled at Jarin, and in that smile Jarin saw a love he never knew existed.

He got down on one knee and bowed his head. "My Lord and my King, I swear my fealty to You for all eternity."

When he glanced up, the man was gone, but Jarin knew he would never be the same.

Cristiana gazed up, mesmerized by the ribbons of maroon and gold fluttering across the morning sky. A breeze twirled one of her curls across her cheek, tickling her skin, and bringing the scent of lavender, rose, and horseflesh to her nose.

Sky? Why was she outside?

The world spun. Someone steadied her with a touch. Nausea gurgled up her throat. She glanced down and pressed a hand over the most lustrous azure silk gown she'd ever seen. Gold filigree trimmed the edges of her bell sleeves along with the slits that opened down her sides.

Blinking, she attempted to focus on her surroundings—the chatter of a crowd standing around her, the familiar shuffle of servants' feet hurrying to and fro, the neigh of horses and grunt of pigs. A crackling sound brought her gaze to torches lining the front of the chapel. *Chapel?* The outer bailey of Luxley Castle.

The blurred shape of the bishop in his white tunic, silk-embroidered vestment, a tall red mitre cap on his head, appeared before her, an open book in his hand. Pressure on her arm brought her gaze to her right where Sir Walter stood beside her.

"If you please, Bishop, let us proceed," he said with impatience.

Wait! Nay! She was marrying Sir Walter? A nightmare. It had to be. She lifted a hand to her head wherein surely a blacksmith hammered an anvil over and over. Pain radiated down her back with each strike.

"I cannot," she finally muttered out.

"Oh, I assure you, my lady." Sir Walter smiled her way. "You can."

The bishop cleared his throat. "Blessings and merry meet, gentle lords and ladies. Their banns having been published, we are here today to join the fair Lady Cristiana D'Clere and the noble Sir Walter LeGode together in matrimony."

Banns? When had Cristiana agreed to this union?

"Sir Walter, art thou here this day in pledged troth of thy own free will and choice?" the bishop continued, his voice muted and distant, as if from a dream.

"Aye, father," Sir Walter said.

"Lady Cristiana D'Clere, art thou here this day in pledged troth of thy own free will and choice?"

Nay, nay, nay! Her insides screamed, her voice unable to function due to the bile rising in her throat.

"The lady says aye," Sir Walter said.

"In as much as this nobleman and fair lady have pledged their troth to be married this day, we call upon heaven to bless this union. Therefore, if anyone can show just cause why they may not be joined together, by God's Law or the Laws of the Realm, let them now speak, or else hereafter keep silent for all time."

Cristiana's thoughts spun into a cyclone of misery, angst, and confusion. Surely someone would say something! Wouldn't they? Mayhap 'twas a nightmare after all.

All have abandoned you.

The voice rang clear through her addled mind. Clear and true. Everyone *had* abandoned her. Her mother, her father, her sister, Seraphina, and now Sir Jarin. Even Thebe. Where was that dear child?

"God, help me," she whispered.

"What say you?" The bishop leaned toward her.

"She says to proceed, Your Grace." Sir Walter glanced over the crowd. "The lady is anxious to consummate the union, no doubt."

Chuckling ensued.

Attempting to catch her breath, Cristiana's legs turned to mush, and she reeled, longing to fold to the ground and disappear. Firm hands gripped her and kept her standing.

"Do you Sir Walter LeGode take unto thyself as wife Lady Cristiana D'Clere and pledge unto her before God and these witnesses to be her protector, defender, and sure resort, to honor and sustain her, in sickness and in health, in fair and in foul, with all thy worldly powers, to cherish and forsaking all others, keep thee only unto her, so long as ye both shall live?"

God, where are you? Have you abandoned me as well? Cristiana felt her thigh for the Spear, but 'twas gone. Without the Spear, the power of God no longer rested on her. Did His love also no longer abide with her? Yet hadn't He protected her over the past year? Hadn't He shown His faithfulness and His mercy?

"I will," Sir Walter answered.

The bishop released a sigh, as if he were bored, ere continuing. "Do you Lady Cristiana D'Clere take unto thyself the nobleman Sir Walter to be thy rightful lord and pledge unto him before God and these witnesses to honor him, to cleave unto him, in sickness and in health, in fair and in foul, be his one true and lasting counselor and solace, and forsaking all others, keep thee only unto him, so long as ye both shall live?"

Think, think, think! If only Cristiana could gather her wits, her thoughts, her strength, she could speak up, deny this hideous farce, and order her knights to toss Sir Walter and the bishop from her castle...her land...her estate!

If only God would heal her as He had done to so many others she had touched.

But without the Spear....

"My lady? What say you?" The bishop's tone was ice.

Holding a hand to her stomach, Cristiana lifted her chin. "This is what I say. In the name of Jesus the Christ, I am healed!" Though her voice lacked the strength of her words, she jerked her arm from Sir Walter's grip and closed her eyes.

Laughter rumbled over her from the crowd. Sir Walter growled. The bishop let out a sigh of frustration.

"Clearly, your excellency, the lady calls to Christ for His blessing on the union."

"Very well," the bishop said. "Heavenly Father, Creator of all things both in heaven and earth, we humbly ask thee to bless this union..."

But Cristiana wasn't listening anymore. As if a strong wind blew away all the dust and fog from her head, her mind began to clear. The world settled. As did her breathing, along with her stomach as a wave of strength swept down her body.

She opened her eyes. God had healed her! Even without the Spear. How could that be? She gazed up at the stunning blue sky—as the bishop droned on—and began to laugh. "You love me? You find me worthy of your love and blessing?" She could hardly believe it. All her life, she'd lived cowardly and meek in the shadow of her courageous sister. Everyone had abandoned her as unworthy. But not her Father in heaven. He had always been with her, always loved her, with or without the Spear! She knew that now.

Sir Walter obviously thought she spoke to him, for he leaned toward her, a pleased grin on his face. "You may not be worthy of me, my lady, but I grant you the favor of becoming my wife, withal."

Nausea brewed in her belly again, but not from any illness.

The bishop cleared his throat. "Shall we proceed?"

Cristiana squared her shoulders and said with the authority of her station. "Nay. We shall not! I would not marry Sir Walter were he the king, himself."

Gasps and laughter tumbled across the assembled crowd, silenced by one look from Sir Walter.

The bishop scowled.

Sir Walter gripped her arm so tight, she let out a shriek. "'Twas not my intention to resort to this, but you give me no choice, my lady." His whisper wafted putrid on her neck. Then, turning her slightly, he gave a nod to a knight standing by the front gate. From within the tower, the man yanked a child and held her beside him.

"Thebe!" Cristiana started for her, but Sir Walter's pinched grip held her back.

"Cristi! Cristi!" Tears streamed down the little girl's cheeks as she struggled to be free from the knight. The anguish and fear on that precious face nearly caused Cristiana to fold to the ground.

"She's just a babe, you devilish fiend!"

"Marry me, and she will be safe. If not"—he shrugged—"I will order my knight to run her through with his blade."

CHAPTER THIRTY-NINE

Jarin struggled against the rope binding his hands in front of him as the knights led him from the dungeon, up a winding stairway, and then out a door into the back courtyard of Luxley Castle. A faint glow lit the horizon, streaking the sky in colors so vibrant, Jarin could not imagine executing anyone with such a glorious dawn as backdrop.

But off to hang him they were.

In good sooth, with ten well-armed knights as escort! Just for little ol' him. He smiled. No doubt Sir Walter had heard of Jarin's skill with a blade, for in truth, with freed hands and a good sword, he *could* defeat these men. Especially now with God on his side.

A God…*the* God… he supposed he was to meet soon enough. Yet he bore no fear, held no doubt that he would be welcomed. Not for his many good deeds, for he knew he'd be found lacking in that area. But simply because Jarin had finally committed his trust to the One who had paid the price for all his errors, his wrongs…his sins. Would that he had more time to honor his new Lord by serving Him here on earth, but that, too, was not in Jarin's hands. In truth, during the long night, he'd discovered that naught had ever really been in Jarin's control. Naught save his free will, which he'd used to choose poorly.

Not anymore.

He smiled at the knight escorting him on his left, and confusion crossed the man's eyes ere he offered a scowl in return.

"Lovely day for a hanging," Jarin said.

"Shut your mouth!" a knight walking in front of him shouted over his shoulder as they exited a back gate and began the descent down a hill behind the castle.

No doubt Sir Walter wished to hang Jarin in private and not in the village as was the custom, for many of the villagers would recognize him as a friend of Alexia. 'Twas for the best. Jarin had no desire to have an audience for so demeaning a death.

They wove through a small copse of trees, and Jarin peered around branches and leaves, searching for his friends. Surely they had heard of his imprisonment by now. Or mayhap not. He had no idea whether Ronar, Damien, and Alexia still lived in Emerald Forest, or if they were able to obtain any information of the happenings at Luxley.

Dawn's light angled through the trees above, shifting light and dark over Jarin as the scent of pine and moss, and the sweat of the knights mingled beneath his nose. He slowed, wanting to savor his last moments alive, to remember the beautiful sights and rich smells of this place.

The knight behind him shoved him forward.

He stumbled into a clearing. A gallows stood in the center. A hooded man dressed in black stood waiting at the top.

Jarin's heartbeat thumped in his ears. *Th-thump, th-thump, th-thump.* Time seemed to slow.

The call of a heron sounded. Odd.

He glanced around. Something shimmered beyond the trees.

Whoosh! Whisk!

The knight beside Jarin toppled to the ground. An arrow protruded from his leg. Before the man could even cry out, another arrow split the morning air and took down a knight in front of Jarin.

"Run for cover!" one of the knights shouted and the men dove back into the trees.

Jarin dropped beside the first fallen knight and reached for the knife stuffed in his belt.

A war cry that could only come from Damien echoed through the clearing. One of the knights grabbed Jarin by the arm and jerked him away.

But not before he grabbed the blade.

The chime of a sword being drawn forced the knight around, and he released Jarin. Blades met high, glinting in rays of the morning sun. 'Twas Ronar! His friend fought with the knight, striking blow after blow, first high, then low, then to the side, sending the knight spinning. Finally Ronar struck the man's head with the hilt of his blade, dropping him to the ground.

Jarin sliced through his ropes just in time to look up and catch a sword Ronar tossed his way. Gripping the hilt, he grinned. "Your timing is impeccable, my friend, though a little sooner would have been appreciated."

"We like to make an entrance," Ronar returned between heavy breaths, both their gazes drawn to the clearing where Damien fought off three more knights. No time to help him as four more warriors rushed toward them.

Jarin whirled just in time to dip his sword in defense against one of two knights charging him from behind.

Ronar thrust his blade toward another knight on his left, slicing his leg, then pulled out his stiletto and flung it at the other. It embedded in the man's chest, expertly positioned between two plates of armor. The man howled and stumbled backward ere rushing back toward the castle.

"Pity. I liked that stiletto," Ronar commented as he took on the remaining knight.

Jarin whirled his sword aloft then cleaved the blade downward in a hissing sound that ended with a mighty *clang* as it met the knight's sword. The other knight charged from Jarin's left, but Jarin ducked, sending the man tumbling into a tree trunk.

An arrow whizzed past them and pierced the man's shoulder, pinning him to the tree.

The other knight swooped down upon Jarin, but with a snap of his blade, he flipped the man's sword from his grip and flung it into the trees, then held the tip to the man's neck.

"Are you quite finished, or do you wish to play some more?" Jarin asked.

The knight, a young man with barely a whisker on his chin, glanced over Jarin's shoulder at Ronar, who was no doubt quickly dispatching the final knight. Turning, he sped off through the trees.

By the time Jarin faced Ronar, the last opponent was lying flat on the ground, blood spilling from his arm.

"My friend!" Jarin gripped Ronar's shoulders, then pulled him into an embrace. "'Tis good to see you."

Pulling back, Ronar smiled. "And you! 'Twas unclear you were ever returning to us."

The ring of blades drew their gazes to Damien. One of his opponents lay unmoving on the ground, but the other two came at him like battering rams.

"Do you think he needs assistance?" Jarin asked.

Stabbing his sword into the ground, Ronar leaned on the hilt. "Nay. No doubt he would resent the intrusion."

Damien went blade to blade with one of the knights, a man as large as he, whilst the other one plucked out a knife, intending to stab Damien from behind.

Ere he could, two arrows flew through the air, one so fast after the other, it seemed they were fired together. One struck the man's arm, forcing him to drop the knife, whilst the other struck his thigh.

Damien quickly dispatched his opponent, then wheeled to face the other man, disappointment marring his features when he saw he'd already been defeated.

Lady Alexia D'Clere, dressed in leather vest and breeches, dropped from the trees beyond the clearing and headed their way.

The woman had the strength of a warrior and the beauty of a goddess, and Jarin could see why Ronar was so smitten. In truth, his friend's eyes never left the lady as she made her way to them.

Damien slipped beside her. "I could have handled the other one as well," he complained to the lady.

"I have no doubt, Sir Damien," she responded with a grin. "Alas, time is of the essence. Good to see you, Sir Jarin."

"And you, my lady." He gave a bow, but she drew him close and hugged him.

When she released him, Damien gripped his arm. "My friend."

Jarin nodded toward the large knight, overjoyed to be amongst his companions again.

Ronar handed him a leather strap, two knifes, and a heavy cloak.

"What news of Cristiana?" Jarin slipped the baldric over his head, sheathed his sword, and flung the cloak over his shoulders. The others donned hooded cloaks as well.

"We must make haste." Swinging her quiver and bow over her shoulder, Alexia pushed past him and rushed toward the castle. "Sir Walter is marrying her at this very moment."

Cristiana had no choice. She must marry Sir Walter. For Thebe's sake. With her eyes never leaving Thebe's, she addressed the monster beside her. "Give me your troth that the girl can remain here at Luxley under my care."

His thin lips puckered as he adjusted the ruby brooch at his neck. "You have it. Now, I beseech you to proceed, Your Grace."

The bishop continued the ceremony, droning on in a rather annoyed tone, but Cristiana wasn't listening. Smiling, she nodded toward Thebe, hoping the child understood that all would be well.

A sound akin to thunder rumbled across the bailey. The loud crackle of fire met Cristiana's ears. Screams ensued. Smoke filled the air. Knights drew blades and charged into the middle of the courtyard, ready to meet their enemies.

At least ten massive barrels, set on fire, rolled toward the crowd! Coughing and hacking, hands to their noses, people darted off in every direction. Screams blared. Horses whinnied, chickens squawked.

Grunts, shouts, and the ring of blades added to the cacophony.

More blazing barrels rolled across the bailey.

The bishop ducked into the chapel. Cristiana yanked her hand from Sir Walter's—who stood in shock—and bolted toward Thebe. Though the smoke was thick, 'twas not hard to find her, for her cries were like a beacon to Cristiana's heart.

A man grabbed her ere she reached the child.

"Release me at once!" She pounded his chest and kicked and clawed, but he was far too strong.

"Be still, my lady!"

That voice, that sultry, rich voice. She stopped struggling but couldn't see his face beneath his hood.

A knight came at him from the right. Without releasing her, he pulled a sword from beneath his cloak and pierced the man's shoulder. Screaming, the assailant stumbled backward.

The clang of more blades echoed in the courtyard. One of the barrels struck the stables, setting it on fire. Soldiers ran to get water. More smoke billowed through the air. Arrows parted the fog and met their mark in flesh. Warriors screamed and toppled to the ground.

Cristiana couldn't breathe, couldn't think.

Hastening her forward, the man plucked a crying Thebe from the ground and then darted across the bailey, shoving and pushing through the hysterical crowd and blazing barrels to the entrance of the kitchen.

Inside, he halted. Meat roasted over a fire whilst pots bubbled with stew, but the cooks and maids must have abandoned their posts in fear, for the room was empty. The man removed the hood of his cloak and smiled her way.

Jarin! But of course 'twas Jarin.

"You came for me," was all she could think to say.

He lifted her hand for a kiss.

"Jarn! Jarn!" Thebe squeezed his neck so tight, he choked.

"'Tis all right now, little one." He pulled her back. "Come! Make haste!" Without hesitation, he dashed through the kitchen into the pantry and then out into the main hall, pulling Cristiana along beside him. Sweet angels, why were they running back into a castle full of enemies?

After a quick look around, Jarin ducked down a corridor to his left, through a series of storerooms Cristiana knew all too well, and then down another set of stairs into the wine cellar.

They were trapped! Terror begged her to grab Thebe and run back outside—to escape while they could. But an aura of confidence and courage clung to Jarin, as it normally did, and she realized she had come to trust him with her life. The smell of mold, dirt, and fermenting grapes wafted around her as they halted before two large barrels.

Jarin set Thebe down and began shoving aside the barrels when footsteps on the stairs alerted him. Drawing his blade, he whirled about.

But the most beautiful sight Cristiana had ever seen descended those stairs.

Her sister, Alexia.

They couldn't get to each other fast enough. The smell of her, the feel of her, Cristiana hugged her so tight, she doubted they'd ever be able to part.

"'Tis you! 'Tis really you! Dear sister!" Cristiana sobbed.

Alexia pushed her back, tears in her eyes. "Finally, you are safe, dear one." Behind her, two men descended.

Sir Ronar and another large knight she remembered as Damien LaRage. He nodded his greeting to her but said naught.

"And, pray, who is this?" Alexia knelt to gaze upon Thebe, then looked up at Cristiana with a wink. "Surely, you haven't been gone *that* long."

Cristiana chuckled as Thebe shyly answered, "I am Thebe."

"Well, Mistress Thebe." Alexia smiled. "Welcome to our party."

The girl giggled as Cristiana looked up and smiled at Ronar. "Sir Ronar. Have you been taking good care of my sister?"

By the way he smiled at Alexia, she had her answer.

Footsteps and shouts thundered above them.

"Alas," Ronar said, "as sweet as is this reunion, I fear we must be on our way."

Damien helped Jarin shove the barrels aside and much to Cristiana's surprise, the entrance to a tunnel appeared. Within minutes, they had crawled through and found themselves several yards from the castle in a patch of thick maples.

Horses awaited. No one spoke a word. After helping Cristiana and Thebe onto the back of a brown palfrey, Jarin leapt behind them. Then grabbing the reins with one hand, he held onto them with the other, and they all took off at a mad gallop.

"Ahhh, Devil's blood!" Sir Walter fisted hands to his temples and uttered every curse he knew into the stagnant air of his study.

Bishop Montruse stood calmly before him, eyeing him with the same evil intent he oft saw in Drago's eyes. "I suppose this means you no longer have the Spear of Destiny?" His tone was caustic.

Sir Walter slammed his fists on his desk, shaking the trinkets, pens, ink, and candles that sat thereon. Including the open box with the key still in the lock.

The *empty* open box.

"'Twas right here!" He pointed toward the velvet cloth lining the inside of the box. "I checked on it right before the ceremony this morn. 'Twas safely wrapped inside. Then I locked it and hid it behind the loose stone on my wall!" He glared at the bishop. "How would anyone know where it was?" He took up a pace, unwilling to believe this was happening. "Devil's blood! The box was still locked!"

"Fatuous goosewit!" the bishop said, seething. "Seems you have once again disappointed me. Not only me, but His Majesty, the king." His placid face became twisted and gnarled. "You should have given it to me the moment you took it from that wench!"

Sir Walter retreated from the man's fury and wrung his hands together. "I needed you to perform the wedding, regardless of the lady's hesitancy."

"And I did." The bishop adjusted the embroidered sash, then twisted the sapphire ring on his finger.

Sir Walter growled. "Now that Lady Cristiana has her wits about her, 'tis quite possible she could return to Luxley, convince the guards and servants to join her, take power, and cast me from this place."

The bishop blew out a sigh. "What is that to me?"

The man's stupidity never failed to astound Sir Walter. He gave a tight smile. "Should she be so bold, Your Grace, you may never retrieve the Spear. Only if she and her friends remain outlaws do we have a chance to find it."

The bishop stared at him, confused.

Sir Walter repressed a growl of frustration and added, "They will have need of its power to defeat us. Should there be naught to defeat, it will go into hiding."

The bishop snorted. "Then I shall proclaim her a witch like her sister. Will that satisfy?"

"Aye." Sir Walter smiled, then whirled, his tunic flowing behind him. "To the devil with those knights!"

"'Twould seem they continue to get the best of you." The bishop's nose pinched as if he smelled something foul. "No Spear, no lady. I grow weary of this dung heap of an estate. Someone of my stature should be in the palaces of London, not here in the muck and mire with such vulgar plebeians."

"Then prithee return home, Your Grace. I will continue my quest here." Sir Walter would do anything to rid himself of this muck-spout! In truth, if the man lingered further, Sir Walter might have Drago cast a curse on him.

The bishop blew out another snort. "Nay. I've had enough of your incompetence. I will send word to the king, requesting more troops. We will find these Knights of the Eternal Realm and their Spear. And when I do, I will burn the lot of them at the stake."

Cristiana had never seen the likes of such a magnificent chamber beneath the ground. As all six of them entered with shouts of glee and praises to God, she could only stare in wonder.

"You lived here all those years we were apart?" She glanced at her sister, who was placing her quiver and bow on a table.

"Aye, with the friar." Alexia gestured toward an older man in a brown robe with a gold crucifix hanging about his neck and a look of enviable peace and love on his face.

"Friar, we have found my sister." Alexia placed a kiss on his cheek, eliciting a blush.

"As I can see." He approached Cristiana and took her hands in his. "God's blessing be upon you, my child."

"Thank you." She longed to also thank him for taking such good care of her sister all these years, but Jarin's laugh brought her around to see him, Thebe in his arms, speaking with Ronar as they put their weapons on the table.

He glanced her way, a look in his eyes that bespoke promise and hope.

"Where's Seraphina?" Alexia asked.

Damien marched up to join them, glanced around, and then headed down a hallway in the back of the chamber.

Ah, yes. How could Cristiana have forgotten that her good friend was here? Elation soared through her as she waited to see Sera again.

Jarin came to stand by her side, and Thebe reached out her chubby little arms. Taking the babe, Cristiana lowered to sit on the sofa, suddenly feeling weak from all the excitement.

Damien stormed back into the room and approached the friar. "Where is she?"

Friar Josef gave him a kind look. "Gone. Left nigh two hours past."

"Where?" Damien demanded.

The friar glanced over them all, a slight furrow in his brow the only indication of any angst. "Forgive me, but I fell asleep. I thought...well, here." He moved to a desk, retrieved a piece of parchment, and handed it to Alexia.

Unfolding it, she began reading it aloud.

"My dearest friends,

I am away to see the king with Sir Walter's confession. I beseech you, do not be angry with me, nor the friar, for you see the Spear appeared in my hand, along with the sign on my wrist. And I knew 'twas God anointing me with the task of clearing all your names and restoring Luxley Castle to its rightful owners. Hence, I am on that very mission. Prithee, do not search for me. I hope I shall return anon with good news.

Ever your loyal friend, Seraphina DeMowbray."

Damien growled and fisted his hands.

Cristiana lifted up her sleeve and glanced at her wrist. "She's right. I no longer have the mark." She held up her hand, amazed that she had not felt it depart.

Alexia set down the letter and leaned back against the desk. "The Spear has chosen her to be its protector now."

Damien started for the table. "And I have given myself that task as well." Retrieving his sword and knives, he shoved them into scabbards around his leather baldric.

Ronar followed his friend. "He's right. We cannot allow her to travel alone."

"Finally, a rational voice." Damien smiled at his friend.

Jarin headed their way. "If you two are going, then I am as well."

Alexia fisted hands at her hips. "Alas, you all intend to leave us? Break up the Knights of the Eternal Realm? Leave us at the mercy of the bishop and Sir Walter?"

Ronar smiled her way. "When have you ever been at anyone's mercy, my love?"

Cristiana closed her eyes and hugged Thebe, her emotions torn between longing to protect Seraphina and yet not wanting Jarin to leave. Silently, she prayed for God's will to be done.

The three knights continued to line their belts with weapons.

"Jarn!" As if sensing he was leaving, Thebe reached out for him, and Cristiana put the child down. The little girl dashed toward Sir Jarin, and he swept her up in his arms.

Alexia smiled at the sight, as did everyone. "We have come to love her as our own," Cristiana offered, slowly standing.

The friar smiled. "Then she is welcome here in our humble home."

"Home?" Thebe's gaze shifted between the friar, Cristiana, and Jarin.

Cristiana made her way to the little girl, still in Jarin's arms. "Aye, darling. This is your new home." Though she had no idea whether Jarin would continue to assume the role of father. By the look he was giving the girl, 'twould seem so. Still, he had made no promises to her or to Thebe, and she feared he would break both their hearts.

Finished with arming himself, Damien started for the door.

The friar raised his voice. "Nay, Sir Damien. We must allow her to have her own journey."

The knight faced them. "Alas, you have said the Spear contains no power in itself."

"Indeed, 'tis true." The friar gripped the cross around his neck. "The power is found only in Christ Himself."

Cristiana glanced at Jarin. "As I have learned as well."

He gave an understanding smile in return.

"In truth? Then, by your own words, she is putting herself in grave danger." Armed with more blades than a battalion, Damien opened the door. "Join me or not. I am going to find her." And out he marched.

Ronar hesitated, exchanging a look with Jarin ere facing Alexia.

"Leave him," the friar said. "Mayhap 'tis his journey as well."

"He's right." Ronar sighed. "We have work to do here."

"I do not gainsay it." Handing Thebe to Cristiana, Jarin returned his weapons to the table. "Damien can handle the protection of one lady." He turned to face them. "Yet, what shall we do in the meantime?"

"What we have always done." Alexia took Ronar's hand in hers. "Show God's love in the village and God's power to Sir Walter and his warlock."

Warlock? Cristiana swallowed a burst of fear. Alas, Cedric had been right. "Mayhap our first task is to convince the guards and servants of my ability to rule. If they side with us, I can assume my proper place as lady of Luxley and send Sir Walter on his way."

Alexia's face lit with excitement. "'Tis true! You are not wanted by the law! Why had I not thought of that?"

Ronar nodded. "That only leaves the warlock to be dealt with."

The friar shrugged. "'Twill be no trouble for God."

Ronar lifted his blade in the air, and nodded at Jarin, who retrieved his sword and raised it high. "For the glory of God, to the Knights of the Eternal Realm!" Ronar shouted.

Alexia grabbed her bow and handed a knife to Cristiana with a wink.

Thebe in one arm, Cristiana raised the blade in the other as Alexia lifted her bow.

"For the glory of God, to the Knights of the Eternal Realm!" they all shouted.

Thebe giggled and lifted her hand. "Tonight with ternal reem!"

Lowering their weapons, they all laughed.

CHAPTER FORTY

Cristiana lowered to sit on the soft, green moss and dipped her hands in the water. Cool and refreshing, it tickled her fingers as she moved them back and forth, creating little wavelets in the otherwise still pond. To her right, lit by the moon, streams of silvery water tumbled over a cliff into the pool, the gushing sound soothing her.

Beyond the waterfall, in their underground hideout, Cristiana had left the friar reading, Alexia, Jarin, and Ronar deep in conversation, and Thebe asleep. Unable to sleep herself, she had slipped out for some time alone—to think and to pray.

Above, stars winked at her through treetops, whilst from their branches an owl hooted. A frog leapt onto a log beside her and stared at her with dark round eyes ere croaking and jumping away. The scent of summer lilies filled the fresh night air, and Cristiana drew in a breath of it, pondering the amazing events of the day.

To think she'd almost married Sir Walter! 'Twould have been a life sentence of torture and misery for both her and Thebe. Even worse, Jarin had almost departed this world forever, taking her heart with him. But God rescued them all. Including Thebe, who now had a home of her own and people to love her.

"Thank you, Lord!" Cristiana stared up at the stars, wondering how far up heaven was and whether God could see her. But she knew the answer. God could always see her. He had never left her and never would.

In truth, they still had troubles. Luxley remained in the hands of evil men, Alexia and the knights were wanted for treason, and Seraphina was on a mission of great danger. But they were alive and safe, and God was on their side. Good would always win over evil in the end. She knew that now.

But what of Sir Jarin? How was she to endure living and working by his side day after day, knowing she would never be his? He had rescued her over and over, cared for her, protected her, and, dare she say, even loved her. But he had never asked for her hand. Alas, he had made it plain from the beginning he was not a man to settle down. Yet, against her will, against all reason, she had fallen so deeply in love with him, she knew she'd never find her way out.

A breeze stirred leaves around her into a gentle dance, and she hugged herself. "Lord, help me. Give me strength to merely be his friend."

Jarin was well aware when Lady Cristiana left the underground chamber. Instantly, both the room and his heart mourned her loss. He'd longed for a moment alone with her, but the day had brought such excitement, and Ronar insisted they catch up on all the happenings since they'd last seen each other. Indeed, 'twas good to hear of all the miracles God had performed on their behalf at Luxley. Nothing surprised Jarin anymore when it came to God's love and power. They, too, were astonished to hear of all that God had done through Cristiana, and of how he had touched Jarin.

"I'm so pleased to hear of my sister's great faith and love." Alexia snuggled up beside Ronar on the sofa. "Her heart has always been twice the size of mine."

Jarin smiled, for he knew that all too well.

Alexia scanned the room. "Where is she? I should go find her." She started to rise, but Ronar pulled her back down and winked at Jarin.

"I'll find her, my lady," Jarin said. "I have something I wish to discuss with her." Leaving the two lovers alone, Jarin plucked a knife from the table, sheathed it, then headed out the door and through the tunnel.

He found the lady sitting on a bed of moss beside the pond, her gown spread around her, caressing the water with her fingers. Moonlight shimmered over her in glowing silver and set a halo of glittering diamonds around her head.

An angel, a creature filled with so much love, the world was unworthy of her.

Jarin swallowed. *He* was unworthy of her.

Careful not to frighten her, he leapt from a boulder onto the ground and made his way to her.

She turned at his approach and smiled—that smile that stormed through every sense, bringing each one to life. She started to rise, and Jarin extended a hand to help her.

"'Tis been quite a day," she said, staring at him curiously.

Jarin nodded and stared over the water. *Nervous*! He could command an army against an overwhelming force, but he stood here before this woman, as nervous as a squire at his first tournament. Now that she was back home with her sister, he feared she'd had time to realize she deserved far better than him, feared 'twas only the danger of their journey and her need for his protection which made her feel anything for him at all.

"Thank God for your friends," she said. "I almost lost you, and I...I..."

He met her gaze, searching her eyes, hope rising.

"Could not bear it," she finally said, looking down, and drawing a hand to her nose.

He took that hand in his and raised it for a kiss, drawing her eyes to his again. A world of promise lived within their brown depths, if only he could dive in and drown in the love he saw therein. He opened his mouth to pledge his love to her, his devotion, but found himself speechless once again, enchanted by this precious woman before him.

They searched each other's eyes, the bond between them growing deeper and deeper. Jarin ran the back of his fingers over her cheek and moved his thumb over her lips, so soft and sweet, he longed to kiss them.

Her breath caught. Her chest rose and fell, and she took a step back, breaking the moment. "But we are finally safe," she said.

"Aye, God watched over us. I see that now."

"You are no longer angry at Him?"

"Nay." A breeze tossed his hair, and Jarin glanced over the dark thicket of trees surrounding the pond. "He has shown me the world beyond this one—the real world. Where my parents and sister are now, happy and alive."

She pressed a hand on his arm. "I am so pleased, Jarin. I, too, have discovered that God never left me, that He loves me…that he loves *us* so much."

Jarin smiled. "'Twas you who helped me see His love. It shines through you so brightly, naught can contain it."

She lowered her gaze. "We both learned much on our journey."

"I leaned other things as well," he said. Pressing a finger beneath her chin, he raised her eyes to his once again. "I leaned that what I thought was living was not living at all, but a mask for my unhappiness. I also learned what an astounding woman you are."

She stepped back from him. "You flatter me, Sir. I can see why so many women have fallen for your charms."

"But only one has won my heart." Jarin went down on one knee and gazed up at her. His heart galloped in his chest, his future teetered on the edge of bliss or despair. "I am only a knight errant and you the daughter of a thane, but I must ask you what my heart begs. Will you become my wife?"

She stared at him, wide-eyed and mouth slightly open for what seemed like an eternity—an eternity in which Jarin's hope began to fade, his future slipping into despondency.

Tears pooled in her eyes "I will not force you away from your life of freedom and adventure, Jarin. I will not do that to the man I love."

He took her hand and kissed it. "Love? As I do you, with all my heart!"

Hope appeared in her eyes, even as a tear slid down her cheek.

Rising, Jarin wiped it away with his thumb. ""My lady, I no longer wish that life. My only desire is to be by your side—to protect, to honor, to love you forever."

"And Thebe?" Her smile was hesitant, her eyes sparkling with love.

"We will raise her as our own."

Ere he finished the words, her lips were on his. Wrapping his arms around her, he drew her close and drank of this precious woman until he was full of love and life and hope.

Gripping her shoulders, he drew her back. "Is that a yes, my lady?"

"Aye, Sir Jarin, a forever and ever yes!"

MaryLu Tyndall

About the Author

AWARD WINNING AND BEST-SELLING AUTHOR, MARYLU TYNDALL dreamt of pirates and sea-faring adventures during her childhood days on Florida's Coast. With more than twenty-five books published, she makes no excuses for the deep spiritual themes embedded within her romantic adventures. Her hope is that readers will not only be entertained but will be brought closer to the Creator who loves them beyond measure. In a culture that accepts the occult, wizards, zombies, and vampires without batting an eye, MaryLu hopes to show the awesome present and powerful acts of God in a dying world. A Christy award nominee, MaryLu makes her home with her husband, six children, four grandchildren, and several stray cats on the California coast.

If you enjoyed this book, you might enjoy the 1st book in the series, ***She Walks in Power***.
Look for book 3, ***She Walks in Majesty***, coming in 2020!

If you enjoyed this book, one of the nicest ways to say "thank you" to an author and help them be able to continue writing is to leave a favorable review on Amazon! Goodreads, Barnes and Noble, Kobo, Itunes (And elsewhere, too!) I would appreciate it if you would take a moment to do so. Thanks so much!
Comments? Questions? I love hearing from my readers, so feel free to contact me via my website:

http://www.marylutyndall.com

Or email me at: marylu_tyndall@yahoo.com

Follow me on:

FACEBOOK: https://www.facebook.com/marylu.tyndall.author
TWITTER: https://twitter.com/MaryLuTyndall

BLOG: http://crossandcutlass.blogspot.com/
PINTEREST: http://www.pinterest.com/mltyndall/
BookBub: https://www.bookbub.com/authors/marylu-tyndall

To hear news about special prices and new releases sign up for my newsletter on my website Or follow me on Bookbub!
https:///www.marylutyndall.com
https://www.bookbub.com/authors/marylu-tyndall

MaryLu Tyndall

Other Books by MaryLu Tyndall

SHE WALKS IN POWER

THE REDEMPTION

THE RELIANCE

THE RESTITUTION

THE RANSOM

THE RECKONING

THE RECKLESS

THE FALCON AND THE SPARROW

THE RED SIREN

THE BLUE ENCHANTRESS

THE RAVEN SAINT

SURRENDER THE HEART

SURRENDER THE NIGHT

SURRENDER THE DAWN

FORSAKEN DREAMS

ELUSIVE HOPE

ABANDONED MEMORIES

VEIL OF PEARLS

PEARLS FROM THE SEA DEVOTIONAL

CENTRAL PARK RENDEZVOUS

TEARS OF THE SEA

WESTWARD CHRISTMAS BRIDES

WHEN ANGELS CRY

LIBERTY BRIDE

WRITING FROM THE TRENCHES

CPSIA information can be obtained
at www.ICGtesting.com
Printed in the USA
FSHW011706200619
59265FS